Songs from the Heart

Violante Publishing House

This book is a work of fiction. Any names, characters, incidents, places are the work of the author's imagination. Any resemblance to any characters, or events, living or dead, is coincidental.

All rights reserved. In accordance with the U.S. Copyright Acts of 1976, the scanning, uploading, and electronic sharing of any part of this book without permission of the publisher is unlawful piracy and theft of the author's intellectual property. Prior written permission must be obtained if you would like to use any material from this book. The author thanks you for the support of their rights.

Copyright © 2022 by YS Reffitt

All rights reserved. Published by Violante Publishing House 2022

Printed in the U.S.A

SONGS FROM THE HEART

Contents

Dedication	VII
Foreword	VIII
Epigraph	IX
1. Chapter 1	1
2. Chapter 2	13
3. Chapter 3	29
4. Chapter 4	37
5. Chapter 5	53
6. Chapter 6	61
7. Chapter 7	73
8. Chapter 8	77
9. Chapter 9	83
10. Chapter 10	97
11. Chapter 11	105
12. Chapter 12	121
13. Chapter 13	127

14.	Chapter 14	137
15.	Chapter 15	147
16.	Chapter 16	155
17.	Chapter 17	171
18.	Chapter 18	187
19.	Chapter 19	195
20.	Chapter 20	209
21.	Chapter 21	231
22.	Chapter 22	243
23.	Chapter 23	257
24.	Chapter 24	263
25.	Chapter 25	271
26.	Chapter 26	283
27.	Chapter 27	293
28.	Chapter 28	305
29.	Chapter 29	313
30.	Chapter 30	323
31.	Chapter 31	331
Acknowledgments		338

For my parents

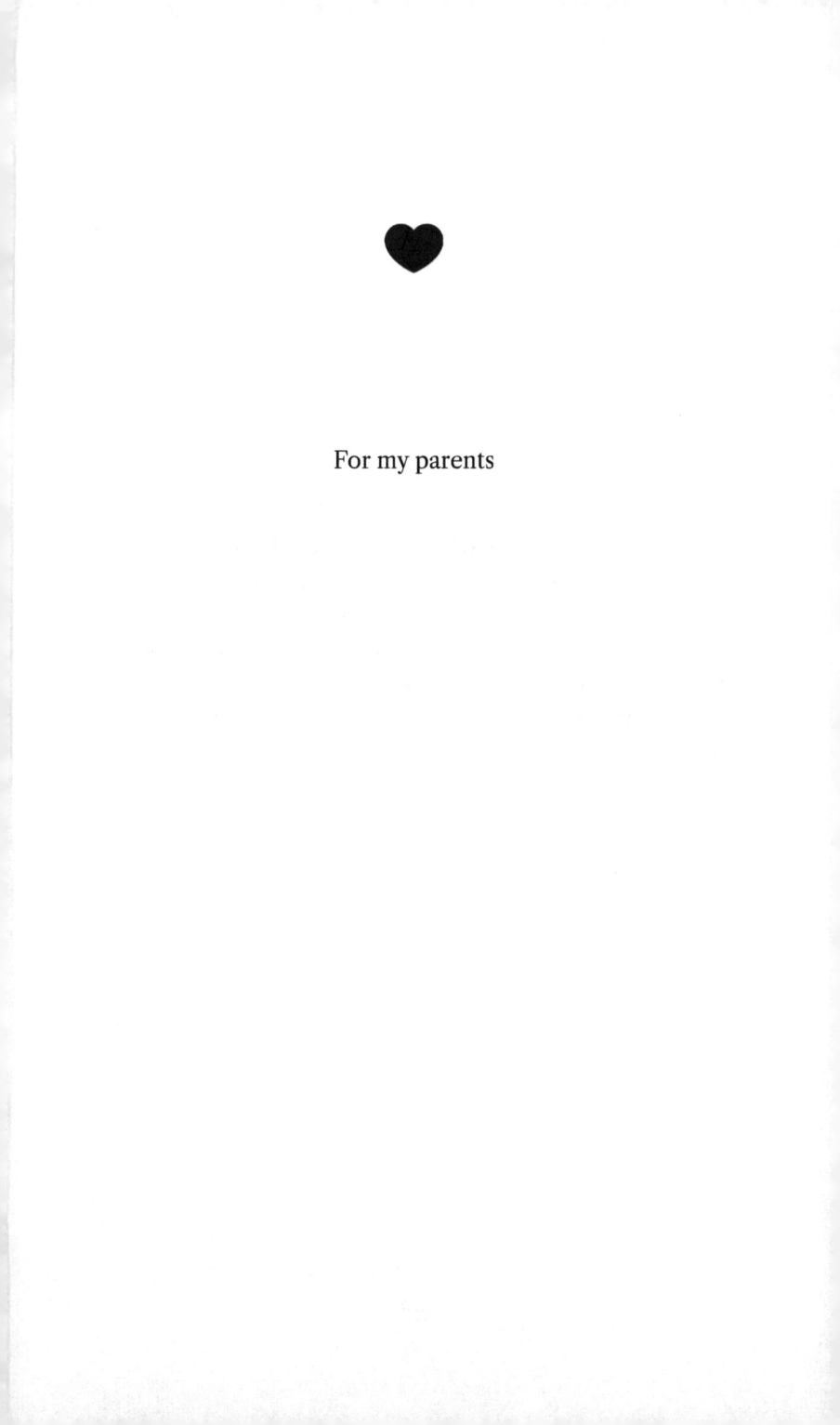

YS Reffitt is an educator, wife, and mother of two based in the eastern US. Since childhood she has written poems and short stories and dreamed of someday writing stories that readers would fall in love with. Now that her boys are grown she has made time to finish her debut novel, Songs of the Heart. She hopes to imagine more stories in the future that readers will love just as much as this one.

"Love is composed of a single soul inhabiting two bodies."

-Aristotle

One

♥

"Rayna I can't believe I let you do that?" Anna said as she ran her fingers through her short hair and shook her head.

I laughed. "Like you could have stopped me." I took my bag from Anna and dug for my wallet.

"I just know that your mom would freak out if she knew I went along with this."

I put my money and ID back in my wallet and threw it in my bag.

"Do you see my mom?" I looked around the perimeter. "You didn't go along with anything. I made the decision to go parasailing and I'm glad I did. It was exhilarating." I tucked Anna under my arm and smiled at her as we walked. She fit easily under my arm with her tiny 5 foot 4 inch stature. The soft sand under my bare feet energized me.

"Why would her mom be mad at you?" Dave looked over at Anna as he raised up from grabbing a shell from the sand.

I drew my eyes down at Anna and shook my head. "Because my mom is a worry wart. She pleads with Anna to keep me safe." I laughed hoping that Dave wouldn't ask more questions.

"So what was it like being up in the air like that?" Anna asked.

At least she was trying to change the subject.

"It was awesome!" Dave said with a grin.

"It was Anna. You should try it with us next time."

"Not a chance." Anna said.

We all laughed and continued our short walk back to the house.

"So how was it?" Rick asked when we made it to his beach spot.

"Awesome!" Dave and I answered in unison. We both laughed. Rick laughed at us for answering together.

"You're back." Travis said as he walked down the steps from the house. He smiled at us, more at Anna but he looked at all three of us. His eyes glistened when he smiled at her.

It warmed my heart and made me smile seeing these two fall for each other. Hopefully one of us could live happily ever after.

"Come on Rayna, you're my partner," Dave said. He pulled my hand toward a setup field in the sand.

"What do you wanna play?"

"Bucket ball. That's what they played while we were gone. Rick and Jeff are undefeated. We have to beat them!"

"And you think we can do that?"

"You said you played sports in high school. Well this is just like basketball and beer pong put together." Dave picked up a ball.

"You just toss this ball down there into one of those buckets. If you get the ball in the bucket the other team has to remove the bucket. Just like beer pong."

"I've never played beer pong."

"What?!!" Dave looked at me like I was an alien. "What do you mean you never played beer pong? Didn't you just graduate college?"

"I did, but I did most of it online. Remember I told you I just moved out of my mom and dad's and moved in with Anna."

"So you never went to parties?"

"No, I didn't". I took a breath and braced myself for his laughter. He didn't laugh. He just looked confused.

"Let's get this game started!" Dave yelled.

Dave didn't pry. I liked that about him. I wasn't sure what to expect when I met him a few days ago. He made me feel comfortable.

Jeff and Rick hurried over to their buckets and picked up the balls.

"Losers first," Jeff yelled.

"I'll show you loser," Dave said. "Go ahead Rayna." I tossed the ball and missed. Dave tossed his and missed. Rick and Jeff harassed us. The game went on for a while. But in the end Dave and I beat them.

"Who is the loser now?" Dave chuckled.

Jeff flipped Dave the bird and walked toward the house. Dave laughed again and put the balls in the bucket.

"Guys, we need to get ready if we're gonna play the show tonight." Rick pointed at his watch.

"Always the slave driver." Dave shot back at him with a grin.

We gathered our things and started for the house.

"Give me that stuff." Dave threw his towel over his shoulder and took my bag from my hands.

"Thanks." Good looking and a gentleman. I locked arms with Anna as we followed the guys up the steps to the house.

The guys quickly showered and dressed.

"We need to get the equipment set up and do sound check so we'll see you later," Rick yelled as he opened the front door.

I stuck my head out of my room. "Okay, see you there."

"Bye Rayna. I'll see you in a few hours." Dave waved at me. I waved back.

I showered and dressed. Anna's music blared from her room. She was making the final touches to her makeup when I walked in.

"You look fantastic! That leather mini skirt shows off those long tanned legs and those blue eyes of your pop with your tan! I love it! You're gonna give someone a heart attack looking like that," Anna said.

I smirked at her and did a little spin. Dressing up in sexy clothes did make me more optimistic. "Thanks." I grinned at her. "You look kinda fabulous yourself."

"Thanks, I hope Travis thinks so too."

I shook my head at her and smiled. "Let's go see Travis." I joked.

Anna put her mascara down and grabbed her purse from the sink. She followed me out the front door to the car. I drove almost a mile.

"We could have walked you know. My heart won't fail from a little walk." I gave Anna a disapproving look as I locked the car doors.

Anna grimaced at me. "Walk in heels and break a sweat after all the hard work on our hair and makeup? Never!" A look of astonishment on her face.

I laughed and locked arms with her as we walked across the street toward the club. My phone rang.

"It's my mom Anna. Hold on a minute. Hi mom. "I held up a finger to Anna.

"Rayna, you didn't call me back."

"I know mom, I'm sorry. Anna and I lost track of time and almost forgot about the show tonight"

"Rayna be careful being out with only Anna."

"Mom, we are here with Rick and his friends, we aren't alone. I have my mace." I smiled at Anna. "Remember, you raised a smart girl."

"I know Rayna. I worry too much I guess. Your fragile condition doesn't help my nerves. I will always worry. Text when you get back to the house so I know you are in. Be safe and I love you. Enjoy yourself."

"I will. I love you too mom. And tell dad I love him." I hung up the phone and put it in my small leather purse. I grabbed Anna's arm and gave her a big smile. "Let's go have some fun girl."

The club was nearly packed. We paid the cover charge and pushed our way through all the young faces toward the stage to find Rick. People were everywhere. Some played pool while others gathered around the bar or tables causing a sea of unrelenting chatter. You could hardly hear yourself think. After looking for a few seconds I spotted him.

"Hey Rick," I yelled over the music coming from the jukebox. He glanced over his shoulder and waved us over to the side stage.

"I wondered where you two were," Rick said. He continued hooking up cables and wires to speakers and lights. "I thought maybe you got lost," Rick teased. "The band is gonna start in about ten minutes. I reserved a table for us up front." He yelled over the noise and pointed to a table close to the stage.

"We had to make ourselves beautiful, Rick" Anna grinned at Rick.

"And you both are. I'll fetch you two beautiful ladies a soda, be right back."

"I can't wait until the band starts. I'm so excited for you to see them. You should have gone with me when I saw them a few months ago," Anna stated.

"I wanted to, but you know I wasn't up to par then, and when I'm fatigued, it's hard to force myself out of the house. My doctors figured my medicine out now. And that helps with the fatigue. I'm ready to start having some fun before it's too late. I mean, all that money my grandfather left me, I need to spend some right."

"Hey, we're not going to talk about sad things tonight. We're gonna have a wonderful time tonight and the rest of the week. When Seer starts playing, you'll be ready to get your groove on and be free of all the worry," Anna said. She sounded like she was barking orders to me. But I understood she only volunteered encouraging words.

The band took the stage and started to play an interesting guitar riff. My attention was perked. I enjoyed rock music and loved to lose myself in the rhythm. And Anna was right. The guys looked amazing; all of them.

"Woooooooo!" Anna yelled and clapped her hands.

I could feel the drum and the guitar pounding in my chest. Anna always gave off incredible vibes. I gave her an evil grin and she knew I was ready to have fun.

The band finished the first song and the singer, Dave's brother that I hadn't met yet, introduced the band members. His voice came out low and sexy when he sang. You wouldn't think that deep raspy sound would come out of such a young looking face. He was cute, but the drummer Dave was the best looking in my opinion. Dave's skin tone was the same as the singer's; but Dave's hair was shorter. The singer's eyes were darker and when he smiled, he exposed straight white teeth. Anyone could tell they were brothers.

"I see that smile. I told you the band was awesome?" Anna smirked. "And we get to spend the entire week with those fine looking guys."

SONGS FROM THE HEART

I smiled at Anna and raise my glass of coke to give her a toast as the band started playing a slower tune. It sounded just as amazing as the first song. The band played a few more songs and I grabbed Anna's arm and dragged her to the dance floor with the others that decided they liked the music. I felt free and young instead of the old grumpy cat I had become in the last few years. I enjoyed this carefree experience. Anna and I slowly moved to the front of the stage as we danced. We danced to every song.

As I glanced up at the band, I made eye contact with the singer, Nick. His deep brown eyes were shockingly intense. When our eyes locked something happened that I'd never experienced before. It was like I had known him all my life. I couldn't pull my eyes away. A magnet kept pulling my eyes to his.

I thought I'd given up on guys because of the heart break with the last one, but if he would step off the stage right at that moment and asked me to leave with him, I would have. I never believed in love at first sight, but I thought I might be experiencing it; right there in the club in front of hundreds of people. I continued moving to the music, but I sensed I was in a trance. Nick turned his eyes away and released the trance he pulled me into. He had some kind of power over me.

The band finished the song and the crowd roared.

"Thank you everyone for hanging out with us tonight," the singer said and took a bow. "We'll be playing on the other side of town in a few days if you want to come join us again."

I brought my thoughts back to reality and glanced at Anna. She was looking at me with a confused expression. We walked over to our table and stood by our chairs. I had never been drunk, but I bet it felt something like this.

"Rayna, are you okay? You look goofy," concerned, Anna examined my face.

I kinda smiled at her not knowing if I was okay. "I'm not sure. I've never experienced that before."

"What! What haven't you experienced before?" Anna demanded as she squeezed my arm.

"This instant attraction to someone, like I would follow them around the world.... like I have known them for years. Like...."

"Your soul mate? I saw you two lock eyes. I knew something was happening." Anna let go of my arm.

"Ssshhh, they're coming over here," I whispered to her.

Anna gave a little squeeze to my hand with a big smile on her face. Rick led the group of guys. They all walked toward us with immense confidence and huge smiles on their faces; except the singer Nick. His face showed annoyance.

Travis walked directly to Anna and stood by her. Dave chose the spot beside me and Nick beside him. Rick did formal introductions.

"This is Nick Perry, our singer and Dave's brother. Nick, these beautiful ladies are Anna Cass and Rayna Taylor."

"Hi," Anna and I said at the same time.

"Hi,' Nick repeated as he threw his hand up to wave.

He moved his eyes away quickly not acknowledging me. He leaned on the table with one elbow and glanced around at the crowd. His white tank top showed off his dark skin and defined biceps and shoulders. The soft hairs on his chest stuck out of the top of his shirt. I glanced at him again, but he still wouldn't meet my eyes. I felt as if I had a stupid little girl crush on someone that didn't even know I existed. Maybe he was pretentious.

I could sense Nick looking at me and I peeked up and smiled. He forced a smile and looked away again. Everyone talked and laughed around the table, but my mind was elsewhere. My stomach churned with those butterflies and my skin rippled with electricity having Nick so close to me. I wanted to reach out and touch his skin. Touch the tattoo of a cross on his shoulder.

"We better pack this stuff up and get it in the van," Nick said. "I'm not feeling so good." He chugged his water, turned, and hopped back into the stage to begin the tear down.

"Yeah, let's get this stuff together and head back to the house where we can relax and hang out. It has been a long day," Travis said.

Travis, the lead guitarist, and Anna hadn't stopped talking since the band finished playing.

"I better help." Dave winked at me as he stood up to go to help take stuff down.

Dave had the same dark mysterious eyes as Nick, but I noticed every detail in Nick's face. It was so beautiful. He tucked his long, shaggy, brown hair behind his ears. Even though he didn't smile but once, I couldn't stop looking at him as he worked to clean the stage.

"Let's help them load up," Anna bought me out of my hypnotic state.

Anna and I wound up black cords and carried them out to the van. Nick was already in the van packing things. He took the cords from me and our skin touched. The electricity from our skin touching was too much. He jerked the cord from my hand in haste. Our eyes locked again. I wanted to jump into the van and press my lips against his. He made me nervous, but it didn't matter. The way I felt around him was intoxicating. It was different than anything I ever experienced. I couldn't figure out what this feeling was. It scared me.

"Thanks," Nick said. I blinked out of my trance.

He quickly looked away. He didn't smile this time. He appeared annoyed. That's when I bolted and almost ran back into the bar. I finally desired someone again. A warmth rose through my body so intense it scared me and he barely said more than one word to me. It must have been wishful thinking on my part because I had been out of the dating loop. Why did he act like I was just any other girl; like he wasn't interested in me? I could have sworn some kind of connection was between us. I bumped into Anna as I walked stupefied across the wooden floor of the club.

"What's up, Rayna? You seemed dazed," Anna said as she gave me a confused look.

"He ignores me.......like I don't exist!" I said. My frustration must've been obvious.

Anna took my arms and led me to the table. She pushed me to my seat.

"Nick avoided my eyes and he only said like one or two words to me. And these butterflies won't stop dancing in my stomach.

"I knew it. You both had a weird expression on your faces. Like you are entranced," She swooned.

"I'm not......... entranced with him," I stuttered, "just dazzled." I scrunched my nose and grinned.

"Remember when we were little and Johnny liked you? Remember when he used to annoy you and we figured out he was just trying to get your attention?"

I shook my head yes remembering.

"Older boys act goofy too when they like a girl; instead of annoyance, it's avoidance. Get to know him a little more and you'll see. I can tell that he likes you. You make him uncomfortable. That's why he's avoiding your eyes," Anna said. She did make me feel a little bit better.

We followed the guys back to the house in the car and talked about it some more. Anna kept coaching until she had me smiling again. When we walked into the kitchen for a drink, we saw the guys outside on the deck goofing around. It looked as though they were giving Nick a hard time.

Anna and I walked out onto the deck. The sound of the ocean filled my ears. The waves beating on the shore were one of my favorite sounds. The ocean breeze blew my hair around my face. I looked over at Nick while he stared out at the dark ocean. He resembled a Greek god standing there. I wanted to walk over and touch him. But he seemed unapproachable and untouchable; far away in his own world.

"Hey guys, you got here quick," Anna said. They all glanced up and smiled at us. Everyone started talking about the night and how amazing the band played. Nick said few words.

"I'm gonna head to bed," Nick said.

"What?" Dave and Rick said. They looked at Nick in shock.

"I'm not feeling well. I must be tired from the plane and playing tonight." Nick said.

"Catch you in the morning?" Dave questioned.

"Yep, goodnight everyone." Nick wave his hand and hurried into the house.

"He's off tonight man," Travis said. "He hasn't acted right since the middle of the show when I played that long riff." What's the matter with him?"

"He usually is the last one to bed and the life of the party," Dave said. "But tonight, he was just plain goofy."

"He's probably just tired. He told me he wrote an entire song on his plane ride down here. Hopefully tomorrow you girls will see the real Nick. You'll love him." Rick explained.

I thought I already did. The guys just told me what I guessed. He was acting strange. This made me feel even bleaker.

"Did you like the band tonight?" Dave asked. He took a drink of his beer.

"Yes, you all did an awesome job. I love all the songs." I said. I gave him a reassuring smile.

"Nick writes all of our music. When he was still in the Marines, he had already written a lot of the lyrics. When he got out, we had lost our lead singer and we asked him to sing for us," Dave said.

"How long has the band been playing?" I asked as I watched Anna laugh while she listened to Travis, Jeff, and Rick talk about something I couldn't hear.

We've been together for about a year now. We made an album with help from some of our friends about a month ago. It turned out amazing."

"I wanna buy one." I smiled

"I'll find you one tomorrow morning." He grinned.

"Sounds good."

"Rick said you just graduated from college too. What did you study?"

"I studied journalism. I hope to find a job in editing. I love books." I gave him a frivolous smile because most people think I'm crazy for liking books so much.

"Maybe I could market some of your books that you edit. I graduated with a marketing degree. Maybe it can help with marketing the band." Dave laughed.

Even though I thought Dave was the best looking in the beginning and he was giving me quite a bit of attention, I couldn't stop my mind from thinking about Nick. I looked at my watch and saw that it was midnight. I excused myself and went into the house to put myself and my crazy mind to bed. As I got dressed for bed, I still couldn't figure Nick out and couldn't drive the way he affected me out of my head. Just thinking about him lying down in a bed on the floor above me gave me goose bumps. I drifted off to sleep with Nick hanging onto my dreams.

Two

I opened my eyes to bright sunlight and the alarm clock showing 9:00 a.m. My first thoughts were, wow.... I slept late. My second thoughts were of Nick. Hopefully everybody would already be up and outside. I wanted to gather my thoughts before I had to speak to anyone. As I put on my robe, I thought of the dream I had about Nick. He's a nice guy in my dream and I think of him as a friend. Then yesterday's memory of him avoiding me made me cringe.

I walked into the kitchen and I couldn't find anyone; thank you God. I found warm coffee still in the pot. I poured some for myself and carried out to the balcony. I looked out at the ocean and saw Anna lying on a beach towel reading a magazine. I drifted off into my own thoughts as I drank my morning cup of java and tried to figure out how I should behave around Nick.

Instead of being an amazing and wonderful week, I started to dread the week ahead. I'd never been drawn to the opposite sex so much. And one that avoids me. It frustrated me. I tried to remember what Anna said about him avoiding me because he's "interested in me." It made sense but I still tried to think of ways to avoid Nick.

"Good Morning".

I jumped and spilled coffee on my new white silk robe. On guard, I turned toward the intruding voice and saw Nick standing in the doorway with a big gorgeous smile on his face. We locked eyes and this time, I turned my eyes away from his. He wore white swimming trunks that hung right at his hips with a pale blue tank and no shoes. The pale colors enhanced his olive skin and dark eyes. His eyelashes were so dark and long; you would think he had on eyeliner. And those trunks; they hung just right. My God he was beautiful.

"Good, good morning," I stuttered as I looked away back out at the ocean. I couldn't meet his eyes directly for long without getting nervous or antsy. I didn't want a repeat of last night. He had been so cold.

"Everyone's down at the beach. Go put on your suit and I'll heat you up some breakfast. We can go down to the beach after." He smiled and turned to go back into the house. I followed him, trying not to run to the bedroom to avoid him. I was hoping he was kidding about breakfast. But he was already warming my plate.

"I'd like to grab a shower to wash away the sleep before I go down," I shyly said.

"I'll wait. I need to talk to you anyway." He leaned against the counter. "I was rude last night and I need to apologize. So go take your shower but make it quick," he gave me his irresistible grin again as he ran his fingers through his long hair brushing it off of his forehead.

I never noticed last night, but when Nick smiled, his eyes lit up. He had a dimple on his left cheek when he smiled........ I blinked and shook my head because I caught myself doing it again; falling for this guy. Get it together Rayna, I told myself. This guy is not interested in you. Something kept turning my brain to mush. Something about him drew me to his every move, his every word, and his every glance.

I smiled, turned, and hurried to my room. With haste, I dug a bathing suit out of the drawer and raced to the bathroom. I jumped into a cold shower to force myself back into reality, but the cool water didn't wash away my thoughts of Nick. I saw his beautiful smile and those dazzling eyes. That's what it is! He dazzled me. I wondered if he was doing this on purpose. Did he realize he was driving me crazy? I needed to stay away from him. I knew touching should be off limits; remembering the electric current when I barely touched him. I needed to focus my thoughts. Get my head straight before I went out to the kitchen. I just met this guy. So far he was a real jerk.

I turned off the shower and wiped my body with a towel. I pulled my bathing suit on a half dry body and twisted my hair up with a clip. Toothpaste helped to scrub the morning out of my mouth. Grabbing a beach towel I opened the bedroom door pausing while I took a deep breath. My feet moved down the hall like a sloth.

"Pull up a stool," Nick said as he set his coffee cup down. He placed a plate of food in front of one of the stools. He glanced at me and smiled.

I smiled back. "Thank you." I tried not to look at him very long. I found it challenging.

"This looks good, did you make it?" I asked as I scooted onto the stool.

"No, Rick cooked this morning. I cleaned up the dishes and saved you a plate." He took a sip of his coffee and glanced at me with those smoldering eyes.

"Thank you again; I didn't think you remembered me." I said. I gave him a playfully sarcastic smirk. "You didn't speak much last night. You kind of made me think you didn't acknowledge my existence." I was being offensively provoking.

Nick gave me a repentant smile. "I was rude, I know. But, I do remember you Rayna. You are a very hard girl to forget,"

Nick said. He spoke with authority. I blushed, I think, and turned my eyes away. I took a bite of food so I didn't say something else horrible and impolite.

Nick took his last drink of coffee and grinned at me. He rinsed his cup and put it in the dishwasher. I continued to eat and said nothing. He seemed a lot friendlier today. It appeared he had a sense of humor too.

"Let me grab my towel and we'll go down, okay," Nick said and left.

I took another bite of food. I rinsed my plate and smiled as I thought about the day so far. Last night I thought this week was going to be a disaster, but today things were looking up.

Nick walked back in the room with his towel around his neck and his flip flops on. "Are we ready?"

"Yes, I am ready," I said and smiled up at him.

Nick followed me out toward a beautiful sunny day. Our group was set up like they had been here all day. The umbrella and chairs were set up. The cooler was full of drinks and a blanket laid out on the sand. Anna was laying in a beach chair and reading her favorite magazine. She glanced up when she saw us and smiled.

"Hey, you two finally made it down. I didn't want to wake you Rayna. Nick was writing so he told me to go ahead down and he would be there when you woke up." She gave me a crooked smirky smile.

I knew that smile so well. She was up to something. I would pry it out of her. I narrowed my eyes at her and gave her a quick grin. Nick and I laid our towels on the chairs and I sat down beside Anna. He pulled off his shirt and then headed toward the waves with the guys. I imagined running my hand up his fit stomach and chest.

"Rayna, ...Rayna, do I even need to ask what you are dazed about," Anna giggled. "I thought you and Dave were hitting it off this past week. What happened?"

"This week has been great. Dave is just a friend. But Nick.....Nick is something else. Last night when I gazed into his eyes, I felt as if we were looking into each other's souls. It's frightening, exhilarating and spiritual all at the same time. I'm not sure what I am experiencing or why. The connection between us seems deep. Kind of stupid right?"

"Have you ever heard of a soul mate? This morning at breakfast, Nick seemed concerned about the impression he made on you last night. I think he likes you. He could be experiencing the same thing you are and it's freaking him out."

"Someone you're supposed to be with; the other part of your soul? I don't believe there's a predestined person for each of us." I smirked.

"You may wanna read this then. It talks about the same things you're saying you're experiencing. I do believe in soul mates or twin flames," Anna finished, as she handed me the magazine.

I took it and started reading the article. Every once in a while I would sneak a peek at Nick. He looked like he was having a good time passing a football and falling into the crashing waves. He moved like an athlete. I caught him glance up and I waved. I started reading the article again. The article said,

"The Truth About Twin Flames: When first meeting one another there is an instant connection and immediate bond. The feeling is as if you have known each other before and there is a perception of familiarity. Whether you have both met in physical person or not, there is most often a peculiar sensation--an intuitive knowing-- The eyes are the windows to the soul. When twin flames gaze into one another's eyes

there is a profound intensity. Making eye contact with your twin flame can seem unusual at times because it is as if you are staring into your own soul. Twin flames can experience moments when there is an overwhelming sense of unconditional love. The emotion can be intensive. The love can be absolutely explosive and expands one into a sense of oneness with their twin.

"All emotions, whether negative or positive, is amplified between twin flames. Feelings are often exaggerated compared to other relationships. When things are good it feels exceptional! But when things are not going so well, the feelings can be agonizing. There is more emotional and energetic intensity between twin flames because things are experienced on a soul level. Since twin flames are often emphatic with one another, it can become an overwhelming emotional roller coaster at times when they are absorbing each other's emotions alongside feeling the intensity of their own.

"There may be similarities and synchronistic patterns found within each of the twin-flames birth dates, anniversaries, addresses, phone numbers, anniversaries and major life events. Both twin-flames may have unusual dreams involving the other and telepathy often occurs between twins in the dream state. Many twin-flames have shared or reoccurring dreams of one another, often prior to meeting their twin.

"Twin flames are connected even at a distance. Telepathy and empathy are common between the twin flames. Each twin may pick up on the others thoughts they may find themselves often calling, texting, or emailing around the same time and also finishing each other's sentences. Synchronicities and unusual parallels often occur within the lives and daily events of each of the twin flames."

There could be something to this. Nick's mood last night affected mine and I did feel like we were looking into each other's souls. Maybe the feelings were too intense for him. The more I read, the more frightened I became. I looked back at the ocean and Nick and the guys were approaching us. His long hair was wet and the water dripped down onto his shoulders. I didn't think I could fight this intense magnetism.

Dave grabbed a bottle of water from the cooler and guzzled it down; but not before he drizzled some of it down my back.

"Wow!! That's cold!" I said. I threw my magazine at Dave.

He laughed and jumped out of the way of the flying book.

"Are you girls gonna enjoy the ocean today or what?" Dave asked.

"Let's go!" Anna jumped up out of the chair and dropped her magazine on her towel.

Nick grabbed a bottle of water out of the cooler.

"Throw me one," Travis yelled.

"Me too." Jeff chimed in and held up his hands to catch it.

Anna and I waited for the guys to drink their water and then we all ran to the water. When the water touched my toes, Dave grabbed me with both of his arms and carried me deeper into the water.

"Don't you dare!" I laughed.

"I dare," Dave teased.

And under I went. He brought me up for air and laughed as he let go of me. I splashed water on him and dove deeper into the water. It didn't bother me to be dunked, but I would've preferred it to be Nick who wrapped his arms around me.

"Heads up," Nick yelled and threw me the football. He tossed it more than threw it.

"Throw me the ball Rayna," Dave yelled.

I looked away from Nick and threw it the best of could.

The next time I tried to catch the ball under I went. Everyone razzed me.

....

Around five we decided to head back up the house to figure out dinner. We all worked together to gather things up from the beach that might blow away. We left our chairs and umbrellas at the beach for later. We hung towels on the veranda outside and Rick's phone rang.

"Hello,......... yeah......that would be great. See you in a few. Love you too." Rick hung up his phone and we followed him into the house.

"That was my Mom. She is bringing Chinese for us around seven. So if you are hungry, grab a snack."

"Your mom is cool," I cheered. "She told my mom she would check in on us this week."

"Yeah, she just got off the plane a little while ago. She's taking care of some renovations that John's doing on a condo he bought. He loves buying real estate as you can see." Rick laughed as he put his hands up presenting the house.

"And we love that he loves it," teased Anna and she danced into the kitchen to retrieve a bottle of water.

I followed Anna to the kitchen and pulled out a bar stool and sat down. Nick came ran into the kitchen and grabbed an apple and yelled, "Heads up Rayna."

I caught the apple he tossed over the counter at me, and he retrieved another apple for himself. He took a bite and kept his eyes on me as he leaned on the counter across from me. I glanced down at the apple and took a bit of mine. His attention was making me a little bashful.

"Thank you," I said after I swallowed the first bite. "How did you know I needed a snack?"

"Intuition, I guess. You looked hungry." He shrugged his shoulders and showed me his beautiful smile.

Rick's mom, Samantha, brought dinner at seven. We talked, and laughed. We all sat around the pool. Nick and I watched each other most of dinner. I found it hard not looking at him.

I wanted to know everything about him; I wanted to be part of his reality. I wondered, would I fit into his world?

Around nine o clock, Nick finally walked over and sat beside me on the bench. He leaned into me and whispered, "Would you like to take a walk with me? We can grab some ice cream."

"That would be nice," I said with a smile. "Can I grab a pair of shorts first?"

"Yeah, I'll walk up with you and grab a shirt."

We walked up to get our clothes. As I grabbed my shorts and did a quick check in the mirror the butterflies danced in my stomach again. Nick and I would be alone. Well, not alone, but without the group and anyone else to talk to or distract us. Just the two of us. The sun had given my skin a nice glow that brought out my blue eyes. I ran a brush through my hair and left my room.

Nick waited for me at the door. We walked down to the pool. Everyone stared up at us like they didn't realize we had left. It didn't surprise me with all the intense conversations going on when we walked up to the house. Rick's mom was still here. I walked over to her.

"Samantha it was wonderful to see you. Thanks again for allowing us to stay in the house and for the amazing dinner." I said.

"No problem. You kids are always welcome. I love that Rick has such wonderful friends." She stood up and gave me a huge hug. "Are you leaving us?" she questioned.

"Nick is taking me for ice cream. So you might be gone when I come back."

"Isn't that wonderful." She smiled and then kissed my cheek.

Nick gave Samantha a hug as well, and then thanked her. I glanced over my shoulder as Nick placed his hand on the small of my back and I waved at Anna. She waved back. I moved in the direction Nick guided me. With his hand on my back I felt as if I was a puppet and he was the master. My body was clay for the molding of Nick Perry. We strolled across the bridge and down the steps to the beach silently. I kicked off my shoes and Nick bent down and picked them up.

"I could have gotten those, I whispered as I run my fingers through my hair.

"But I wanted to," Nick gazed deep into my eyes.

We stood still looking into each other's eyes for what seemed only a second, but I knew it had been longer. I could get lost in his eyes and live happily ever after. I wanted to learn the secrets behind those eyes. Who was he? What made me experience this strange connection to him without really knowing him? So many questions unanswered. I moved my eyes away from his looking down the shoreline. We started toward the pier. The sun began to set turning the sky a beautiful orange and pink.

"So, are you in school?" I probed, as we walked barefoot in the sand. I had forgotten what it felt like to be attracted to someone. The sensations woke every nerve ending in my body. The exhilaration could be as addictive as a drug.

"No, I work full time at a collision center. I do body work repairs on vehicles."

"Have you always done that?"

"No, I got out of the Marines a year ago. I also write the music for the band."

"Where do you live?" I pushed, trying to find out as much about him as I could during our beach walk.

"I have a little place just outside of Pittsburgh. It's not much but the old couple that own it leave me alone and let the band practice there, so it's perfect," Nick stopped to pick up a seashell and handed it to me. "Why all the questions?" Nick asked with apprehension on his face.

"I want to get to know you. Is that okay?" I answered his question with more of my own questions.

I moved my eyes up from the sand and over at Nick. The longing in his eyes made my heart skip a beat. Maybe I wasn't crazy and thinking that I only had a crush.

Nick and I didn't speak the rest of the way to the pier. We enjoyed the quiet time walking together with the breeze blowing our hair and the warm salt water bathing our feet. I glimpsed over at Nick several times to steal a peek at his gorgeous profile. Each time, Nick caught me looking at him or I would catch him gazing at me.

The sun had completely set by the time we purchased our cones. We walked out onto the deck of the pavilion and found a table. The place was busy for a Sunday night. Children were playing video games in the arcade and people were having a late snack or cocktail at the bar. The warm breeze and the soft music playing calmed and seduced your senses.

"I can't believe we both love raspberry ice cream. Most people I know like chocolate." I said and then licked my ice cream.

"Wonder what else we have in common. Where is your favorite place to be?"

"That's easy, the ocean at sunset.....like now."

Nick chuckled and shook his head. "Guilty." Nick raised his hand. What is your birthday?"

"October 4. ----Yours?"

"April 10th----Wow!"

"This is kinda awesome and weird at the same time." I took another bite of ice cream.

We sat and talked even after we finished our ice cream and discovered we had a lot in common. We also had some major differences. My family was a wealthy loving family. Nick came from a poor home with an alcoholic stepfather.

"Do you see your dad much?" I asked.

"My father died when I was ten."

"I'm sorry."

"Thanks. I struggled with losing my father for a long time, especially when my mother remarried. I got in trouble a lot at school because of my father passing and because I locked horns with my step dad."

"I can't imagine what losing a parent is like."

"My step dad got hurt at work. After that he started drinking all the time. And then he started hitting my mom. She hid it for a long time. When I was fourteen I saw him hit her one night and I lost it. I hit him and he called the police. I was almost sent to juvenile hall. But he never hit my mom again."

"Wow. You had a tough childhood."

"Some parts were, but some parts were great----Like Samantha. When her and Rick moved to Pittsburgh, Dave and Rick became best friends. She let us both spend a lot of time at her house. She was like a second mom. She helped me and my brother stay out of trouble and pushed me to finish school." Nick chuckled.

"I didn't realize you were so close with her."

"We stayed at Rick's a lot. My stepdad spent his days drinking and his nights being cantankerous and criticizing everyone near him. I can't wait to get my mother out of there."

"What do you mean?"

"She has nowhere to go except some apartment. I want to buy her a house so she can leave that wretched existence behind."

"Sounds like you really love your mother." I smiled and took a drink of water.

"I do very much. I can't wait for you to meet her."

"That would be wonderful." It made me smile that he saw me in his future.

"Are you ready to head back? It's getting late." Nick looked around then stood up.

I hadn't noticed that we were almost alone. Most of the people had disappeared while we were deep in conversation. I stood up and follow Nick's lead.

The mood on the way back to the beach house was lighter. We talked about our likes and dislikes. We laughed a lot and enjoyed each other. Nick really did have a great sense of humor. He was captivating. We swapped trivial stories and almost past up the house. I was disappointed that our walk was coming to an end. I pulled my phone out of my pocket to check the time as we approached the stairs to the house.

"It's already midnight," I yelped, as I gazed up at Nick with surprise.

"Wow, I didn't realize I kept Cinderella out past her time," Nick joked with a little laugh.

A smile formed across my face as I slapped his chest. Nick chuckled even bigger this time. The sound of his chuckle made me feel safe. I threw my shoes down and held onto Nick's arm as we slipped on our shoes. He took both of my hands in his and looked into my eyes. His gaze was penetrating. I felt like we could read each other's thoughts.

"Thanks for going with me tonight. I like spending time with you.

"I am glad you invited me."

I would like to do something else with you tomorrow. It doesn't matter what it is. Just as long as I am doing it with you," Nick confessed. He gave me a grin and his eyes lit up. He almost looked like he was embarrassed.

"Last night, I thought you wanted as far away from me as you could get. It left me a little more than confused. But tonight was wonderful, Nick." I couldn't believe I was being so honest with him. With Nick, it's easy to express my emotions. I hoped he couldn't hear the nervousness in my voice.

"Again I'm sorry about that," Nick smiled and let go of one of my hands. He led me up to the pool. Everything was quiet. I was thankful there wasn't anyone to harass us. Maybe we dodged the bullet tonight. Anna and Travis were cozied up on the couch watching a movie when we walked in. Anna glanced up when she realized we had walked in.

"I wondered if you two were coming home. I was about ready to call 911 and tell them Nick abducted you," Anna said. she smirked as she moved a little closer to Travis.

"Who's to say I didn't abduct him," I said harassing Anna as I threw a pillow from the chair at her. She giggled and caught the pillow. The light in her eyes and her body language told me she really liked Travis.

Nick smiled at our joke and then asked, "Where are the others?"

"They went to bed a little while ago," Travis said. "I think the sun took it out of them today. We were all discussing perhaps going sightseeing tomorrow. You two in?"

"Yeah," Nick and I said in unison. We gazed at each other and both laughed.

"That sounds like a plan," Nick yawned.

"I'm worn out too. I think I am going to head to bed so I can be an earlier riser tomorrow. I will see you guys in the morning."

"I'll walk you to your room," Nick replied.

"Night, Travis and Anna," again Nick and I spoke in unison. This time we just looked at each other with a look of awe. Nick walked me down the hall. I was tired, but it made me gloomy that my time with Nick was over for the evening. He reached down for my hand and brought it up to his lips while gazing into my eyes.

"Goodnight, Princess Rayna, thank you again for the wonderful evening." Nick let go of my hand with ease as he lowered it back to my side. He left me standing by my door in a daze....Dazzling me once again. How does he make me all jittery inside with just a gaze, a smile, or a word?

"Goodnight," I whispered as Nick walked away.

I turned and went into my room. Once again, Nick engulfed my thoughts. I snatched my night clothes and headed for the bathroom for a quick shower. I washed the salt from my body as I thought about Nick's lips on the back of my hand. My nerve endings were still tingling from the sensation. I swiftly dried off, pulled on my silky pajamas, and walked to the bedroom where I crawled under the lush beige comforter. I shut off the lamp and thought about my night with Nick. I was beginning to enjoy this trip more and more, and Nick....... more and more. I couldn't wait to fall asleep so the sun would rise on another day with Nick. I felt like a child at Christmas. I closed my eyes and fell into dreams of Nick.

Three

The morning sun kissed my eyelids, I didn't open my eyes. I wanted to relish in my sweet dream of Nick. But the aroma of the rich coffee and the strange sense I wasn't alone, forced me awake. I opened my eyes to the sun and turned over with apprehension. Anna sat on my bed, staring intently at me, drinking a cup of hot coffee from a white mug. I jumped, almost causing her to spill her coffee on the beige down comforter. Anna laughed and started in on me.

"Sooooo,.......give me the scoop," she demanded. Anna bounced the bed.

"What scoop? Me and Nick?" A sheepish grin formed on my face and then developed into a full blown smile. "You want full disclosure and I haven't even had a sip of coffee?" Anna picked up a small designer pillow and threw it at me. Then reached over on the night stand and produced another cup of hot coffee. I sat up and took the coffee appreciatively. I took a sip and smiled.

"Since you brought me coffee in bed......I guess I can give you a few details," I giggled.

"You better spill the beans for that cup of coffee.

"Where are the guys?"

"Still in bed. I'm the first one up Rayna, It is only 7:30." Anna made a silly face at me.

"Wow, why did you wake me up?" I laughed when Anna drew her eyes down at my comment. "I feel great. I must have slept like a baby."

"Okay, enough small talk. Spill the beans girl." Anna eyed me trying to penetrate my brain.

I smiled and reflected on last night with Nick; remembering his soft lips on my hand and the intense feelings I experienced when we were together. I took another sip of coffee and then a deep breath.

"He is amazing. We have so many things in common. We walked on the beach and just talked and laughed. He opened up and I got to meet the real Nick. He's funny and passionate." I looked down at my cup. "And.....I have never felt this way before. This connection I have with him is sometimes so overwhelming; it's almost scary. I hope I don't scare him away. I worry I need to reel in my feelings for him or he'll disappear."

"Rayna, stop thinking that way; I watched him yesterday and the way he looks at you. I think he feels the same intense connection. It's probably why he acted so weird Saturday night; it took him by surprise and it scared him."

"You really think so?"

"I noticed him looking at you all day yesterday; he looked at you with so much longing and affection. You need to be yourself and go with the flow. Don't hide yourself and don't be scared. Just follow your heart with him." Anna put her hand on my arm.

"What are you talking about? He will think I am a stalker and run." I pulled my eyebrows up into a concerned look.

"I'm not telling you to act crazy. I want you to be yourself. You've been out of the dating loop for too long."

"You think?" I rolled my eyes and took another drink of coffee.

"How long has it been? Sixteen months, that's how long. You went out on a few dates and they all ended after a few weeks because you kept your guard up. You need to put yourself out there and stop trying to protect yourself Rayna. You'll never fall in real love if you keep a wall up," Anna said with frustration. "You need to take a chance. You can't be scared of getting hurt. I think you'll be surprised."

I thought about what Anna said as I took a long sip of coffee. I needed to be open and find out where this connection might be going. I had protected myself for too long; it may be safe, but it's also boring.

"Okay, you're right. I'm gonna put myself out there and try to enjoy this week with Nick. No locks, an open book. Now, tell me about Mr. Travis," I teased. I poked her in the chest with my finger.

Anna smiled and told me all about Travis and how much she liked him.

"I'm gonna take a walk on the beach, want to join me?" I got out of bed and stretched.

"No, go ahead. I'm gonna make breakfast. I hope the guys will be up soon to eat." Anna stood up to leave my room. "Don't be long; I'll have breakfast ready in a jif."

I brushed my teeth and hair and dressed before I left my room.

"I'll just be a little while. I want to clear my head and think a little about our conversation." I refilled my coffee cup and headed down to the beach. I wore my bright pink bikini since I was in such a positive mood. I had a white crocheted cover over my bikini; it didn't cover much, but it added to the outfit. I hoped to impress Nick of course.

The beach was mostly quiet at 8:15. A few people sat up their spots for the day. I walked the beach and searched for seashells as I wandered up the shore. I thought about Nick and what might happen with him. I could end up hurt again. Of course I wanted to move forward with Nick, hopefully. But my past relationship still lingered in my head and the aftermath of it after it ended. I never wanted to be that emotionally involved again. But I also remembered the good times; the feelings that swam in your body while you are falling in love. And then I remembered the old saying, "it's better to have loved and lost than to not have loved at all." It made sense. What Anna said made sense. And really what choice did I have? Nick was a magnet that kept pulling me toward him.

On my way back, I made up my mind to take Anna's advice and let the Nick thing play out and put my feelings out there. I planned on taking a chance to see where this relationship went; even if it meant getting hurt. As I walked up the steps from the beach, Nick stood on the veranda. He waved and smiled at me. I waved back and gave Nick a huge grin. My heart pounded just seeing Nick for the first time today. I'm glad he wasn't close enough to hear it.

Anna was cleaning up some dishes when I walked into the house. Rick, Dave, Travis, and Jeff were finishing up their breakfast.

"Hungry?" Nick ran his fingers down the back of my hair as he walked passed me into the kitchen.

"Yes, very. Did you eat?"

"No, I wanted to wait on you," Nick said. He smiled and took two plates out of the cabinet and scooped Anna's famous casserole out of the dish.

Anna glanced over her shoulder as she wiped off the counter and gave me a smiling smirk that said, "I told you so." Nick set the plates in front of me.

"Thank you." I gazed at him and smiled. He smiled back and looked at me with his brown smoldering eyes.

"You're welcome." Nick poured two glasses of orange juice and then sat down beside me.

I could get used to a guy paying attention to me. It was so sweet. He was so sweet; and gorgeous. And his scent...... every time he walked past me or came close; I would detect a hint of citrus and musk. The scent was wonderful; it smelled of Nick. I wanted to be closer to him so I could inhale deeper.

The next couple of days were wonderful. We played in the sun; window shopped, relaxed by the pool, and enjoyed everyone's company. Nick and I got to know each other better. I learned he loved to write music and hoped one day to make a career out of it; whether he sang his songs or someone else did. He was also a very sought after body man and he did beautiful custom paint jobs.

I divulged a little of my medical condition to Nick. I disliked revealing my heart condition to new people because I didn't like to be treated differently. People treated me like I might break when they discovered my heart might fail. But the connection I made with Nick was powerful. And I sensed the almost instant bond would be virtually unbreakable.

On Wednesday, Rick planned a deep-sea fishing trip for the guys, so Anna and I did some shopping. It was sort of nice to sneak away from the guys and have some girl time.

We were famished from our day out, so we grabbed dinner and headed back to the house around seven. The house was empty. I hoped Nick would be back from fishing. I missed him. I missed his beautiful brown eyes and the way he looked at me. I missed his long brown hair and the way he tucked it behind his ears. I missed his smell. I missed the way he moved when he walked, rugged yet sensual. I missed everything about him which seemed a little crazy. Why did I miss a guy so much that just met a few weeks ago? Then I reminded myself even though it had only been a few days, I knew him better than I knew most people. Maybe the twin flame or soul mate thing Anna talked about might be real. I couldn't think of a better answer for the deep connection I had with him.

I was out on the veranda, sitting back in a chair, thinking about Nick when he snuck out and whispered in my ear.

"Hey beautiful, how was your day?" his low sweet voice sounded like heaven. An electric shock tingled down my body causing goose bumps to rise on the back of my neck and down my arms.

"Good, how about yours?" My brain froze because of his proximity to me.

"We had fun, but I'm glad to be back looking at you," he said. He smiled his warm sweet smile and rubbed my shoulder with his hand.

I smiled, enjoying his touch.

"I'm glad you're back looking at me. The storm's moving in and it sounds like a big one."

"Yeah, the boat captain said it was gonna be a terrible storm so we grabbed some movies and snacks. I think the guys are worn out from the fishing trip today. I'm gonna grab a quick shower because I know I stink of fish and then we can watch one."

"Sounds good."

Nick gave me a wink and headed off to take a shower. I sat a few more minutes out on the veranda and enjoyed the final breezes before the rain started to come down.

Upon inspection of the movies the guys brought home, two of them were thrillers. I hated thrillers. Nick rented a drama, which was more my style. He said he didn't care much for thrillers and something told him I didn't either. He said it was intuition again.

"You want to watch this in my room?" I asked Nick as I picked up the movie and waved it in the air. I was hoping to spend some quiet time with Nick, just being close to him was all I wanted tonight.

"Thought you would never ask," Nick grinned and took the movie from me, and grabbed my hand.

"Have fun with your horror flick," I said spookily to the gang as I waved and let Nick lead me to my room.

Anna stuck her tongue out at me as she moved in closer to Travis on the couch.

Nick laid the movie on the oak dresser and turned around to face me. We just stood and stared into each other eyes. I realized at that moment I was falling for this guy; and fast. The emotions that stirred in me were wonderful and frightening at the same time. I trusted Nick with my heart and soul. I couldn't explain it, but from the first time our eyes met, I knew.

Nick gently took my face into his hands while still looking into my eyes. He slowly lowered his sweet lips to touch mine. The warmth from his lips flowed down my neck and radiated down my body into my toes. I wrapped my arms around Nick's waist as our kiss lingered until I was lost in the aura of Nick. My adrenaline began to increase, causing my heart to bang against my chest.

Nick took his time as he pulled his lips from mine and whispered seductively.

"I have been waiting all day to do that," then he smiled and kissed me again before I could regain my composure.

We finally separated so he could put the movie in the DVR. I turned on the television and fluffed all the oversized decorative pillows and put them against the wooden headboard so we could lean on them while watching the movie. I jumped on the king size bed and got comfortable. Nick hit start and crawled onto the bed beside me. He opened his arm up for me to slide in against him. I wasted no time moving over and snuggled up against him. I fit flawlessly beside Nick. He kissed the top of my head as the movie started. I never wanted to leave this spot. I decided I'd like to stay here forever, in his warm, strong embrace listening to Nick's beating heart. It was the safest place I'd felt in a very long time.

I opened my eyes and realized I'd fallen asleep; on Nick's chest. It was still dark outside and the movie was over. I looked up and Nick's eyes were closed. As I lay against his chest, I heard his heart, and I realized my own heart was beating with the same rhythm as his. I needed to use the restroom. I crept out of bed so I wouldn't wake him. He was so peaceful sleeping, like an angel.

When I moved, Nick groaned and opened his eyes. "Where are you going?"

"To the restroom, be right back." I peeked at the clock as I moved off the bed. It was one in the morning.

"Do you want me to go to my room?" Nick gazed at me with sad eyes and a worried look.

"You better be here when I come back," I demanded as I smiled and grabbed my pj's.

I hurried into the bathroom and came back out. Nick had moved down in the bed into a more comfortable position. He had one arm under the pillow under his head as he carefully observed me walk over to the bed. He smiled and patted the spot beside him. I dashed back into bed because I couldn't wait to curl up back beside Nick. He was warm and comfortable. I snuggled into Nick's welcoming arms. I closed my eyes and tried to imprint this moment into my mind. Being in Nick's embrace, smelling his skin, and feeling his warmth was where I wanted to be. I didn't want to leave. He held me like he didn't want to let go, and I was fine with that.

Four

I woke to the sun shining through the blinds and Nick looking at me intently. "What?" I asked, puzzled, wondering what he could be thinking and why he didn't wake me.

"Just watching you sleep. You look so peaceful and happy. I like watching you sleep." Nick traced the contours of my face with his finger.

"I am happy..... in your arms." I said. I wasn't sure if I should have let the last part out. I wanted to let him know exactly how I felt. So I went on. "I'm glad you didn't leave last night, just being in your arms makes my world better." I wondered what he might say now that I had revealed my true feelings to him.

"I'm glad you didn't kick me out. I didn't wanna let you go. But sadly, I must let you go now so we can get ready for the show."

I had forgotten the band had a show today. They mentioned it on Saturday, but I'd been concentrating on Nick all week, not the band.

"That's right....I forgot about it. What time do we need to leave?"

"About ten or so," Nick said as he brought his sweet lips to mine again. He kissed my forehead and crawled out of bed. He took my hands and pulled me off the bed and into his arms.

He held me for a minute. I savored the moment. Nick let go and gave me a quick kiss and left to dress for the show.

We had to drive to Key Largo for the show. It was an afternoon concert for the start of summer. The rain the night before stopped and it had turned into a beautiful sunny day. The concert was right off the boardwalk, so there were crowds of people everywhere. Anna and I decided to stay close to the stage so we didn't lose our spot. I wanted to be right in front so I could see Nick perform and Anna was dying to watch Travis play.

The band had the crowd alive and dancing by three in the afternoon. Nick owned the stage. I could listen to his voice all day. I heard whistles in the crowd and an urge of jealousy nudged at me. I smiled thinking about myself being jealous of Nick. I liked it.

While we waited for the guys to pack their gear in the van after the show, Anna made me fill her in on last night because she saw Nick come out of my room this morning. I also admitted to her that I thought she might be right about the twin flames. It was the only conclusion to explain my feelings that Nick and I were experiencing. Anna admitted she wasn't sure if she believed there was anything to "twin flames" until she watched me and Nick together. Now she believed.

"The way he looks at you.........with such affection........ longing. And the way you two react when you are together. You respond to each other like you know what the other is thinking. I've never seen two people so in sync. You two have only known each other a few days. It is amazing."

"You can really see that when we are together?"

"Yes, it is a little disgusting and it makes me jealous," she wrinkled her nose and laughed as she gave me a huge hug. "Rayna, I am so happy for you. If anyone deserves to find their twin flame or soul mate or whatever it is, it's you."

"Do you honestly think we were meant to be together?" I needed reassurance from my closest friend.

"If you two weren't meant to be together, then love is a big joke the universe has played on all of us." Anna was firm on this point.

We spent the rest of the afternoon and the evening in Key Largo. We stopped in little shops and enjoyed all the activities on the boardwalk. The boardwalk was busy with people going here and there. Nick held my hand most of the day. When he didn't hold my hand, he kept his arm over my shoulder or around my waist. I loved the attention. I couldn't get enough of him. My body was alive with an electric current and adrenaline when Nick touched me.

It was past eleven when we got back to the house. I was worn out from all the tourist activity. I hoped Nick would stay with me again tonight. He was beginning to become my addiction and I needed my fix.

Nick led me up the steps and into the house.

"Night guys, see you in the morning," Anna said as she walked to her room.

"Good night Anna." Nick and I said together.

As we walked into the great room I gazed up into Nick's deep brown eyes. I could lose myself in his gaze. "I'm tired too, how about you?" I asked, hoping he was.

"Exhausted." Nick caressed my cheek with the back of his hand as he stared deep into my soul.

"Stay with me," I said more as a demand than a question. Nick said nothing. He took my hand and led me to my master suite. Snuggled in his warm, electric embrace, I drifted off in seconds to a dream land where Nick was forever mine.

I awoke in the morning before the sun fully rose. It started to peek through the drapes and spill some of its rays on Nick's face. I must have slept soundly because I hadn't moved all night. I was still in Nick's arms. He was even more beautiful when he slept. His face was peaceful and content. I was afraid to move for fear of waking him. I moved my head slightly so that I saw his angelic face better. Nick wrapped his arm a little tighter around me and a little moan crept out of his throat, but he didn't open his eyes. I enjoyed admiring him without him knowing. I tried to imprint every line of his face into my memory before he roused. I would have two more days with him to spend exclusively and I intended on making the best of them.

Realizing our week was almost over made me anxious. I was spoiled by seeing Nick every day. Getting back to the real world wouldn't change the feelings I had for Nick; I only hoped it wouldn't change anything for him.

As I thoughtfully gazed at Nick, his eyes opened and looked directly into mine. Nick smiled blissfully, showing the dimple on his left cheek. I moved in and gave his lips a peck.

"What's going on in that beautiful head of yours, Rayna?" Nick's voice was barely a breath. He moved a piece of hair out of my face.

"Just taking in the gorgeous views," I said. I smiled and blushed at the same time.

Nick smiled and gave my lips a quick peck. "Likewise baby."

My heart raced and my lips warmed from the touch of his lips on mine. This man was going to drive me insane. I couldn't get enough of him. I guess this is why they call it falling in love. You actually do have a sense of falling, but the fall is breathtaking and scary at the same time. The emotions involved with falling in love are the most euphoric sensation I ever experienced, the daunting part is hoping they fall with you and not let you crash.

I looked at the clock, it was 7:05. "Don't move," I demanded as I jumped out of bed and ran to the bathroom. My bladder was full and I wanted to erase my morning breath. I hurried hoping Nick wouldn't escape.

I ran back into the room and climbed back onto the bed. I sat facing Nick. He was stretched out with his hands behind his head. I leaned over Nick with my arms braced around his body and stared into his eyes. I slowly placed my lips on his to kiss him more deeply than I ever had.

Nick responded by parting his lips and cradling my face with both of his hands. Our breathing grew heavy and erratic. Nick rolled me over on my back and continued kissing me for another moment. I ran my hands up under his shirt and caressed his strong smooth back. Nick kissed me deeper and more passionately. I moved my lips to Nick's cheek and worked my way down the side of his neck breathing in his scent. Nick pulled his head back and allowed my lips to move down his neck and let out a sigh. He turned and kissed my neck and continued up to my lips where he placed a long sensual kiss.

"You're going to be the death of me Rayna," Nick spoke in a whisper.

I smiled and studied those possessive eyes, "Likewise baby." I raised my head and gave him another kiss.

"Let's get moving, I want to spend my last two days here enjoying you on the beach." he climbed out of bed.

"But I wanna stay here with you all day." I pouted. I wanted Nick all to myself. I didn't want to leave his warm embrace.

"I would enjoy that also Rayna, but if I don't start moving now, our relationship is going to move to the next level and I'm being honest when I say I want to savor this part of it." His face was sincere and he spoke with affection. I gazed at him with amazement. I was speechless.

Nick walked around the bed and pulled me to him as he wrapped his arms around my waist. "Say something Rayna." I didn't look at him because I was trying to understand what he just said.

Nick's hand raised my chin so our eyes met. "Have I upset you?"

"No.....I am trying to comprehend what you just said. I've never heard a guy say anything like this before. Not that I've had many experiences, but most guys move fast. I am just surprised....." I felt a little embarrassed talking to Nick about this, but I trusted him.

"Yeah,............well, you're not most girls. You're worth the wait." Nick smiled and kissed me.

I slid my arms under his, wrapped them around him, and squeezed as I laid my head on his chest. This guy is wonderful. He wanted to be with me not just have me. I appeared to be in heaven.

"Hey, how about a picnic breakfast on the beach?" Nick suggested.

"That sounds kind of cool." I smiled.

"Get dressed and I'll pack us a breakfast to go." Nick gave me a quick kiss and left my room.

Anna was leaning on the counter drinking coffee as I entered the kitchen.

"Travis and I are going out for breakfast. Do you wanna join us?" Anna asked.

"No thanks. Nick is taking me on a picnic for breakfast." I smiled

"Wow.....How romantic," Dave teased walking to the refrigerator. Anna smacked the back of his head and I stuck my tongue out at him. Dave laughed at us.

"You could learn something from your big brother," Nick said as he walked into the kitchen. "Ready?" He looked at me for an answer.

"I guess I should pay attention. After all, you are the one with the girl. But for now, I'm off for a run. See ya." Dave saluted us and left.

"Did we miss something?" Rick and Jeff asked as they walked into the kitchen.

"Dave being Dave." Nick chuckled as he grabbed a thermos off the counter and walked over to me.

"We're going out for brunch if you two wanna go with Anna and me." Travis offered to Rick and Jeff. "Rayna and Nick are taking a picnic to the beach."

"Yeah, we'll go with you," Jeff said. Rick agreed with a head nod. Everybody laughed.

Nick forced us out of our little secluded world and out into the real world. He led me down to the beach and carried a picnic basket in his other hand. He took out a blanket and spread it on the sand. We both sat and set up our picnic.

"How long have you lived with Anna?" Nick inquired. He spread a bagel with cream cheese and set it on a plate in front of me.

"I moved in with her in August. Just before school started. I lived with my parents before that."

"What made you move out of your parents' house?" Nick poured coffee. He handed me a cup.

"I should have moved out when I started college but I was still depressed about my heart." I popped a strawberry in my mouth and chewed. "My parents were upset that I moved out but I needed to get my life moving."

"Are you happier now?" Nick took a bite of his bagel.

"Moving in with Anna was the best decision I've ever made. She brought me back to life. I wouldn't be sitting on this beach without Anna."

Nick and I watched the waves as he fed me the rest of my breakfast.

The sun started to get hot by the time we finished breakfast, so we gathered our things and headed to the pool. After cooling off, Nick and I sat on the bench in the pool without talking. He held my hand while he traced my palm with his finger.

"Haven't you two had enough of each other?"

Nick stopped tracing my palm and we both glanced up and saw Rick looking down at us from the veranda.

"Not even close," Nick grinned and said with conviction. I squeezed his hand and he looked at me and smiled.

My blood pumped through my veins as my heart beat faster. A butterfly flipped in my stomach.

Dave walked out. He said, "Leave the love birds alone, I think they're cute."

It was kind of embarrassing everyone witnessing what I was feeling, but I ran my hand up Nick's arm as I tighten my fingers around his. Then he leaned in and kissed me while the guys watched. They all let out a disgusted moan. I felt dizzy and I almost forgot to breathe.

We all enjoyed a wonderful day at the beach and decided to go out for the evening. We had dinner and then went dancing at the club down the street. Nick was a surprisingly good dancer. Our bodies moved in unison and he made me feel like the only girl in the place. He never took his eyes off me and continued to make sure our bodies were connected in some way; whether our hands were entwined or his arms locked around me.

Anna and I hadn't spent any girl time together in the last couple of days, so we had a quick chat in the bathroom.

"What is going on with you two?" Anna inquired with a huge smile as she elbowed me at the sink while I looked in the mirror adjusting my hair.

I took a deep breath, turned, and smiled at Anna. "I think I'm falling in love!" My voice was faraway and dreamy.

Anna squeezed both of my hands and smiled with genuine love. "I am soooo excited for you girl. You deserve this. Nick is a wonderful guy. Not only because of the way he treats you, but from what I overheard the guys talk about."

"I want to hear about that. But, the guys are probably waiting on us, so we better go. We need some girl time," I said. I walked toward the door and glanced back and smiled at Anna.

"You know you are glowing don't you?" Anna said as she followed me out the door.

"It shows?" My voice full of surprise.

"Like the sun in the morning," Anna said without skipping a beat.

We walked back to our table. Nick peeked up and greeted me with a grin and a kiss as he wrapped his arm around my waist. I was loving life. He pulled me to the dance floor for a slow song. I laid my head on his shoulder to savor his intoxicating scent and to feel his body move with mine. Nick sang the song in my ear. I could let him sing to me all night. I nuzzled his neck with my nose and then kissed it. Nick let out a breath as he pulled me closer. I didn't want the song to end. Nick pulled his head back so he could plant a kiss on my lips. I was in a dream world with my emotions and electricity was pumping through my veins.

The evening ended like the night before; me falling asleep in Nick's arms. And again in the morning, I didn't want to leave his embrace.

Nick hadn't shaved since yesterday so he had a five o'clock shadow. The stubble on his face made him irresistible. I ran my fingers over his cheek, then his chin, and last his upper lip.

"You like that huh?" Nick said with more of a statement than a question.

"It is sexy," I whispered as I kissed him.

· ♥ · ♥ · ♥ · ♥ · ♥ ·

Nick pulled me back to reality again where we all spend our last day in paradise. We enjoyed a buffet style lunch and dinner from what we found left in the fridge. Nick and I couldn't keep our hands off of each other. I sat on his lap, we held hands, and walked hand and hand all day. So Anna and I still didn't have any girl time yet. But I knew tomorrow on the plane we would have plenty of time to talk. I wanted to enjoy every minute I had left with Nick by my side and he appeared to feel the same. Whichever way or where ever I moved, Nick moved with me. When he moved, I moved. This happened naturally, without even thinking; like magnets pulling each other together.

The sun had set and the gang hung out at the pool. Anna and Travis were in the hot tub talking intently. Nick lay back on a lounge chair with his feet on the either side of the it. I sat in front of Nick lying back on his chest, relaxing.

"Take a walk with me?" Nick asked. He didn't smile. I sat up and gazed at him, not sure if I was comfortable with his tone; a little too dark for me.

"Okay." I said in a quiet and reserved tone.

Nick took my hand and led me across the patio, over the bridge, and down to the beach. We walked slowly down the shoreline; our hands connected. Nick didn't speak and I patiently waited. The longer the silence continued, the more frightened I became. What was Nick thinking? What did he want to say to me? Nick stopped and let go of my hand to sit down on the sand. I sat beside him hoping he would speak.

SONGS FROM THE HEART

"Rayna, I wanted to talk to you about the first night we met." Nick didn't meet my eyes; he continued looking out at the ocean. The breeze blew his long hair away from his face. The sound of the ocean made our spot more private. I glanced at him and then looked down at the sand, not wanting to speak, for fear of messing with his train of thought.

"You are probably going to think I'm crazy. I want to be honest and completely open with you.... That first night when our eyes met.....when I stood on the stage, something happened. I can't really explain it. I've never experienced anything like it. It scared me........." Nick paused for a moment. I didn't say anything.

"I felt like you could see my soul. When our hands touched.........electricity sparked. When I said I was ill and I went to my room, I didn't lie...... I was telling the truth. Whatever happened between us at that moment, confused and scared the hell out of me. I needed to be away from you so I could think."

Nick's finger touched my chin and he raised my face to stare into my eyes. A tear leaked from the corner of my eye and he wiped it away with the back of his finger.

"Rayna, what's the matter? Am I scaring you?" Nick questioned. Nick stared at me trying to penetrate my eyes with his intense gaze.

"No, just the opposite."

Nick stared at me with confusion on his face, so I continued.

"I felt the same way, but you acted like you didn't want to be around. That confused me even more. Now I'm relieved," I said. I smiled at him.

"I didn't want to be around you that night. The feelings were too intense." Nick turned away looking out at the ocean but continued to talk. "Last summer, my girlfriend of two years decided she wanted to be with someone else. I guarded myself after that. Then here you are. Flipping my world upside down with one glance. I can't stay away from you. And I can't understand the pull you have on me. But it really doesn't matter because I am already falling for you." Nick seemed relieved but uneasy about his response.

I couldn't say anything. Nick's honesty sent me over the edge. Emotionally I thought Nick couldn't move me more, but he just did. Another tear slid down my cheek.

"Nick," I said in a whisper.

I moved closer and kissed him. All my fears vanished and I let my last guard down. He had me. Nick returned my kiss with more passion than before and more intensity than I had ever experienced. Every nerve in my body awoke and ignited ready to burst. I climbed into Nick's lap and straddled him as we kissed and I ran my fingers through his hair. Nick moved his hands up and down my back. I breathed in his air and he breathed in mine. I wanted this man, all of him. Nick took my face into his hands and pulled away.

"We need to slow down. I want to take "us" slow," Nick whispered.

I looked down and bit my lip. I wanted to go slow too since I had not been with a guy, but I couldn't help myself with Nick.

"Are you mad at me?" Nick asked as he raised my face to gaze into his eyes. A worried look formed across his face.

"No. But since we are being honest I should tell you something."

"You can tell me anything. princess." Nick kept our eyes locked.

I looked down. "I'm..... Nick....I'm a virgin." The words spontaneously came out. There was no better way to say it. "That is the reason my ex broke up with me. We dated for two years and he was ready to have sex and I wasn't." I was petrified of what Nick might say. I moved my eyes away from his and put my head down again; scared of what I would see in Nick's eyes.

Nick pulled my face back up to his again and waited for my eyes to meet his. "Rayna, don't be embarrassed. You should be proud. He must've not been the right guy for you if you weren't ready. He didn't deserve you if that's why he let you go."

Nick kissed me and then stared into my soul.

"I think I am ready with you."

"Precisely the reason I want to take it slow with you. I want to know everything about you before I know you that intimately," Nick said.

He stared into my eyes for a while. The heat and electricity between us was more than I could take. I kissed him and snuggled into his neck. Nick and I sat for a long time, just holding each other, not speaking.

It was a relief talking with Nick this way. We bared our souls to each other and exposed our innermost fears. Even though we were waiting for sex, he and I shared more intimacy on the beach that night than most people share in a lifetime.

"Let's take a midnight swim." Nick stood up and pulled me to my feet.

"In the ocean?" I was a little surprised by his sudden energy.

"Yes....in the ocean, silly girl." Nick gave me a quick kiss and pulled me to my feet.

The warmth of the water was tranquil as we waded into the ocean. This was a first for me. I'd been to the ocean many times before, but I had never swum at night. It was very sensual. It was euphoric; being in the ocean with our skin touching and Nick kissing me.

"Okay, ...if you want to wait, we need to get out of the water and put some clothes on before I lose my mind." I gave Nick a stern and serious face.

He laughed and agreed. The chilly air brought goose bumps to my exposed skin when we got out of the water. We had no towels. We ran back up to the house to find our towels. Everyone was gone from the pool. Nick grabbed my towel from the chair and wrapped it around me. He rubbed my arms vigorously before he wrapped his towel around himself.

We went into the house and changed our clothes. I jumped into bed and under the covers. Nick came back down to my room and found me waiting for him.

"Can I stay tonight?" Nick stood at the side of the bed with a white t-shirt and silky blue basketball shorts on. He was sexy in anything.

"Now that you have clothes on and if you promise not to tease me." I patted the bed beside me as I pulled the covers up further as I shivered.

Nick smiled and crawled over me instead of walking around the bed. "Back at ya baby."

Nick crawled under the covers. "You're cold," he said. He moved closer. I snuggled into him to steal his heat. Nick leaned in and kissed me. "Goodnight princess Rayna, Nick whispered. He smiled and then kissed my forehead.

"Goodnight prince Nicolas." I closed my eyes and drifted off to sleep. Safe and secure in his arms.

In my dreams that night, I dreamed Nick was lost and I couldn't find him. I woke up in a fright and woke Nick. He pulled me closer and held me tight chasing the demons away.

The morning rays of sun woke me along with the sensation of my arm being rubbed. Nick stroked my arm with his fingers. I rolled over on my back so I could see into Nick's eyes.

"Good morning beautiful," Nick said. He kissed my forehead.

"Yes, it is with you here." I smiled and caressed his cheek and ran my fingers through his hair. He was my beautiful, strong prince that I found when I hadn't been looking. Nick had to leave today and I wanted to remember this feeling right now, so it could keep me happy when I couldn't be with him.

"I need to put my things together. The guys are gonna want to leave soon. Want to help me?" Nick played with my hair and caressed my arm.

"I can do that." I pushed myself up on my elbow and leaned in and kissed him as he fell back on the pillows and pulled me closer.

This is what I wanted to savor; to keep me going for the next day. This was the only place I wanted to be, in Nick's embrace and with my mouth devouring his. I came to my senses and fully sat up and grabbed a pillow to smash Nick with. He laughed and grabbed me and threw me down on the bed for one more, long kiss.

"Let's pack up my things before I'm in trouble with the guys," Nick said. He smiled and pulled me out of bed. He led me to his room to start packing him up.

The reality of Nick leaving hit me in the gut. I became gloomy and silent. I tried to act cheerful. I stole one of Nick's shirts he had worn out of his bag.

"What are you doing Rayna? I'm trying to pack," Nick chuckled.

"It smells like you. I wanna sleep with it." I hugged it to my chest.

He laughed and shook his head. He kissed me on the top of the head and continued packing his things. I had a small inclination that Nick would let me get away with a lot and I smiled inside.

The van was packed and ready by eight a.m. All the guys were in the van waiting for Nick.

"I'll call as soon as we get home. I have work this week but I'm free in the evenings. We can do something." Nick held me in his arms.

"What day do you think?" I peeked up at Nick.

"Monday around 6. I figure I'll need to work a little later Monday to get caught up."

His kiss was not long enough, but when the guys started to harass us, it was difficult to continue with an audience. I reluctantly let Nick go and waved as they pulled out of sight. My heart broke.

Five

♥

Anna and I landed in Pittsburgh around 4 p.m. the next day. We drove straight home. As I shut the front door my phone notified me that I received a text. It was Nick. He wrote four little words, "I miss you already." These four little words warmed my heart more than anything I ever read. Tears swelled in my eyes and I took a deep breath to wash them away before they could slide down my face and expose me. I didn't need to give Anna more fuel to convince me I was in love.

I showered after I unpacked. I was exhausted from the last week. My phone rang around ten. I was lying in bed holding his shirt missing him.

"Hello," I said with relief. I was happy to hear his voice; knowing he made it home safe.

"How are you beautiful?" His voice tired but sexy.

"Tired, I'm in bed, just waiting for your call. So you made it home safe." I said.

"Yes, I'm home safe. Am I keeping you awake? I can let you go," his voice full of sensual teasing.

"You hang up and I'll have to get up and drive out of this city to find you," I said demanding but yet humorous.

Nick laughed. "Maybe I should hang up then if that's how I'll be able to see you."

"I've missed you all day. It's weird not seeing you. I don't know how I'm going to make it until tomorrow." I hoped I didn't scare him away by being so honest. But I needed him to know my feelings. "I'm sleeping with your shirt," I said and then laughed a little.

"I'm jealous of my shirt." He laughed. "I missed you today too. The drive was so long."

"I bet. I'm glad you're home safe."

"Thanks. Think about what you want to do tomorrow and call me around noon. I'll be on break. Plus I don't think I can go all day without hearing your voice." Nick sounded so sincere, my heart melted. I didn't think this guy could get any better, but he surprised me every day.

"I wish you were here and not the shirt, but it helps." The shirt smelled like him. "It'll help me sleep." Nick and I talked for over an hour and I grew sleepy. He needed to be up for work tomorrow, but it was hard to let him go.

"Sleep well Rayna and dream of me." Nick's caressing voice sent shivers up my spine and made me miss him more.

"I doubt I sleep well because you're not here. I know I will dream of you because I do most nights."

"Really, now that's flattering. I am honored to be the man of your dreams." Nick chuckled.

"Nick, stop laughing. You are the man of my dreams." I laughed a little myself, he was always so goofy.

"You are the girl in my dreams as well. Goodnight Princess Rayna. See you tomorrow."

"Night," I whispered and hung up the phone.

Monday dragged on forever. It seemed like the hands on the clock would never reach six. I messed in my closet trying to find the perfect outfit to wear. I decided on a pink mini skirt with a frilly white tank top and pink sandals. I painted my toe nails and finger nails and after they dried, got a shower.

With my hair and makeup finished, I decided I liked the way I looked.

The doorbell rang and I froze. Nick arrived a little early. I checked myself in the mirror once more and headed out of my room. I took a deep breath and opened the front door. He smiled that beautiful smile that made me melt. I grabbed his hand and pulled him inside. The butterflies danced in my stomach, so I took another deep breath and smiled at Nick. He leaned in and touched his lips to mine. I melted.

Anna was in the kitchen cooking something for dinner. She had invited Travis over.

"We'll be back later Anna," I yelled.

"Hey Nick," Anna peeked around the corner.

"Hey yourself. How are ya?" Nick waved at Anna as I opened the door to leave.

"Good. Just cooking dinner for Travis," she smiled.

"Tell him I said hi. See ya later," Nick said. Anna waved bye to us.

Nick held the truck door open for me. He drove an older Toyota Tacoma, but he took care of it. It was an attractive sapphire; possibly his favorite color. I didn't even know his favorite color. There was a lot I needed to learn about Nick I decided as I watched him walk around the truck to get in. As he started the truck, I leaned in to kiss Nick. He parted his lips slightly and allowed me to have my way for a minute. My stomach growled and interrupted the moment. I pulled away and laughed.

"Somebody's hungry," Nick said. He laughed and put the truck into drive.

I had him drive to a small restaurant I loved with delicious food and a quiet atmosphere. I asked a million questions. He answered everyone. I found out that we both loved red and steak medium well. We listened to a lot of the same music. We shared a piece of cheesecake for dessert. It was nine when we left the restaurant. We sat on the balcony off my living room for nearly an hour. The weather was warm and the stars were out.

"When can I see you again?" Nick's voice just above a whisper

"Any day is yours. Remember, I'm free until I find a job." I grinned with a little shyness.

"In that case, can I fix you dinner Wednesday? I think you need to have a look at my place before you decide if you like me."

"Too late." I smiled and hugged him. "Wednesday sounds great. What time?" Nick smiled and kissed me.

He stood up and pulled me up to him. "I finish early, so how about five or so? I'd invite you tomorrow, but I work a little later and I need to wash some laundry and clean up a bit. I don't want you to think I'm a total slob." He laughed.

"I can't wait."

Nick led me to my front door. He kissed me one final time and left me at the door watching him leave.

The next day I decided to try some shopping to keep me busy. I hadn't bought many new clothes in a few years. Shopping helped make the time pass. I wondered what he was doing the entire time.

Nick and I talked on the phone on Tuesday evening for hours. He called again right before he turned in for bed. He said he liked to hear my voice before he closed his eyes. Tomorrow evening couldn't come soon enough. I already missed him. That night I dreamed of Nick. We were walking on the beach at sunset and he declared his love for me.

Nick gave me the address of where he lived. I had never been there before, but I knew the area. It was not that far from me; about fifteen minutes without traffic. I drove up toward a huge gray brick house and spotted the garage Nick said he lived in. It was an ordinary concrete block building without paint. There were only two windows on the side with the door. Nick's blue truck was parked outside.

I knocked on the door. I took a refreshing breath as my stomach flipped.

"It's open, come on in," Nick yelled.

I opened the door and went in. Nick stood in the kitchen area, cutting vegetables up. He looked up and waved me over. I walked over and he put the knife down. He pulled me into his arms and kissed me.

"That is what I've been missing," he whispered in my ear as he pulled me into a hug.

I smile up at Nick, loving the attention. He touched my cheek as he gazed into my eyes for a moment and kissed me again. He let go of his embrace on me and finished cutting up the vegetables.

"So, what are we having for dinner?"

"Lasagna, salad, and garlic bread. Do you like?" He glanced up at me for an answer.

"One of my favorites. Nice place you have here; suits you well." I kept an eye on Nick as I walked around and examined his pad. He continued cooking. "I like it."

Everything was open. The kitchen, dining area, and living area were under a loft. As Nick prepared dinner, I walked around his living room trying to get a sense of who he was. He had a few pictures. One picture was of him, Dave, and a very pretty older lady; I assumed it was his mother. Nick's hair was buzzed off in the picture. He looked better with his shaggy hair. I couldn't find any signs of a female touch. It was all high quality furniture, just a little rough around the edge; like Nick; rough around the edges. But I felt comfortable here.

I worked my way back to the kitchen where Nick continued to work on our dinner. He tossed the salad and prepared the bread for the oven.

"So, what do you think?" He wiped his hands on a kitchen towel and took a drink of his glass of water.

"About what, dinner?"

"No, about my place?" He moved his hand around his apartment like he was a game show host showing the prizes.

"I like it. It suits you." I grinned and walked around the island to wrap my arms around his waist. He wrapped his arms around me and kissed the top of my head as I snuggled my head into his chest.

"You look beautiful tonight Rayna. Of course you always look beautiful; when you wake up in the morning is when you are the most beautiful."

I peeked up at Nick so I could gaze into his beautiful brown eyes. He kissed the tip of my nose and then my lips. He pulled away, but I wanted more. I had the feeling he did too, but was trying to squelch the flames before we both were engulfed in the moment.

"I better take the lasagna out and put the bread in if we're going to eat tonight." Nick chuckled and gave my lips a quick peck as we both released our hold on each other.

I walked around the counter and sat on a stool at the island so I could watch him work. He wore tan cargo shorts and a plain black tank top. He was barefoot and he looked oh so sexy walking around like this. I enjoyed watching him while he worked but would prefer touching him. The electricity between us moved back and forth from across the bar. It was as intense as always.

When he started to dish out the lasagna onto our plates it brought my mind back to reality.

"Parmesan cheese?" Nick asked as he held up the grater with a chunk of cheese in it.

"Yes please. You thought of everything." Wow! Is all I could think. What guy buys fresh cheese and grates it onto your food? I had found the most wonderful guy in every way.

I took a bite. "This is delicious. Who taught you to make it?"

"My mom. She is an excellent cook. The secret is in the sauce." Nick winked at me before he dove into his food.

After dinner, I helped Nick clean up the dishes. He wanted me to sit and not help, but I liked working with him. Being with him is what I wanted and it was a joy to work with him as a team. Nick washed and I dried. We finished the dishes, put away the food, and decided to watch a movie. We picked a light romantic comedy.

The movie finished a little before eleven. I knew Nick had to be up early the next morning for work, so I stretched a little and started to stand up.

Nick pulled me back down on the couch and into his arms. "You're not leaving are you?"

"You have an early morning. I figured I better let you go to bed."

"Stay with me. I sleep better when you're next to me." Nick pleaded with his eyes. I couldn't resist those beautiful, intense eyes, nor did I want to.

"Are you sure? My voice barely above a whisper, but hopeful.

"Yes, I want you with me always." Nick put his hand through my hair and behind my neck and pulled me into him for a kiss. The kiss deepened and I ran my fingers up his muscular back. His mouth grew more aggressive against mine. I leaned back and pulled his head with me causing us both to be lying on the couch. Our kissing and caressing went on for a few minutes until Nick kissed my neck and then a quick peck on my cheek;

simmering our passion. We both caught our breath while we just held each other.

Nick pushed himself up and kissed the tip of my nose while he still hovered over me and turned the television off. I watched his tantalizing body move across the room and wondered how much longer we could go without taking our relationship any further. It was very hard touching and kissing him and then stopping. I wanted him completely. I had never felt these emotions before and I started to become frustrated with my own body and feelings. I should be able to control this. But it was beyond my reach.

Nick led me upstairs to his loft. He had a full size bed with a simple headboard of dark wood. A small wooden nightstand set on either side of the bed and a mix matched dresser with a small mirror set adjacent to the bed. There was no comforter, just a basic blue and white quilt for the cover.

"Do you want one of my t-shirts to wear? Nick said as he pulled his shirt off.

"I will take that one please." I smiled as I pointed to the shirt in his hand.

Nick smiled from ear to ear and threw the shirt across the bed at me. I pulled my shirt off and pulled his shirt over my head. I peeled off my jeans and pushed the blanket down as Nick dropped his jeans and stepped out of them. I stopped and stared of course. I couldn't help myself; his body was so perfect and sculpted. Nick standing there in his boxer briefs tantalized me without him knowing it. He crawled into his bed and I followed suit. He held his arm out for me and I moved over to be wrapped up in his warm strong arms. This was my favorite spot. My world felt complete when I was with Nick.

Six

♥

Nick finally took me to meet his mother. Even though he didn't live more than thirty minutes from his mother's, he didn't visit often. He planned our visit when he was sure his stepfather would be sober.

"Mom this is Rayna," Nick introduced me when we walked into the kitchen of his childhood home.

"You are just beautiful," his mother said in a soft voice. She held her arms out from her thin body for a hug. "I am so happy my son finally brought you to meet me."

I stepped into her arms for a warm and loving hug. "Nice to meet you Olivia." I smiled as she let go of me. She continued to hold my hands and smile at me. Her thin body looked tired.

She let go of my hands. "Get your mamma a hug." She reached over to Nick.

He leaned down and hugged his mother lifting her off her feet. She kissed his cheek.

"Sit down. Let me fix you something to eat."

Nick pulled out the outdated wooden chair for me to sit. He grabbed two waters from the refrigerator and sat with me at the old wooden table.

"Don't worry yourself mom. We didn't come to eat we came to visit. Where is he?"

"At the bar."

"Hopefully he gets lost," Nick said.

"Oh Nick." Olivia swatted his arm. "Nick tells me you just graduated college."

"Just a few weeks ago." I smiled.

"What are your plans?" Olivia closed the cabinet door. She pulled a chair out and sat with us.

"I want to work in publishing, but we'll see."

"Hopefully you find what you're looking for."

"I'm not in a hurry. I've worked so hard the past three years. I wanna take a little break." I took a drink of my water.

"Only three years?"

"Yes. I started college early. I never took summer breaks so I finished early." I smiled at Olivia.

"Beautiful and smart." Olivia smiled at me and then Nick. I blushed.

"Mom, you're embarrassing Rayna. What have you been up to?"

"Oh, the same old things. Work and putting up with John."

"Maybe one day I'll get you out of here," Nick said. Olivia smiled at Nick and place her hand on his.

The rest of June flew by quickly. I started a part time job editing for a local magazine. I even helped Nick work on his motorcycle. Or should I say I handed him tools and relished in his amazing body as he worked to rebuild it. We became inseparable. My love for him grew deeper and deeper every day; although neither one of us revealed this to each other, we felt it. I sensed when Nick would call or somehow knew what he would say. The only time we were away from each other was when he worked. On those days, I helped with getting gigs for the band. Some of my classmates from college helped get me connected. I started to book them some incredible gigs. Rick started traveling a lot for his advertising firm. It didn't leave him with much time to manage the band.

I procrastinated letting Nick meet my parents. They didn't realize I was getting serious with anyone. They knew I was dating. I couldn't hide the way I felt about Nick and I wasn't ready for their criticism yet.

A few weeks into the updated gigs the guys put on a great performance for a huge crowd. The crowd showed their appreciation with loud hoots and hollers. When the band finished, the crowd demanded more. The guys went back on stage and performed another song. This happened a lot. People loved the band whether this was their first time seeing them or not. Most became fans.

Anna and I stood up and applauded with the crowd. We both beamed with pride. Nick walked off stage over to us. He cracked his towel at me, picked me up and swung me around, pressing me again him.

"You are sweaty." I grimaced and wrapped my arms around his neck. His delectable aroma spilled onto me. I liked it on me.

"You mean you don't like me like this?" Nick chuckled and leaned in to kiss me.

"It is kind of sexy." I gave him an admiring look with a huge smile. I always melted when he kissed me.

"We need to pack the equipment, up you two if we are going to enjoy the fireworks. You can do that later." Dave glared at us with disapproval and then he gave us his cute endearing smile.

"Okay, okay." Nick put me down and wiped the sweat from his face. He jumped back on the stage and started tearing the equipment apart. All the guys razzed Nick about me, teasing him. He smiled at them and let them continue with their joshing.

Anna and I packed our chairs up and took them to the van. As we started to walk back toward the stage, Anna elbowed me.

"Who the hell is that?" Anna demanded as she pointed to the stage.

I glanced up and a beautiful blond sauntered toward Nick. He had his back turned as she prowled up behind him. She said something and he turned around. She threw her arms around his neck and didn't let go. Nick placed his hands on her waist. They parted and stood talking. This woman wore a pair of daisy dukes and a white tank top loaded with silver sequins. She was beautiful. She tossed her long blonde hair back as she flipped her head back and laughed at whatever Nick said.

"Who the hell is that?" Astonished at how this woman flirted with Nick. I stood and watched the conversation unfold. Dave came over and gave her a hug and the other guys came over to talk. Anna and I stood there, wondering who this beautiful flirty woman could be. And why did her hands keep touching my man. A surge of jealousy engulfed my body. I didn't like the stirring in my stomach.

Watching Nick smile at her while she talked brought out an emotion I was not comfortable with; it frightened me. I wanted to storm up on the stage and shove her away from Nick. I was sure that wouldn't be the thing to do. I needed to find out about this mystery woman first. So I waited. Right before she left, she moved in to kiss Nick goodbye. Just before she reached his lips, he turned his head and she kissed his cheek. She hugged him and walked off the stage. She waved as she walked away.

"I hope that's his cousin or something." Anna hissed. She grabbed my hand and pulled me to the stage.

Anna appeared to be as upset as me. I took a deep breath to wash away the jealousy. I didn't want Nick to see me this way.

"Anna, don't say anything. Let me find out who she is first, okay." I stared at Anna, pleading with my eyes; hoping she would keep quiet.

"Okay, I'll let you find out the answers," Anna reassured me. Anna locked arms with me for support as we walked up the steps to the stage to help with equipment.

"It's about time you two showed up to help," Rick teased. He smiled at us and gave me a wink as he carried a speaker passed me.

I didn't say anything to Nick. I wanted him to disclose the identity of the woman to me without me asking. I worked on winding speaker cords and tying them up. We all worked together and got everything cleaned up and packed away quickly. Nick still hadn't said anything about his visitor. I grew angry when he didn't mention anything about her.

Nick and the rest of the band changed their sweaty shirts at the van so we could enjoy the other bands and the fireworks. We grabbed some food and a picnic table. Nick straddled the seat, pulled me into him and wrapped his arms around me as we sat. I was relieved that everyone had a conversation going on because I didn't want to talk. I started getting pissed that the visitor had not been mentioned yet. Anna kept giving me glances; watching my face I guess. She probably guessed my mood by the anguish on my face. I put my back against Nick. It was nice because he couldn't see my pouting face. In his arms, I still couldn't shake the jealousy I had when I remembered the way the other woman touched him. It still brewed inside of me.

We got back to Nick's house around ten thirty. I hadn't said much the entire evening after I witnessed the blond woman.

Nick said nothing about her. This bothered me even more. Why had Nick not said anything to me? I hoped she wasn't anybody to worry about. But it still clouded my mind.

"Everything okay?" Nick pulled me close outside of Anna's car. I was glad I decided not to stay with Nick that night. I was still upset with him. I promised Anna to help her at work tomorrow and Nick had to work in the morning.

"Just a little tired. I think I'm going to bed as soon as I get home." I lied. I didn't want to sound paranoid, telling Nick I had been jealous about the blond. I couldn't shake the vision from my mind. Maybe I needed some rest to clear my head.

"You sure? You've not said much since the show, Rayna."

"I need some rest that's all. I promise." I leaned in closer to Nick and laid my head on his chest. He pulled me tighter and held me.

I raised my head up and kissed Nick's soft lips. He always smelled so tantalizing. The warmth of his lips on mine brought some relieve to my gloominess, but didn't erase it altogether. I still felt uneasy; like he was keeping something from me. I sensed it.

"Are you ready, Rayna?" Anna said as she walked toward her car.

I glanced down at my watch and realized it was almost eleven. "Yes, whenever you are." My mind drifted; not thinking about the moment.

"You have work tomorrow Nick, you better get yourself in bed and get some rest." I kissed Nick again and he opened the car door for me.

"Call me when you're home." Nick's face held a worried expression. He gave me a weak smile.

"I will." I forced a smile for him and closed the door. I waved to him as Anna backed out of the driveway. My thoughts drifted far away, wondering about Nick and the blond.

"Rayna, are you with me?" Anna probed.

"Yeah, still wondering about that woman." I stared out the window of Anna's car, not looking at anything in particular.

"Nick never said anything about her?" Anna sounded surprised.

"No, and I never asked. I hoped he would bring her up." I said; frustrated and uneasy.

"Travis told me that she's his ex, Karla." Anna blurted out.

"What?" Surprised, my head swung to stare at Anna.

"Yes, the one that broke it off with him for some other guy; the one that broke his heart about a year ago." Anna kept her eyes on the road as she gave me the news with a pained face. "I can't believe he never said anything. It is possible he doesn't want to bring her up. I mean, what's the point; he loves you."

I gave Anna a disapproving look. "His ex; wonder what she wanted?"

"Travis said she was touchy feely and acted happy to see Nick, but he was stand offish with her. He said that Nick wondered what the heck she wanted and why she even bothered to say hi. Travis thinks she got a little too friendly."

"From what I observed, I think she was a little too friendly as well." My head became dizzy and my stomach turned to knots hearing the news that this was Nick's ex-girlfriend that caused him to react in fear of me when we first met. Was Nick glad to see her? Did it bring back feelings? Did he miss her? Why didn't he say anything to me? Could he be trying to hide it from me? These questions drove me crazy and made me insecure.

"Rayna, Nick loves you. That old girlfriend can't change anything." Anna tried to be reassuring to me.

My face showed the pain I had in my heart. "He hasn't told me he loves me. How would you know that?" I questioned.

"Anybody can tell he loves you, Rayna. It's hard to hide it; the way he touches you and looks at you. Not to mention the attention he gives you. You have to know that he does." Anna glanced over at me with a concerned look.

"I sense he does. He expresses it to me in different ways. I know I love him."

"Have you told him you love him?"

"No. I haven't got the nerve to tell him yet. After being hurt before, it's hard to open yourself up like that."

"Maybe he feels the same way Rayna. He could be scared of being hurt again."

"I would never hurt him," I stated with passion.

"I realize that, but he doesn't. Maybe he's scared to reveal his true feelings to you as well. When you tell someone you love them, you let them know they have the power to hurt you or protect you. When you love someone, they have a hold on you."

We didn't say much else. Anna drove and I thought about the blond and my feelings and how Nick might feel.

"Talk to Nick about it. It may settle your mind, if nothing else; just to know one way or the other." Anna gave me a reassuring smile that helped to ease the ache in my heart a little; but it didn't wash away all the doubt.

I hurried in the apartment so I could call Nick and tell him we made it home safe. I hoped to confront him about his ex-girlfriend.

"Hey girl." Nick's voice calmed me a little.

"I made it home safe."

"I can always sleep better when I know you're safe."

"I'm glad, but I don't think I'll sleep well tonight."

"I grasped that something was bothering you. You're not just tired are you, Rayna?"

"No." I became quiet. I didn't know how to bring this up. I guess I needed to blurt it out; get it off my chest.

"Rayna?"

"Why didn't you tell me your ex-girlfriend, Karla came to see you today?"

"Because seeing her isn't important to me. Who told you?" Nick's voice soft with concern and worry.

"Anna told me. We saw her with you. It really upset me seeing another woman touching you like that. I was hoping she might be an old friend or relative. I had a sense that it was your ex. Anna confirmed it for me........What bothers me the most is you didn't say anything." My voice was low but full of the emotion I was trying to hide.

"Rayna, I'm so sorry. I didn't think you saw her. You didn't say anything; I didn't want to mention it for fear of causing you any confusion or hurt. I wished I had known you saw her. I would have told you who she was."

"What did she want?" Not quite sure my heart would endure the answer, but I needed the iy.

"She said it was wonderful to run into me; that she'd been thinking about me. She also asked if she could see me again. I told her I was seeing someone and then she kissed my cheek and told me to call her if it didn't work out."

"Do you think you'll ever call?" The question was probably insensitive, but I needed to hear the brutally honest truth from him. I wanted to know exactly how he felt about this woman.

"No, Rayna...... Even if I never met you a month ago, I still wouldn't call her. I am completely over her. I dislike her because she almost cost me you. I almost didn't give you a chance because of the hurt she caused me...... If she hadn't found someone else, I wouldn't have met you. I'm glad she broke up with me. It freed me to find you."

A smile formed on my face. My mood brightened a little and my heart warmed. Nick always made me the center of his world. I didn't understand why I doubted him now. "Thank you...... Thank you for being honest with me; even if it would have hurt me a little."

"I wish you had asked me when you were still here. I hate that you went all evening worrying about this..... That upsets me Rayna..... Promise me next time something is bothering you, you will ask me. Don't let it cause you so much pain. I never want to hurt you Rayna..... I wish I was holding you right now."

"I promise Nick. I wish I could be in your arms and not sitting here alone." I enjoyed talking with Nick like this; it brought me closer to him. This was intimate for me; letting my feelings out and accepting his warmth. I grew more in love with him, but wasn't quite strong enough to tell him that I loved him.

· ♥ · ♥ · ♥ · ♥ · ♥ ·

The next weekend the band had a gig for a larder music festival. Nick had been writing new music and they planned on performing some of it. The band gained a huge following the past year and Rick's mom had connections through her social and work networks that helped get the band booked.

The band was a nervous wreck. They'd never played for such a large venue; but they had thirty minutes to play the songs Nick wrote.

Nick paced back and forth while Dave was biting his nails. I was a bunch of nerves for them, but I didn't let it show; I knew they would be great.

"Are you okay?" Anna asked Travis when he came back from the bathroom.

"I feel a little better after I threw up." Travis gave Anna a weak smile.

"Take a deep breath," I told Nick and Dave.

"I'm so glad you're here. Nick held me tight and didn't seem to want to let me go.

"I'm glad I'm allowed to share this with you." I held on to Nick as long as he allowed me. These were the best times; the times I could just "be" in his arms.

Nick kissed my head and squeezed a little tighter. "Never let me go Rayna." His voice filled with emotion.

"Never," I said. I closed my eyes because Nick's words made me euphoric; just knowing our feelings were mutual. He let go of his hold on me to kiss me. The emotions that erupted with his kiss were so powerful that they sometimes scared me.

"Gotta go," Travis exclaimed as he patted Nick's back.

Nick stared deep into my eyes for a long moment. "I love you, Rayna." He turned and walked out to the stage leaving me with my mouth dropped open.

I stood there in shock. All I could do was stare after him, wanting him to come back. I loved Nick, but I hadn't confessed this to him yet. He blurted it out and left before he let me say anything.

"Good luck," Anna and Rick yelled as the band walked onto the stage. Anna had a questioning grin on her face. "What's wrong?"

"Nick just told me he loved me." I couldn't take my eyes away from Nick as he began singing one of his songs.

Seven

"I knew that," Anna replied and stared at me like I was clueless. I elbowed her. We both laughed. We enjoyed the rest of the band's performance and they nailed it. They sounded superb. Nick's voice was strong and accurate. The crowd roared and applauded. The guys returned to us full of adrenaline and pride. They couldn't hide their smiles.

A man approached Nick and asked him if he could speak with him for a moment. We watched as they talked for a moment.

"Who's that?' I asked.

"I don't know. Do you know?" Dave asked Rick.

Rick shook his head no. We watched Nick and the man shake hands. Nick smiled as he walked back toward us.

"That was the manager for Reckless. They want a CD from us. They liked the songs and might want to record one." Nick said.

We all looked at Nick in disbelief.

"What?!?!" Dave yelled in surprise.

"That's amazing!!" Travis said.

"Wow!" Jeff said.

"I'll go grab one now," Rick ran to the side stage.

I hugged Nick. Anna wrapped her arms around us both. Then one by one each band member joined in for a group hug.

Rick's mom took us to dinner at an upscale downtown restaurant in celebration of the guys playing with famous bands. The food was superb and the company exceptional. Everyone was so excited about the idea of somebody recording one of Nicks's songs, but not more than me. I over flowed with pride and love for this man; so much happened today. I smiled as I watched him and the band discuss the idea of possibly having one of his songs recorded.

Nick's dreams seemed to be coming true as well as mine. When Nick confessed his love for me today, I wanted to tell him I loved him, but I needed to be alone with him. I loved him and I was ready to take this relationship to the next level.

After dinner, Nick drove me back to my apartment so I could grab a few things. I sometimes stayed with him on the weekends and he stayed with me through the week since he worked in downtown Pittsburgh. It made it difficult to stay with Nick and not take our relationship further. But I didn't like sleeping without him either. I decided I was ready to take our relationship to the next level so I planned on making the move tonight. I had been planning this night in my mind for a while.

When we got to his place, I excused myself to go to the restroom. I didn't want to waste any time tonight. I loved this man and he loved me. I prepared myself in the bathroom. I took a quick, hot shower and prepared myself for my big night. I primped a little and brushed my teeth. I put on the racy white nightie I recently bought, I examined myself in the mirror and I took a deep breath, swallowed my fears, and opened the door.

Nick sat on the couch scanning the TV channels.

"You want to watch some TV?" Nick said as he set the remote on the coffee table.

I bolted over to the couch. I hoped I could make it to the couch before he turned around. As I approached the couch, Nick turned around.

"Rayna, put some clothes on." Nick's mouth fell open with wide eyes.

"Absolutely not." I grinned from ear to ear and continued to walk around the couch to face Nick. I sat astride him on the couch, leaned down and kissed him. Nick placed a hand on each side of my face and pulled my head back to gaze into my eyes. "I love you, Nick."

"I love you Rayna." Nick breathed in a whisper.

I smiled and looked into Nick's brooding eyes. "I love you and I want you," I said.

Nick never stopped kissing me. His kisses traveled down my neck as he wrapped his arms around me. His lips traveled back to my lips as he took my face into his hands. My body was on fire.

"Are you sure?" Nick caught his breath as he looked into my eyes; searching for my answer.

"Never have I been more certain of anything in my life." I kissed Nick aggressively as I pulled his shirt up. He lifted his arms for me to take it off. He pulled me close and held me as he kissed my shoulder.

"You intoxicate me Rayna. I love you so very much." Nick whispered as he continued kissing my shoulder and moving up to my lips. The sensation of his bare skin on mine intoxicated me. Nick made love to me that night. The emotions I had for him overwhelmed me to the extent that a single tear of happiness flowed down my cheek.

Nick and I slept late the next morning. I woke up and I left my eyes closed remembering the night before. The night was magical and only deepened my bond with Nick. Being in Nick's arms once again brought joy to my heart. I treasured each and every time I could be in his warm embrace.

Nick rustled and opened his eyes. "You are here, it wasn't a dream," he moaned a sensual moan and brought his lips to mine. Nick made love to me once more. The scent of his body, the warmth of his skin beneath my fingers, and his sensual touch drove me over the edge.

"I love you," I breathed.

"I love you princess, always." Nick held me for a while. Neither of us said a word. There were no words to say. The lovemaking said it all. I couldn't explain the love I had for this man. I wouldn't ever be able to live without him. Without him, my world would be void.

Eight

♥

We finally pulled ourselves apart to eat some breakfast. We enjoyed the rest of the day lounging around his house watching movies and talking. I couldn't bear being away from Nick now that we confessed our love to each other and connected ourselves in every way possible, so I asked Nick to come and stay at my place tonight. Nick helped me cook dinner and then clean up the kitchen. We cuddled on the couch out on the balcony and watched the sunset.

Anna came home after work and ate a plate of food I left for her in the microwave. She talked a little to us and then retired for the evening. She had been working long hours trying to make enough money to put back before school started. I hated seeing her work so hard, but she insisted on not allowing me to pay more than I already was. I fixed dinner for her often and I even washed some of her laundry. She appreciated everything I did, but wasn't happy I did so much for her; I loved her, she was like my sister. She knew I would continue to help her, so she didn't put up much of a fight; she knew I would win.

Nick and I retired early. He had to work the next day. I made the best of the evening and made love to Nick again that night. I couldn't get enough of him. I was addicted. Life was wonderful and I was so happy with myself for taking a chance on Nick. I didn't think life could be more perfect.

"I'm glad we waited." Nick brushed my hair behind my ear and kissed me as we showered.

"Me too, it was magical. I love you so much Nick." I fell asleep in Nick's strong arms that night, not wanting to ever leave.

Nick made love to me again in the morning before he left for work. Morning love with him was incredibly delicious. I wanted to go shopping and buy some things for Nick. So after he left for work I went shopping. I was on the war path for some clothes, a necklace, and maybe even a bed. Nick's bed was ridiculous; uncomfortable and low quality. If I was going to be making love in his bed, it needed to be a superb one. And of course, new Egyptian cotton sheets.

Nick came in from work that evening while I set the table for our dinner. I grabbed some Chinese from the best Chinese shop in town. He came in all sweaty and dirty from work. He wrapped his arms around me from behind and kissed my neck.

"Mmmmm. You smell delicious." Nick groaned."

"You are dirty." I twisted around in his arms and wrapped my arms around his neck. "You smell delicious though."

"Rayna, I'm sweaty from work today." He chuckled.

"I know, and I love your scent." I kissed his lips and smiled.

"I'm going to grab a shower." Nick let go of me and swatted my butt.

"I bought you some things today. They're on my bed. You should try some on. I think you'll like them," I called to him. I had laid everything out on the bed for Nick to find; even the necklace, I placed the appointment card for the studio time on top of the clothes.

After about 30 minutes, Nick came out of my room with one of the new outfits on. He had on black leather pants and a silver silk dress shirt. Man, he was hot!

"Wow! I didn't think you could get any sexier." I walked over to wrap my arms around Nick's waist and I planted a kiss on his lips.

"What's this Rayna?" Nick held up the necklace and the appointment card; confusion on his face.

"I wanted to buy something for the man I love." I smiled up at him.

"Rayna, can you afford this? I mean the studio time must be extremely expensive, let alone this gold chain and the clothes." Nick pulled his eyebrows down and together.

I looked up at Nick and realized I had to tell him how I could afford these things. I thought I would be able to sneak it by him. Then again, Nick was incredibly smart; I should've known he would question it. I needed him to know I had money coming out my ass. I took Nick's hand and led him to the couch and sat down. He sat beside me.

"Nick, I have a trust fund. My grandfather left me with more than enough money for the rest of my life. I haven't spent any of it except for college because I didn't have anything to spend it on. I wanted you to have these things.... I love you........

"I love you Rayna, but you don't need to buy me things. I have a job".

"My car didn't give it away?" I gave a weak smile. I couldn't believe he hadn't realized by the expensive Lexus I drove.

"I just assumed your parents bought you the car."

"I know I don't need to but I want to give you things. Besides, after you start selling your songs, you're gonna wanna spend money too. You and the band needed the studio time so you can sell your songs..... Don't be mad at me. My bank account is starting to overflow. I can afford this; let me please." I pouted at Nick hoping to force a smile from him.

"I'm not mad at you. It just doesn't feel right having you buy me things. I am supposed to buy things for you." Nick grinned and touched my chin with the tip of his finger.

"And you will, but right now, I wanted to buy these things for you." I gave his lips a peck with mine.

"Leather pants?" Nick made a gruesome face.

"These are for when the band plays. If you are going to be a rock star then you gotta dress the part." I tugged on his pants and let them snap back to his skin. "Get used to me buying you things now that I love you. I buy things for people I love." I kissed Nick again and stood up from the couch and walked over to the counter to take our food out of the packages.

Nick gave up so he came over to help fill our plates. Anna came home from work looking exhausted.

"Are you hungry?" My voice was full of anguish for Anna. She looked like she hadn't slept in a week.

"Starving!" Anna hung her purse on the coat rack on the wall beside the door and slipped off her shoes. "What is the occasion? You look like you just got off stage."

"Rayna bought these clothes for me. She says I gotta dress the part."

"She's right; you look hot in those leather pants." Anna raised her eyebrows and smiled at Nick as she walked over to the dining table.

Nick rolled his eyes and scooted his chair from the table. He stood up and walked to the kitchen cabinet. He grabbed a plate, utensils, and a drink and set it on the table for Anna.

"Thank you; I can see why Rayna loves you so much." She smiled and sat down at the table.

"You are very welcome Anna. I know what it feels like to be that hungry and tired." Nick kissed the top of my head before he sat back down to finish his dinner.

"Are you able to go to my mom's July 4th party with us on Saturday? Or do you have to work?" I said between bites.

"No, I'm off. Travis and I both can go. I need a day of relaxation." Anna grinned and took another bite.

"Good, because I will need you there for moral support since this will be the first time my mom and dad meet Nick."

"Why do you need moral support for that?" Nick questioned.

"Because her mom can be very controlling Nick; you'll see. Rayna has always tried to please her mom and dad until she moved to Pittsburgh with me. That's the first time she upset them"

Nick looked from Anna to me as he chewed his food. I took another bite trying to avoid questions.

"She's their little girl and they still try to protect her from everything by trying to make her decisions for her," Anna added.

"Oh; so do I have anything to worry about?" Nick tried to make a worried face but held back a smile.

"Nothing I can think of." I forced a smile. I knew my mother wouldn't be happy that Nick didn't earn a college degree; that he had long shaggy hair, and a tattoo, not to mention he was the singer for a rock band. She would find fault in something or everything about Nick. I could only hope that one day she would see the real Nick that I knew.

Nine

My mom's July 4th bar-b-que for family and friends was the perfect time to introduce Nick to my parents. I asked Anna and Travis to be my buffers. Anna was excited about the idea because she'd not seen my parents for a while either and she loved parties. The house would be full of family and friends, so my mom couldn't give Nick the great inspection; asking questions about his family, what he did for a living, and what he planned to do in the future.

We arrived a little early for the party since this was the first time my parents would see Nick. I'd not told Nick my parents made a lot of money, just that I had a trust fund. I didn't want him to think of me as an uptight rich chick. When we got out of the car, his face turned puzzled after seeing the house. I shrugged my shoulders and smiled as I entwined my hand with his and lead him into the house.

My mom was in the kitchen finishing up all the preparations when we arrived.

"Rayna, baby." My mom dried her hands on a beige dish towel and wrapped her arms around me and then kissed my cheek. She pushed me back from her to get a better look at me I guess. "You are more beautiful than a few months ago at graduation."

"I know I haven't been around lately. Sorry mom, but I have been busy having fun. Mom, this is Nick. Nick, my mom Carrie." I held my hand up gesturing to each of them. I smiled and hoped for the best.

"It is wonderful to finally meet you Mrs. Taylor." Nick shook my mother's hand and gave her his beautiful smile.

My mother loved a handsome man, so she was probably impressed with Nick.

"Lovely to meet you Nick. Call me Carrie." My mom gave Nick an impressive smile. "I'm glad Rayna decided to bring you here to meet us."

"Anna, you look wonderful as well. Don't stay away so long." My mom kissed Anna on the cheek and gave her a warm hug too.

"Mom, this is Travis, Anna's boyfriend."

"Hello, Travis. It is nice to meet you as well. I hope you two enjoy yourself today. Please make yourselves at home."

"Would you like some help with anything, Carrie?" Nick offered his services to my mother.

Wow, he was really going to impress my mother. But that's what I loved about Nick. He didn't try to impress her; this was Nick. He was such a wonderful person inside and out.

"If you wouldn't mind, you guys could carry this stuff out." My mom pointed to the plates, silverware, and cups on the counter. "You could also carry those drinks out and pack them in the ice in the coolers out there."

"Come on Travis, help me out. You two girls visit with Carrie while we take this stuff outside." Nick gave my cheek a peck before he grabbed a couple of cases of soda and beer to take outside.

"Looks like you two are serious," my mom said as she took bagged cut up vegetables out of the refrigerator and arranged them on a platter. She looked at me with a straight face; no smiles.

"Yes, I guess we are kind of serious mom." I smiled as I shook my head in response. I'm sure my face gave away more than my words did. Anytime I spoke of Nick or thought about him, I spoke lovingly and my face lit up.

"Well, don't go too fast Rayna. Make sure you take time to get to know each other well."

"Nick and I are very close, Mom. We talk every day about real life." I took the vegetable dip out of the refrigerator and handed it to my mom.

"Nick is a wonderful guy Carrie." Anna came to my rescue.

"I'm sure he is Anna, I just don't want Rayna hurt again. I don't want anything to jeopardize her health."

"Actually, Rayna has been better than ever since she met Nick." Anna gave me a reassuring smile. I smiled back to let her see how much I needed her right now and how much I appreciated her sticking up for Nick.

"Mom, I have started living my life now. I go out every day and I forward to waking up every morning. I'm not down or depressed anymore. I want to live life to its fullest."

"Well, he is handsome. I hope he's as sweet as he looks." My mom smiled and gave me another hug. "Rayna, I need to talk to you sometime today before you leave okay?"

"Okay, go ahead."

"I would rather do it in private." The expression on my mom's face told me I wouldn't be happy about what she had to say or tell me.

"I'm gonna tell Anna anyway, so you should go ahead and say it." I shrugged my shoulders and threw my hands up in defeat.

My mom glared at me trying to decide whether to say anything in front of Anna. "Alright then, Rayna, I noticed you spent a large amount of money in the last few weeks. You're not giving money to this guy are you or spending money on him?"

"Yes. I bought some things for Nick and the band. I enjoy buying things for him mom. It upsets him when I buy him things, but has now accepted that I will do what I want. I have it, why shouldn't I spend it? I can't take it with me, so I'm gonna spend it on people I love." I gave her no room to question me.

"You love him? Rayna, you just met him."

"Yes I love him. I may have just met him, but I know him better than I know some people I've known for years."

"Rayna, how can you be sure he isn't dating you for your money?"

"Really mom? You think so little of my judgment? Nick didn't even realize I had any money until a few weeks ago. I didn't say anything to him about it and he never asked. We loved each other before the money was ever brought up." I raised my voice a little. She started to aggravate me. She needed to leave this alone. "Mom, I don't want to discuss this. My money is my business. I don't tell you how to spend yours and you shouldn't tell me how to spend mine. I'm a smart girl."

"I worry about you honey." My mom grabbed the sides of my arms and pulled me to her to wrap me in a hug. "I want to protect you from everything."

"I realize that mom, but I'm a big girl and you need to have faith that you raised a bright and intelligent woman." I hugged my mom back.

"I did raise an intelligent woman, but love can blind you baby."

"I love him and he loves me, unconditionally."

"Okay, okay, I'll leave this alone. Now you girls take the food out of the refrigerator in the garage and take it outside for me. People should start arriving and I want to be out of this kitchen and out by the pool. Go."

After my confrontation with my mother, my clan and I enjoyed the rest of the afternoon. We swam in the pool and enjoyed the wonderful food my mother ordered from her favorite restaurant. My mother and father treated Nick with respect and acted like they liked him, but I could still tell my mother wasn't sure if she trusted him. And even if she did trust him, she would probably find something wrong with him. I ignored the thoughts so I could enjoy my time with Nick, Anna, Travis, and the rest of the company. My aunts, uncles, and cousins all seemed to love Nick and seemed fascinated by the fact that he wrote music and had a good chance of selling a song.

Nick had no problem showing his affection for me in front of my family. He held my hand, put his arm around me, and kissed me anytime we separated for any reason. My mom watched this closely, even though she tried to be discreet. It made me laugh. She acted like I was a child with my first boyfriend. Anna even picked up on my mom's behavior. She also thought it was comical. That only made me lay it on a little thicker and sometimes I would grab Nick's butt or just hold my hand on it.

"Rayna, we are at your parents' house," Nick said. His voice was a whisper and scolded me with his eyes.

"I can't help myself," I giggled and wrapped my arms around him. He kissed my cheek and hugged me tightly. I cut him a little slack and tried to keep my hands to myself.

My dad and uncle bought fireworks to set off. The fireworks lit up the night with beautiful colors and made it magical. Everyone was impressed. Nick and I sat with our legs dangling in the pool as we enjoyed the beautiful array of colors of red, blue, white, orange, and purple light up the night sky. Nick held my hands as I leaned my head against his strong shoulder.

After the fireworks, we gathered our stuff together to head back to Pittsburgh.

"Rayna, I made you some packages of food to take with you. Your father and I will never eat all the food that is left. I noticed Nick and Travis especially liked the potatoes and pulled pork." My mom smiled and patted Nick's arm.

"The food was delicious Mrs. Taylor." Nick grinned as he rubbed his belly.

"Yes, superb," Travis also said.

"I told you to call me Carrie." My mom grinned and shook her head.

"Sorry, Carrie. Thank you for inviting me to the party today. I really had a wonderful time. I'm glad I had the opportunity to meet you as well." Nick smiled as he put his arm around me and gave me a little squeeze.

"You are more than welcome Nick and I'm glad Rayna finally decided to bring you around. I like to be informed of who my daughter is hanging out with. I'm a protective mother if Rayna hasn't told you."

"I understand that you love her and you worry about her." Nick gave her his gorgeous smile and batted those beautiful brown eyes at her. "I will take good care of your daughter, Carrie, I love her too."

We talked to my dad a little before we left. My dad is usually quiet, but he did speak to Nick about cars and sports. Other than that, my dad didn't have much to say. He was happy to see me and acknowledged I looked radiant and wondered how my summer was going and asked that I visit a little more often. I said I would and kissed and hugged him and my mom goodbye. My mom made sure she sent enough food for an army with us.

The band's studio time was tomorrow morning so when we got to my apartment, we all retired for the evening. The party at my mom's house made the day fun but exhausting.

I crawled into bed and cuddled up to Nick after I brushed my teeth. He was warm and strong and I fit perfectly in his little nook. I buried my face in his neck and breathed deep to inhale his scent as Nick wrapped his arms around me. He kissed the top of my head.

"You told my mom you loved me."

"Why wouldn't I? It's the truth. Your mother should be informed about my feelings for you."

I kissed the crook of his neck. "I love you," I whispered and then snuggled in and entwined my legs with Nick's and closed my eyes.

"I love you princess Rayna, always."

I woke up tangled up with Nick. I moved a little and peeked up at his warm brown eyes watching me sleep. He smiled and kissed my lips. I loved waking up like this, in Nick's arms. I always woke up well rested when I slept in Nick's arms.

"What time is it?" I said as I yawned and stretched a little.

"It's eight, beautiful; time to start moving." Nick raised himself up and over me and kissed me again before he turned and rolled out of bed. "I'm getting a shower to help wake me."

I lay in bed thinking how much my life has changed in the last month. I had been single and depressed for so long, I forgot how amazing it felt to love life. I looked forward to every day knowing I would be with the love of my life. When he was at work, I couldn't wait until he got off. An ugly thought would sometimes sneak into my head that maybe my strong attraction to Nick was somehow unhealthy; that maybe we spent too much time together and my life was dependent on him. But then I would push those thoughts away because this love thing was too wonderful, too right.

I heard the water shut off in the bathroom, so I jumped up and ran in to make some coffee. After I got the coffee started, I went back to my bedroom and gathered my clothes for my shower. Nick came out of the bathroom with nothing but a towel on. Man, he was easy on the eyes. I walked in his way so he had to stop. I took advantage and wrapped my arms around his waist and gave him a hug. He wrapped his arms around me and held me for a minute...or two.

"You smell incredible!" I gazed up at him and smiled and he leaned down and kissed me passionately. I let go and walked into the bathroom leaving him looking after me.

Jeff, Dave, and Rick showed up at the apartment while I was getting dressed, I could hear all of them talking and laughing. You could hear the excitement in their voices. I wondered if they were nervous. If I was recording music for the first time, I would be a wreck, but I guess that is why I'm not a performer.

"Hey guys, are you ready for this?" I said as I walked over and took a mug from the cupboard and poured me some coffee.

"No, just excited to get a chance to record these songs. Thanks Rayna for making it happen." Dave said before he took a sip of coffee. His voice was genuine. I could tell he appreciated this.

"Yeah, Rayna, thanks for doing this for us." Travis and Jeff added.

"You guys deserve this. You are a remarkable band and Nick's music is too exceptional not to record."

"I'm buying the first album." Anna giggled and gave us all a bright beautiful smile as she finished the scrambled eggs she made for us.

I made toast to go with our breakfast and dished out the sausage she finished frying. We all ate a hearty breakfast and the guys helped Anna and I cleaned the kitchen before we left. The session started at ten and we were right on time to leave.

Plus, Nick's bed would be delivered today. He didn't have a clue about that, so I had to keep everybody on time so we could be at his apartment this evening when they delivered it.

The band played every song to perfection. None of us had ever been in a real recording studio, so the guy making the recording needed to instruct the band all the way. It took several attempts for them to get the hang of everything. Anna and I only slipped out once to grab some coffee.

Nick was in heaven; singing his songs to be recorded on an album; his face full of pride and joy. I never felt happier than to be able to give this to him. This is where he belonged; singing his songs. The lyrics to his songs were deep and inspirational as well as upbeat. I could lose myself in his music and sweet voice.

A few hours into recording, the band took a break from playing to watch the mixing happen. It was amazing watching all this come together. By the end of the day, they made an album. More mixing would be done and they would have the album in hand to send to the manager of Reckless within a week. We were all so excited. We decided to celebrate by grabbing some Chinese takeout and heading to Nick's house.

Shortly after we arrived, the furniture company came with the new bed I bought for Nick.

"What is the big truck for?" Jeff said as he came in from outside.

"What truck?" Nick got up from the table to go check outside. I grinned and took a drink of soda and set it down on the table. I got up and followed Nick out the door.

"I bought you a new bed."

"Rayna, I told you not to buy things for me." Nick gave me a reprimanding glance as he grabbed my hand and lead me to the truck.

"It's for us. Your bed is uncomfortable and lumpy. If you want me to stay, I need another bed." I smiled at him and kissed his cheek.

"If you bought it for you, then....okay." Nick kissed my hand and smiled.

The company unloaded the bed and mattress into the house and left.

"Can you guys carry this upstairs and put it together, please?" I asked as I smiled at Dave, Rick, Travis, and Jeff with pleading in my eyes.

"Of course, Princess Rayna. It would be a privilege, but can we eat first?" Dave gave a bow to me and I punched him lightly in the gut. The guys always teased me about Nick calling me a princess.

"Yes, I'm starving and I'm sure you are too." I smiled and walked over to the kitchen table to help myself to my favorite Chinese meal of lo mien noodles and garlic chicken with rice.

We all filled our empty stomachs and chit chatted about the day at the recording studio and the hope that an artist would buy a song from Nick. We all debated on which songs we thought they would choose. We all had different ideas, but we all agreed at least one would be purchased. I feed Nick noodles and he fed me wontons while I sat on his lap.

Dave rolled his eyes, "Rent a room, you two are ridiculous."

"That is what I'm trying to do as soon as you guys put this new bed together." My tone was sarcastic and I smiled an evil grin as I hand feed Nick another noodle, holding it above his head and lowering it into his mouth, and finally kissing him. Nick threw a wonton at his brother and everyone laughed as we enjoyed our friendships and the wonderful food.

The guys carried the bed pieces upstairs and got busy putting the bed together. Anna and I cleaned the kitchen and ran out to grab a movie and snacks for later.

"So Rayna, our lease is up in September and Travis asked me to move in with him." Anna blurted out as she picked up a bag of chips.

"Are you going to move in with him?" I glanced over at Anna with shock on my face. I mean I realized they were getting close, but I didn't think they were that close yet.

"I love him Rayna, I think he is the one." Anna beamed with loving affection. I knew the look, I had it often when I spoke of Nick and I could see it in Nick's eyes as well.

"Anna, he lives with three other guys."

"He wants to rent a place for me and him. He got the promotion at his job when he graduated from school in May and he is ready to find his own place. He wants me to move in with him. What do you think?" Anna pushed the cart to the next aisle.

"You still have one year of school left, how are you going to do all of this?"

"Travis doesn't want me to pay anything. He is going to pay the rent. I won't have to work so much. He just wants me to go to school and work a few days a week."

"You won't let me pay all the rent."

"That's different Rayna. You are my friend and he is my boyfriend.....hopefully more soon." She smiled and giggled.

"I am happy for you Anna." I placed the soda in the cart and gave her a huge hug.

"So you're not mad?"

"Of course not, I'm sure Nick and I am are moving toward that as well. I bought a new bed for his place for crying out loud." We both laughed and then finished our shopping for our evening movie.

After the movie, everyone said their goodbyes and headed home. I was staying at Nick's for the night. I wanted to try out the new bed. We both decided it had been a long day and we were both exhausted. Nick even put the new Egyptian cotton sheets on the bed. They felt wonderful under my skin as I ran my hand over the silky cream colored material. A new bed, new sheets, and a new boyfriend to make love to me; this was my new life and I loved it.

I woke up feeling wonderful, well rested, and wrapped in the warm arms of the man I love. I savored the warmth of Nick's skin against mine as he held my head pressed to his shoulder with one arm; his hand in my hair and the other wrapped around my arms like a cocoon as he lay on his side. The sound of his heartbeat against my ear comforted me; it matched my own.

As I lay there quiet and still, I relished in the dream I woke from. I was living with Nick. We had made a home together. We lived in his garage apartment, but I had redecorated and added some of my things. It seemed comfortable and mine. I smiled at the thought of it. Nick and I had only met a month and a half ago, but our souls were connected in a way I couldn't explain. It felt wonderful to be this connected to someone. I didn't understand how I knew, but this man was my future, my life.

· ♥ · ♥ · ♥ · ♥ · ♥ ·

While Nick made breakfast, I sat drinking my coffee and reading a magazine.

"I had a dream about us last night. He turned and smiled at me. "You were moving in with me."

"No you didn't!" I dropped my book on the bar while I held my coffee in midair looking at him astonishment.

"Yes I did. I dreamed that the guys helped move all of your stuff in and we were putting things away and you were trying to redecorate." Nick laughed as he turned the bacon in the skillet.

"I had a dream that I'd already redecorated and I was moved in." I raised my eyebrows and a grin grew across my face. "We need to quit having the same dreams." I took a sip of coffee and went back to my magazine.

"It's weird isn't it?"

"Very weird; I think you can read my mind, even while I'm sleeping."

"You know Anna is moving in with Travis when school starts." Nick continued to flip bacon and stir the eggs.

"Yes, she told me last night. She hoped I wouldn't be upset with her." What was he getting at? Was he ready for me to move in? Was I ready to move in? We pretty much lived together already, but I still had the safety net of my own place.

"Well?"

"Well what?" I glanced up from my magazine and looked at Nick.

"Will you move in here? We practically live together now."

"Um......can I think about it?"

"Sure....take all the time you need; but the sooner the better. That way I can have you beside me all the time."

Ten

♥

The band's popularity picked up after June. They had gigs two to three times a week. I went to every one of them. We drove four or five hours for some shows. Sometimes we traveled north to Cleveland, west to Columbus, south to Morgantown, WV, or east to Harrisburg, PA. I loved watching Nick sing and listening to the band play. Anna came to most shows, but sometimes she had to work. Travis wasn't happy about this; he wanted her to be with us. We were all like a big family. Rick, Dave, and Jeff met some girls they dated on and off and they sometimes came to the shows with us. The girl Dave sometimes dated liked him more than he liked her I think. She clung to him. He did show her attention and affection, but nothing compared to what Nick showed me. I would catch her sometimes staring longingly at Dave.

July was non-stop for the band. They practiced a few nights a week and played a show a few nights a week. Nick and I didn't have as much alone time anymore, but we were together every day. During the day, Nick worked his job and I helped Rick with the promotions for the band. I spent half of the day on the phone with promoters setting up gigs and negotiating prices for performances by the band. It kept me busy while I was away from Nick and I enjoyed helping the band.

A few weeks after the July Fourth holiday, Nick wanted me to go out to dinner with him, his mom, and Dave, but I promised my mother I would have dinner with her and my father. Nick was sad I couldn't spend the evening with him, but he understood. While I got ready for the six o'clock dinner date with my parents, my mom called and had to cancel because a friend of hers mother had passed away and she needed to be with her. I decided not to call Nick and just drive over to surprise him.

When I arrived at Nick's, an unfamiliar blue car sat in the driveway. It must be somebody from work. Nick always left the door unlocked. I opened the door and went in. I walked over to the couch to set my purse down. I heard water running, so I knew Nick was still in the shower. I headed to the bathroom to surprise him, when something caught the corner of my eye. I turned my head to the left and spotted the blond sitting at the table. I stood in shock. What the hell was going on? Before I could say anything, Nick came out of the bathroom with a towel wrapped around his waist.

"Rayna, I thought you couldn't make it." Nick smiled.

I stared at him for a second and then glanced over at Karla, the blond. Nick's smile disappeared and confusion replaced it when he saw the anguish on my face. Nick turned to where I had looked. His face turned to anger and he glared at Karla.

"What the hell are you doing in my house?" Nick screamed.

I turned and ran for the door. I could hear yelling behind me, but I didn't stop. I ran out the door and to my car. I needed to get out of there. Tears welled up in my eyes as I tried to unlock my door. They streamed down my face and I couldn't see through the tears in my eyes. My heart ached.

"Rayna, stop!" Nick yelled as he grabbed my door before I could close it. "You're not leaving. You promised."

I peered up and Nick stood at my door with the towel around his waist and no shoes. Nick's face held fear and confusion. What was Karla doing here? I was so confused. I trusted Nick, but it made it hard to trust him when I walk into his house and his ex-girlfriend was sitting at the table like she lived here.

"Get out of the car Rayna." Nick demanded.

Nick reached in and took my hand to help me out of the car.

"Why is she here?" I asked through sobs.

"I have no idea, but SHE is leaving. I don't want her in my house."

I reluctantly let Nick take me back inside his place. Karla stood just inside the door, gathering her purse.

"What are doing in my house?" Nick demanded from Karla with wide eyes and an irate face.

"I wanted to visit you and you didn't answer when I knocked. The door was open, so I came in."

"Did you ever think that I don't want you to visit? This is Rayna, the love of my life. Nothing is going to change that. You need to leave now." Nick gritted his teeth and pointed his finger toward the door.

Nick spoke horribly to Karla. He was always so sweet and passive. I had never seen the angry side of him. It made me a little uneasy seeing him this way. He was aggressive and passionate at the same time. He didn't release my hand, even as he introduced me and motioned for Karla to leave.

"I'm sorry I upset you Nick. Call me sometime." Karla said with a slight grin. She walked past us and looked me up and down before she walked out the door.

"Karla, I am never going to call you. Please leave my house and leave me alone. Do not call, do not stop by. We are over and we have been over. Goodbye." Nick slammed the door behind her.

The way Nick said her name made me shiver. I didn't think he had a mean bone in his body. I hoped he would never speak to me in that tone. It was upsetting. And she behaved like it didn't bother her he was so angry with her. Nick took a deep breath and gazed at me. His eyes lost the anger and slowly turned to worry.

Nick held my face in his hands with such gentleness and stared into my eyes searching for something. "Rayna....I'm sorry for that. She should have never been here."

"You were so mean and angry. Where did that come from?"

"Right here." He touched his heart as he continued searching my eyes. "Rayna, I never want anything to jeopardize us. You mean too much to me. And for her to come into my house and do that to you brings out a different person in me. Anybody that would try and hurt you makes me extremely angry. I saw the hurt in your eyes when I came out of the bathroom. It set something off in me to see you hurt. I love you."

I didn't think it was possible, but at that moment, I fell deeper in love with this man. The love I felt for him at that moment was so overwhelming, my heart ached. He looked so sexy standing only in a towel; hair still wet from his shower and the love in his eyes. I wrapped my arms around him and placed my lips on his soft warm lips. I ran my fingers down his back and pulled his towel off of his waist.

"I need to become angry more often," Nick said. He smiled between kisses that he trailed down my neck. He scooped me up and carried me to the couch.

"We are going to be late for dinner with your mother." I joked

"You started this Miss Taylor. Are you changing your mind?" Nick's voice was jokingly sarcastic as he gave me a delicious evil grin.

"Never about my love for you." I grinned as I shoved him down on the couch. He fell backward onto the couch laughing and pulled me with him as he fell.

"I love you more than my own life." It sounded like the first time he said it. He gazed deep into my eyes for a long moment and didn't make a move.

"I love you." My voice barely above a whisper as I got lost in his loving brown eyes. Butterflies danced in my belly. I leaned down and kissed Nick's neck and traveled to his ear lobe. He sighed and pulled my lips to his.

We finally made it to dinner with Nick's mom and Dave.

>>>>>>>>>>>>>>>>>>>>>

Nick called me in the afternoon from work about a week later and told me that he had some exciting news to share with me and he wanted me to meet him at his house when he got home. I'd been helping Anna a lot so he knew that I would be with her until evening. He didn't say to dress up, so I put my usual cutoff jeans and a tank top on and packed a nicer outfit in case he had different plans for us.

When I pulled into Nick's he was getting out of his car. He had a bag from our favorite Chinese take-out in his hand.

"Hey beautiful." Nick called as I got out of my car.

I walked up to him and placed a hand on each side of his face and kissed his wonderful sensual lips. "Hello yourself; I missed you today, but that's not unusual. I miss you every day that I'm not with you. So what is this exciting news?" I put my hands in my back pockets and rocked on my feet feeling anxious about his news.

"You'll need to wait a few more minutes. I need to grab a couple of things from inside." Nick grabbed my hand and led me to his French doors. We went inside and he told me that he'd be a minute. He came back downstairs with a blanket and walked over to the cabinet and pulled out two plastic cups.

"What are we doing?" I gazed at Nick with wonder in my eyes. He always tried to surprise me.

"We're going on a picnic. It's a beautiful day outside and we haven't done this yet. Come on little lady." Nick put the cups in the bag from the restaurant and the blanket under his arm. He took my hand with the other hand and we walked to the door. I assumed we would be getting into his truck, but he started leading me to the back of his garage.

"Where are we going?"

"To one of my favorite spots. It has beautiful views so the sunset is miraculous. You are going to love it Rayna."

"Sounds wonderful Nick." I let him lead me up a path through the woods. It was about a five minute walk on a small incline, but when the trees cleared out, it was worth the walk. The views were spectacular. High up on a hill where it seemed you could see for miles; it was breathtaking. The rolling green hills and valleys expanded on forever. Nick glanced over at me and just smiled and I returned his infectious smile.

Nick laid out the blue blanket and took my hand to help me sit down. He was always a gentleman. I sat down and pulled my legs beside me. I watched him as he sat down and took the food out and placed it in front of us. He kept his smile on his face.

"I got a phone call today." Nick continued setting out our dinner with forks and napkins, he even brought a bottle of wine.

"Who was the call from?" I took a glass of wine from Nick as he looked at me with his joyful eyes and beautiful smile.

"A record company. They want the band to come to New York. They want to talk with us about possibly signing us Rayna. I thought the call would be about one of my songs. The man who asked us about giving him a demo because they wanted to buy our songs actually liked the band, not just the songs." Nick took a drink of his wine. I held up my glass to clink for a toast.

I toasted Nick's glass. "This is the most amazing news. I am so excited. When do we leave? When will the album come out?" I pulled myself up on my knees and threw my arms around his neck almost causing him to fall backward.

Nick laughed out loud. "I don't know all the details yet. They told me they'd be in touch in a few days. They want me to discuss it with the band first.

I released Nick and sat back down on the blanket. "Looks like your dreams are coming true."

"Only part of my dream. I am still waiting on your answer." Nick took a bite of his food but continued to look at me.

"Well, I've been thinking about that and I decided that I'd love to move in with you on one condition." Nick stared at me waiting for the condition. "You need new appliances and I'm gonna buy them if I'm moving in. I'd also like to get some new rugs or have carpet laid and we'll be moving my new furniture in so you'll need to decide what we're gonna do with your current furniture."

"I agree that we need new appliances and you can move your furniture in, but it is still in question as to who is going to buy the new fridge and stove, but we still have a few weeks before we need them." Nick gave me his gorgeous smile and kissed me.

"Thank you Rayna for making this decision, you have made me the happiest man in the world. You can decorate the place as you see fit, just as long as I can share my life with you. This has turned out to be the second best day of my life, the first being the day I met you."

We finished our dinner and then lay back on the blanket to watch the sunset. We talked about the plans for the move and what a record contract could mean for Nick and the band. I was so happy for him. His dreams might finally becoming true. His songs were amazing. His voice, his words, and the music went so beautifully together. And we were moving in together. I would start sharing my life with him completely.

When the sun started to set, the sky looked magnificent with the pink and purple hues in the sky. It let us know that tomorrow would be another beautiful day. As I lay in Nick's arms, I knew this would be an amazing life with Nick.

Eleven

A few weeks passed and we all prepared to go to New York City. The record company booked us round trip air fare and a hotel. Our meeting was Friday with the executives of the record company. We planned to stay the weekend in New York to do some sightseeing. Nobody had ever been to the Big Apple. I drug Anna to the store before we left for a small shopping spree. She needed a couple of new outfits and so did I. She bucked me all the way, but I refused to listen to her crying about me buying her stuff. I did it anyway.

When we boarded the plane, we were bumped up to first class. This company must have really wanted the band to sign with them. The plane took off at eight in the morning. We arrived in New York City around nine-thirty. A long black limousine waited for us. The chauffeur took our luggage and drove us to the Four Seasons Hotel.

I traveled with my parents a bit, but I never stayed in New York City. This was a treat for me as well. When we checked in, the bell boy took our luggage and guided us to our room. He unlocked the door and held it open for us.

"Holy shit!" Dave said.

"Dave," I reprimanded. I drew my eyes down and shook my head.

He looked at me and shrugged his shoulders. Nick slapped him in the back of the head as he pulled out his wallet. He handed the bellboy a tip. The others guys snickered.

"This definitely is a bit fancier than I expected," Rick said.

"I for one am going to enjoy staying in this luxurious suite." Anna smiled from ear to ear.

"I'm glad it's paid for," Travis responded.

"You got that right. It's probably more a night than I make in a week," Jeff chimed in.

After we investigated our palace for the weekend and unpacked, there was a knock at the door. Dave answered it and a waiter stood in the hall with carts full of food.

"We didn't order anything did we?" With a look of surprise, Dave scanned each of our faces for an answer. We all shook our heads no as we glanced around at one another.

"Compliments of Mr.Delong; he wanted to make sure you had something to eat before your meeting," the waiter announced as he pushed the carts over next to the dining table. He removed the cover from each dish and set some of the items on the table and placed a plate at each setting.

I moved over to tip the waiter and he held his hand up.

"It has been taken care of Miss." After he finished setting our meal up, he asked if there might be anything else we needed. Everyone shook their head no.

"A car will be ready for you at 12:15," he said and then left the room.

Mr. Delong was the CEO of the record company we were meeting today. He sent up a light lunch of wraps, a fruit and cheese tray, a vegetable and humus tray with pita chips, and shrimp cocktail. We were all famished and sat down at the table to dig in. The food was exceptional. We finished up with our lunch around 11:30. We all retreated to our separate bathrooms to freshen up a bit.

We arrived at the record company's office building after a short silent ride. The anticipation made everyone a little nervous. The glass door opened for us and a man directed us into a huge reception area. Nick took lead and walked up to the counter and let the secretary know who we were and who we came to see. We took the elevator up to the top floor. The receptionist ask us to sit on the leather brown couches in the lobby and told us it would be a few minutes. Nobody said a word as we waited for the fate of the band to be established.

"Mr. Perry, Mr. Delong will see you now," the receptionist said. She walked out from behind her huge mahogany desk and waited for us to follow her. She led us across the huge foyer/waiting room and down a wide hall. Our shoes clacked on the shiny gray granite floors and made an echo through the hall. When we reached two large cherry wooden doors, she stopped and pulled on the huge brass door handle. She held the door open as she motioned for us to go in.

The office was outlandish. I looked up and down the glass walls that went from floor to ceiling on two walls in the corner office. The city sprung out in front of us with its skyscrapers made of concrete, glass, and mirrors. We walked toward a huge glass top table that sat in the center of the room with eighteen chairs. Four executives stood up as we approached. The band shook hands with each of the executives as they introduced themselves. The executive that introduced himself as Mr. Delong, motioned for us to take a seat. We sat down in the tall back burgundy leather chairs and the meeting began.

"Your album was brought to our attention by a friend of ours and so we sent one of our executives out to view one of your shows. We believe your band can become a huge success with your lyrics, your music, and our promotional influence. So we asked you to come today to see if we can come up with a mutual agreement and possibly sign you and begin your career." Mr. Delong's face exuded power and self-confidence. I wanted to shout at the top of my lungs. This was incredible news. Wow! They wanted the entire band, not just a song.

"I flew out to Pittsburgh and watched two of your shows. Your presence on stage is enormous and your lyrics are deep. I was thrilled I traveled down to view the band in person. You did not let me down. Bottom line is, you impressed me and that is difficult to do on first impressions." Mr. Swiger, one of the other executives, wore a huge smile on his face showing his brilliant white teeth. He was a handsome man with dark brown hair, cut short and stylish. He wore a contemporary black suit with a purple tie.

My palms grew clammy and I'm sure my armpits showed signs of perspiration as well. I was nervous and not even part of the band. I was nervous for Nick. This was the big break he'd been dreaming about; wondering and hoping that one day it would come true. I smiled inside to hear the band impressed someone of such importance in the music industry.

"We have what we think is an excellent proposal for the band." We would like to sign you to a two album contract. This means we would work together for two albums and after that time, we would all meet again and decide if we wanted to move forward with more albums. A two album contract can take us anywhere from two years to five years; depending on the sales and the marketing for live performances."

"Usually we start at the beginning and record an album, but since you took the initiative and recorded the album, we can skip that part and move right to promotions and marketing. We would like to remix the recorded album with our own people. We would remix and review the new album, including the sound, the cover, and the credits."

The band members sat silent. Nick nodded his head in understanding. Dave glanced over at Nick and then at Rick. Rick stayed focused on what the executives said.

"We would like you to take the contract and read it and have all of you meet back with us on Monday morning to let us know if we can move forward." Mr. Delong got right to the point but in a friendly manner.

Mr. Delong was a businessman, but he seemed genuine in his statements. Some of these executive types move fast and the band is left in the whirlwind.

"I think we can do that. Thank you for meeting with us and giving us the opportunity to show you our talents." Nick kept a blank face, but hopeful. I could sense he wanted to shout from the rooftops about this record company wanting to sign the band, but he kept himself reserved in front of the execs.

"We took the liberty and made arrangements for you to stay through the weekend at the Four Seasons. You also have reservations in the restaurant for the weekend. We would like you also to use our car for sightseeing and enjoying the city. The company is at your disposal this weekend; we want you to feel like part of the family. If you need anything else, please call my secretary and she will arrange it for you." Mr. Delong stood up and put his hand out to shake Nick's hand. He also shook Dave's, Travis's, Jeff's, and then Rick's. He nodded at Anna and me and told us to take care of the "boys."

"Monday morning at nine." Mr. Delong repeated as we stood up to leave the room.

We all kept our composure until we got out of the building.

"Oh, my gosh." Anna squealed with delight.

"Wha-hoo!" Dave yelled and the other guys joined him.

Nick grabbed me up into his arms and spun me around in a circle. I held tight around his neck. His dreams were coming true. I pulled my head back so I could kiss Nick. I glanced at the huge smile on his face before I planted my lips on his. Adrenaline pumped through everyone's veins. After all the anxiety and the waiting to hear what the record company offered, the release of the emotions was exuberant.

"Let's celebrate," Rick said as he smiled from ear to ear.

"Sounds like a plan," Nick said, agreeing with him. "Let's go back to the room and relax for a few."

"We can order some champagne and celebrate and then dress for a dinner celebration. I could use some rest and relaxation after all this stress," I said. I was exhausted but didn't want to alarm Nick. These past couple of weeks had been busy and stressful for me. I realized I needed to slow down a bit some days. So I hoped everyone would agree with me for a little relaxation time.

"I could use some time to relax and a hot bath." Anna agreed. She sensed my exhaustion.

"Okay, we can go back and enjoy that fabulous room and celebrate at dinner," Nick said. He smiled and took my hand and led me toward the limo that waited by the curb. "We need to fax this contract to Rick's mom so her fiancé can take a look at it for us. We can do that at the hotel as well."

"I would also like to fax a copy to my father and let him read over it as well," I said.

"Two opinions are better than one; wonderful idea Rayna." Travis winked at me as he got into the limo.

The limo took us back to the hotel and we all climbed on the elevator. When we got to the room I ordered champagne and some snacks. I called my dad so I could ask him to take a look at the contract the record company offered to the band.

"Rayna, did you make it to New York safe?" My dad's voice sounded chipper.

"Yes dad. We are staying at the Four Seasons. The record company has put us up in a superb suite and has a limo waiting at our beck and call," I said. I laughed at how silly I must sound. "The record company offered the band a contract and I was wondering if you would take a look at it for me?"

"I would love to do that for you honey. Fax it over and I will read it tonight. Glad you called. I wanted to talk with you Rayna."

"About what dad?"

"Well, it's about Nick. A friend of mine and I talked the other day and he asked about you. I told him you had a boyfriend. A few days later, he called me about Nick. He said he remembered the name, Nick Perry. He said he dug through his old files and found Nick. He almost sent him to juvenile hall Rayna for domestic violence a few years back."

I didn't say anything. I couldn't believe my dad was bringing this up. It seemed like he was spying on him. Nick told me about this.

"Rayna, I am worried about you. I am not sure you are safe with Nick. I hope your silly romance ends soon."

"Dad, Nick told me about juvenile hall. Did your friend forget to tell you the domestic violence was against his alcoholic stepfather who hit his mother?"

"Rayna, it just shows he can be violent." My dad's voice raised in volume.

"There isn't a violent bone in Nick's body; a protective and loving bone; but not a violent one." My mood went from happy and joyful to defensive and protective in a split second. My mother didn't care for Nick because he didn't have some savvy degree and now my dad was moving against Nick. This is just more ammunition for my mother not to like Nick. I didn't want to listen to their critical words.

"Dad, I don't need to discuss this now or ever. I love him and nobody can change my feelings. End of discussion. Do you still want to look over the contract?" I said with sarcasm.

"Yes I'll read over the contract; for you and the band. I'll be keeping my eyes on you two Rayna. You are my only child and I will protect you no matter what. I love you." My dad's tone now subdued.

"'I'll fax the contract shortly. I love you too Dad." I hung up the phone and took a deep breath. My parents loved me and wanted to protect me, but I was a grown woman with excellent decision making skills. I wasn't an idiot; although they often treated me like one. I refused to let this ruin my time in New York, so I put a smile on my face and pushed my dad's accusation from my mind. When the time was right, I would talk with Anna.

"Everything all right?" Nick asked as I came out of the bedroom and into the living room.

"Yeah, a little tired from all the excitement." That was the first time I lied to Nick, but I wasn't about to tell him about my father's mistrust and witch hunt.

"We have champagne!" Rick yelled as he held the bottle up. He popped the top. The cork flew into the air as bubbles foamed to the top of the bottle and down the sides.

"Wahoooo!" Everyone shouted.

Rick poured glasses of champagne and we all gathered around the small bar in the suite.

I held up my glass to make a toast. "To the band; you all have worked hard to make your dreams come true." I clinked glasses with Nick and then with Anna and the rest of the band.

"Watch out world, here we come." Dave held his glass up in the air after the toast and finished off what lingered in the glass.

Nick took a drink and put his arm around my waist and pulled me into him as he planted a kiss on my lips. The electricity traveled through my body and I had to catch my breath, again.

"So you think you guys are going to sign the contract?" Anna looked around at each person looking for a reaction.

"It sounds wonderful, but I think we need to wait to give that answer until Rayna's dad and Samantha's fiancés get a chance to examine the contract. But at least we know they want us, we can always negotiate." Nick pulled me tighter to him as he spoke. "We probably should fax the contract to them right away." He gazed down at me.

"I think I am going to try and take a power nap. Why don't you and Rick go down to the front desk and ask the clerk to send it." I hoped this wouldn't give me away. I didn't want Nick to know how tired I really was. Over the past week, I noticed I was more fatigued than usual. I didn't want to cause concern to anyone during such an important time in their life.

"I think we can take care of that," Rick said as he finished his champagne and set his glass down.

Nick peered down at me with concern in his eyes, but he didn't mention anything. "Okay, sounds good. Lie down and rest up; I don't want you getting sick." He kissed me again on the lips and then on the top of the head. I slid out of Nick's embrace and turned for the bedroom.

When I woke from my nap, I still felt a little tired. The clock on the nightstand read 5:06. I could have slept more, but we had dinner reservations at 7:00 and Nick would worry if I slept more. He already worried about me too much and tried to hover over me when he thought I didn't feel well.

After my shower, I dressed and walked out into the living room of our suite. Nick, Dave, Jeff, and Travis all sat on the two couches enjoying a beer. They glanced up when I entered the room.

"Whoa, you are ravishing Rayna." Jeff examined me with his big blue eyes and smiled.

"You are beautiful princess." Nick stood up and walked toward me.

"Thank you," I said and smiled and spun around for them to see every angle. I wore a short black dress that opened in the back with two pearl stands that hooked on each side of the back of the dress. My black glittering heels complimented the dress.

When Nick met me he took my hand and kissed the back. He pulled me in for a kiss on the lips as he wrapped both of his arms around my waist. "We have dinner in 45 minutes so I better go clean up." Nick kissed the tip of my nose and reluctantly released me to go take a shower.

Dinner was spectacular. The company, atmosphere, and the views were wonderful. The stress of anticipation about the meeting melted away, our excitement still high, but it settled some. It was nice sitting with the band and Anna. Only a few short months ago, I sat in my apartment with only Anna living in a gray world. Now I felt like I had an extended family that brought color to my monochrome world. The guys in the band had grown on me and I sensed we would all be close. It was wonderful being able to share this excitement with them.

We discussed what being signed to a record company would mean and they all seemed enthusiastic about making this their job; traveling the country promoting the album and playing their music every night.

Nick kept his eye on me during dinner. My little nap had his radar on. He kissed my hand a few times during dinner and I found him watching me while we socialized and had a few drinks. I ignored his worry. Watching Anna and Travis being affectionate and expressing their love brought happiness to me. The band's excitement gave me a reason to press on for the night.

The next day the guys wanted to check out some music stores. So Anna and I decided to do some shopping of our own. We shopped most of the morning and then found a wonderful little café to eat lunch. It was great getting some girl time with Anna. We hadn't got to do this in so long, I didn't realize how much I missed her company.

"How are you feeling? And don't lie to me; I've known you too long." Anna was sober now.

I knew I couldn't slide anything past her. She could see through me and I felt Nick could as well.

"I've been tired lately; trying to keep up with everything."

"You need to go to your doctor and have everything checked out if you are more fatigued than usual. You know what happened last time."

"Last time I just wasn't fatigued, I was getting dizzy and breathless. I've only been fatigued. I might be pushing myself too hard. When we get home things will slow down and I'll see the doctor, just to make sure."

"Okay, I believe you; but don't put the doctor appointment off." Anna reached across the table and squeezed my hand.

I smiled at her thinking about how grateful I was to have such a wonderful friend. I loved and missed her. I really enjoyed our girl time.

When we arrived back at the suite with all the things we had bought that afternoon, the guys were already there.

"What's on the agenda for tonight?" Anna inquired as she moved to the couch to snuggle up beside Travis.

"We found a rooftop restaurant we want to try and then maybe some sightseeing of New York during the evening. We got some remarkable tips on things to do in New York; maybe a Broadway show." Nick's voice sprung with excitement as he spoke of this evening. He smiled and pulled me toward the sofa.

I pushed off my shoes and pulled my feet up on the couch as I snuggled into Nick and laid my head on his should. He placed his hand on my leg and squeezed. He kissed the top of my head. I could stay where I was for the evening, close to Nick with his protective hands on me. But we were here to enjoy New York and celebrate with the band.

"My mom called this afternoon and said the contract looks excellent. We'll be keeping most of the creative control and a large amount of any decisions made," Rick sounded positive as he described the analysis of the record company contract.

"I'll call my dad and make sure he agrees." I felt a sense of energy as Rick spoke of the positives of the contract. Maybe this was going to be a phenomenal deal. I could only hope for the band's sake; especially Nick's. He could finally take care of his mother like he wanted; him and Dave together.

• ♥ • ♥ • ♥ • ♥ • ♥ •

Dinner tasted exquisite. I had never eaten such decadent food. The conversation was just as tantalizing. The guys talked about going on tour and quitting their current jobs. I didn't believe any one of them would miss going to work each day. Each and every one of them loved playing music and performing for a crowd.

After the waiter cleared our plates, we all decided on an after dinner drink. I chose an expensive wine as my gift to the band for being handpicked by a record company. We needed to celebrate with the best.

"To all your dreams coming true." I raised my glass to all of my friends and smiled the most ridiculous smile because I was so happy for them. Everyone raised their glasses and we clinked.

After everyone sat their glasses down, they grew quiet. I looked around at each one and they all looked at me. What had I said that had their attention? When I peeked over at Nick, he was on one knee looking up at me threw his long dark lashes. My heart skipped a beat.....maybe two. I took a deep breath and stared down at what he held in his hands; a small, simple, black satin box.

"Rayna Marie Taylor, you are my best friend, my lover, my soulmate; will you do me the honor of marrying me?" Nick swallowed as he spoke with a soft voice; just loud enough for me to hear. A bead of sweat formed on his forehead. His gaze never left mine.

I brought my hand to my chest and took a breath. Tears of joy swelled up in my eyes. Of course I would be his wife. He was everything I ever wanted. He was the man of my dreams. I looked from the box up to Nick's warm loving eyes, back down to the box waiting for him to open it. Tears escaped both eyes and ran down my cheeks.

"Rayna, say something." Nick's alarmed voice brought me back to the here and now.

"Yes, of course I will marry you." I slid out of my chair to wrap my arms around Nick. I held tight around his neck. I was so overfilled with joy at the moment I forgot we were in a five star restaurant.

"Let's see the ring." Anna spewed out. "I've waited all day for this to happen and I would like to see the ring." Her smile full of excitement.

"Oh, me too," I said and laughed as I let go of Nick. I sat back in my chair.

Nick kept his eyes on me as he opened the tiny box. I looked from him to the box and inside laid a beautiful emerald cut diamond. It had to at least be a carat or more. On each side was a baguette diamond. It was set in platinum. It was exquisite. I put my hand over my mouth; I was speechless. Nick held his hand out for mine. I placed my hand into his and he slid the ring on my finger. It was a perfect fit. I stared at the ring now adorning my left hand. Joy rushed through every cell of my body; I couldn't be any happier at this moment in time. It just kept getting better. Nick stood up and pulled me to my feet. His lips touched mine. He kissed me tenderly but left me wanting more.

"Forever." Nick gazed into my eyes and smiled.

"Forever," I repeated after him and grinned from ear to ear.

The crew stood up and cheered and clapped; making a spectacle of our table. Everyone in the restaurant stared around at our table.

"She said yes!" Nick yelled to the patrons of the restaurant.

Everyone in the restaurant clapped and cheered. It was a little embarrassing. Nick and I turned and smiled at them and then sat down.

Anna ran around the table to give me a huge hug. "I love you and I'm so happy for you; congratulations." She whispered as she squeezed.

"Thank you. I love you." I whispered back. She released me and gave Nick a congratulatory hug as well.

The rest of the crew congratulated us too. Then they discussed their day helping Nick pick the perfect ring. I was astounded he had just bought it that day and they were all in on it. I would ask him about it later and try and find out if he went into debt for this huge rock, but now was not the time.

SONGS FROM THE HEART

We enjoyed the rest of the evening with great company. but I couldn't wait to take my fiancé back to our suite.

Twelve

We got back from New York Monday afternoon. Exhausted from the trip, I needed some rest, but I still needed to finish packing the rest of my stuff. I needed to be out of my apartment by August 30; that left me two weeks to move everything, so I decided to contact a moving company to do all the work. I wouldn't be able to handle the stress.

I promised Anna I would go look at apartments with her the next day and I still had a few articles to read by Friday. I made the arrangements with the moving company, did some reading, and went to bed early.

I woke in the morning to a bright room. I rolled over and found a note and a fresh daisy lying on Nick's pillow.

"Good morning beautiful. You looked too peaceful to wake. You needed to rest so I didn't wake you. I love you. XOXO. Nick."

My heart suddenly warmed. This was the reason I love this man so much. It was the little things. He always thought of me first. As I smelled his flower and held the note, I stared at my left ring finger. The diamond Nick placed on my finger was beautiful. The ring itself didn't deepen my love for Nick, our love was as deep as the depths of the ocean; it just verified our commitment and bond to each other. My heart belonged to him and his belonged to me; nothing would ever break our bond.

After spending the day finding Anna and Travis a great apartment, she drove me home.

"I'd like to plan a congratulation party for the band and an engagement announcement."

"When?" Anna asked as she pulled into Nick's driveway.

"Well, I figured I needed to tell my parents I got engaged and I think a congratulation party at our house would be the perfect time to tell them. Nothing too big; just our close friends for dinner. I'd like to do it this Sunday if you think we can pull it off." I opened the door to get out.

"I think it is a wonderful idea. I think we can make it happen. I work the next two days, but after that I'm yours." Anna said. I smiled and got out of the car.

I had about an hour to spare before Nick got home. I made a few calls about food for Sunday and then I started dinner. It felt wonderful getting so many things accomplished.

I told Nick my plans for the dinner party and he thought it a superb idea. He said it would be wonderful to bring our friends together to celebrate the band getting signed and our engagement. I made the calls to invite everyone while Nick took a shower,

My mom, still upset after I told her last week about me moving in with Nick, agreed to come to our house for Sunday dinner. If moving in with Nick shocked her, then the announcement of our engagement would send her over the edge. It had to be done. At some point and time, they needed to accept the fact I planned on being with Nick; now they must accept he would be their son-in-law.

Nick ran out of the bathroom. He grabbed me into his arms and spun me around. I wrapped my arms around his neck and held tight, laughing the whole time.

"I love you," I said between giggles and kissed his cheek. Nick always made me smile.

He stopped spinning around and set me down. He stared deep into my eyes and became quiet for a moment. "I love you more every day Rayna. You are the love of my life and you've made me the happiest man alive." Nick leaned his head down and kissed my lips so tenderly and passionately. "God made you just for me."

I stopped breathing for a moment. "I think he made us for each other." I touched Nick's cheek with the back of my hand and he closed his eyes and inhaled.

"I want you to know that since the first time I laid eyes on you, my world has changed. I look at the world differently now. I can't wait until we start living our life as husband and wife." Nick gazed at me with intent and sincerity. He ran his hand up and down my back as he spoke these words to me. He sent a shiver down my spine.

"Nick, you're the reason my life is so full. I can't wait to wake up every morning to open my eyes to you. You're my soul mate and I love you."

"The connection between us is incredible. I sense what you feel, even when we are apart. When we're apart, I'm lost." Nick brushed my hair off of my left cheek.

I smiled up at Nick because I knew exactly what he meant. "I know."

"If anyone listened to our conversation right now, they'd think we are nuts. But I guess we are nuts; nuts about each other." Nick laughed his throaty laugh and leaned me back into a deep dip and kissed me again.

"Okay Romeo, let's clean the kitchen up." Nick lifted me to a standing position and released his arms from around me.

"Alright slave driver. I'll wash and you dry." Nick swatted my butt as I turned to head to the kitchen. I turned around and smiled at him with an evil eye.

The next couple of days went by fast. The moving company moved mine and Anna's things from our old apartment to our new homes and we returned the keys to the landlord. Officially, I now lived with Nick. The sectional and new appliances arrived and I had most of my things put away and hung up. When Nick came home from work and saw everything he thought he had the wrong house.

"You've made this old garage look amazing. I love it," Nick said before he gave me a kiss.

"Thank you sir. A little money and a female touch can make anything look good."

I ordered a few more things for our apartment and then I would be finished. I wanted everything to be perfect for the party on Sunday. Anna came over to help me and she seemed impressed at what I had done with the bachelor pad. We both thought it had come a long way. The brown sectional fit amazingly in the open floor plan. It spaced the area out incredibly well.

While I looked over my masterpiece and finished up some final touches the day before the party, Nick came out of the bathroom from his shower. He turned on the radio. He walked over to me and took my hands and placed them around his neck and started slow dancing with me.

I smiled up at him and he smiled back. I laid my head on his shoulder and the warmth of his body warmed mine as he wrapped his strong arms around me and held me close. Our bodies moved as one; in total sync. Our bodies, hearts, and souls one.

"You make me the happiest man in the world Rayna," Nick whispered as he continued to lead me in his dance.

I peeked up at him and into his warm chocolate brown eyes. "I never realized love could be this way Nick; you are my everything."

Nick leaned down and kissed me gently and then stared into my eyes. We spoke with our eyes; we didn't need words. He took my breath away with one gaze.

"It's late princess. You might turn into a pumpkin if I don't put you to bed." Nick smiled and kissed the tip of my nose as he swooped me up into his arms and carried me to bed.

• ♥ • ♥ • ♥ • ♥ • ♥ •

I woke up with a start. Still dark outside, I reached for Nick, but his side of the bed was cold. I got up and pulled my robe around me and walked downstairs. Nick sat at the kitchen table writing on a tablet of paper. I didn't want to disturb him, but the stairs creaked and he turned my way.

"What are you doing up?" he asked. You need your rest."

I walked over to Nick and he opened his arms for me to sit on his lap.

"I guess I could sense you left; even in my sleep. Writing a new song?" I asked as I glanced down at his music journal he carried everywhere.

"Yes. I woke up and had these lyrics in my head and I wanted to put them down before I forgot them. I'm finished now, so let's put you back to bed." Nick put his pen down and closed his journal.

I stood up, but grasp his hand, making sure he came with me. Nick kept a hold of my hand and followed me back to bed. I snuggled into Nick's open arms and laid my head on his chest.

"What is your song about?" I whispered as I ran my hand up to Nick's neck and left my hand there.

"You and how much I love you. I can't wait to run it past the band and get their take on it."

"When can I hear it?"

"Soon." Nick ran his fingers lightly up and down my back. He knew this would lull me to sleep.

"Are you nervous about Sunday?" I wanted to see the expression on Nick's face, but I was too tired and comfortable to raise my head.

"Not at all, are you?" Nick said with confidence and pride.

"A little. I'm anxious about telling my parents about our engagement. I'm sure they'll find something negative to say about it. I want everyone to be as happy as I am about it."

"Everything will be fine princess, I promise. Now get some rest." Nick kissed the top of my head and continued to run his fingers across my back as he hummed a slow melody.

Thirteen

The band continued to perform while they waited for the album to be re-mastered, so Friday and Saturday brought late nights. Saturday before we left for the show, I did the finishing touches to prepare for the party on Sunday; the day for the big announcement. The butterflies fluttered around in my stomach with the thoughts of it.

Sunday morning I woke up early to prepare for our company. Nick and the band helped set up tables and chairs on the lawn so we could be outside in the beautiful August weather. Anna helped me inside set up the food I had ordered.

"Are you okay girl?" Anna asked as she opened packages of plates and napkins.

"A little nervous. My parents didn't appear too happy I moved in with Nick, so I'm pretty sure they will be gloomier about the engagement."

"It might be a shock to them at first, but give them some time to digest it. I prayed the news of the band getting signed will encourage them to be a little happy." Anna laughed.

I drew my eyebrows down at her in doubt. "I wanted to tell them with other people around; this party is my safety net. They can't yell too much at me today. It doesn't matter if I marry Nick next week or in two years, I'm still going to be with him. I don't think they realize how much we love each other."

I continued setting out the condiments from the refrigerator and the packages from the restaurant.

"You would have to be blind to not see how much you two love each other; how Nick tends to your ever need. "

"I know, but I don't think anybody will ever be good enough for my parents."

"I don't think your parents have gotten to know Nick enough to appreciate the love he has for you. When they realize he brought you back to life and he would die for you; surely they will accept him. Give it some time." Anna walked over and hugged me tightly.

She knew I needed her support and love now more than anything. And she willingly gave it. With Nick and Anna in my life, I could make it through anything.

"Thank you for being here and being my best friend," I said with newfound confidence and a smile on my face.

"Hey you two; we have company." Dave peeked in the door to inform us of the arrival of our first guest.

"On our way," I yelled over to the cute smiling face looking through the open door.

"Where is your ring?" Anna asked as she pulled my left hand up to examine it.

"Nick and I decided I wouldn't wear it until we announced our engagement tonight. We didn't want people asking questions before I told my parents." I shrugged my shoulders and put my arm around Anna's waist to guide her to the door.

"Good thinking." Anna smiled and followed my lead to greet our guest.

Rick's mom Samantha and her fiancé arrived first. She took time to give everybody a hug and wanted updated on the latest news. Anna's mom and the guy she dated arrived shortly after. She had only met Nick a few times but seemed to like him enough. Anna's mom, a very accepting person, encouraged

Anna to go after her dreams with a passion. Although she worried about Anna often, she had enough faith in Anna to make the right decisions.

A few more of our closest friends arrived and then my parents. My mother ran immediately over to me to wrap me in her protective arms. She pushed me away from her but kept her hands on my shoulders to check me over.

"Rayna, you seem tired honey. Are you okay?" She had worry and concern on her face and voice.

"Mom, I'm fine; wonderful actually. How are you?" I gave her my biggest smile; for her reassurance.

I never felt better in my life. I was the happiest I had ever been in an extremely long time; a little tired, but happy nonetheless.

"Rayna, you are beautiful as usual." My dad kissed my cheek and gave me a tight squeeze. "I'm glad you invited us, I've missed you honey."

"I missed both of you, but we've all been busy. That's why Nick and I thought having a party would be a wonderful idea. And I wanted you two to see my new place."

My mom made a face of disapproval but didn't say anything.

"Let me show you around before you start mingling with everybody." I held my hand up to show them toward the French doors.

My mom was impressed with what I had done to the garage. She liked the open floor plan and the updated appliance helped to make the place more modern.

Outside, everyone enjoyed themselves immensely. My mom and dad joined in the fun and started relaxing and socializing. Maybe this wouldn't be as bad as I had thought. My parents even socialized with Nick. Nick introduced my parents to his mother. My mother appeared to like Nick's mother. I hoped this would help break the ice with Nick and my parents. I stood back and watched to see if I could get a vibe from them; hoping they would finally start to like Nick more; I wished even love him like I did.

After about two hours, Nick came over to me and put his hand on my back. "Do you think it is time for the band announcement?"

"Yes and the engagement announcement as well. I feel solid about everything right now. I want to get this out in the open." I gazed up at Nick with hopeful eyes. He touched my cheek with the back of his hand and then kissed my forehead. "Let's go tell the world."

Nick led me to the center of our guests where they all congregated on the concrete patio.

"Rayna, the band, and I would like to thank all of you for coming to our house today. We invited you here to help us celebrate the signing of the band with a major record company. You should be hearing one of our first songs on the radio soon."

Everybody cheered and clapped. Questions came from all of our friends. My mom and dad even seemed incredibly happy about the announcement.

After our friends and family calmed down a bit about the band announcement, Nick called for their attention again.

"Can I have your attention again, please? Rayna and I have an announcement of our own."

Everybody got quiet and all eyes were on us.

"While the band visited New York, I asked Rayna to be my wife and she accepted." Nick spoke with confidence and pride. He smiled and pulled me into him. He kissed the top of my head.

Everyone stood speechless for a moment. Anna glanced from me to my parents and I kept my eyes on my parents. My mother's face showed no emotion. I think she was still registering what she heard. My father scowled at my mother with a shocked face.

"Rayna, how wonderful to have you for a daughter." Nick's mom came first to congratulate us. She hugged us both and told us how much she loved us and how happy she was for us both.

"I am so happy for you both." Samantha smiled and hugged me and then kissed my cheek. Nick leaned down to give her a hug. "I want to help with the wedding; I have a lot of connections." She winked at me and took my hand to peer at my ring.

"Stunning; amazing choice Nick." She smiled at him with pride written all over her face.

"Thank you Samantha." Nick kissed her cheek as she squeezed his hand.

"Yes, thank you Samantha. I'll be taking you up on the offer." I smiled a genuine smile of happiness even though I had a huge ball of nerves in the pit of my stomach.

I wanted my parents to be happy for me; but wasn't sure that dream would come true, at least not today.

Everyone wanted to see the ring Nick had given me. I wanted to share this wonderful moment with my parents, but I didn't want to push it on them; so I waited for them to approach me. I was happy and sad at the same time; euphoric because I would spend the rest of my life with a man I loved deeply and loved me; but sad because my parents didn't agree with who my heart chose.

My parents moved quickly to be the first to leave; which didn't surprise me much.

"Congratulations Rayna and Nick." My mom's face didn't show any signs of happiness, but she tried to make an effort. She gave me a hug and told me she would see me soon.

"Thank you Carrie." Nick said before she could pull away from me.

"Thank you for inviting us to your celebration." My mom put on a forced smile and patted my shoulder.

"You have a nice place here. Thanks for inviting us to your party and congratulations on your news." My dad shook Nick's hand and showed a persona of disapproval toward him.

"Thank you, Mr. Taylor. It means a lot that you two came today to celebrate with us. I hope you will join us again." Nick smiled at my parents with confidence.

My dad gave me a hug. "Come see me soon. I miss you."

"I miss you dad." I smiled. "I'll call you tomorrow; I love you." I called as my parents turned to leave. I understood my parents disapproved of the engagement, but didn't what to speak their objections at the party. My stomach twisted in knots. Would they come around before the wedding or would they stay in mourning?

"We love you Rayna; talk to you soon." My parents gave me a reluctant smile and turned to walk to their car.

The next morning, I slept later than usual. When I woke up, Nick was gone. I made it down for coffee and found a note with a few wildflowers from the backyard.

"I couldn't find the heart to wake your beautiful sleeping face. See you this evening. All my love, your future husband, Nick."

He always knew how to make my eyes tear up and my heart skip a beat.

Nick and I didn't talk about my parents' reaction to our engagement announcement. He knew I would talk to him about it when I was ready. I still needed time to digest my feelings about it.

Nick got home late because he needed to finish some cars before he quit his job to go on tour. He spoke with excitement when he got home because the record company had called and told him they planned for a photo shoot this week in town with a local photographer. The photoshoot would supply the band with pics for the album and some photos to promote the tour.

With the thoughts of touring on my mind, I wondered how tough it would be for the band traveling and playing every night. I'd be able to go with them but didn't have any real concept of a touring schedule. I wanted to be with Nick during his touring and I could do that because I edited articles for my job online. I had money in the bank that allowed me to be gone for long periods of time. But Nick and I would always be in a group; we wouldn't have any "us" time. I thought about this most of the day and eventually came up with an idea.

I discussed my idea with Nick.

"When does the band start the tour?" I asked while we ate dinner.

"We don't have the exact date, but we are looking at a couple more weeks. Probably the first of September." Nick said between bites of his stir fry.

"Well, I wondered if you and I could pull off a mini vacation before the tour starts. After the tour starts, who knows how long before you get a real break and before we find any downtime." I gave him my sad eyes, hoping he would give in easily.

"I don't see why not. They know I'm not taking on any more jobs. If I need to work late to finish them, I can. I do whatever I need to make you happy. What did you have in mind princess?"

"I thought maybe Jamaica, Cancun, the Bahamas, or a cruise." I glanced up from my plate and raised my eyebrows waiting for his response.

"I can't afford an exotic vacation this quick Rayna. I don't wanna spend the money from the record company yet."

"I want to help or maybe pay for it all; my gift."

"You need to stop this. I told you before; I don't want you spending your money on me," he said with a stern tone.

"It's not just on you. It's for me too. You pay my rent; let me pay for this vacation. We're engaged now, like a married couple, so my money is your money." I smiled up at Nick hoping he would return my smile.

"Your parents already think I'm with you for your money; this will send them over the edge."

"Please? If it makes you feel better, you can pay me back as soon as the band makes it big." I begged. I got off my chair and went over and sat in Nick's lap, wrapping my arms around his neck. I gazed deep into his dark brown eyes with my pleading eyes. We encountered a sort of standoff. I hoped I'd win this battle.

Nick continued looking at me and gave in. "Oh, okay. Whatever you want princess. Where are we going?" I defeated Nick and he realized it.

I smiled from ear to ear. "Thank you. We need this; I need this! This is going to be wonderful. I;ll have everything booked and ready tomorrow." I babbled. I gave Nick a thank you kiss.

"You're welcome. You're like a kid in a candy store," Nick laughed as I moved from his lap to my chair.

"Are you alright with how my parents reacted yesterday about our engagement?" I asked after I chewed my bite of food.

"It's not the best reaction, but I'm more worried about how their reaction affected you." Nick looked up from his plate. "I don't think they're being fair to you; it upsets me. How are you feeling about it?" Nick set his glass of water down and placed his fork on the table to give me his complete attention.

I never had to try to get Nick's attention; I just had to speak and I had his undivided attention. That's one of the things

I loved about him and one of the things that bothered me because he was always so receptive of me. Sometimes it made me nervous.

"Well, it bothers me they don't have enough faith in me that I can make smart choices. It makes me a little angry and I want to scream sometimes. I hope they come around soon because I am going to marry you whether they like it or not." I took my last bite of food and sat back to hear what Nick had to say.

"Well, it sounds like you understand what you want and how you're going to handle this. I'll let you work with your parents and I'll try not to do anything to make them dislike me more."

"I don't think they dislike you; they don't like "me" being with you. They like you as a person, but in their eyes, nobody will ever be good enough for me. I hope they come around soon. I'm going to go on with our plans so they better catch up with us." I smiled and finished my drink.

Fourteen

♥

The next day I moved in full swing making our plans for our mini vacation. While Nick went to work, I scanned the internet for places to go. I wanted to go someplace exotic, but I didn't want to spend half of the trip on a plane or at the airport. I found the perfect spot in the Bahamas. Sandals at St. Lucia, Bahamas had the most beautiful rooms. I didn't show Nick because of the price. He would argue with me, but I wanted a relaxing vacation with him before the tour started.

The Beachfront Grande Rondoral Butler Suite had a private pool outside of the room, with the beach right off of the pool. Since we both loved the beach so much, this would make the perfect spot for us. We wouldn't need to leave the room with a private butler. This was just what we needed since we would be surrounded by people the entire tour. I was booking the room as soon as Nick gave me the dates. The excitement about our trip made it hard for me to finish reading the articles I needed to finish by Friday, but I forced myself to complete some work. Nick would be working late, so I ordered a pizza and tried to work late as well.

Finally, Nick came home around 7:30. Even though he ate earlier he still enjoyed some pizza. He looked exhausted.

"I have to work late again tomorrow if I'm gonna be off early Wednesday for the photo shoot," Nick said between bites of cold pizza.

"You look tired." I finished emptying the dishwasher. "Go grab a shower. We can relax and watch a movie in bed."

"Sounds good to me." Nick kissed my cheek and headed to the shower.

The movie ended and I turned off the TV. "I love you," I whispered. But the only thing I heard was his soft breathing. I closed my eyes and drifted off to sleep.

I woke up to Nick's breath on my face. I was having a wonderful dream of us on a beautiful beach. I smile up at him as he leaned down hovering over me.

"I didn't mean to wake you; I just wanted to give you a kiss before I left." Nick gave me an apologetic smile.

"Never be sorry to kiss me." I pulled him down to my lips to give him a better kiss. "I was having a wonderful dream of us floating in the blue waters of the salty ocean."

"I must've been having the same dream. We were in blue green waters and the sun warm. You had a sun kissed tan and your beautiful brown hair blew in the salty air."

"We always do this." I giggled. "I wonder why?" I stared deep into his eyes

"I think maybe because our souls are so connected----we connect even in our sleep." Nick kissed me again. "Gotta get to work beautiful. I'll see you this evening."

"Any special request for dinner tonight?"

"Anything you decide to fix will be fine with me." Nick winked and blew me a kiss as he turned to go down the stairs.

I lay there thinking about the wonderful man that was part of my life. My life was wonderful in every way. I loved him for who he was and for making my world such a wonderful place.

I had only talked to my parents once since the party and they didn't say anything about my engagement. It seemed like they were trying to deny my engagement by not talking about it. I made plans with my mom to have dinner with my parents next week. Even though Nick and I hadn't talked specifics on our wedding I needed to start the conversation with my parents.

Nick called in the afternoon to let me know he was on his way to the photo shoot. He had no idea how long they would be taking pictures, so he said he would call when he had a chance. I finished reading articles for the evening and decided to start on dinner.

I invited Anna to come over since Travis would be with Nick. She ate dinner with me while we caught up on things. We discussed the band going on tour and her trying to work her school schedule into the band's touring. She knew it would be difficult, but she would be able to be at some shows.

Nick called around eight and said the band was going over the pictures with the photographer so they wouldn't need to meet again. He told me they should be finished around ten. The photographer would be sending the approved pictures to the record company for them to use on the album and promo posters.

"I'm sorry about dinner baby. I'll make it up to you."

"It's fine. Anna ate dinner with me. You can take leftovers tomorrow in your lunch. Take all the time you need to pick out the best pictures for the album. I love you."

"I love you. See you in a bit." Nick hung up the phone.

Anna and I had some wine and I told her about our plans for a mini vacation. She was happy we would be spending some quality time together. She only wished she and Travis could get away to a beach, but they had decided to take a weekend trip to a cabin; which sounded kind of amazing as well.

My phone dinged. It was from Nick.

"Check out these pictures." I handed Anna my phone.

"Wow, those are awesome. I love them." Anna flipped through the photos. "I'm impressed. These are better than I thought." Anna smiled and handed my phone back.

"I know right? These are really gonna help promote our guys. It's so unbelievable, only a few months ago we didn't even know this band. Now we're starting a life with them and they're getting a record deal. How life can change almost instantaneously. Anna, I am so happy right now. Every day I get to wake up to this wonderful life. Thank you for making me go to the beach this summer." I leaned in and gave Anna a hug.

"You deserve this. I'm happy you finally listened to me." We both laughed and she poured us some more wine.

"I invited my parents to come up to Pittsburgh to have dinner at their favorite restaurant on Wednesday," I said.

Anna set her glass on the table. "That's nice.

"I want to clear the air about my engagement before I leave with the band." We might not have a break before Christmas and I want to do this in person."

"Is Nick going?" Anna took another sip of her wine.

"I didn't think I should subject him to the drama." I rolled my eyes.

Anna smiled. "I think he should go. He is part of your life now so this concerns him.

"You're right. As usual." We both laughed and finished the bottle of wine.

SONGS FROM THE HEART

· ♥ · ♥ · ♥ · ♥ · ♥ ·

Wednesday came and I was a nervous wreck.. I remembered how they acted at the party. I hoped and prayed for some acceptance of our engagement.

Nick appeared to be in an ecstatic mood on the way to the restaurant. He tried to keep me talking about the tour and our vacation, but all my brain would think about was my parents accepting him into the family. I wanted my parents to love Nick as much as I did. I always wanted my parents to be proud of me. Sometimes I felt they had no faith in me.

"It's going to be okay, Rayna." Nick tried to reassure me as he squeezed my knee.

"I hope." I smile up at him and lay my head on his shoulder and wrapped my arms around his arm, glad I had him with me for support.

"Did you book our vacation?" Nick tried to distract me from the upcoming dinner as he drove my car to the restaurant.

"Yes I did. I can't wait until we are there. I will need a stress free weekend."

Nick laughed and kissed my forehead.

"During the tour are we driving the van around and staying in hotels?"

"I guess. I never thought about it. Why?"

"Well, I was thinking, hotels and eating out all the time will more than likely take most of the band's beginning profits. What about investing in a used RV? A mini-bus until the band can afford a bus. Someone can drive while others sleep, take a shower, and pull over anywhere to rest and cook." I raised my head off of Nick's shoulder so I could see his face.

"That might be a superb idea. We should run the idea by the guys when we get home. Have I ever told you how smart you are?" Nick smiled down at me.

I smiled up at Nick and nuzzled back down into the comfort and safety of his shoulder, thinking about the dinner.

We arrived at the restaurant and Nick got out of the car and walked around to open my door. I decided to wear a new dress I hadn't worn yet; a simple little black dress, it fit perfectly in all the right places.

"By the way, you are stunning tonight." Nick said as he took my hand to help me from the car. He kissed my hand and then pulled me into him.

"Thank you; you are rather handsome yourself." I wrapped my arms around Nick's waist and held him tight as he wrapped his arms around me like a cocoon.

The restaurant was crowded for a Wednesday night, but most of Pittsburgh's businesses were usually pretty busy every night. The host took us to our seats after we told them we expected two more. He took our names and assured us he would bring my mother and father to our table when they arrived.

My nerves started to get the better of me now. When the waiter came to our table to fill out water glasses, I ordered a bottle of wine. A drink might calm my nerves. He brought the bottle and filled our glasses. I drank my glass rather quick and refilled it.

"Thirsty?" Nick laughed.

"Haha." Just my parents driving me to drink.

My parents arrived and Nick stood to welcome them. He shook my father's hand and moved to help my mother with her chair.

"Thank you," my mother said. Nick nodded and sat down. My father kissed my cheek then sat in his chair.

"Thanks for inviting us to dinner Rayna and Nick." My mother said as she took a sip of her water.

"You're welcome. I haven't seen either of you since our party." I said. I took another drink of wine.

"You two kind of took us by surprise." My dad said as he poured himself some wine.

"I love your daughter Mr. and Mrs. Taylor and I want to spend the rest of my life with her." Nick's face was a statute.

"We understand young love." My dad peered at my mom and took her hand and kissed the back of it. "But just because you're engaged doesn't mean you will be married next week. It took us some time, but we've come to terms with the engagement." My dad glanced from me to Nick.

"Yes, we want Rayna to be healthy and happy," my mom said.

"I am both. I'm the happiest I have ever been in my life. And no, we didn't set a date yet. But it does make me feel better that you accept my decision. I love you both and I want us to all be a big happy family."

The waiter came back and took our orders. We discussed the fact that I wanted a small wedding with family and close friends. My mom tried to encourage a bigger to do than I wanted, but I put my foot down.

We enjoyed dinner and the conversation. My parents listened with interest in the band's tour and what getting signed to a record deal meant for them. They acted truly happy. My mom watched Nick and me as we showed our affection for each other. Nick filled my glass and shared his dessert with me. She seemed impressed.

"Are you going to be staying at Nick's by yourself while he is away? Why don't you come and stay with us while he's touring?" My mom said between bites of her cheesecake.

"I'm going with the band on tour. I'm gonna help Rick with the managing and selling merchandise."

"Rayna, do you realize how rough living on the road will be?" My mom put her fork down and scowled at me.

Yes, but I refuse to be away from Nick. I don't sleep well when I am away from him. He's part of me and I can't be without part of myself.

"Are you okay with this?" My dad questioned Nick.

"I want Rayna with me. That's why I asked her to marry me. I can't live without her either. I need her to be near me."

"Is it healthy to be together all the time?" My mom took another bite of cheesecake.

"It's unhealthy for us to be apart. I'll be fine." I leaned in and kissed Nick.

My parents left the conversation there. We enjoyed the rest of our evening with my parents and I promised to come for dinner at their house before we left for our mini vacation. It made my mom happy we would be visiting, but still a little bothered I'd be going on tour for a few months. I could tell that my going on tour made her a little nervous.

On the drive home, rain started to fall. I stared out into the dark rainy night and thought about how well the evening went.

"That went well." Nick glanced over at me.

"Maybe a little too well. It just seems odd at how quick they are okay with our engagement." I held Nick's hand on my lap.

"Don't look a gift horse in the mouth. After it settled in, they might have realize they're being silly."

"I hope you're right. I want my parents to accept everything about me and you. Maybe you and my dad could do something together. Go to a game or go golfing." I laughed.

"Haha, golfing.....right. We really should discuss setting a date. We don't need to set the actual date, but a time reference; winter, spring, summer, or fall. What do you think? I'm happy with tomorrow." Nick pulled my hand up to his lips and kissed my fingers.

"I don't want anything giant. Like I said at dinner, family and close friends. We could rent a place for a weekend wedding. We could check the tour schedule and try to make a date. Spring would work for me, that's about eight or nine months. Or would you like to tie the knot sooner?"

"I'd marry you tomorrow without any of the frills, but I wouldn't want to take a beautiful wedding day from you. Can we think about winter? That's only six months." Nick gave me his pleading eyes.

"I want a honeymoon, so if February will work into the tour schedule, it's a go. I think I can pull a wedding together in six months, even on the road. Now you made me excited."

"Baby, I've been excited since the first day I laid eyes on you, and it hasn't let up. I knew the moment our eyes met, I was going to marry you. That's why I freaked out, I realized my world would change and I had no idea what to expect. I love you now and forever."

"I love you Nick, and I can't wait to be your wife" I laughed and snuggled into Nick's arm as he drove down the four lanes.

"Hey while we're talking about our future and the tour dates, what day is your check up with the doctor? You promised to make an appointment before we left on tour to make sure everything was okay with your heart."

"It's Monday at three, why?"

"Because I wanna go with you. I want to make sure I am informed on everything about your condition. Plus it'll help me feel at ease."

"It'll be boring, but if you insist, you can hang out at the doctor's with me." I smiled up at Nick. It warmed my heart to know he wanted to be a part of my life in every way. This confirmed his love for me----taking care of me in every way.

Fifteen

♥

We got off the plane in the Bahamas around eleven on Thursday morning. The beautiful light blue sky allowed feathery white clouds to dance here and there. The warm breeze blew through my dark brown hair. Nick pulled our bags from the airport to the Rolls Royce that waited for us. We packed light since we would be spending most of our time in the room. The next four days would be fantastic.

Our driver opened the door for us and then placed our bags in the trunk. Nick and I took in all the views as we passed small brightly colored houses. The drive to the resort was relatively short, about fifteen minutes. When the car pulled in, the resort staff greeted us with exotic drinks in blue keepsake tumblers. We drank these while we waited to check in. A host introduced us to our personal butler which gave us a lemongrass heated towel to freshen up after our flight. He served us champagne while we checked in and guided us to our room. A bellhop delivered our luggage. The next few days would be amazing, laying in the sun, splashing in the waves, all while being with the love of my life.

Nick held my hand as we followed the host down the sidewalk to our room. Beautiful pink hibiscus flowers and lush greenery lined the walk on both sides of us. All the foliage and flowers took my breath away and the smell of the salt air exhilarated my senses.

"Would you like me to unpack your luggage?" The butler stood at the door with his hands clasped together in the front.

"No, that won't be necessary." I smiled at him. "But I think we would like to have something light to eat please."

"Of course mam. What would you like?"

"What do you recommend?" I asked the butler as I walked over to scan the menu.

Nick leaned against the door jamb as he gazed out at the ocean.

"Nick, what would you like?"

"May I suggest the chicken salad sandwiches with a strawberry salad, mam?"

I glanced over at Nick who still leaned against the jam lost in his own thoughts.

"That would be fine thank you." I nodded to the butler and he bowed slightly, turned, and left the room.

"Hey." I walked over and rubbed Nick's arm. "Did you hear me?"

"Sorry, what did you say?" Nick turned to me and showed me his beautiful smile. He wrapped his arms around my waist.

"I ordered lunch and wondered if you had a preference."

"I trust you to order something delicious." Nick smiled and kissed to the top of my head.

I knew he had something on his mind, he'd tell me when he felt ready. He was probably worried about the tour, maybe nerves.

"Let's put our swimsuits on and go out to the pool." I smiled up at Nick. He smiled and kissed my lips.

"Sounds wonderful."

We changed and went out to our patio with the pool, lounge chairs, a hammock, and a Jacuzzi. The beautiful blue-green water of the ocean and the white sand were amazing views from the pool. It was wonderful. Nick held me in his embrace in the pool while we stared out at the ocean and said nothing; just enjoying holding each other in our own little secluded world. This vacation had been just what we needed; a chance to be alone and appreciate each other.

"Sir, where would you like your lunch?" The butler asked.

"There on the table is fine," Nick motioned.

"Very good. Would you like dinner brought in as well?"

"Yes please," I smiled. The butler held up a towel for me as I got out of the pool.

"Thank you." I took the menu out of his hand that he offered. "We would like the steak for dinner tonight please." I handed the menu to the butler.

"Very good. Dinner will be served at 8." The butler turned and left.

After lunch, we decided to head to the beach. Neither one of us had ever seen white sand beaches. They were stunning and the warm water welcomed us as it caressed our bodies. We played in the waves and watched fish swim. The water was so clear you could see the bottom even chest deep. The gentle current and the soft waves calmed our spirits.

"I could stay and live here forever," I said as I floated in the ocean.

"You aren't kidd'in. I could get used to this," Nick smiled and pulled me to him. His smile left quickly.

I could still tell something bothered him. He acted like he was in amazing spirits, but I read his face and something was on his mind. I figured I'd approach him about it at dinner. I didn't want his mind anywhere but here at this amazing place.

We spent the rest of the day at the beach. In the early evening, we took a shower and dressed for dinner. Our butler brought us white wine, Caribbean steaks, mashed potatoes, a mandarin orange salad, and key lime pie for dessert. Light music played in the background. It was wonderful being taken care of in such a beautiful place. Dinner under the stars at the ocean was my favorite way to have dinner.

"What has been bothering you all day?" I asked as we ate dessert.

"What do you mean?" Nick set his glass of wine down with a fake confused expression on his face.

"Nick, you know you can't keep anything from me, I can sense your feelings and sometimes know your thoughts." I placed my elbows on the table and put my chin on top of my crossed hands as I smiled at him; showing him I waited for an answer.

"Rayna, you have enough stress on you right now with your parents and the stuff you do for the band. I don't want to bother you with this. It's nothing for you to worry about."

"We promised to never keep anything from each other Nick. Now tell me what's been bothering you all day." I sounded a little more demanding this time.

"Okay, you're right. But I don't want you upset. I don't want our vacation ruined. You promise?"

"I promise." I refused to allow anything to ruin this vacation. I couldn't be sure when Nick and I would enjoy another one.

"Yesterday afternoon your mother came to my work. Long story short, she offered me fifty thousand dollars to leave you and go on with my tour. She told me you would find someone else eventually and tried to convince me to take the money. Of course I didn't take it which made her unhappy with me." Nick paid close attention to my reaction.

I sat back in my chair speechless; not moving. I contemplated what he just said; trying to comprehend it. It was almost unbelievable that my mother would do this. I got up, took a deep breath and walked to the banister to look out at the ocean. My parents truly didn't want me with Nick. And they honestly thought he wanted my money. I wondered what they thought now that he refused their money.

"Rayna, are you okay?" Nick asked as he placed his hands on my shoulders. I put my hand on his hand and held it on my shoulder.

I didn't answer at first, but he allowed me time to answer. He knew this would hurt and anger me.

"Marry me this weekend!" I turned and fell into Nick's warm embrace.

"Rayna," Nick pulled my chin up with the tip of his right hand. He gazed into my eyes. "You don't want a wedding with all of our friends and family?"

"No, I want to marry you now without everybody else. We can have a party later. My parents are never going to except this." I shook my head. "Trying to plan a wedding with my mother will only be more stressful. I am ready to start my life as Mrs. Nick Perry."

"Are you sure? I don't care how I marry you, as long as I marry you."

"Let's get married here in this beautiful place." My eyes pleaded with Nick as he held his gaze on me. "It would make me the happiest girl in the world. I wanted to marry you the first day I met you and I don't want to wait any longer to be your wife." I smiled up at Nick and stood on my toes so I could kiss him.

"Ok, I'll marry you tomorrow Princess Rayna, but I'm paying for the wedding." Nick grinned and picked me up and spun me around.

Our kiss lingered for a long while; Nick turned our embrace into a dance as we moved to the music and the sound of the ocean. Our butler came to clear our dishes and turn down our bed.

"What would we need to do to have a wedding here before we leave?" I asked our butler when he came to take our plates away.

"We have wedding packages. I could bring the information if you would like."

"Yes please. Could I see it tonight?"

"Just one moment mam. I'll be right back." He smiled and left our room.

We danced to another song and gazed at the stars. The butler returned with the information and cleaned up our dining table while I went through the packet. I filled out the paperwork, picked out flowers, and the clothes we would wear.

"Do you think this can happen tomorrow at sunset? I handed the papers to the butler.

"Yes mam. I checked before I came back. I'll take care of everything. I'll let you know in the morning what time you need to get ready."

"Thank you so much for everything you're doing for us," Nick said.

"My pleasure. If there is nothing else, I'll let you two enjoy your evening." He nodded and pushed the diner cart out the door. We enjoyed each other the rest of the evening.

• ♥ • ♥ • ♥ • ♥ • ♥ •

The next day was busy. We had breakfast by our pool. The butler brought an itinerary for our wedding day. We had a couple's massage scheduled and then a fitting for our wedding clothes in the afternoon. He explained to us that the resort would supply our two witnesses for the wedding and then after our dinner we would be the special guest at an outdoor party.

At 5:30 I had appointments for my hair and makeup at the spa. Thinking about the wedding in a few hours had butterflies dancing every so often in my stomach. But the staff at the spa kept me busy talking about how Nick and I met and how beautiful our wedding was going to be.

When the staff completed their work of art on me they gave me a mirror. My mouth fell open. I looked like a walked out of a fairy tale.

"You have outdone yourself. I love what you have done." I smiled and admired myself in the mirror.

"We had a beautiful canvas to work with." They all smiled.

"Now it's time to get dressed." The young staff girl smiled as she presented my dress.

I smiled and followed her to the dressing room. She helped me put my dress on. It was a long white dress with spaghetti straps. The front was cut deep and the back was open. The rest was form fitting with a small train. The white lacy beach shoes had no sole. They hooked on my toe and tied around my ankle. They were delicate and beautiful. I almost didn't recognize myself when I looked in the mirror.

"You're a beautiful bride." The staff girl said.

"Thank you," I smiled at her in the mirror.

"You are going to take your groom's breath away."

I looked in the mirror one last time. Butterflies flip flopped in my gut. She handed me a beautiful bouquet of fuchsia orchids. I took a deep breath and was ready to meet my future on the beach.

She walked me to the beach where I would be married. An arch was put up on the beach with sheer white material wrapped around it. The same orchids in my bouquet were placed in different places on the arch. It looked so romantic.

Nick stood under the arch with the minister. He wore an off white pair of slacks and a white button up shirt with an orchid boutonniere. His hair blew in the ocean breeze. He kept his eyes on me as I walked down the white wooden walkway that had been placed in the sand for me.

Nick took my hand. "You're gorgeous." He smiled.

"Thank you handsome," I said.

He held both of my hands as the minister began. We continued looking into each other's eyes. We were married at sunset. We celebrated with a wonderful dinner, a small cake, and our first dance as Mr. & Mrs. Nick Perry.

Sixteen

There was an RV parked in the driveway with the trailer on the back when we arrived home. Anna and Travis were loading some things into it.

"Hey you two, how was your vacation?" Anna ran over to the car door to hug me as I got out of the car.

"Amazing. It was beautiful Anna. I wish I could stay forever." I hugged her tight because I'd missed her. "I see they got the RV. What are you loading?"

"We're putting some kitchen items in the RV that we collected from friends and family so you guys can eat. Come check it out, it's pretty awesome. You'll need some sheets and blankets, but I figured everybody would bring their own." Anna grabbed my hand and pulled me around the RV to the side door.

We stepped up into the RV. It was tiny, but actually very quaint. It was clean and polished; it looked close to brand new. At least we wouldn't be riding in the van. Nick stepped into the RV and whistled.

"This is a cool ride Travis. You guys did well." Nick checked all around the RV and opened cabinet doors and the refrigerator.

"You and Rayna can have the bed in the back. I don't really feel like sharing a bed with one of the guys." Travis pointed to the back of the RV and laughed.

"Well, thank you Travis." I smiled and told Anna to come in the house with me.

She followed me into the house and flopped herself onto the couch.

"Did you take any pictures of that beautiful place?" She looked up at me.

"Of course I did." I smiled and walked over to the counter to remove my phone from my purse. I also pulled out our wedding photos. I walked over to the couch.

"I'm going to share something with you because you're my best friend. But you have to promise to keep it quiet; at least for now." I stood looking down at her waiting for her promise.

"I promise, cross my heart." Anna sat up straight and crossed her heart.

I handed her the picture without saying a word. She took a moment and flipped through them. She set them on her lap and glanced up at me with a huge smile.

"You did it! You got married." She jumped from the couch and embraced me with a bear hug. "Did you two plan this before you left? Is this why you took a mini vacation before the tour? You eloped?

Anna let go of me and waited for my answer.

"No, we just decided to do it. It probably helped that my mom tried to give Nick fifty thousand dollars to break up with me," disgust on my face.

"What?"

"My mom went to Nick's work last week and gave him a check. She told him to use it for the tour or the band, but to break it off with me. He refused of course. She must have thought he would take the money. I mean, she does think he is after my money. So I decided I didn't want to deal with trying to plan a wedding with my parents and what better place to get married than at the beach? I just wish you could've been there with me."

"Me too. Are you glad you did it?" Anna stared at me seriously now.

"I've never been happier Anna. The stress with my parent's refusal to accept him has been lifted." I gave her a big smile and another hug. "We're going to have a big reception after the first part of the tour. I figured after we're on the road, we'll set a date and I can make the arrangements over the phone with your help."

"Of course, I'll do anything to help. But first and foremost I'll keep a tight lid on the news." Anna gave me her best mischievous smile.

I trusted my life with this lady, so I knew my news of marrying Nick would be safe with her until I was ready. I would be lost without Anna and Nick. They were the mortar to my bricks, holding everything in my life together. I was sorry Anna couldn't be the maid of honor at my wedding, but she would still play her part by helping to create a wonderful reception. During the tour, Nick and I would set a date and the planning would begin. I would skype, email, and text Anna the whole time to make sure everything about our wonderful day would be set.

"Do you want to go with me to my parents' house? I need to visit before I leave. I could use the moral support. I need someone there to help me not go crazy on her." I gave Anna my best pleading eyes I could muster up.

"Yes, I'll go. It'll be refreshing to visit your parents. It's been a few weeks since I saw them."

"We can grab her dessert from her favorite restaurant and order some pizzas for dinner." I said as I grabbed my overnight bag and took it into the bathroom. I needed to refresh it since we were leaving tomorrow.

As I pulled into my parent's driveway I took a deep breath. I was still extremely upset with what she'd done; it would be hard to be diplomatic about it. I wondered if my father was in the loop about what she did. He wouldn't approve of it I know. I hoped Nick not accepting her money would show her he didn't care about money as much as she thought he did.

"You ready?" Anna glanced over at me with worried eyes.

"Ready as I'll ever be. Let's go." I opened the door and got out of my car. I stood looking at the beautiful house I used to live in. I grabbed the three pizza's from the back seat and Anna grabbed the dessert.

"You made it." My dad stood at the front door with his hands in his pockets smiling from ear to ear. "I see you brought a present." My dad pointed to Anna as he walked down the patio steps to take the pizzas from me and kiss my cheek. He kissed Anna's cheek as well.

"Hi dad, how are you?" I smiled at my dad as he turned to walk up the steps.

"Glad to see you for sure. How have you two ladies been? "

"Great."

"Good." Anna said. She wrapped her arm around my waist as we walked into the house. It was a protective arm; like she guided me into a hostile situation. It made me smile knowing my best friend was that protective over me.

"Dad, do you mind grabbing the bag out of the trunk too? I thought I would do my laundry while we visited."

"Sure honey. Let me put these pizzas on the kitchen counter and I will." He carried the pizzas down and turned around to me. "You are so grown up honey. You look beautiful. Where did the time go?" My dad pulled me into a huge hug. He didn't let go for a minute or so. When he did, he scanned me again and kissed my cheek before he let go and walked out of the kitchen.

My mom walked into the kitchen. "I thought I heard voices down here." My mom smiled as she held her arms open to hug me. I hugged her tight. I loved my mom very much, but I was still upset with her right now. She kissed my cheek and then hugged Anna.

My dad carried the bag of clothes into the laundry room right off from the kitchen.

"Let me throw a load of laundry in and then we can eat and visit." I pointed to the laundry room. "I figured I could kill two birds with one stone."

"I knew I raised a smart girl." My mom patted me on the back. "Let's find some drinks and plates Anna." My mom moved to the refrigerator while Anna went to the cabinet to grab the plates.

I threw jeans in the laundry first. I sorted the rest. I walked back into the kitchen where they had everything ready for dinner.

"Thanks for bringing my favorite dessert Rayna. You know I love it." My mom smiled.

"You're welcome. I brought enough so you can have leftovers for tomorrow." I pulled the chair out and sat down.

We all dug into the pizza and conversation. We talked about Anna and her plans after school and her mother. We talked about my part job working for the magazine and we talked about the band. Anna and I filled my parents in about the record contract, the album, the merchandise, and then the tour the band would be embarking on. I could tell when the conversation turned toward the tour, my parent's expressions changed; concern on their face. But Anna and I spoke with such enthusiasm about the band; I think some of it rubbed off on them. They seemed impressed when we told them one of the songs off the album started playing on the radio a few days ago. Anna and Travis had already heard it, but since Nick and I were away, we didn't get a chance to hear it yet.

Between eating and conversation, Anna and I had successfully accomplished the task of doing the laundry. We were eating dessert by the time I had the last of the laundry washing and it was close to nine in the evening. We talked about when I'd be back from the tour and what I'd be doing with the band.

"How's Nick?" My mom asked after a while. She took dishes from the table, rinsed them, and put them in the dishwasher.

"He's wonderful, you should know mom; you saw him last week." My adrenaline started to build in the pit of my stomach. I didn't know how she would respond to what I said, but she needed to know that I knew what she did. She stopped rinsing dishes for a moment and then began again.

"He told you I saw him?" She kept her back to me and continued to load the dishwasher.

"We don't keep anything from each other, Mom. He told me you came to his work and offered him fifty thousand dollars to break it off with me. Did you honestly think he would take the money mom?" I needed to get this out. I sat at the table without moving.

Anna got up and went to the laundry room to finish up. I think she realized this visit would soon be over.

"What did you do?" My dad's face now full of shock while his voice turned low and surprised.

"He didn't take it. I just wanted to test him to make sure he wasn't after your money." My mom turned around and walked over to the table. She sat down.

"I'm not worth very much to you mom." My words came out flat and without emotion.

"Rayna, you are worth everything I have. But I'm glad he didn't take it." My mom smiled.

"Are you really. If you're glad, why did you even do something like that?"

"Why would you do it Carrie? I can't believe you would do that to Rayna." My Dad pushed for an answer.

"I just wanted to make sure he loved her for her and not for her money. I'm sorry Rayna. Even though Nick seems to be an okay guy, I think you could do better for yourself." My mom just kept talking. She kept pushing my anger.

"Mom, stop! I don't want to hear anymore. I will be with Nick and there's nothing anyone can do to change that. I love him." My voice rose as I stood up from the table getting ready to leave. I realized I better go before I blurted the news of my marriage out.

"You didn't set a date yet right?" My mom probed.

"No, we do not have a date yet." I wasn't lying because we never set a date for the reception yet.

"Good because I think we need to discuss a prenuptial agreement if you're absolutely going to marry him."

"I think I better go. I don't want to discuss this anymore; I love you both and I'll call you." I walked into the laundry room to help Anna gather the laundry. I got angrier by the minute and I needed to get out of this house before I blew up on my parents. I walked back into the kitchen and hugged both of my parents. I told them I loved them and started for the door.

"Oh, I almost forgot; I ran into Tom the other day. He asked about you. I told him I'd have you call. He misses you Rayna." My mom stood in the foyer as I headed for the door; her arms wrapped around her. My dad opened the door for us as she said this. He turned and gaped at her with surprise.

I turned around with my arms full of laundry. Anger filled my emotions and I could tell she saw it in my face. "Tell Tom to go to hell." I turned and walked out the door.

"Rayna!" My mom yelled as she walked to the door where my dad stood.

"I love you both. I'll call in a few days." I opened the door and tossed the clothes into the back seat. Anna set the clothes on the backseat. I needed to get out of there. I got into the front seat and started the car and backed out of the driveway. I drove down the road and pulled over. I burst into tears. I felt pain rise in my chest but it didn't surprise me, since it started doing this a few weeks ago whenever adrenaline would surge through me.

"Are you okay Rayna?" Anna put her hand on my back as I leaned over the steering wheel."

"No, not really." I continued to let the tears fall down my cheek. "I'm having some angina, but it'll go away in a minute.

"What?! Let me take you to the hospital." She said as she opened her door and got out. I could hear the stress in her voice. She suddenly appeared at my door. She opened it and persuaded me out of the driver's seat. She walked me to the passenger side and put my seat back for me to rest and tried to get me to relax.

"Rayna are you sure you don't want to go to the hospital?" Worry and concern frozen on her face. She put her seat belt on.

"No, just give me a minute and it'll subside. I've had this a few times. When Karla was at Nick's and when we made the announcement about our engagement." I lay back in my seat with my arm raised over my head.

"So you've been having this pain. Have you told Nick or the doctor?"

"No, I haven't said anything to Nick, but I go to the doctor tomorrow before we leave for the tour. Nick's going with me so he will find out there." I laid for a few minutes and we were both quiet.

"Are you okay for me to start driving?" Anna still worried, turned to look at me.

"Yes, go ahead and take us home please."

Anna drove us home without too much talking. I felt better, but thought if I started talking about my parents again it would cause the pain and anger to come back. I just stayed with my seat back for the ride home. As we got closer to home I raised my seat up. I pulled the mirror down from the visor to check the state of my face.

"Ugh. I look awful." I fixed my makeup around my eyes with a tissue I took from the glove compartment. "What do you think?" I glanced over at Anna.

"Your eyes are a little red. I have some visine in my purse.

I dug through Anna's purse and found the visine and placed a drop in each eye. I didn't need to worry Nick anymore. When I got home and to Nick, I would feel better anyway. I held my eyes closed for a few minutes and then checked them again. They started to look better. By the time we got to my house, the red would be gone.

"Rayna, are you gonna talk to your doctor about your attacks tomorrow? Please don't keep that from him just because the band's leaving for the tour." Anna glanced over at me with concerned eyes.

"Yes, I'm gonna tell him. I know he'll tell me it's the adrenaline when I am nervous or upset. He told me before this might happen. Actually, it surprised me that I haven't had any episodes yet. He'll probably give me something for it."

Anna scrutinized me like I might be deceiving her.

"I promise, I'm going to tell him." I felt like a little kid being reprimanded for an infraction.

We pulled into my place around ten in the evening. Lights shone through the windows in the garage, so I knew Nick was home. Everyone had left except for Travis. He stayed to wait for Anna. When we walked in, the two guys were at the counter in the kitchen having a beer talking about the new song on the radio.

"Hey you two lovely ladies, you're back." Travis bellowed out.

"Yeah, we made it back safely." Anna glanced over at me as we carried in the laundry and set it on the table.

I walked over and wrapped my arms around Nick. He set his beer down and wrapped both of his arms around me.

"Did you miss me?" He asked.

"Very much." I leaned in and kissed his warm lips. Just being in his arms relaxed me and made my heart calm. I hoped he couldn't tell that I had been upset. He could always sense my moods so I deliberately tried to hide my grief.

"Do you two want a beer or some wine?" Nick offered.

"No, I'm okay, just tired. I think I'm gonna take a shower and go to bed." I tried to deliver my anguish as exhaustion and it seemed to be working.

"Yeah, I'm a little tired too Travis." Anna followed my lead.

"Thanks for going with me today. It was great spending time with you before we leave." I let go of Nick to give Anna a tender hug.

"Thanks for having me girlfriend. I enjoyed our time very much." Anna hugged me back and kissed my cheek.

"Are you coming to see us off tomorrow?" I asked Anna as I let go of her.

"Yes, I'll bring Travis over tomorrow evening. I'll tell you bye tomorrow." Anna smiled. "Now get some rest."

"Yes mam." I walked over and kissed Nick and turned to walk to the bathroom to grab a warm shower. I needed to wash all the misery from today out of my mind.

"I'll be up in a little bit. I love you." Nick said as he kissed me again.

"I love you."

I stayed in the shower longer than I had expected, but the warm water helped to relax me and wash away the day. Nick even came in to check on me. I told him I was fine and I was just enjoying a real shower since we would be taking showers in the RV. He laughed and then left me alone to dress.

Travis and Anna were gone by the time I came out of the bathroom. Nick was packing his clothes and I went to lie down in bed until he came up.

I must have fallen asleep as soon as my head hit the pillow. I woke up and got up for a glass of water. I saw Nick had packed all of his clothes and some of mine as well while I slept. He was such an amazing guy; always taking care of me.

My doctor's appointment the next day went well. He increased the milligrams on some of my medicines and told me the adrenaline was affecting my damaged heart. He wanted to keep a closer eye on me. So he wanted to see me more often. He released me to go on tour. He told me to make sure I got enough rest and not to overdo anything and above all, try and keep stress to a minimum. Nick smiled when the doctor gave me clearance to go on the tour. He even turned a little smug when the doctor encouraged him to keep an eye on me as well. I just hoped he didn't start becoming overprotective instead a support system.

We left for the tour in the RV around six that evening. We all said our goodbyes to Anna and we both cried. I told her I would call her every day and even skype with the band. And then she lets us leave. She stood in my driveway and waved at us until we drove beyond her view.

Travis drove for a few hours while Rick slept. We pulled over and took a small break at a rest stop and Rick took over. I climbed into bed while Rick drove and when I woke up in the early morning, I lay wrapped in Nick's strong arms while the RV sat in the parking lot of our first performance.

I lay still, knowing if I moved I would wake Nick. I wanted him to be well rested for his first show. I closed my eyes and enjoyed being in my husband's arms. My husband, I really liked the sound of that. I nuzzled into him and he let out a little sigh. I enjoyed hearing that sound come from Nick. I closed my eyes and relished in my bliss for as long as possible.

When Nick opened his eyes, he kissed my lips gently. It seemed he was trying to kiss me without waking me. I surprised him by meeting his kiss.

"Were you already awake?" Nick chuckled.

"Yes, I was laying here blissfully in your arms until you kissed me." I giggled and kissed him again.

I heard the door shut in the bathroom and knew one of the guys was awake. Nick and I lay wrapped in each other's arms for a few more minutes and then decided to get up and grab some coffee once we smelled the delicious freshness of it being brewed.

"Ready for tonight?" Dave asked as we came out of our little hole in the RV. He held the coffee canister while pouring himself a cup of coffee.

"Yes sir I am." Nick's smile spread from ear to ear. He didn't seem a bit nervous, just full of confidence.

I poured a cup of coffee and handed it to Nick. I took another cup out of the cupboard and poured myself a cup and leaned against the counter. Travis rolled over in the bed made from the couch and glanced up at all of us.

"Good morning sleepy head." I smiled down at Travis and set my coffee cup down and poured some for Travis. He got up, folded his blankets, and put the couch back together. I handed Travis his cup of coffee and then we all sat on the couch drinking our morning potion. Rick and Jeff climbed out of bed last, poured a cup of coffee, and made another pot.

"I am powered up for tonight. I can't wait to be on that stage." Jeff was all smiles and full of energy.

"Where are we anyway?" I scanned the room waiting for someone to answer me.

"Philadelphia, silly girl," Dave answered and then took another drink of coffee.

"Sorry, I didn't receive a schedule." I smiled and got up to refill my coffee cup. Dave stuck his tongue out at me.

"We go on at nine tonight, so we should set everything up right after the doors open around noon. That way we can rest before the show." Rick chimed in. "Rayna, we'll wait to put merchandise out until later this evening when we'll be there so that nothing gets snatched."

"Sounds good to me. I can make some food while you guys set things up."

"Well we have a few hours until they open so let's make some grub." Dave got up and went to the fridge to pull out food to cook.

We ate breakfast and cleaned up. The guys unloaded all of the equipment and then started setting things up at the venue. It was a small club. We were told that they sold out. So tonight would be a full house. My nerves were a little on edge for the band. I took a shower while they set up for the show. It gave me a little more privacy having the RV to myself while they worked.

The first show of the tour went off without a hitch. CDs and t-shirts sold like hot cakes and the band did a meet and greet for every fan that wanted a picture or autograph. While the band met fans, Rick started packing the equipment up and I sold merchandise. Then we were off to the next show.

A few weeks into the tour we had a few days off so we stopped at an RV park

"I had to call the agent at the record company to get more merchandise. We're about sold out," Rick said as he walked back to his lawn chair by the fire.

"Already?" Jeff asked.

"Yep, the fans are crazy for the stuff. They let me know that our song is still climbing the charts. It's number 16 this week."

"Wow! I hope it goes to number one," Dave said as he put another log on the fire."

"That's great guys," I smiled. "I'll be back in a few. I'm gonna go throw a load of laundry in and grab a shower in the shower house."

"I'll walk you over." Nick got up with me.

Nick helped me carry the laundry over and put it in the washer. He kissed me and left me at the shower house. I took a long overdue hot shower. Nick was waiting for me when I walked out of the shower house.

"I need to put the laundry in the dryer."

"Done," he said. He smiled and took my hand as we walked back to the campsite.

"I'll go get them shortly."

"I got it," Nick smiled.

"In that case, I think I'm gonna retire for the evening if you don't mind."

"Not at all Princess. We've been going nonstop for a few weeks. You need your beauty rest."

"Thank you. Night everyone. I'm calling it a night." I waved at the guys as I walked into the RV.

"I'll tuck you in," Nick said with a smile and followed me in.

I slept in more often and I felt tired most days. Late nights were starting to wear me down so I took advantage of our few days off.

The stress of my parents and the tour started to take a toll on me. I became more exhausted with dizzy spells. I hid these from Nick. I smiled a lot and encourage the band after every performance. They were having the time of their life and making their dreams come true. I refused to spoil that with my sickness. We had a few more stops and then we would be back home for a couple of weeks. I planned to call the doctor as soon as we got home. I was determined to help Nick with his dreams without any interference from me. I was strong; I could push through a couple more shows. I just needed to rest.

Seventeen

We enjoyed a day off between shows, so Nick made reservations for a birthday dinner. He found a quiet Italian restaurant for us to enjoy our favorite food; lasagna. It was fun to get out and be alone for the evening. Nick arranged for a car to pick us up and take us to the restaurant. He ordered champagne to celebrate my twenty-second birthday. After we ordered our food, Nick took out a gift box and handed it to me.

"Happy Birthday my love," He handed me a beautiful gold box and sat back and watched me open it.

Inside were two gold infinity necklaces. I covered my mouth with my hand because they were both so exquisite. I gazed up at Nick and he smiled.

"One for you and one for me; to wear close to our hearts."

"They're beautiful, Nick. I love them. Thank you." I smiled. I looked on the back of each necklace and read an inscription, "My heart forever." My eyes became glassy from the tears welling up. I loved this man with all of my heart and every day the love and bond between us grew deeper and deeper.

He stood up and walked over to my side of the table and leaned down to kiss me. He took one of the necklaces out and placed it around my neck and then he kissed me again.

"I love you so much. Every day you bring me joy just being you. Without you, my life would be void." Nick stared deep into my eyes and I felt our souls connecting as they often did.

"You are my life, Nick. You brought me back to life. My love grows for you more each and every day."

We ate our dinner and then shared a dessert. After dinner, Nick took me upstairs to a hotel room that he booked for the night.

"I thought you would enjoy an evening without the guys." Nick smiled down at me as he let go of my hand and unlocked the door.

In the beautiful honeymoon suite Nick reserved, a bottle of champagne and pink and red rose petals waited on the bed for us. In the bathroom, a tub of bubbles with warm water had been drawn for us. I felt blessed that I married a man that took such wonderful care of me.

"I love you." I smiled and wrapped my arms around him. He leaned down and kissed me with his warm soft lips. I took advantage of the time with my thoughtful and incredibly sexy husband.

· ♥ · ♥ · ♥ · ♥ · ♥ ·

When we got back to the guys the next day, they presented me with a birthday cake and they sang to me. I had a superb bunch of guys in my life.

For the rest of the month we played show after show. The band did radio and television interviews throughout the day and performed at night. We traveled from one city to the next. I slept every night even though we rode cooped up in an RV. I even grabbed naps while the band set up and did sound check. I felt like I couldn't get enough rest.

A week into October, the band was ready to perform their last show in Columbus. Anna wasn't able to make the show because of school. I was a little disappointed, but I'd see her tomorrow. I tried to hide my fatigue from Nick, but he started to question me. It was hard to keep this from him since we were so connected. My acting skills really kicked in. I slept more than anyone else, and I put it off to not resting well. Nick let it go, but he kept a sharp eye on me.

The band finished their set with one of the most incredible performances of the tour. The venue was packed. I could barely see the end of the crowd when I gazed across. I was working the merchandise stand.

"Hey Rayna. How we doing over here?" Rick asked as he stepped in and started to help.

"Busy." I continued working. I was exhausted but needed to keep going just a little while longer.

"Nick wants you to help with the meet and greet tonight. You look tired and most of the people are already waiting in line." He smiled and started helping customers. I looked at him odd because I'd never helped with this before. I assumed this was Nick's way of keeping his eye on me. Actually, it was a much easier job. You stood by the band and took pictures for the fans. They didn't want me to do it before because they always worried about crowd control or a rowdy fan, so I thought that it was odd that they would have me do it tonight, but I agreed.

I walked over to the table where the band would be coming out and prepared the area for the meet and greet. The band came out after they cooled off in the RV and got a drink. I smiled at Nick. He gave me a huge hug and kissed me.

"Great show baby." I grinned from ear to ear. I was very proud of my man and the guys.

"Thanks, princess." Nick kissed me again and then gave my nose a peck. The guys all sat down at the table to sign autographs and take pictures with the fans. The line of fans to meet the band seemed like it would never end. I took pictures with people's phones and their cameras. Most people wanted pictures with Nick; especially the girls. Dave was the next favorite for pictures. And some people wanted a picture with the whole band.

Fatigue started to set in. I felt a little dizzy but I had the table to lean on. We had another twenty minutes with the meet and greet and then I could lie down.

As I stood there accepting phones and cameras from the fans, another dizzy spell started to come on. I reached out for the table for support..

....

I opened my eyes to Nick looking down at me. I was lying on the table and Nick held me in his arms and Dave held my hand.

"Rayna, you blacked out baby," Nick said. "We are taking you to the hospital."

"What? I don't want to go to the hospital. The meet and greet and the band."

"No, you need to be checked out by the doctor." Nick caressed my forehead. I glanced up at him, worry and determination in his eyes. I glanced around at Dave, Rick, Travis, and Jeff for assurance that I was going to be fine, but I found none. They all had a grave look of concern on their faces. Anxiety and fear seeped from Nick.

"The guys are going to load the RV up and you and I are going to the hospital. We called an ambulance for you. You are white as a ghost and you were out for a few minutes." Nick whispered.

I didn't say anything. I just gazed up into Nick's worried eyes.

"Rayna, how often have you been getting dizzy?" Nick asked.

I didn't answer at first.

"Rayna," Nick spoke in a firm voice. One that I hadn't heard often.

"A couple of times this week; but I figured I'd be fine until we got home tomorrow."

"Rayna, you're the most important thing to me, not this performance. I need to take care of you first and the band second. If I lose you, I lose everything. I love you." Nick's eyes were becoming watery. And a single tear slid down his cheek.

"I love you. I'm sorry."

Nick pulled me into him and held me tight. I started to cry. I knew that he loved me and I hated putting him through this. I trembled with fear. I just visited the doctor and he told me that everything appeared okay, and now this. What would happen? Was my heart finished?

The ambulance arrived. They took my vitals and then worked a little faster. Nick walked with the stretcher as they wheeled me across the grass and into the ambulance; he never let go of my hand.

We arrived at the hospital. Nick filled them in about my heart condition. They took my condition very seriously. They had me hooked up to every machine and they drew blood until I thought I wouldn't have anymore. The doctor came in and told me they were going to transport me from Columbus back to Pittsburgh. The hospital had spoken to my doctor and he wanted me brought to Pittsburgh. They would transport me in an hour or so by ambulance. Nick called my parents to inform them I was being moved and to meet us.

It was a long drive, but the medicine they had me on helped me sleep most of the ride. Nick stayed by my side the entire ride, holding my hand. The hospital staff took me immediately to the Step Down unit when I arrived where they hooked me up to a different heart monitor. My doctor wanted me observed for 24 hours. My parents were waiting in my room when we arrived.

My blood work and EKG weren't normal and my doctor wanted to run more tests in the morning. My parents stayed until I was settled in my room. The nurses assured them I would be fine for the night. I was hooked up to every monitor possible, so the nurses would be alerted if anything went wrong. Nick and my parents exchanged pleasantries, but nothing more.

Nick wanted to stay, and I would love to have him with me, but he needed his rest. He looked tired and worried. I needed him here tomorrow for me. So I convinced him to go home after three in the morning. The request didn't make him happy, but he did it for me. I didn't sleep well in the hospital with the nurses waking me up every few hours and my heart monitor going off several times during the night.

In the morning, the nurses had me whisked off for more tests before my parents or Nick arrived. More blood tests were required and an MRI of my heart. I missed breakfast because of the test. By lunch, my stomach growled loudly. Before lunch they took me back to my room where Nick and my parents waited for me. Nick still looked exhausted.

"How are you?" My mother ran over to the wheelchair before the nurses had a chance to move me back into bed to give me a hug. My dad followed her. Nick stood against the wall assessing me.

"Better, I had some chest pain last night and they gave me nitroglycerin and it helped; but other than that, tired and hungry." I forced a weak smile. I hoped my worry didn't show on my face. I always prayed this day never came. The chest pain and knowing my heart might be failing chilled me to the bone, but I wanted to be strong.

"Your lunch will be here shortly mam. The doctor will be here in the afternoon to go over your test," the nurse said as she helped me back into bed.

Nick walked over to the side of my bed but said nothing. He took my hand and gazed down at me with despair. I must look incredibly awful because he never looked at me with such pity.

"Rayna, we want to be here when the doctor arrives, so your Mom and I are going to go grab some lunch. We'll be back in a little while. We wanted to see you when you got back so we waited. Would you like to join us Nick?" My Dad offered with a smile.

"No thank you, I grabbed something before I got here. I'll stay here with Rayna." Nick smiled at me.

My mom and dad kissed my forehead before they left to grab some lunch. Nick leaned down and kissed me as soon as my parents walked out of the room. I wondered why they invited Nick for lunch. Did they feel bad or were they just being cordial?

"You look tired." I touched Nick's cheek and examined his face.

"I didn't get much sleep last night. I couldn't stop worrying about you. You scared the shit out of me last night Rayna. I'm still scared." Nick brushed my hair behind my ear and touched my cheek.

I didn't want to admit to him my fear. My eyes gave me away, they welled up with tears. I tried to look down before he saw my eyes, but it was no use. Nick pulled my chin up so I had to look into his beautiful worried brown eyes. A tear slid down my cheek.

Nick wiped away the tear. He sat down on the side of the bed and took me in his arms. Nick's embrace and love caused the tears to flood down my cheeks.

"I love you, Rayna."

I held him tighter, allowing the fear to escape through my eyes. Nick held me until I finished crying. He said nothing about my sudden outburst. Nick being able to sense what my soul felt without saying a word was all I needed. He was all I ever needed.

My lunch came and I ate what they brought me even though it wasn't that appetizing. I offered some to Nick but he declined. He knew the food probably tasted as bad as it looked. But being hungry helped it go down a little easier. Nick and I didn't talk much, we didn't need to.

My parents made it back just in time for the doctor. Doctor Adkins had been my heart doctor since I'd been diagnosed with my condition.

"How is everyone today?" Dr. Adkins always appeared to be in a good mood, so you couldn't tell if he came here bringing bad news or good.

"Fine, Dr. Adkins. Just a little worried," my dad replied as he shook Dr. Adkins' hand.

I reached up to take Nick's hand. I needed his support for whatever Dr. Adkins was about to tell us. My mind reeled and my body flooded full of adrenaline. I was a nervous wreck but tried my best to hide it with a weak smile.

"Rayna, there is no other way to say this." Dr. Adkins glanced around the room at everyone and then back at me. Your blood test shows your peptides are way too high and the other test shows that your condition has worsened. The left ventricle of your heart has thickened and it can't pump your blood efficiently. That's why you passed out. The medications can't do anymore. We need to put you on the list."

The blood rushed from my head. I lay back on the pillow, afraid I would pass out. I feared this day. I held Nick's hand tighter, hoping he wouldn't let go. My mom covered her mouth with her hand and my dad gazed at the floor. Nobody said anything for a minute.

"What list?" Nick questioned the doctor.

"The heart transplant list." Dr. Adkins glanced at Nick and then back to me without any emotion. "I'm sorry Rayna, but your heart isn't doing its job anymore.

My parents and I already discussed this with Dr. Adkins when he diagnosed me. He told us that one day this might happen, but we all hoped it never would. Nick was the only one who was clueless.

"How long will she be on the list?" Nick questioned Dr. Adkins as he glanced over at me.

"We don't know. It could take months or years. We need to wait for the right donor. Everything must match."

"What do we do in the mean time?"

"I have to stay here Nick." A tear snuck out of the corner of my eye. My mom walked to the side of my bed and touched my arm.

"Not anymore Rayna. We now have an artificial heart pump that will allow you to go home while we wait for a donor. It's called a left ventricular assist device or an LVAD.

"How long will that last? How does it work? " I still had a some hope but still a huge amount of anxiety. I didn't want to live in the hospital waiting for a heart or waiting to die.

"It can last years, Rayna. You can go on living your life while you wait for a heart. You'll need open heart surgery. I would place the LVAD in your chest outside of your heart. It's a device that assists your heart in pumping blood. After the surgery, you can't see or feel it."

"When can we do it?" I tried looking hopeful at Dr. Adkins.

"I would like to send someone up to discuss everything with you about the device and the surgery before you make any decision. Someone can talk with you today and then if you decide to do the surgery, we can do it tomorrow."

"Send them up, please. There is no sense in waiting around." I felt defeated. My heart couldn't work anymore and I needed a new one. You can't buy a heart; somebody had to die for me to live. Thinking about this didn't make me feel any better. But at least they made something to help my heart work in the meantime. Nick still held my hand and I wasn't about to let go.

"I'll go and make sure everything is set up. Rayna, you're going to be okay." Dr. Adkins gave me a reassuring smile and patted my leg before he left.

"Rayna, we need to really think about this before we make a decision, honey." My mom rubbed my arm as she tried to convince me to hold off and think about all this.

"What is there to think about? I need a new heart. There isn't one right now and I refuse to live on my back while I wait for one. I want to live my life mom; not lay here waiting around for a heart or maybe waiting around to die." My voice got louder showing the irritation she caused me. "I'll listen to everything they're going to tell me, but my mind is made up. If this thing can help me live as close to a normal life while I wait for a heart, then that's what I am going to do."

"Rayna.....let's listen to what they have to tell us and then we'ill discuss this." My dad's voice was calm and gentle.

Nick stayed quiet; his face unreadable and pale. "Excuse me; I need to go to the restroom. I'll be right back Rayna." Nick kissed my forehead and left the room.

"If you decide to do this, you're going to need to slow down and rest more. You've been trying to do too much with work........ and Nick." My mom turned away when she said Nick's name. She knew my reaction wouldn't be pleasant if she looked at my face.

"Nick has nothing to do with my heart health. If anything, he's helped it. I'm not discussing this with you two right now. I'm twenty-two years old and I hope you'll both support my decisions." I used more authority in my voice than I ever had with my parents. When it came to Nick, I was very protective. They still didn't know that we had married.

When Nick came back, I could tell he didn't feel well. I could see it on his face and feel it in his soul. He had a bottle of Coke and looked frazzled. The heart staff came in and explained the procedure to us. They told us how long the surgery took, how long I would be in the hospital, and the things I would need to do once I went home. It sounded like I would be able to live my life pretty normally after I got out of the hospital. Even though I was nervous, knowing Nick would be by my side helped me have courage.

Nick's mom and Dave stopped in to visit me. Anna came by a little while later to check up on me. I told them what the doctor planned to do tomorrow. They all seemed optimistic about my situation. Anna cried and she held me for a few minutes. She told me she loved me and that she would be here before my surgery tomorrow. I made my decision and sent everyone home by the end of visiting hours. Nick stayed a while longer. I wanted to spend some time alone with him.

"Thanks for staying with me." I reached up and touched Nick's stubbly cheek. He hadn't shaved since the day before yesterday. I kind of liked this new style. It made him even sexier; like that could even be possible. He'd been quiet most of the day and avoided my eyes. He still sent shivers down my spine, sitting on the bed holding my hand.

Nick gazed up into my eyes. "Where else would I be? Rayna, you're everything to me. I have nothing without you." Nick placed his hand behind my head and brought his lips to mine; his kiss long and gentle. He pulled my face to his chest and wrapped his other arm around me. "I love you," he said in a whisper.

"I love you, Nick. I'm going to be fine. I have faith." I pulled away so I could look into his eyes. I needed to see what he was feeling. He looked lost and terrified. "I need you to make sure you get some rest tonight. I want you here and healthy when I wake up tomorrow. I want your face to be the first thing I see. I need you to promise me."

"I'll try to get some rest."

"Nick.....promise me. I need you to be healthy and strong for me. I'm going to need you. And I want you to promise me we'll set a date for the wedding announcement when this is over."

"Okay. I promise."

"Promise what?" I grinned.

"I promise I'll get some sleep and be the first face you see when you wake up. And we'll set a date for the wedding announcement party when this is over." Nick's voice was convincing. He finally gave me his beautiful smile. He touched my cheek and kissed me again.

Nick stayed until around ten. I was getting sleeping and I saw the circles getting darker under his eyes. I convinced him to go home so he could be here early in the morning. I wanted to see him before they took me to surgery. Nick left reluctantly; promising me he'd rest tonight. I didn't show any more distraught emotions while Nick was there. I wanted him to sleep well tonight and not be worried about my being scared and nervous; he worried enough.

I tried to sleep. I tossed and turned most of the night with worry. This was one of the most terrifying things I have ever been through. My chest would be cut open tomorrow in the hopes of saving my life. I still had chest pains and the nurses gave me more nitro. This helped me sleep some. When I fell asleep, I dreamed of Nick. We walked on a beautiful beach with clear blue water and white sand. The ocean breezes blew our hair around our faces. And the warm water washed our feet. We walked down the beach holding hands. We both had huge smiles on our faces. I could never make out what either of us said, but I knew we were talking because our lips moved and we laughed and embraced.

I opened my eyes to see Nick looking down at me. I smiled and he touched my cheek. He brushed the hair from my forehead and leaned down and kissed me with a light touch. The dark circles still shone under his eyes, but not as severe. He had shaved and he smelled wonderful; like body wash mingled with his scent.

"Good morning, beautiful." Nick's voice sounded a little more confident today; rest was what he needed after all that had happened the last two days.

"Did you eat?"

"Rayna, yes I ate. Quit worrying about me and keep your mind strong." Nick sat down next to me and took my hand. "I need you to keep your mind positive. Okay?"

"Okay. But you are my life and I don't want you getting worn out worrying about me. I'm gonna be fine, but I'll need you strong after this surgery."

"I slept great and I'm ready to help you with anything you need. I'll be here when you wake up. I love you and need you to be alright. Okay." Nick kissed me again.

My parents walked into the room in front of the nurses that came to prep me for surgery.

My mom came over and kissed my cheek and squeezed my arm. "I love you Rayna. Your dad and I will be here when you wake up."

My father stepped around my mom and kissed me on the forehead. Rayna, everything is going to be okay baby." He smiled and touched my cheek.

"I know dad." I smiled. "I love you both. Be back in a few." I smiled a weak smile and looked at them both. Their faces filled with worry and concern. They both tried to keep a brave smile for me, but I could see they hid their distress under their smiles.

The nurses began hooking things up and moving in and out of the room when Anna showed up. She came straight over and hugged me and kissed my cheek. "Good luck, I love you girl." She gave me an encouraging grin and moved over beside Nick.

An orderly came in to move me down to surgery. My parents walked on one side and Nick and Anna on the other. Nick never let go of my hand until we reached the door where I would have my heart surgery. The medicine started to kick in and I started getting groggy. The orderly paused so everyone could tell me they would see me soon. My parents kissed me on the forehead and told me they loved me again.

Nick leaned down and kissed my lips. He whispered in my ear, "I love you Rayna Perry. I'll be waiting for you." He stared deep into my soul as I closed my eyes.

"I love you Nick Perry." I whispered as I fought to keep my eyes open. He kissed me and touched my cheek again. The orderly pushed me through the doors as Nick let go of my hand.

The room was cold. I remember being moved from my bed to a hard table; the table even colder. A nurse stood over me and asked if I needed a blanket. I mouthed yes. She wrapped me in another blanket and told me to count backward from twenty as she placed a mask over my mouth and nose. I started at twenty, nineteen. My eyes began getting heavier, eighteen ....seventeen.....sixteen..

Eighteen

I opened my eyes to a groggy world. I made it through; I'm still here. A slight grin crept onto my face. I scanned the room and spotted Nick to my right. I turned my head slightly and realized that he held my hand.

"Hello beautiful." Nick leaned in and kissed my forehead.

I smiled up at Nick and gazed deep into his worried eyes. I survived I thought. I tried to speak, but my throat was dry and my voice weak.

"You did it baby, I love you. Rest, you need to heal." Nick leaned down and kissed my lips.

Knowing I survived through the surgery, the meds, and having Nick there, helped me feel safe and I closed my eyes and drifted back off to a restful sleep. The room was dark and quiet when I woke again. I wasn't as groggy, but still sleepy. Nick and my parents must have gone home to rest, I was sure it was a long day for them. A nurse came in to check my vitals and meds.

"Did they go home?" I whispered.

"No honey. They are all still here."

"What time is it?"

"It's after midnight. Now close your eyes and rest, you need it. The doctor will be here to check on you in the morning and I'm sure your visitors will be anxious to see you rested up."

I listened to her advice and closed my eyes. The medicine still kept me sleepy or maybe it was the trauma my body just went through. All of the contraptions they had hooked up to me, made it hard to get comfortable, but the nurse gave me another dose of medication in my IV that helped me to relax and made it easy to drift off to sleep. I drifted in and out of sleep the rest of the night and most of the next day. I remember my parents being in the room and seeing Nick off and on.

On what I guessed to be the third day, I woke up and felt a little more alert. Dr. Adkins came into the ICU and told me some of the contraptions would be taken off today and I would be moved to a regular hospital room for the rest of my recovery. That sounded amazing because my visitors could stay in my room most of the day; not just a few minutes at a time.

Nick came in to visit me and let me know my parents would be in to see me in my new room. They ran home to get showered. He said he planned to stay until tonight. He wanted to spend time with me without all the junk hooked up to me before he could relax enough to go home and sleep. He always made me feel wanted and loved in so many ways.

Our intense connection was a wonderful thing most of the time, but I understood what he meant when he said he wouldn't be able to relax at home until I was completely out of the woods. He said that while I was in surgery, he felt disconnected in some way. He said he couldn't really explain it with words, but he was empty and lost while they had me under the heavy medication. He said he already started to feel whole again with me being more alert.

The hospital moved me out of the ICU and took me to a private room because my father requested it. My parents knew I would be more comfortable without someone else in my room. They also knew I would have plenty of visitors and didn't want to disturb another patient. I was actually going to get some food by mouth today too. Even though I would eat a liquid diet today, it would be wonderful to be well enough to drink some water and broth. Nick stayed with me until the nurses came in to give me a sponge bath. He excused himself and said he would use this time to grab something to eat himself. He didn't want to eat real food in front of me since I couldn't eat anything solid yet.

I had a bandage over my sternum and on my left side. The procedure had come a long way and you didn't need your entire chest cut open. I did have a wire hanging out that needed to be plugged into a little box.

I lay in the hospital for the next week and a half. I slowly regained my strength back. I had rehab every day to help me recuperate. Anna visited and filled me in with the latest gossip and my mom and dad kept me busy with everyday chatter. Nick and his family filled in the gaps. Nick wrote lyrics while I did rehab. We ate lunch and dinner together most nights. Sometimes he would meet me for breakfast. He'd bring me some of my favorite food if the doctor allowed him. I told him he didn't need to spend every waking hour with me although I loved him being there.

"Rayna, you're my life; there is no other place I want to be but right here with you. The record company set the tour dates back a couple of weeks until you are out of the hospital. It took some doing, but they reset all of the dates. The entire band refused to leave again for the road until you're home." Nick pulled my hand up to his lips and kissed the back of my hand.

"You didn't need to do that." I smiled at him because I was glad he did.

"I wouldn't be able to perform well without knowing you were home and healthy. Record sales are soaring; we're okay just adding a couple of weeks to our break. I'd like to try and have our announcement party planned before I leave on tour again though. Are you up to helping me plan this?" Nick pulled his eyebrows up.

"Of course, yes. Where should we have it?"

"We could have it at one of the hotels, or at the house. What do you think?"

"I wouldn't mind having it at the house, but I'd like to hire a company to come in and set up a beautiful area and have it catered."

"That sounds great to me. I'll find some numbers and we can make some calls tomorrow. Now, let's make a date."

Nick and I decided to host the party the weekend after he came back from the second part of the tour. I couldn't go with him this time because I needed to be within two hours of the hospital in case a donor became available. But it would give me and Anna time to make sure everything was ready for our reception.

It was a relief when the doctor finally let me come home for the night. Nick stayed with me in the hospital, but being in his arms, in our bed, meant so much more. Lying in Nick's arms gave me a restful night of sleep. I realized he would be leaving soon, so I relished in every minute I had with him. Nick took care of my every need when I got home. He cooked, cleaned, and went shopping for things I might need while the band toured. He didn't want to leave me, but he had to finish the tour. It would be detrimental to their success if the band postponed any more dates

Their second single received a lot of radio time and more albums were being sold daily. The song was like an overnight success. The entire band floated on a career high and I was elated for them. I was disappointed I wouldn't be able to finish the tour with them, but grateful their dreams were coming true. The band would be gone for three weeks this time.

My mom wanted me to stay at her house when Nick left for the tour but I insisted on staying at mine and Nick's. Anna moved in with me for three weeks. She went to school most days and I slept a lot. We ate dinner together and enjoyed the live shows that Rick recorded. I skyped with Nick every day. My parents and Anna's mom visited every couple of days. Nick's mom came to visit a few times a week and sometimes she would stay and enjoy the band's performances with us. She was proud of her sons.

Anna and I met with an event planning company that would take care of everything from the tent, lighting, and flooring, down to the linens, food, and cake. I just sat and picked everything out. We invited family and close friends only but that list included over fifty people. Nick trusted me with all the details and he got excited when I told him what we planned.

I didn't sleep well at night, so I took naps during the day. I tossed and turned most nights not having Nick by my side. I had weird dreams as well. I'd wake up scared he was gone; I couldn't find him. I'd search every night for him in the woods, in the mall, in a field, but could never seem to find him. One night I tossed and turned half the night and then fell into a deep sleep. When I dreamed that night, I dreamed I was wrapped in Nick's arms. I used my arm to pull his hand up to the side of my face. I kissed his hand and pulled him in tighter.

I didn't open my eyes when I woke up. I wanted to retreat back to my dream. And then I realized I was snuggling with an arm and a hand up to my cheek. I abruptly rolled over and stared into Nick's beautiful sleeping face. He smiled and a small sigh came from his chest. I kissed his lips and he kissed me back. The kiss lasted longer than most. Then I pulled away and he opened his eyes and smiled.

"What are you doing here?" I whispered with a smile on my face.

"You have me for a few days. The band doesn't play until Wednesday, so Travis and I caught a plane late last night because we wanted to see you two. I don't need to leave until Wednesday morning." He kissed my nose.

I just stared at him, in shock. So happy he was with me, I couldn't speak.

"Do you want me to leave? I can go now." Nick moved to get up and I pulled him back down and he laughed.

"You better not even try to leave, mister. You said you were mine for a couple of days. Now move over here and kiss me again." I pulled Nick to me and he kissed me like the first time.

I spent every minute of the next two days entirely with Nick. I refused to let him out of my sight. The past week and a half were the longest I'd been away from him and I didn't like it. I needed this short visit to help me cope. We cooked together and watched a few movies and we made love. It was a little difficult with the cord and battery pack on my LVAD, but he made it still just as special.

"I haven't been able to sleep very well without you here. I have nightmares most nights." I told Nick as I lay on his chest before we fell asleep.

"Me neither. I've been dreaming that you're lost and I can't find you. I wake up sometimes in a sweat. I slept sound once I curled up beside you last night." Nick kissed the top of my head.

"So this visit is therapeutic." I turned my head and gazed into those deep brown beautiful eyes I loved so much."

"Most definitely. I love you princess."

SONGS FROM THE HEART

"I love you forever." I lay my head back down on Nick's chest and yawned. I listened to his heart and before long; it matched the beat of my own, even though my beat was artificial. Nick's heart mimicked my heart.

Nineteen

It was hard letting Nick go at the airport. I realized it would only be a week and a half, but it felt like a lifetime being away from him. My heart was weak, but nothing compared to Nick leaving and taking part of my heart with him.

Anna went to school during the day and I shopped for our party outfits. I bought him a simple suit and I bought myself a white cocktail dress with embellishments on it. I also bought Anna a dress, because she would've been my maid of honor. Anna's dress, a short cocktail dress as well, was pale pink with beads sewn on intricately. In the evenings, Anna and I listened to the radio while we cooked dinner. We heard both songs on the radio often. Hearing the band on the radio got us excited and made us miss them at the same time.

It appeared the band was better than a one hit wonder. The band's first album was in high demand and every day the sales went up. The second half of the tour was planned there was talk of another album. We were going to be busy for the rest of the year and well into next year. They would start the final part of the tour right after New Year's.

The band got back from the tour the beginning of November. We had a few days until the announcement party on Saturday at six in the evening. I showed Nick the new suit I bought him and he wanted to see my dress, but I refused at first. I sort of saw the dress as my wedding dress and tried to explain to him how it was bad luck. But he persuaded me to show him. He thought it was beautiful. He always made me happy.

Thinking about Saturday made me nervous and to my surprise, so was Nick. He handled things like this pretty well, but this time he was a little tense.

"What are you worried about?" I asked as I chopped vegetables for dinner.

"I'm worried for you. I hope your parents accept the fact we're already married. I want the party to be a success for you. This is our wedding party. I don't want anything to ruin it." Nick walked around the island and wrapped his arms around me while I chopped the vegetables. He kissed my cheek.

"I think everything will go fine. How are we going to announce this? As soon as everyone gets there or after they eat?"

"I think we should announce it before they eat. Let everyone arrive at the party and drink some champagne and then we can make the announcement; you and me together." Nick let go of me and stole a piece of broccoli. He chewed while he stared at me waiting for an answer.

I stopped chopping and gazed up at Nick's smiling eyes. "Okay, before dinner. Now help me with dinner." I poked Nick in the gut and he laughed.

"How have you been feeling?" He questioned me.

"Besides missing you, I've been great. No pain, dizziness, or fatigue. It's kind of amazing, except for this thing." I pointed at the battery pack hanging on my side. I didn't notice it too often, but sometimes it got in the way. Like this weekend when I wouldn't be able to find a place for it.

"Are your Mom and Dad coming for sure; did they RSVP?" Nick asked after he swallowed his bite of food.

"Yes they did. She wondered why we planned another party. I told her we liked to celebrate with friends and family. She didn't ask anymore."

"I think we should buy a house when we finish this next part of the tour. What do you think?" Nick stopped eating and watched for my reaction.

"Really?" That sounded wonderful. I'm sure my face showed my shock. A couldn't wait to buy a house with Nick.

"This first album is doing better than we thought. I think the band received their big break. We'll be opening for bigger acts and the crowds are getting larger I think we can afford it by then."

"We can afford it now." I laughed. "Where?"

"I'd like to stay close. Is that okay with you?"

"Yes, of course. I want to be close to my parents and Anna. Can we start looking now?" My excitement grew. I would happily move tomorrow. I loved Nick's place, it was him. But I would appreciate nicer amenities; and a bigger yard.

"Yeah, if you want. Let's clean up these dishes and check on the internet." Nick picked up both of our plates and took them to the sink and started the dishes.

We finished the dishes and put everything away. It was wonderful having Nick home, my soul wasn't lonely anymore. We searched for hours on the internet and were impressed with a few of the houses. We also checked a few houses for Nick's mom. We wrote some numbers down so we could call in the morning.

When we called the realtors the next morning, she had a few openings, so we went to tour houses. Dave met us so we could go see the smaller ones for their mom first. We found one we all agreed on. It had two bedrooms and two bathrooms.

We ate lunch with Dave and discussed it some more. We were ninety percent sure we wanted to put a deposit on the house. Nick's dream of buying his mother a house was coming true. We hoped to close on it before Thanksgiving.

· ♥ · ♥ · ♥ · ♥ · ♥ ·

The big day arrived for our wedding reception and I was a nervous wreck. The company brought the tents and began setting everything up. The food would arrive around four with two waiters and a bartender.

The tents were canopies with twinkling lights on the ceiling. The entire place would be lit up like stars in the sky when night fell. The company did a wonderful job of creating the atmosphere. The tables were all set with white linen table clothes and white chairs. Everything was classy.

Anna and I escaped around noon to have our nails, hair, and makeup done. We wanted to be gorgeous; especially for the pictures. I hired a photographer so we could have amazing memories of the reception. They always said a picture is worth a thousand words.

Nick had showered by the time I got home. Still dressed in regular clothes, he was cleaning the bathroom so everything would be tidy. I went up to dress. I put on the pearl necklace my grandmother had given me and the earrings that matched. The stylist had pulled my hair up and placed small pearls in my hair; so the jewelry added to the delicate aspect I went for. I pulled my dress out of the closet and slipped into it.

"You're beautiful Mrs. Perry." Nick walked up the steps and stopped to admired me.

I smiled from ear to ear. "Thank you." I glanced away with a little bit of embarrassment. I don't know why; I think maybe because of the expression on Nick's face.

Nick walked over and pulled my chin up with his index finger and gazed into my eyes. "Everyone will know today that I am the luckiest man alive. I wanted to shout it to the world; it's been hard to keep it a secret. I want everyone to know you are my wife." Nick leaned his head down and kissed me softly, being sure not to mess up my hair or makeup.

"I guess we're both the luckiest people in the world since we found our true soul mate. Not many people are given that opportunity. I love you and I want everyone to know you are my husband. Now go get dressed Mr. Perry, your bride awaits you." I laughed and swatted his butt.

"You better watch it. I'm a married man." Nick laughed and kissed me again and walked to the closet to grab his suit.

By five thirty Anna and all the guys had arrived. We headed to the tent so we would be there to welcome guests. We could hear the DJ playing music. Even though there was a chill in the air since it was early November, the tent was pleasantly warm. We walked around and gazed in awe at how beautiful everything was. I was impressed. The waiters were getting trays of champagne ready for guest when they arrived.

The first to arrive was Dave and Nick's mother. She wore a simple black dress and heels. Her hair was pulled up. She wore a simple strand of pearls around her neck. She was beautiful. I understood where Nick and Dave got their attractiveness. Nick, Dave, and I greeted her after she was served champagne. She embraced both of her boys and congratulated them on their success. She took my hands and scanned me.

"Rayna, you are exquisite; like an angel. I'm so glad Nick found you." She smiled at me and squeezed both of my hands.

"Thank you. You look beautiful as well." I grinned from ear to ear feeling only love coming from my new mother-in-law.

She pulled me in tight for a warm embrace. It was a wonderful experience being accepted by Nick's mom. I knew we would grow closer and I wanted to be part of helping her get out of her bad relationship.

"Where is your husband John?" I asked when she released me.

"The same place he always is; at the bar drinking. My boys aren't important to him and never have been. I just wish I could get away from him." Olivia said with loathing in her voice.

"That may be happening sooner than you think," Nick said. He kissed his mother's cheek and went to greet Samantha and her fiancé as they walked in.

"Why?" She asked shocked.

"We'll talk later. Go find our seats." I kissed her on the cheek as well and turned to greet guests.

Our friends and family rolled in quickly. Thankfully Anna, Travis, Jeff, and Rick started helping us greet the newcomers as they were offered champagne. Hugs and kisses were given with the word "congratulations" echoing off the walls.

Travis and Anna made a picture presentation that showed pictures of the band before they signed with the record company, the photo shoot for the album, and pictures of the band performing on tour. Anna and I also made a presentation of my and Nick's wedding video and photo to show after the announcement. People gathered around watching the presentation, chatting in small groups, and sitting at tables enjoying conversations.

My parents arrived a little after six. They congratulated each of the guys. My mom gave Rick and Nick a hug. I knew the hug she gave Nick was superficial for all the guest. My father shook their hands.

"How are you feeling Rayna," my mom asked as she hugged me. My dad followed suit.

"I've never been better; besides carrying this thing around." I pointed to the battery pack I had slung over my shoulder like a purse. "No dizziness, fatigue, or breathlessness. It feels wonderful to have all this energy all of a sudden." I smiled and led them to the table where Nick's mom sat talking with Samantha. I introduced my mother to Nick's mother and they appeared to hit it off. My parents sat down at the table as the last guest arrived.

"It is about time Mrs. Perry," Nick whispered in my ear from behind as he wrapped his arms around me.

"Are you ready?" I whispered with a forced grin. Butterflies fluttered in my stomach; not sure if they danced around because of the excitement of telling everyone or being nervous about my parents' reaction.

Nick and I stood in the middle of the dance floor and motioned for the band to join us. Everybody had enough time to congratulate everyone and see all the pictures on the PowerPoint presentation that was accompanied by the band's new album; now it was time to thank everyone for sharing in this celebration and then Nick and my announcement.

"I would like to thank everybody for coming to help us celebrate the success of the band. We just started on our journey and we have a long way to go. We'll be on a heavy tour schedule to promote this album after the holidays. It'll take us into the spring and after we are going back to the studio to record our second album. So, we're going to be really busy and we wanted to share our excitement with our friends and family that have supported us through the years and put up with all of our crazy music playing. From the entire band, we would like to thank you." Rick said this with such authority as he raised his glass of champagne. He really sounded like a band manager. It made me smile.

Everyone clapped. Dave took the mike and made a little speech; and then Travis, Jeff, and last Nick. They each thanked somebody special in their life; their mother and father or a friend. Nick thanked his brother Dave, his mother, Rick for getting the band gigs, and then me for believing in him.

Everyone in the room stood and clapped as the band took a bow. I even heard a few whistles and hoots and hollers. My heart started to pound as the crowd started to sit back down. Nick squeezed my hand. He still held the microphone.

"Before everyone starts with dinner, Rayna and I would like to share another announcement with you." Nick's voice was calm and articulate. The crowd oohed and aaahed, probably because they thought we would tell them the date of our wedding.

"We also invited everyone here tonight to celebrate something else with us."

Nobody said a word. They looked around at each other for an answer but sat in silence. Nick pulled a ring out of his pocket, took my hand, and placed a wedding band on it. He then handed me a ring to put on his left ring finger; a wedding band. This part was a surprise even to me. My eyes welled up with tears. I smiled at Nick and took a deep breath to keep the tears from running down my cheek and ruining my makeup. Everyone sat in silence. I think they were unsure what was taking place. They appeared a little lost and confused for a minute.

"I love you Rayna Perry; more than life itself."

"I love you more," I said in a soft voice barely audible.

"Let's call it a tie." He smiled and turned to finish his speech.

"Rayna and I married before the band left on tour when while we vacationed in the Caribbean. We would've liked to have had a formal wedding so all of you could share that with us, but it was such a beautiful place, we just decided to unite ourselves in paradise. We did bring some pictures for you though." Nick let the mic drop to his side. He pulled me into him and kissed me the way he kissed me at our wedding.

The crowd clapped and cheered, the sound was deafening, but it warmed my heart. Anna dropped the band's sign and revealed a wedding banner; "Congratulations Nick and Rayna Perry."

My mother's mouth fell open and my father closed his eyes.

Anna started the wedding DVD and everyone continued to cheer and clap. That gave Nick and me a few minutes to catch our breath after the announcement.

"That wasn't so bad was it?" Nick whispered in my ear as he still held me close in a protective embrace.

"That was because you made the speech. I haven't spoken to my parents yet. The pressure will be on then. Did you see their reaction?" I whispered back.

"I did. I looked both of them right in the eye when Anna exposed the sign. I think the shock has dissipated, but they are still not pleased. My mom is talking to them and she looks ecstatic."

After the video played, everyone started standing up to form a line to congratulate us. The DJ started playing soft music while we met with our friends and family. I felt relief that our secret was out. It was so hard trying to keep this under wraps until tonight. My parents mingled with other guests; trying to avoid me or just waiting for the crowd to clear, I wasn't sure.

The DJ asked for the bride and groom to dance their first dance. Not sure if it was our first dance as husband and wife, but it was our first dance as a couple for our friends and family. Nick took my hand and led me to the dance floor and swept me into a wonderful waltz. He learned a little bit from his mother. I kept my eyes on him and his were on mine. I loved looking into his eyes and speaking with his soul. It was so intimate. It was like Nick and I were the only people in the room. I got lost in his eyes and almost forgot where I was. And then the song ended and Nick kissed me.

The DJ announced he would like the bride and her father and the groom and his mother to dance. My father got up from his table and Nick went over and took his mother's hand. He guided her as gently as he guided me to the dance floor. Anyone could see Nick loved his mom very much. My father met me on the dance floor and put his right hand at my waist and took my other hand in his.

"Rayna..Rayna." He shook his head.

"What Dad?" I understood what he meant, but acted oblivious.

"I wanted to be able to give you away one day. I'm not ready for this. I mean, Nick seems like an okay guy, but you just met him six months ago." My father held a frown; his face shrouded in disappointment.

"Dad, I love him. He loves me. I didn't want to wait anymore. I don't know how much time I have. It seemed if I tried to plan a wedding with mom and you, I would've just been more stressed out. I know you guys didn't want me to marry Nick; you never kept it a secret." I kept my face stern but soft.

"You're my little girl; my one and only child. I love you and only want the best for you."

"I believe that Dad, but Nick is the best for me. Ever since I met him my world and soul have changed. I wouldn't survive not being with him. I need to be with him. He's my soul mate whether you and mom want to accept it or not."

"Please don't be upset. I'm not happy about how you went about this. I want to trust that you're right for your sake Rayna, but I'm here if you're wrong or right."

"I know I'm right. I'm sure about Nick. I have never been surer about anything in my life."

"I love you honey. Always have and always will." My Dad pulled me into a hug. He appeared to be holding back his tears.

"I love you too Dad; with all my heart." I hugged him back and didn't want to let him go. I wanted him to be happy for me. I hoped one day that would happen.

The song ended and my father gave me a tight hug and kissed my cheek. Nick's mom came over and gave me another hug.

"I'm so proud to have you for my daughter-in-law. I'm so happy my son found someone he loves so much and that loves him back as much. Welcome to the family darling." She smiled from ear to ear, kissed my cheek and gave my hands a tight squeeze. She walked back to the table smiling all the way.

Everyone ate dinner and chatted while the DJ played soft music. It turned into quite a party. I sat at the same table with both Nick and my parents along with Dave and a girl he'd been dating. Anna, Travis, and her mother joined us as well. My mom talked a little but listened mostly to the conversation at the table. Dave and Nick talked about the band and Nick and I talked about our wonderful tropical vacation where we married. We laughed and joked. Everyone appeared to enjoy themselves. My parents talked with Nick's mom; trying to find out more about Nick I suppose. But his mom only talked positively about Nick and Dave. You could tell by the way she spoke about both of them that they meant the world to her and she was proud of them both. I started to relax and enjoy myself celebrating me and Nick. I scanned the room at all the family and friends that were happy for me and Nick and enjoyed helping us celebrate. It was an amazing experience of pure joy. I floated on a cloud.

When I came out of the bathroom though, my mother quickly brought me down to earth.

"Rayna. Why did you do this? I thought we were going to plan a wedding for next year. Did he push you into this?" She didn't appear angry just agitated.

"No! I was the one that encouraged the wedding. I didn't want any more stress about me marrying Nick. When he told me you tried to pay him money; that did it. I planned on waiting, but you pushed me over the edge."

"I'm sorry Rayna, but I'm only looking out for your best interest. I'm your mother, it's my job; to protect you."

"There was never anything you could do to make Nick leave me. We were eventually going to be married no matter when. I'm glad we got married. I didn't want to wait any longer to be with Nick in every way. It's done. There is nothing you can do about it." I tried to keep my anger contained. I realized she meant well, but she needed to learn to deal with the fact I was a grown woman.

"That's what I'm worried about; how close you two are. I don't think you take care of yourself when you're with him. You wouldn't have the battery pack on you if you weren't with him. You're not thinking correctly." My mom put her head down and wiped a tear from her eye.

"It's not Nick's fault this battery pack is helping my heart pump. I'd still be living in a depression if Nick hadn't saved me. He brought life back into me. He gave me a reason to live, Mom." My mom raised her head and gazed at me. I stared into her eyes pleading for her to accept this. She didn't say a word. She only stared back at me and shook her head.

"I love you mom and I hope one day you'll believe in Nick and me."

"I love you Rayna. Have fun and please be careful." She kissed my cheek and pulled me into her arms. She held on for a few minutes. It felt like a goodbye hug. I needed my parents to accept my marriage, but I didn't want to push it right now. I hoped that over time, they would see how much Nick loved me and how he brought me to life.

My Mom and Dad left shortly after that. They told everyone goodbye at the table. My Dad shook Nick's hand and my mother even gave Nick a hug; for show no doubt. She said something to him, but I was too far away to hear what she said.

Everyone danced and seemed to have a genuinely great time. I was happy, even though I had some words with my mother. I danced my feet off with Nick and Anna. I had the time of my life. This night turned out to be better than I had hoped for.

Around eleven at night, people started to leave and the catering crew had cleaned up. They started taking down some tables and packing them in a truck parked outside. The band and Anna were the final guest. The tent would be taken down tomorrow. We all came into the house and Nick and I gathered pillows and blankets for them. Travis and Anna took the extra bed. Dave took the couch. Rick and Jeff had blow up mattresses. It was wonderful having everyone back together like we were at the beach house.

Twenty

The next week was full of other secrets. Dave and Nick bought the house for their mother. They were excited and planned how they would show her. They didn't know if they should wait until everything was final and they had the keys or show her early. They decided on telling her early. Dave picked her up and we all met at the house. She was under the impression she would give her opinion on a house for me and Nick. We arrived early so we had some time to fill the real estate agent in on our little secret.

"Oh, Nick this is a beautiful house. I love it." Olivia smiled and patted Nick on the arm as we entered the front room.

"We hoped you'd like it." Nick grinned. I stood beside my new mother-in-law, Olivia. I smiled because we made her happy. It brought so much happiness to my heart.

"Do you think it's big enough? I mean, will there be enough room for my grandchildren?" She gave a sneaking grin to Nick and then winked at me.

"It'll be fine. Let's look at the rest." Nick encouraged.

"Oh, this kitchen is just beautiful. I'd love to cook in here Rayna. You'll need to let me cook for you two." Olivia ran her hand down the granite counter top. She searched around the kitchen in cupboards, the oven, and the dishwasher. She moved out of the kitchen and down the hall to the bedrooms and bathroom.

Nick and I exchanged knowing smiles. He took my hand and squeezed it. Dave followed his mom after he threw us a smile. Olivia checked everywhere and inspected everything for us.

"So do you approve?" Dave asked after we toured the entire house and the garage.

"Yes, I think you two will be happy here. Are you going to buy it?"

"We already did," Nick answered. "For you. Dave and I signed the papers yesterday. You can move in next week."

Olivia stood in complete silence for a minute or two. She glanced at Nick, then at Dave, and last me. I shook my head yes at her, trying to persuade her to speak. Tears started streaming down her cheeks.

"Don't cry Mom," Nick let go of me to hug his mom.

"You shouldn't have."

"We wanted to Mom." Dave chimed in.

"I've waited for this day. To buy you a house and get you away from that crazy bastard." Nick said with conviction.

Dave hugged his mom when Nick let go.

"Mom we want you to be happy. Nick and I can afford this now. Can I stay with you until we record another album?" Dave said as he held his mom.

Everyone laughed and we all joined in a group hug.

"I don't have any furniture. I don't wanna take anything out of that damn house." Olivia said as she wiped the tears from her eyes.

"We can go shopping tomorrow. I like to shop." I smiled at Olivia

It didn't make her happy about us spending so much money, but I saw the weight being lifted off her chest knowing she'd be out of the toxic relationship. She told us she wanted to wait until she moved in to file for divorce. Nick and Dave told her they would be there to move her things out. They were not going to put up with their crazy stepfather anymore.

Everything fell into place. Nick and I were never happier with our lives, the band's success, and his mother moving on. The only thing that brought discomfort to our lives was me needing a new heart. We understood I might receive a heart at any time or I may never receive a new heart at all. We never talked about it much. The battery pack on my side would always be a daily reminder. Me receiving a new heart also made me think about somebody dying for me to live. I pushed those thoughts aside because they only made me depressed.

A few days before Thanksgiving and it was unseasonably warm still. Usually, the weather required a winter coat, but the last few weeks only required a light jacket. Nick had been busy trying to complete his motorcycle. He wanted to try and finish the bike before he left on tour again. My mom and dad were away at my uncle's for Thanksgiving. We spent Thanksgiving dinner with Dave and Olivia.

After Thanksgiving, Nick and Dave closed on their mom's house and moved her in. They got Jeff, Rick, and Travis to help. She only took her personal things, so they almost had her out of the house before John walked into the door. Nick told me he threw a fit because so many people were at his house. And when he realized Olivia dared to move out, he lost it. He started throwing and breaking things. He got so angry he started to go after Olivia. Nick and Dave told him he would be making his last mistake. So he decided to yell profanities at them and told Olivia she would never make it without him. I stayed at Olivia's house because Nick refused to have me around such violence.

Over the next few days, Nick finished up his motorcycle and I went to Olivia's new house when she got home from the dentist's office to help put things away and decorate. She enjoyed my help and the company. She loved her new home and continued to thank me every day for the gifts, the help, and the company. Our bond grew during this time together, it came easy with Olivia. Nick inherited a lot of her traits; compassion, loyalty, strength, and playfulness.

Olivia and I were finishing up everything in the kitchen when I got a tight knot in the bottom of my stomach. I became light headed and nauseated. I had been feeling tremendously well since they put the pump in. Everything about my body worked great now, so I couldn't imagine why all of a sudden my stomach knotted up into a painful ball. Thirty seconds later, my phone rang. I didn't have the usual vibe when Nick called, so I figured the call came from Anna or my mom checking up on me. The caller ID read Dave.

"Hey whatcha doing, helping Nick?" My voice came out a little weak because of the sudden sickness.

"Rayna, Nick has been in an accident on the motorcycle." His voice rang in my ear cold and flat.

I couldn't speak. The cup fell from my hand and shattered onto the floor. My head spun and I couldn't breathe. My body slid down the counter and onto the floor.

"Rayna, Rayna." Olivia's voice sounded like it came from a tunnel. Her voice moved closer until it was beside me. "Rayna!" I heard the panic in her voice now and it brought me back to reality.

I gazed up at Olivia who squatted beside me with my phone in her hand. Nick had been in an accident. That is all I remembered hearing. Tears ran down my cheeks and I couldn't stop them.

"Nick," was all I could say.

"Yes, Rayna, we need to go to the hospital."

"I never asked Dave where."

"I talked to Dave. They took him to UPMC. We need to go now honey." The concern in Olivia's eyes told me more than she was going to.

The drive to the hospital seemed to take forever with the traffic when in reality it was only about fifteen minutes with Olivia's driving. She got me there quickly. The entire drive, I prayed silently Nick would be okay. I didn't know the extent of his injuries, but the urgency in Dave's voice told me it was serious. Olivia had to pull over for me twice because I needed to throw up. My body ready to break, I tried to hold on and push the fear away from me. I needed to be strong.

The hospital ER waiting room was quiet when we arrived. I scanned the room for someone familiar, but I saw no one. I went to the nurse's desk and asked about Nick. Dave came out of the ER door while the nurse looked up the information.

"Rayna, Mom, you made it. Nick's asking for you. Come on." Dave full of concern and worry, tried to give me a reassuring smile, but I saw the fear in his eyes. "Rayna, Nick looks better than he is. The doctors are worried about a possible bleed in his brain. He has a few cuts and bruises, a broken arm, and a few cracked ribs. The doctors are getting him ready for a CT scan. You got here just in time to see him."

I gazed at Dave with tears building in my eyes. He was alive. I couldn't tell if the tears were from fear or joy. Fear of seeing Nick hurt or joy he was alive and breathing.

"Take me to him Dave. I need to be with him." I pulled what little bit of strength I had left out of me to be strong for Nick. He couldn't allow him to see me falling apart.

"Nick." I breathed and held back the tears. I went to one side and Olivia to the other of his hospital bed.

"Rayna." Nick held out his hand to me as I made it to his bed. He looked so fragile lying in the hospital bed with no shirt and a white sheet covering him. His arm looked severely distorted and his hands were cut up. The white sheet had smears of Nick's blood. I wanted to grab him and pull him close to me but didn't because of fear of hurting him. I held his hand and brushed the hair back from his forehead. I leaned in and kissed him on the lips gently and then I touched my lips to his forehead.

"You scared me to death. What were you doing?"

"Trying the bike out. We finished it today and was coming to show you. The next thing I realized, I was laying in the road wondering what happened. They said a car ran a red light and broadsided me." Nick spoke just above a whisper.

"I love you," I whispered in Nick's ear as I leaned down to kiss his cheek.

Nick raised his good arm around my back and used the last of his strength to pull me close to him. His face winced in pain. But he must've known I needed him to hold me.

"Rayna, I'm going to be fine. They're going to run some tests and you'll see everything is going to be fine. I love you."

"Mr. Perry, we're ready to take you for the scan. After the scan, we'll get that arm set and wrap your ribs," the nurse said.

She turned and glanced at me, "after we take care of his injuries, we'll let you know where he'll be."

I shook my head as she continued to talk.

"Give the nurse at the desk your cell phone number so we can locate you. It should be an hour or so."

I kissed Nick once more before they wheeled him away.

"I love you."

"I love you, princess Rayna."

The hour or so in the waiting room turned into pure hell. I never thought ninety minutes would take so long. Dave filled me in on that accident. He was following Nick over to Olivia's when the car hit him. Nick's helmet had a crack in it. That's why they were doing the CT scan. Nick also complained of a headache. That's what Dave meant when he said he appeared better than he was. The broken arm and ribs would heel, but a brain injury might last for life.

Anna and Travis showed up along with Jeff and Rick. The whole crew was here. They each gave us a hug asking about Nick. I tried to think of happy memories with Nick and not the accident while I sat in the waiting room. Trying to occupy your worried mind was harder than I thought. I tried to push away abysmal thoughts by telling Dave and his mom that Nick had been writing songs and they sounded great. Actually, we all tried to keep our minds preoccupied with small talk rather than Nick and his accident. My mom called to ask about Nick as the news traveled.

A doctor came out around eleven or so. He asked for Nick's family. I stood up with Dave and his mom. He told us the CT scan came back that Nick had a concussion, and he wanted to keep him for a few days for observation, just to make sure no complications arose. He said he should recover fully, but he was still concerned because of the headache. His arm had been set and his ribs taped. The doctor went on to say Nick would be closely monitored for the next few days. Nick, now in his room, would sleep most of the night, but we could see him for a few minutes.

Although I was relieved the doctor allowed us to visit Nick and he was okay for now, I was still scared something might happen to him. This man was my life. I needed him well and healthy.

We walked into Nick's room. There were IVs and monitors hooked up everywhere. I hated seeing him like this. My heart broke. His wounds were cleaned and he had a few stitches on his hand and bandages on his elbow. I took a deep breath; I needed to be strong for him and for myself. I needed to have faith he would be fine.

"How bad is it?" I winced when I glanced at his arm in a cast and the tape on his ribs.

"Not as bad now, since they gave me some medication. The drugs are making me sleepy. The headache has gone away some." Nick whispered as he fought to keep his eyes lids from closing.

"They said we could only stay for a few minutes. You need your rest. I am going to stay in the waiting room." I stated bluntly.

"No, you need to get your rest, Rayna. I'll be here tomorrow. I don't want you getting sick. You're still healing yourself." Nick opened his eyes more to help get his point a crossed.

"Nick's right, you need to rest and come back in the morning," Olivia said.

"I want to be right here with you Nick."

"No, you're going home. Come visit me in the morning. I'm going to sleep with all these drugs anyway." Nick gave me a weak smile. "Please, Rayna. Do it for me?" Nick pleaded.

I stood not moving for a second but I couldn't refuse his beautiful face. I nodded my head in defeat. He was right. He would sleep and I wouldn't be any good to him tired.

"Honey, I'm so glad you are okay. You scared me." Nick's mom leaned down and kissed his forehead and touched his cheek.

"Yeah man, I thought I might need some oxygen when I saw the car hit you. You scared the shit of me." Dave's voice full of anxiety but relieved at the same time.

"How's the bike?" Nick made a sour face.

"Mashed. I'm surprised you're just banged up a bit. I think the bike took the brunt of the hit; which is fortunate." Dave stood at the end of the bed.

The nurse came in to check on Nick and bring him some water. She checked his IV and monitors and informed us we could stay only a few more minutes. I smiled at the nurse but was unhappy about the fact I had to leave him.

"Let's give them a few minutes Mom." Dave put his arm around his mom to encourage her to leave.

"Love you bro, see you tomorrow," Dave called out to Nick.

"I love you too; take care of my girl for a few days for me will ya? Make sure she eats and gets some rest." Nick said. "I love you mom, night."

"Goodnight honey. I will be in to visit you tomorrow. Get some rest." Nick's mom kissed his forehead and then smiled at me. She walked around the bed and gave me a hug.

Dave and his mom left the room and I turned to Nick. His eyes were getting heavy, but he pushed to keep them open.

"Squeeze in here with me a minute, before the nurse comes back," Nick said.

I think he sensed I needed his arms around me. Even though he could barely move, he made room for me. I crawled in beside Nick for a few moments. He wrapped his arm around me and held onto me. I wrapped my arm across his chest and around his neck. I tucked my face under his chin. This is the place I liked to be. I could stay here forever. I breathed in Nick's scent and felt his warm skin on mine. I kissed his neck and his cheek. He turned and kissed my lips as many times as he could before his eyes got heavier.

Nick had fallen asleep. I laid still for a minute before I slide out of his bed. Nick squeezed my arm and I gazed into groggy eyes.

"I love you baby." Nick whispered.

"I love you." I kissed Nick one last time before I left. "See you in the morning."

Nick's eyes were closed again and he was sleeping. He was still beautiful even with his injuries. I watched him sleep for a moment. His peaceful look had vanished. His sleeping face held a sort of anguish I couldn't put my finger on. I brought his hand to my cheek and held it there and then kissed the back of his hand before I placed it down on the bed beside him. I forced myself to turn and walk out of his room.

I felt uneasy about leaving Nick, but I knew they would monitor him and I needed rest.

"You guys are still here?' I said as stopped in the waiting room.

"We told Dave to drive Olivia home. We all wanted to wait for you," Anna said as she hugged me tight. I held back the tears that were ready to flow.

"Can you take me home Anna?' I asked. I needed to get home so I could break down. I couldn't hold it together much longer.

"Of course. Travis and I will stay with you tonight." She led me by the hand to her car. It was nearly midnight when they got me home. She made me a bowl of leftover wedding soup. I forced it down. My appetite was gone, but I knew I needed to keep my strength up for Nick. I finally broke down and cried when I crawled under the covers. I didn't sleep that much, but when I did, I dreamed of Nick.

• ♥ • ♥ • ♥ • ♥ • ♥ •

I rushed to get ready and grabbed breakfast for the road. I needed to see Nick; hoping for better news today. Nick had to be okay, he was my life. Without Nick, I didn't exist. Meeting your soul mate is so profoundly intense, it's hard to explain. But when you meet them, you are complete. You have found the other part of your soul you were missing and now you are whole. And now that Nick lay injured, part of my soul was injured as well. Nick hurting physically caused me pain, I couldn't quite put my finger on it, but I didn't feel right. I felt like I had a hole in me and it seemed to be slowly growing bigger.

"I thought you would sleep in today?" Nick lay helpless in the hospital bed. Even though he talked to me and appeared to be more alert, there was something in his face that told me he was in pain.

"I couldn't sleep any later. I needed to be here to calm myself." I wanted better news from the doctor today. I prayed everything was okay with Nick. I needed him home and safe. "I guess I'll be taking care of you for a while. I get to return the favor." I smiled and sat down on Nick's bed. I needed to be close to him and be enveloped in his warmth. I could always feel a difference in my spirit when Nick and I were separated, and having him injured affected my spirit even more.

"Oh, I'm going to eat this up. Having you bath me and feed me; sounds exotic." Nick smiled his sweet grin.

I gazed up at Nick with an evil grin on my face., "Is that a yes?"

"Definitely. I can even buy a little nurse outfit for you."

I reached up and gave Nick a long passionate kiss. He rubbed my cheek with the back of his knuckles and smiled. I lay my head back down on his chest. We were silent. I listened only to Nick's heartbeat and heard my own heartbeat keeping rhythm with his.

Dave snuck into the room while I lay across Nick's chest allowing him to hold as much of me as one arm would allow.

Aware of his ribs, I stayed closer to his neck. But I liked being in the crease of his neck. I had skin contact on my cheek and my lips, and I could inhale his erotic scent.

"As always, you two need to rent a room." Dave joked as he sauntered into the room and took a seat in one of the empty chairs.

"We have one man." Nick threw back at him.

I stood up and wacked Dave in the back of the head.

"What?" Dave chuckled as he readjusted himself in the vinyl chair causing a rumbling sound.

"Are you going to be here long?"

"Yeah, I planned on being here for a while today. I don't have anything to do so I wanted to make sure I stayed here and annoyed him enough today." Dave said with a huge smile on his face. He leaned up and poked Nick in the leg. "Mom said she'll be here as soon as she takes care of some things at the office."

"Good, I didn't want to leave him here alone too long while I slipped out for a few." I'd been feeling odd and I wanted to check in with my doctor but didn't want to alarm Nick, so I didn't mention it to him. It was probably nothing, but I wanted to make sure. I needed to be in good health for Nick. I figured it was the stress of Nick's accident that made me fatigued and nauseated.

"You two act like I'm a little kid. I can take care of myself, you know." Nick chuckled and grabbed his ribs.

I told Nick and Dave I'd be back soon and kissed Nick. I didn't want to leave his side, but I needed to get this done and grab a bit to eat.

At the doctor's office they checked all my vitals, listened to my heart, checked my pump, took a blood test, and urine sample. They said everything looked fine but wanted to make sure. They had me wait in the waiting room while the lab processed the samples. When they called me back in to give me my report the doctor smiled, but his face showed concern.

"What's wrong doctor?" I asked impatiently, needing to get back to Nick.

"Well, Rayna. Everything seems to be fine."

"Okay, so it's just the stress." I smiled and started to get up from the chair.

"There's a reason you're fatigued and nauseaed."

I waited for the doctor to respond.

"You're pregnant."

The wind got knocked out of me for a minute. I was speechless. I took a few deep breaths and forced a smile. Not quite sure how to react to the news. I was elated, but shocked at the same time. I let the information sink in for a few moments. I put my hand to my stomach as the news sunk in.

"Are you okay?" The doctor asked concerned.

"Yes, I'm okay, a little surprised." Knowing I had a new life inside of me sent a wave of panic through me for a moment. Nick's child grew inside of me. The realization made me smile.

"How far along am I?" I stared at the doctor while keeping my hand on my stomach trying to investigate if I had a bump. It appeared a little harder.

"Approximately six or seven weeks. You'll need to make an appointment with an OB/GYN to be more accurate. Rayna, you need to take excellent care of yourself right now. With you being pregnant and your heart condition, you could be in trouble quickly. You need to monitor yourself more. And I'll need to see you more often now," the doctor said with a straight face.

"Yes doctor, I will. Thank you." I shook the doctor's hand and left the office.

I swung by our place and grabbed some of Nick's things so he could clean up. I knew it would make him feel better.

When I got back to Nick's room, I wanted to tell him the news. This was a life changing event. I was still trying to comprehend the news myself, so I wasn't sure how to tell him.

"I brought you some things from home."

"Great you can help shave me," Nick said as he looked in the bag that I brought from home.

"Nick, I got some news today?" I glanced over at him to try and judge his reaction. He always smiled at me so I didn't know what to expect.

"Good or bad news?" He waited for me to respond.

"Not sure. I guess it might be either."

"Let's hear it then." Nick touched my face with the back of his hand.

"I'm pregnant." I didn't know how else to say it so I just blurted it out.

"What?" Nick's voice was quiet. He sat in his bed looking at me for a moment. And then a huge smile formed on his lips. He grabbed both sides of my face and pulled me into a deep kiss.

"Wow! That's amazing news Rayna. I guess this is an unexpected happy moment; me, you, and a little princess." He smiled from ear to ear.

"It might be a little prince." I smiled, relieved he seemed so excited.

"How long before we meet the princess or prince?"

"The doctor said I'm six or seven weeks. I have to make an appointment with my OB/GYN. She'll be able to tell me more. But it looks like this summer."

"It appears I'm going to be flying around a lot. I'm not gonna miss this. The guys will drive the RV and I'll fly back and forth when I can. I love you so much." Nick kissed me again.

The nurse came in and unhooked the monitors from Nick so I could help him clean up. She said she'd give him twenty minutes and she'd be back to hook him back up.

I smeared Nick's face with shaving cream and turned the water on for him. He leaned in and kissed me, leaving shaving cream all over my mouth. It put a smile on his gorgeous face. I left it on my face hoping I would see his sexy little grin again. I got a few of them. After he shaved, he brushed his teeth and gave me a better kiss, so we swapped shaving cream again. Nick wanted to shower, but I didn't know how that would be possible with his arm in a cast and his ribs taped. But he had it all planned out. He had me find a cup and dump water on him from his ribs down, he lathered up and I rinsed him off. I washed his right arm, chest, and back with the washcloth and dried him off. I helped him back into bed.

Nick acted like he was a little better today, maybe because of the shower, the medicine, or maybe because he was going to be a father. He ate lunch and the nurses checked his vitals. I crawled into bed with Nick and we found a movie to watch on TV. Nick and I dozed off for a few hours. When I woke up, I laid and admired Nick as he slept; I loved to watch him sleep.

Nick opened his eyes after a few minutes and smiled at me. I kissed him and remembered to tell Nick about my dream. I wanted to tell him as soon as I got to the hospital, but he was ready for a shower, so I put it in the back of my mind. But I drifted back into my dream from this morning when I fell asleep with Nick and this brought it back to the front of my mind. It made me smile. "I dreamed last night we got married on the beach at sunrise and everyone was at the ceremony."

"It sounds like everyone there was happy and it appears it made you happy."

"Only in my dreams, and yours too it sounds like."

"We did it again; we dreamed the same dream." Nick kissed me. "How do we keep doing this? This is wonderful but crazy at the same time."

"Because our souls are a match; we are twin flames. We connect even while we sleep."

"Rayna, I'm sorry your parents haven't really accepted that we're married. I would do anything to change your parents' minds. It bothers you they weren't there, I'm sorry. We could have an actual wedding if you want; so they could be there."

"It wouldn't change how they feel Nick."

"No, but it might make you feel better. I want to make you happy in every way possible." Nick's eyes filled with sadness.

"Nick, life happens fast and I don't want to put off tomorrow what I can have today. Anything could happen. I think we've both proven that. I'm fine. Yes, I wish they'd be happy for us. But I will never regret marrying you when I did." I smiled at him. I didn't want to spend months planning a big wedding for people to attend. The intimate beach wedding was what I wanted, no frills or big deal. I started living my life with the man I loved and loved me beyond everything. We tied the knot and that would always be enough for me.

Nick gazed at me with concern. He brushed his fingers down my cheek and I leaned into his touch. Nick's expression turned loving with his puppy dog eyes.

"I'm the luckiest man alive. I'm so happy you married me and now you're giving me a child," he smiled. I hugged him tight and kissed him again.

"I'm going to try and rest, my head hurts a little." Nick touched his head and cringed for a moment.

"Okay, close your eyes and rest. I'll be right here." I kissed Nick and then moved over to the chair to let him sleep. I opened my tablet and turned it on with the sound off. He needed his rest if he was gonna be able to finish the tour. Nick closed his eyes and slept. I sat and watched him and thought about our future and our news of a child.

· ♥ · ♥ · ♥ · ♥ · ♥ ·

The nurse cleared her throat when she walked into the room.

"How are you this afternoon Mr. Perry?" The nurse asked as she began her assessment of Nick's monitors and began to take his blood pressure. She wore blue scrubs. She was an attractive older woman with dark hair pulled up in a ponytail and warm blue eyes.

"I'm still hanging on to this headache a little. Can't seem to knock it."

"I'll tell the doctor. Everything else seems to be fine. I'll check on you later." The nurse finished her assessment and walked out of the room.

Olivia and Dave showed up while Nick tried to eat his dinner. It didn't look appetizing; maybe because I still became nauseated when I smelled food.

"How are you today honey?" Olivia walked over beside Nick's bed and touched his forehead.

"Still sore and I can't kick this headache. But Rayna gave me some wonderful news to help cheer me up." Nick smiled over at me and reached for my hand.

Olivia glanced from Nick to me with questions in her eyes. She waited for a response from one of us. I nodded at Nick for him to tell his mother.

"What is it?" Dave chimed in.

"You're going to be a grandma, and you're gonna be Uncle Dave." Nick kept a grin on his face while he held my hand.

I smiled at both of them. This pregnancy thing started to wear on me; knowing I carried a life in my womb. Olivia's eyes grew huge and she covered her mouth with her hand. Excitement was written all over her face.

"Good job bro; congratulations." Dave walked over to shake Nick's hand, and then he turned around and gave me a hug.

"Congratulations you two. I'm so happy right now I don't know what to say. I'm going to be a grandma."

"Looks like we have a reason to celebrate as soon as you're home." Dave was all smiles. He looked so much like Nick more every day. He could almost be his younger twin. Dave kept his hair short, but he looked like he skipped a few hair appointments.

Olivia moved around the bed to give me one of her tight hugs. She was like another mother to me. She accepted me so easily. She often said I was like the daughter she never had. She treated me like one of her children. She worried after me almost as much as Nick did. After she hugged me, she bent down and gave her son a hug. When she stood back up, she wiped away some tears. They were tears of joy.

"I'm the happiest I've ever been in my life. My two boys are successful Rock Stars, I have a new daughter, a new house, and I am going to be a grandma. My life is perfect."

We all spent the evening together. Dave went out and got us dinner and Anna and Travis stopped by to visit Nick. We told them the news. Anna was ecstatic. She was ready to plan a baby shower with Olivia, but I told them to hold off on those plans until I told my parents the news. Nick seemed to be having a wonderful time visiting with everyone.

I planned on telling my parents about the baby as soon as Nick got home from the hospital. They could wait a few more days. They just returned home from their trip to my uncle's. Anna and Travis left later in the evening, Olivia followed them out. Dave was the last to leave. Nick and I were watching one of his favorite shows on TV when my phone rang. I didn't recognize the number. I walked toward the door so I could hear better.

"Hello?"

"Rayna Taylor?" The voice came from a woman.

"Yes, can I help you?"

"This is the transplant department at UPMC.. We need you to be at the hospital within two hours please. We have you a heart."

"I'm currently at the hospital visiting my husband. I don't think it's going to be possible for me to have this done right now. My husband is a patient in the hospital and I just found out today I am pregnant."

"Are you planning on keeping the child?"

"Yes, of course."

"Then you are correct. We cannot do a heart transplant if you are pregnant, the child will not survive. We'll place you back on the list mam. Thank you. Have a good day."

"Thank you." I stood there looking at the phone in my hand. Not believing what I just heard. They had a heart for me. This world could be so cruel.

"Rayna, who was that? What's the matter?" Nick's voice sounded concerned.

"Rayna." Nick said again. A little louder.

I glanced over at him. "They have a heart for me." My voice was almost a whisper, but Nick heard me.

"Good thing you're already here then." His voice was full of excitement.

I shook my head.

"What's the matter?"

"I can't have the surgery. You're in the hospital and I am pregnant."

"You need the heart Rayna. Who knows when or even if they'll have another one? Don't worry about me. I'm gonna be fine. I hope to be out of here tomorrow."

"No, they can't do the surgery without killing the baby. I will not let that happen. I'm doing fine with the pump right now. Another one will come." I forced a smile on my face.

"The call could come too late. We agreed you would take the first heart; even if I was on tour." Nick appeared to be tired and defeated.

"I know, but that was before you got hurt and I became pregnant. I want this child. I don't want to do anything to put his or her life in danger Nick." i placed my hand protectively over my baby bump.

"We can have another child, but you may never receive another heart. Baby, please reconsider this." Nick pleaded with me. But no matter how much begging he did, nothing would change how I felt about leaving his side or giving up this child.

"My mind is made up. You can't change it no matter what. I'm not leaving your side until you're well. I'm going to do everything to protect our child. I love you and I would do anything for you but this. Another heart will come; I believe that; you need to believe it too."

· ♥ · ♥ · ♥ · ♥ · ♥ ·

Nick made me leave again that night. Dave stayed with me; perhaps per Nick's request. I didn't care if he stayed. He left me alone. If it made Nick rest better that Dave kept an eye on me, then I would deal with it. I was restless again. I dreamed of me and a child holding hands; a little girl. We played in a field.

Nick stood off in the distance watching, but never coming over to us, even when I waved for him to come to us. He stood and continued watching. He waved once; he had a smile on his face. Dave was there with us. He picked up the little girl and carried her. He took my hand and we walked away from Nick. I turned around and motioned for Nick to follow us, but he didn't. He waved as we walked away.

Twenty-One

♥

When I got to the hospital after my restless night, Nick slept. I grabbed some coffee and a snack. I hoped he would sleep for a while. This early in the morning the hospital stayed quiet. I hoped the doctor would let Nick go home today. Besides his broken ribs, arm, and headaches he was okay.

When I strolled back into Nick's room, he was awake and a nurse was checking his IVs and his vitals.

"Good morning mother-to-be." Nick smiled even though the pain showed on his face.

"Good morning. How did you sleep?"

"Okay I guess. I had nightmares.

"Me too. But I don't want to talk about it." I walked over and kissed Nick. He looked exhausted and frustrated. "I hope the doctor will let you out of this place today. I want you home with me."

"I hope so. I'm tired of being cooped up in this place."

I spent the morning with Nick while he ate his breakfast. I helped him clean up again. He didn't like having to depend on anyone for anything. After I helped him, Dave came to visit. I took advantage of it and told them I wanted to run out and grab some lunch.

I grabbed some lunch in the cafeteria for Dave and me. I needed to keep my strength up now more than ever. I had a lot to deal with and I didn't want to jeopardize this pregnancy. I grabbed a nutritious lunch of fruit and vegetables. I rode the elevator up and walked back to Nick's room. Dave sat in a blue hospital chair alone. Nick was gone.

"Where did they take Nick?" I asked. The expression on my face showed my concern.

"He still has those headaches and his vision was a little blurry, so they took him for another CT scan," Dave responded with a dry tone and a blank face.

"Oh, God. That is not an encouraging sign. How long has he been gone?"

"About ten minutes. They came to take him right after you left. They said he'd be back within an hour. I called my mom, she's on her way."

Dave stood up and took the lunches from my hands and set the bags on the stand. He put both hands on my shoulders and directed me over to the chair he'd been sitting in. I still hadn't said anything. My mind reeled. Is this good? Is this bad? I couldn't make my mind comprehend which way it was. So much had happened in the last few days. I said a silent prayer for Nick. He had to be okay, he was my world; without him, it didn't make sense.

"Rayna, it's going to be okay. This is just a scan to help the doctors treat Nick." Dave kept his arm around my shoulder for support. I was so thankful for him right now. He'd been such a big help to my mind the last couple of days. He filled in the gaps that Nick's injury caused.

Nick's mom walked into the room soon after and came over to hug me and Dave. Dave filled her in on what was going on.

I realized Nick's mom was reassuring me as much as herself. I closed my eyes and prayed. I prayed for Nick to be okay and for the strength to make it through this trying time. I knew what faith did, and mine was not weak.

Orderlies wheeled Nick back into his room. I immediately rushed to his bedside and leaned down to hold him, touch his cheek, forehead, and finally his lips. When I released him, I kept his hand in mine.

"You scared me to death. You disappeared."

"It's okay. The doctor just scheduled a scan to investigate why I still had these headaches.

We were all a little on edge. We hoped Nick would come home today but now that he had a CT scan, we thought he we thought he'd need to stay. I still had some hope left he would be okay. He had to be.

An hour later, the doctor came into the room to give us news of what he found on the CT scan. The doctor wore a white lab coat over his blue dress shirt and tie and held Nick's chart in his hand. I held Nick's hand and Dave stood with one arm around me and the other one around his mother.

"Nick, the CT scan showed you have a small bleed in your brain. That's why you're experiencing headaches and now having some blurred vision. Yesterday, we didn't find a bleed, but a small tear wouldn't have shown up without bleeding. With a lot of rest, the bleeding should stop with the correct medication. But I don't think you'll be leaving today or tomorrow. We'll monitor the bleeding and pressure on your brain for the next couple of days and then check how you're healing. Do you have any questions?"

"I thought he was okay?" I asked before anyone else responded. Nick squeezed my hand as I questioned the doctor.

"These things happen sometimes. That's why we kept him for observation. Sometimes a bleed doesn't show up for a few days. Just be glad it happened while you were still here and not after we released you."

"Thank you doctor." Nick's mom gave the doctor a weak smile as she hovered beside Nick.

Olivia and Dave stayed the evening with me and Nick. We talked about Olivia's new house and trivial things. Nobody wanted to discuss Nick's condition, it was too daunting.

Nick made me leave the hospital again telling me to go home and rest. With Nick's health taking a turn for the worst, I knew I wouldn't be able to rest. But I had to try for the baby.

Dave followed me home. It was after ten when we got in the house. I called my mom to give her an update on Nick.

"How are you Rayna?' My mom said as she picked up the phone.

"A little tired. I just walked in the door and I wanted to let you know how Nick was." Dave brought me a cup of chamomile tea to help me relax.

"How is he? Ready to come home?"

"We were hoping he'd be home today." I took a deep breath to keep the tears from streaming down my face.

"Rayna, he's a strong guy. He's gonna be okay. I'm gonna come and stay with you tonight."

"No, it's fine Mom. Dave's here with me. I'm going to drink my tea and go to bed. I'll feel better in the morning."

"Are you sure? I can be there in no time."

"I'm sure. I'll talk to you tomorrow. Love you Mom."

"I love you too Rayna."

I hung up the phone and pulled my legs into me and held them. Wrapping my arms around my legs felt like I was holding myself together.

Dave tried to reassure me Nick was a fighter and he'd make it through this. He said Nick would be upset if he left me here all alone. I rolled my eyes at him, but let him have his way. I told Dave goodnight and retired into my big empty bed. I prayed for Nick and for sleep. Nick stayed in my thoughts as I drifted off to sleep. He stayed with me all night in my dreams. Sometimes we walked together and other times he was just out of my reach. I spoke to him, but it was as though he couldn't hear me.

Nick lay sleeping when I arrived at the hospital at 6:30. I checked in on him, but didn't want to wake him, so I just sat and watched as his chest raised and lowered as he took each breath. I loved watching him while he slept. Still tired, I laid my head down on Nick's bed while holding his hand. I must have fallen asleep because I woke up to Nick touching my face.

"Hi," he smiled when I gazed up at him and raised my head. "You look tired."

"I was restless last night. I had nightmares about not being able to find you."

"I had some of those last night myself. I kept calling for you, but I couldn't find you. You were lost in the woods."

"We did it again; I wonder how we do it? I ran in the woods in my nightmare, looking for you. I kept hearing you call my name."

"Remember, you're the one that said we were twin flames?" Nick smiled and pushed my hair behind my ear. He penetrated my soul with his eyes. "I love you so much, Rayna."

"I love you more." I stood up and leaned down to kiss the man I loved; the man that controlled everything about me now. He didn't even know it. He took me to a beautiful place when I gazed into his deep soulful eyes. My body shivered as electricity went through my body from Nick's kiss.

"I'm not sure how that is possible," Nick said in between breaths as he continued to place kisses on my lips.

"How are you today?" I pushed Nick's hair back from his forehead, brushing it with my fingers.

"Still have the headache, but other than those, about the same." Nick gave me a look of surrender.

"Well, I hope the medicine is working and the headaches stop soon. I just want to take you home and have you well again. I don't like seeing you like this." I smiled because just the thought of being his wife warmed my soul.

After breakfast and nurses in and out to assess Nick, he grew tired quickly. I stroked his arm as he drifted off to sleep. I crept away to find myself some food. The couple of days since Nick's accident left me tired and a little weak. I hadn't eaten much the last couple of days and the hunger pangs started to rise. I grabbed some of Nick's favorite snacks on my way out of the cafeteria so we could eat them later and a large cup of coffee for me. I needed something to keep me going.

When I got back to Nick's room, he still slept. He looked like an angel. I sat down in the chair and reclined it back. I closed my eyes hoping to find a few z's.

I awoke suddenly to Nick's anguished cries. "Rayna! Rayna!"

I jumped out of the chair and raced to Nick's side. "What is it?" I was confused and afraid. I saw the fear and pain in Nick's voice. I always sensed Nick's emotions more deeply than anybody close to me whether it was pain, fear, joy, or love. And this feeling haunted me.

"Everything is blurry and my left side is numb. I can't see right!"

"I'll buzz the nurse; everything's going to be okay, Nick." I pushed the call button on the remote.

"Yes," the nurse said.

"He can't see. He can't see!" I yelled into the box. I touched Nick's face and pressed my lips to his forehead to console him. I held him and he continued to panic. I began to panic inside but kept it there to try and keep Nick calm.

"What is happening Rayna? My vision! Rayna, I'm scared."

"I know, I know. The nurse is on her way." I kissed Nick's hand and held it to my face as I tried to console him. I prayed God would let him be okay. He had to be okay. Seeing him with this much desperation terrified me. I felt helpless and confused.

The nurse arrived and assessed Nick and checked his monitors.

"I'll page the doctor. I'll be right back."

Within minutes, orderlies came in the room wheeling Nick out of the room for an MRI, and another CT scan. I walked alongside the bed as they wheeled Nick down the hall and into the elevator. I continued to hold his hand until we arrived at radiology. I let go of his hand now with immense resistance.

"I love you Nick." I leaned down and whispered into Nick's ear and kissed his lips as tears swelled in my eyes.

"I love you baby. See you soon."

"I will be right here waiting for you."

It was nearly four when they took Nick back for the scans. I walked into the small waiting room. An older woman sat alone on one side of the light blue room, in a comfortable looking dark blue chair. There was an empty blue couch, but I chose not to sit. I walked back out into the hall to make a call. I called Dave to inform him of the change in his brother. I told him what happened and he turned his car around toward the hospital. I needed someone to be here with me. I couldn't be alone right now. I was scared beyond belief. An ache in my heart began and a huge knot formed in the pit of my stomach. I paced the waiting room waiting for news or for Dave to appear.

To keep my mind from running crazy, I called Anna hoping she could make it to the hospital. She just walked into her apartment from class and said she'd be right over. I needed Anna's support too. She was my strength, she always kept me together when it seemed like things would fall apart. Since I met Nick, I'd been complete. Now I began a downward spiral and he wasn't able to keep me together, so Anna and Dave became my next option.

I tried sitting on a soft blue couch in the waiting room, but my mind reeled. I decided to move from the room to the hall and back to the room again. It felt like hours had passed, but looking at my phone assured me it had only been fifteen minutes. I looked up and Dave moved fast toward me. Tears welled up in my eyes just seeing his face. All of the emotions I had been trying to keep a hold of threatened to spill out. Dave took me into his arms and the tears streamed down both cheeks. These tears turned into sobs and then uncontrollable gasps. Dave held me tight and refused to let go. I needed his support more than I realized. I fell apart in his arms and he let me.

When I could speak, I explained more about what happened with Nick.

"He panicked Dave. It was so frightening. He said his vision was blurry and his left side numb, he couldn't move his left side. I've never seen Nick falling apart like this. I almost lost it."

"Rayna, the doctors are doing everything they can. Thankfully he was still in the hospital when all this happened." Dave held my hands as he tried to console me with his words. I wanted to believe him, but seeing Nick in the state of mind he was in retched my heart. It tore at my heart and my gut convulsed. My body started to shake and tremble. Dave pulled me close to him and held me as I cried once more.

"But he's getting worse, not better. He has to get better. He's gonna be a dad."

"I know----I know," is all Dave said. He understood he couldn't reassure me anything. I think he was as scared as me, but he tried not to show it for my sake.

Nick's mom showed up while we waited for news on him; worry and exhaustion on her face. She still had on her work clothes as she rushed in to find Dave and me. She held me and we both cried. Dave and I explained what happened since yesterday. Nick's mother was in as much despair as me.

Anna finally showed up with a tray of Starbucks coffee for everyone. I cried again. Anna told me she called my mother and she wanted an update later, which surprised me.

I had a sense something wasn't right. The connection I had with Nick didn't always bring a positive vibe. I could always tell when he didn't feel well or if he was upset. Right now I was experiencing a deep sense of dread. I tried to ignore it, but it wouldn't leave me.

As we all sat quietly praying and waiting for news, the doctor came out. He was dressed in scrubs. His face showed grave concern and this set my nerves on end. We all stood when he approached us. I held my arms tight around my body hoping to hold myself together. My eyes were red from crying and I still held the tissue full of tears in my hand.

"Mrs. Perry?" The doctor scanned our group, questioning which one we were.

"Yes." I responded with only one word. Afraid to speak fearing my voice would falter. Nick's mom simply shook her head.

"We finished our scans, but while we were finishing our last scan, Nick suffered a seizure. He's okay now, but very tired from the seizure. We need to let some pressure off his brain and repair the bleed. The bleeding has gotten worse and the pressure is pushing against his brain. That's why he had trouble with his vision, paralysis, and now a seizure. He's aware of what's happening and he has given consent for us to make a hole to release the pressure and fix the leak."

I dropped my head in my hands and sobbed. I felt dizzy. Dave wrapped his arms around me and held me. His mother joined him. I needed to be with Nick. Things seem to be getting worse and I needed to be with him right now, anything might happen and I needed to touch him and look at him.

"Can we see him?" Dave questioned the doctor. He read my mind I think.

"Yes, but only for a few minutes until they have him ready for surgery. You can follow me back. He's been asking for you Mrs. Perry." The doctor turned to lead us to him. Nick's mom, Dave, and I followed the doctor as he led the way. Dave took my hand as we walked to Nick's room. Having Dave with me helped to comfort me some, but my body shook and became weak inside. I took a deep breath to pull myself together for Nick. I didn't want him to see me this way. I needed to be strong for him, but I didn't know if I could pull this act off. He always saw through me and sense my every emotion.

The doctor led us to the door that held the love of my life. Dave stepped in front of me to open the door for us. I stepped in, afraid of what I would witness. The lights were dim and machines beeped everywhere. Nick was hooked up to multiple monitors. I hated seeing him like this. I moped to the edge of Nick's bed. His eyes were closed. His chest slowly raised and fell as he took each breath. It was beautiful to watch this movement. Nick's mom walked to the other side of his bed and Dave stood beside me; maybe for support. I touched Nick's arm with a tender hand. His warm skin felt wonderful against mine. Nick opened his lethargic eyes and tried to focus. He scanned the room.

"Hi." I slid my left hand down to Nick's hand and placed my other hand against his cheek.

"Hi," Nick whispered to me. He moved the corners of his mouth to try to form a smile for me. "You talked to the doctor?"

"Yes, he told us what happened and what he needs to do." Nick's mom placed her hand on Nick's shoulder. I shook my head.

"They're going to cut my hair." Nick smiled, but the smile was for our benefit. Nick loved his long hair. I loved his long hair.

I bent down and kissed his cheek. He closed his eyes and then opened them when I moved away.

"I'll be right here waiting for you. I'll wait forever if I need to. You're going to be a father Nick. Your precious baby needs you-----I need you." I smiled down at Nick as I gazed into his eyes and into his soul. His fear radiated into my soul.

"I love you." Nick forced a smile.

"I love you." That was all I could force out without breaking into a full blown crying attack. So I kept it short and to the point. Nick and I talked with our eyes so nothing more needed to be said. He knew how I felt.

"We'll all be here waiting for you when you come out of surgery honey. I love you." Nick's mom bent down and kissed his cheek and pushed his hair back from his forehead.

"I love you mom."

"Hey bro, you're gonna be fine. You have a tour to finish, a beautiful baby on the way, and a gorgeous wife waiting for you. I love you bro," Dave leaned in and gave Nick a hug.

As Dave leaned down, I saw Nick whisper something in his ear. He said it so quietly I couldn't hear what he said, but Dave gave Nick a very serious look and shook his head yes, and said I will.

"Let's give them a few minutes mom," Dave said to his mother.

Dave stepped away from the bed and held his arm out to his mother. She kissed Nick one last time and walked toward Dave. Dave wrapped his arm around his mother and led her out of the room.

I didn't ask Nick what he said to Dave. I didn't want to pry. If he wanted me to know, then he would have said it out loud. I'd give him privacy about it for now. I didn't want to leave Nick's side, but I also wanted the doctors to help him, so I tried to make the best of my last few minutes with Nick. I leaned down and wrapped my arms around the man I loved. Nick wrapped his arm around me and held me like he may never hold me again. The tension in his grip left me frightened.

"Rayna, I love you more than my own life. You are my everything. I want to spend the rest of my life with you. I can't even express the depth of my love for you."

"You're my other half, you've made me whole. I love you more." I didn't want to let go, but I wanted to look into Nick's eyes and get lost. I released Nick enough so I could look into his eyes. I escaped to another world when I looked into his eyes. We just silently stared into each other. When hearts and minds connected, you didn't need words. I kissed his warm lips and he returned the kiss with electrifying passion even though he was in pain and very weak. When we separated, we got lost in each other's eyes once more, until a nurse came in to interrupt our love story.

"It's time." She said, her voice just above a whisper.

"I love you baby." Nick whispered as he held my hand. "Be back in a few." He smiled.

"I love you back. I'll be here waiting." I kissed Nick one last time as the nurse wheeled him out of the room. My last thought as Nick disappeared was there goes my life.

Twenty-Two

The rest of the evening drug on for hours and hours, I didn't know what to do with myself. Anna and Dave tried to keep my mind off of Nick. They talked about the tour and the places they would visit. Olivia talked about the baby and what I wanted, a girl or boy. She didn't care either way, she was just excited about being a grandmother. Dave was a little excited as well about being an uncle. They all threw baby names at me while we waited for Nick to come through surgery.

The doctor showed up in the waiting room a little after eleven. It was an exhausting evening. He had his blue scrubs on and a mask around his neck. As he approached us, the expression on his face was hopeful, but exhausted. We all stood up with anticipation when he walked in the door.

"Mrs. Perry, Mrs. Scott, Nick is out of surgery and in recovery. The surgery went well. The bleed was deeper than we thought, so we placed Nick into an induced coma. This will help his recovery. He needs to be asleep while his brain is trying to heal. He will be placed in ICU for a few days, and if everything goes well, he will be moved to a room." The doctor spoke matter of fact without any emotion.

"How long will you keep him in the coma?" My voice shook just above a whisper. But I guessed the doctor heard me. I tried to speak louder, but fear wouldn't allow it. Coma was the word I heard above all the others.

"A few days, a few weeks, it's really hard to tell. We have to monitor him and observe how he responds to the surgery and how well he is recovering."

"Will he make a complete recovery?" Nick's mom questioned the doctor.

"That's something we have to wait to see as well. Within the next few weeks, we should know a lot about his recovery. In a few minutes you can visit him in the ICU, but he's going to be sleeping for a few days and he's in wonderful hands. Are there any more questions for me?"

Nobody asked another question. We all shook our heads no and looked at each other with blank faces as the doctor disappeared from the dim, quiet waiting room.

The ICU was behind a locked door. We had to call back and be buzzed in. They allowed two visitors at a time every three hours for thirty minutes. Dave and his mom took turns so I could stay the full thirty minutes.

Nick lay behind a glass wall with a sliding door. There were four patient rooms in this ICU. Two nurses sat cramped in the small room watching the complex monitors and checking on patients. The sliding door opened when Dave and I walked in front of them. Nick slept. His beautiful brown locks had disappeared. Nick lay in the bed with his head wrapped in gauze, a broken arm, respirator, heart monitors, brain monitors, and IVs. He looked so broken. I wanted to take him in my arms and love the pain away. But the monitors only allowed me to hold his hand and touch his face. He was so helpless but peaceful. Tears streamed down my cheeks. Dave put his arm around me and held me while I held Nick's hand and said a silent prayer.

Ten minutes later, Dave left to allow his mother some time with Nick. I had a few moments alone with Nick. I leaned down and whispered in his ear that I loved him and would be waiting here for him to wake up. I lightly touched his still warm lips with mine. I let my lips linger on his for a few moments and I experienced the same electric current I always felt when our lips touched. It excited me and made me hopeful that Nick was in there somewhere.

Everyone insisted I go home for the night and rest. I didn't want to leave the hospital, but the nurses in the ICU told me I wouldn't be allowed back tonight and Nick was in capable hands. They reassured me they would call if anything changed with him and reminded me I lived only a few minutes away.

Anna and Travis made it to mine and Nick's house before me and she warmed me up some leftover lasagna she made the night before. Anna didn't want to leave me alone tonight, so she and Travis were staying with me to give Dave a break and so he could stay with Olivia.

"Rayna you need to eat," Anna said.

"I know it's just hard when you have no appetite." I forced a bite down.

"Eat as much as you can please." Anna's face was full of concern.

I didn't even want to be here, I should be at the hospital with Nick. I ate what I could and then took a shower. The water warmed my skin and helped to relax me a little. I hoped it would wash away some of the sadness.

I crawled into bed a little after two in the morning. My body and mind were exhausted from the day's events. Just a week ago Nick and I were planning our life together. Now that life was threatened. So much had happened since I met Nick six months ago. My eyes grew heavy thinking about this past year and exhaustion won over and I drifted off to sleep.

Nick and I sat on a cozy chaise on a luxurious bamboo deck looking out at the beautiful blue water as the sun began to set. We sipped wine as we talked about our future plans. The ocean winds were warm and breezy and the sound of the ocean was breathtaking.

"We need to start looking for houses when we get back to the real world." Nick smiled as he placed the wine glass to his lips and took a sip of the tasty wine.

"Yes we do. I'm so glad we're moving to the beach. House hunting will be exciting. I'm thankful our careers are allowing us to live anywhere we chose. I always knew I would live near water." I took a sip of my wine and leaned my head on Nick's shoulder. "I found a few houses online that I'd like to investigate more. They're all right on the water in Florida.

"Our albums have gone platinum so you can buy whatever house you want princess."

I snuggled into Nick's bare chest as he wrapped his arm tighter around me. I curled my feet up on the chaise. We both watched as the sun set down into the ocean.

I opened my eyes to peek up at Nick, but what I found was a lonely bedroom. Realizing I'd been dreaming, I closed my eyes to try and escape back into my dream. Reality hit and reminded me Nick lay in an induced coma in the ICU. I rolled over and glared at the red lights staring at me letting me know it was eight in the morning. I wanted to be at the hospital by now. I jumped out of bed and dressed with swiftness and ran to the bathroom to brush my teeth and fix this crazy looking hair. I pulled it into a ponytail and brushed some face powder on and applied some eyeliner and mascara to help hide my tired looking face.

When I finished getting ready, I found Anna and Travis at the kitchen bar having breakfast. Anna begged me to eat something. I grabbed a granola bar from the cabinet and a protein shake from the fridge as I drank some coffee in their company.

"How did you sleep last night?" Anna inquired with a worried expression on her face.

"I slept pretty well. I had a wonderful dream of Nick last night, I kind of wish I didn't wake up from it." I forced a smile.

Anna took another sip of her coffee and smiled. She walked around the bar while placing her coffee on the counter.

"Rayna, Nick's a fighter; he's gonna pull through this." She wrapped her arms around me and hugged me tight.

This was almost my undoing. I held tight to Anna and a tear escaped my eye. I pulled away and wiped the single tear away and shook my head in agreement. "I better go. Thanks for the coffee."

Anna took the coffee cup from my hand and held my face with her gentle hands before I turned away. I gathered my purse and headed toward the door.

When I got to the hospital, I grabbed some coffee from the café and went straight to ICU. Nick was the same. He seemed peaceful sleeping. I sat and watched him for a little while and held his hand. I rubbed the back of his hand with a gentle thumb, I knew he wouldn't open those beautiful brown eyes to look at me, but I still wished and prayed.

"Get better baby, I love you," I whispered in Nick's ear. I knew he was somewhere in there and he heard me. I told him about my dream last night; that we were on the beach sitting on a comfy couch at twilight sipping wine. Even though I understood he wouldn't respond, it was nice talking to Nick. Just being in his presence and feeling his warm skin gave me a little comfort. It's funny how just being in the same room with someone calmed your nerves and made you smile. Nick would always do that for me, even when he slept.

The nurses let me stay in ICU for about an hour before they kicked me out. I reluctantly walked to the waiting room just outside of the ICU. It was almost eleven and the nurses wouldn't let me back in to visit Nick until one in the afternoon. So I took my tablet out to look for baby names. This helped keep my mind busy and my hope strong.

The doctor kept Nick in a coma for a week. He had first stated he would keep him in a coma for three or four days, but then extended this time for healing purposes. I stayed at the hospital all day and evening until the nurses kicked me out. The nurses were very cordial and often allowed me more time with Nick. I would bring them coffee and snacks as a thank you. It calmed me knowing Nick was in competent, compassionate hands when I couldn't be with him.

Nick stayed the same, sleeping like an angel. I spoke to him every day; I knew he could hear me. I sensed his presence with me when I was in the room with him. I dreamed of Nick every night. Sometimes we walked on the beach (our favorite place) and sometimes we made love in our beautiful home, but every night we spoke and declared our love. I spent my days watching Nick sleep and my nights living life with Nick. I started to prefer my nights over my days other than the fact I knew they weren't real. And I wondered if Nick had the same dream, since we often had similar dreams. The knowledge of us having similar dreams got me through the days.

A week after the induced coma, the doctor wanted to meet with Nick's mom and me to discuss Nick's treatment. The doctor came in to check on Nick after dinner. He wore street clothes instead of scrubs. He had on a pair of tan dress pants and a peach colored polo shirt. Even though the doctor was about my father's age, he was a handsome man. He had a strong jaw and light blue eyes. His hair was dark with a light dusting of gray at his temples.

"I'd like to take Nick out of his coma and see how he reacts after taking him off of the medicine. It might take a little while for the medicine to wear off enough for him to be fully awake.

So don't be alarmed if he doesn't wake up after a few hours. All patients are different, so I can't give you an exact timetable. After I take him out of the coma, I'm slowly going to take him off of the ventilator, but we will monitor his breathing and his oxygen levels." The doctor raised his eyebrow looking for a response from one of us. His voice sounded hopeful.

I glanced at Nick's mom and our eyes met for a moment. She nodded her head and I followed suit. I had a sense of relief that Nick was going to be taken out of his coma. A small smile formed on my face.

"Okay doctor." My voice was soft but strong. Knowing Nick would be awake soon helped me to feel stronger and more encouraged.

"Yes, whatever you think is best." Nick's mom shook her head up and down as she wrapped her small arm around my waist for support or to help support me I didn't know.

"When will you be taking him off of the medicine?" My anticipation ran high now that Nick was going to be awake. I felt relief and anxiety at the same time. This was encouraging news, but I still had some fears deep inside of me.

"We'll do it in the morning, around 8 o' clock."

"Thank you doctor." Nick's mom put her hand out to shake the doctor's. He took her hand in his and gave it a quick shake and nodded his head. As he let go of her hand, he turned and walked out of the waiting room.

Nick's mom and I stayed with Nick the rest of the afternoon and then grabbed a quick dinner at a local restaurant. I told her I wanted to go home because I needed a good night's rest for tomorrow. She agreed with me that we both needed the rest so we would be fresh for Nick when he woke up. We ate and I paid the bill in a hurry. She hugged me tight and told me Nick would be fine and tomorrow would be a new day for all of us; the beginning of his recovery. I held onto her tight for reassurance and support. She was a strong, optimistic woman. I only wished I had half of her strength.

When I got home, I called Anna and Travis to let them know what the doctor said and they were both exuberant about the news. They said they were coming to the hospital right after work tomorrow. I also called Dave. Relief flowed through my soul talking to Dave about Nick because the two of them were so close. He reminded me of Nick and that made me more comfortable sharing my feelings with him.

"What if he doesn't fully recover?" I asked.

"Let's take this one day at a time. You need to focus on Nick waking up tomorrow and then we can think about his recovery. You are letting your mind run wild."

"I know. Thanks for listening to me." My nerves calmed a little talking with Dave.

I showered and crawled into bed. I wrapped my arms around Nick's pillow and held it tight to my body. It helped me sleep better. My thoughts were full of fear and excitement not knowing what tomorrow would bring. I prayed Nick would open his eyes tomorrow. I needed to see those beautiful brown eyes. I had 't seen Nick's soul for so long, my heart ached. Knowing I would be with him when I fell asleep helped me to relax.

We stood on a cliff looking down at the ocean. The waves crashed on the rocks and the sea sprayed up toward us. The sun started to set. The sky was a beautiful pink with clouds slashing through here and there. The sea breeze blew warm on our faces, blowing our hair back. I leaned into Nick and his arm wrapped around me. We gazed at each other and needed no words. Nick's mouth moved, but I couldn't hear him. I read his lips. He said I love you. I said I love you, but I heard my own voice. He touched my cheek with the back of his hand and then pulled my hand to his lips and kissed my palm. He kept his eyes on me and I never looked away. I leaned in to kiss Nick and before my lips touched his, I woke up. I closed my eyes and tried to travel back into my dream, but to no avail. I rolled over and glared at the clock, 6:30 a.m.

I rolled out of bed nervous about today. I made coffee and drank my first cup while I got dressed. I wanted to look good for Nick when he woke up, so I wore one of his favorite outfits; a pale pink dress that could be worn to dinner or to the office. When I looked in the mirror in the bathroom I discovered I needed more than a little makeup. My face was pale and I had dark circles under my eyes. I looked like I hadn't slept in days. I needed a makeover and more sleep. I couldn't let Nick see me like this, so I started trying to disguise the restless nights. While I worked on my face, I heard a knock at the door. I walked out of the bathroom with my empty coffee cup wondering who was here so early. I saw Dave through the glass in the door. He had a white bag in his hand and what appeared to be a plastic grocery bag in the other.

Dave smiled when I opened the door. "Morning."

"Dave, what are you doing here, I thought I would meet you at the hospital?"

"I brought breakfast for you. I know you haven't been eating right Rayna. You've lost weight." Dave closed the door behind him and walked over to put the bags on the counter. He took out bananas and grapes from the grocery bag and breakfast sandwiches from the other bag and laid everything on the counter.

"My appetite has been a little nonexistent." My voice sounded flat as I walked over to fill my cup.

Dave grabbed a cup from the cupboard and poured himself some coffee. "Rayna, you have to stay healthy for Nick and the baby. Please eat something. When he finds out how thin you've become in such a short time, he isn't going to be happy with me or you."

"You? What do you have to do with me losing weight? I peeked up at Dave as I raised my eyebrows and took a sip of coffee.

"He'd be disappointed I didn't keep my eye on you."

"I'm not your responsibility." My words came out sharp as they spilled off of my tongue. I wasn't usually short and crabby, but I was on edge because of fatigue and worry. "I'm sorry Dave. I didn't mean to be short with you."

"I understand, but Nick told me to look after you and I've not been doing a very good job."

"When did he say that?" I drew my eyebrows down as I sat my cup on the counter and waited for his answer.

"Before he went into surgery; he told me to take care of you."

I dropped my head down and put my hands on the counter, wondering why Nick would say this. I held back the tears that threatened to escape my eyes. I took a deep breath and let it out. Dave put his hands on my shoulders and gave them a small squeeze.

"He's going to be okay Rayna."

I gazed up at Dave and a tear slid down my cheek. He pulled me into his arms and held me tight against him. I wrapped my arms around his waist and buried my face into his chest and the tears ran down my cheeks.

• ♥ • ♥ • ♥ • ♥ • ♥ •

Dave and I got to the hospital shortly after the doctor had taken Nick off medication. Nick was still hooked up to all the monitors and the ventilator. We spoke with the nurses and they told us Nick could be awake in a few hours up to a few days; it was just a waiting game. We spent as long as they allowed us with him. Dave and his mom gave me a little time alone with Nick. I held his hand and told him about my dream. Nick lay still as I stroked the back of his hand. It was warm but lifeless. He looked peaceful sleeping but helpless because of the machines. He didn't look like himself with no hair and the bandages still on his head. I bend down and kissed him on the corner of his mouth. I wanted to touch his lips with mine, but the tube in his mouth stopped me from that. I kissed his cheek and then stroked it with the back of my fingers. I whispered I love you in his ear before the nurse sent me away.

Dave and Olivia insisted we have lunch, but I didn't want to go far, so we ate in the hospital cafeteria. The cafeteria was large and open. Three sides were glass. This brought in the natural light which helped make the place more airy and bright. The food wasn't bad either. I ate a green salad with pieces of chicken. Dave ordered a double cheeseburger, large fries, a milkshake, and an enormous piece of pie with ice cream. He ate the pie and ice cream first. The Lord only knew where he put the food he ate. He ate like he was a giant and never gained a pound. We talked about Nick and his recovery and when we thought he'd wake up. We all tried to be optimistic, but it was hard seeing him like this.

I picked at my food, only taking a few bites. Dave pushed me to eat, telling me I needed to keep my strength up. I understood not eating would only make things worse, so I tried to push as much food into me as possible, but I could only stomach about half of the salad. Stress, long days, short nights, and loss of appetite brought me down. I continued to have bouts of nausea that kept me from eating. My medicine and now the pregnancy had a tendency to cause nausea, so I wasn't too concerned. We dumped our trays and headed back to the ICU, hoping for Nick to be awake. He was still out, no change. Olivia stayed for most of the day but left for home around six. Dave stayed with me until after visiting hours. He insisted I go home. I argued with him I had nothing at home. It was empty. I wanted to stay at the hospital so when Nick woke up, I'd be there. The nurses assured me they would call me if he did, no matter what the time. This helped me feel more comfortable. I gave in and let Dave take me home.

"Rayna, I'm going to fix us something to eat. You should go take a hot bubble bath; maybe it'll help you relax some." Dave tucked a stray piece of hair behind my ear and lifted my chin with his index finger so he could look at me. He gave me a warm smile.

I nodded my head assuming he was right. I ran a warm tub of water and added lavender oil. I lit a few candles and turned out the light. The room did seem relaxing. Lying in the warm tub relaxed my tense muscles and helped to relieve some of the stress I'd been going through. But thinking about Nick and not knowing his prognosis, only helped the tears roll down my face again. I lay my head back and let them slide out of the corner of my eyes and down the sides of my face. I couldn't stop them, nor did I want to. It felt good letting them out in the solitude of my own bathroom with nobody around. I was tired of being strong, so I let go. I felt so alone,

I came out of the bathroom after about an hour. Dave had food ready. He made fried potatoes and fried chicken with green beans. One of my favorite home cooked meals. I sat down at the bar with my pink terry cloth robe and Dave set a plate in front of me as he walked around the bar and took a seat beside me. I was hungry tonight, so I finished most of my plate. We ate in silence. Dave smiled. Seeing me eating must make him happy.

"Dinner tasted great Dave, thank you. And you were right about the bath; it did make me feel better."

"I'm glad you feel better Rayna, but your eyes are swollen from crying. I'm moving in for a while." Dave stared at me with a blank face. No emotion, just matter of fact.

"Why would you move in? I can take care of myself." My tone sounded a little bitter, but I didn't care. I was not a child that needed to be taken care of.

"When Nick wakes up, and he sees you like this, he's going to be pissed at me and you both. You're not sleeping well and you barely eat. I told him I'd take care of you and that is exactly what I plan to do. I keep my promises."

"Do what you want Dave." I raised my eyebrows and let out a sigh in defeat. I refused to put up a fight because I realized I'd lose. I didn't have the fight in me. I got up from the stool and turned toward the steps.

"Goodnight Dave," I said as I headed up the stairs to try and sleep. My body was finished for the day, but my mind wouldn't rest.

Twenty-Three

Nick came to me again in my dreams. It was a cool evening and we strolled down a path in a park. I was under his arm and both of my arms were wrapped around his waist as we strolled down the dirt path. The fallen brown leaves crinkled under our feet and a light breeze blew through our hair. The feeling of being pressed into Nick's side was comforting. His scent filled my nose and warmed my chest. We talked about our life and about children. I wanted one and Nick wanted two. We laughed and talked while we walked as dusk fell on us. Nick stopped and wrapped both his arms around me into an embrace and pulled me tight against him. He held me and I never wanted him to let me go.........

I woke up and refused to open my eyes. I wanted to escape back into my dreams; trying to figure out where I am in Nick's strong, warm arms. I squeezed his pillow tighter and tried to make myself more comfortable, hoping I might drift off to sleep again. But I couldn't escape reality. Visions of Nick with tubes coming out of him and the sound of the beeps from the machines haunted my mind and I couldn't push them away.

I forced myself out of bed to begin the same day that I lived over and over for three weeks. It'd been a month since Nick's accident and three weeks since he'd been in a coma. He wouldn't wake up from the induced coma as planned. I went to the hospital every day and spoke with him, hoping he heard me. The doctors kept saying "any day he could wake up," but nothing changed. Dave stood by my side and supported and comforted me. The days grew longer and the nights with Nick in my dreams were too short.

Dave was now a fixture in mine and Nick's home. He moved in for the time being. It was actually great having someone there so it wasn't so quiet. He kept me company when I was home and helped keep my mind busy.

My mom touched base with me every other day. She and my dad visited me at the hospital a few times a week. They weren't thrilled when they found out I was pregnant but accepted it. They knew Nick being sick was affecting my health so they hoped for his recovery. Anna kept a close eye on me as well. She'd bring dinner with her to the hospital a couple of times a week. We'd catch up on the weekly happenings over dinner. She and Dave both knew I wouldn't eat if it hadn't been for them forcing me. Christmas came and went without much celebrating. We had dinner at the hospital and there were no gifts to be wrapped or opened. My parents wanted me to come to their house for Christmas dinner, but I refused. So they brought dinner to the hospital.

I started becoming increasingly more tired. And I'd lost a considerable amount of weight. I kept trudging on. Nick needed me and I needed to be with him every day. Even though he couldn't talk to me, I still held his hand and felt his warmth. I talked to him every day and read reviews of the band's album and concerts.

Dave stood at the stove fixing breakfast like he did every day when I walked into the kitchen. Just as the smell of breakfast touched my nose, a wave of nausea engulfed me. I held my hand over my mouth and ran to the bathroom. I didn't have anything on my stomach, so much didn't come up. Nausea came and went. I hoped it would subside soon. I took a couple of deep breaths and wiped my mouth. I brushed my teeth and when I opened the door, Dave stood there staring at me.

"You okay?" Dave had a look of worry and concern on his face as he stood at the bathroom door.

"Yeah, just a little upset stomach. It'll pass." I walked past Dave and toward the kitchen to grab some coffee.

"Can you hold down some breakfast?" Dave fixed himself a plate with eggs and sausage.

"I don't think I should try anything just yet. I'm still a little queasy. I hope I'm not getting something. I don't want to subject Nick to anything." I took a sip of coffee and waited hoping it would stay down.

Dave had taken to trying to write music while he sat at the hospital. He went through a lot of paper. The record company was on the guys wondering if Nick would be able to go on tour in a few weeks. Rick and Dave informed them of his condition and they called every week to check on him. If Nick still lay in the hospital, Dave tinkered with the idea of him singing for the tour. He did sound like him and he started to look more like him.

"The hospital will call if there are any changes Rayna; you can take a day off you know. Everybody would understand." Dave took a bite of eggs and chewed waiting for my response.

"I'll be at the hospital today. I need to continue with my life and my life is Nick. I have nowhere else to go and nothing else to do." My face was expressionless. "Besides, the doctors are doing a brain scan today on Nick. I need to be there."

"Okay, Rayna. I'll go with you. But you're going to have to take a day off soon."

I just stared at Dave with resignation. I refused to argue with him. I just wanted to go to the hospital before noon. I went to get ready and left him standing in the kitchen staring after me.

It didn't take me long to fix the damage on my face. I applied a small amount of makeup to hide the dark circles under my eyes, pulled my hair into a ponytail, and yanked on some jeans and a t-shirt. I did notice my jeans fit a little tighter around the waist even though I'd lost weight. My stomach started to grow a little bump.

We got to the hospital a little after ten in the morning. It was busy with visitors and staff going in and out of the automatic entrance doors. When we got to Nick's room, he was gone. The nurse at the desk informed us they took him for a brain scan. We waited in one of the smaller discrete waiting rooms for the doctors.

Nick was returned to his room around noon, but the doctor didn't show up until after one.

"There is some brain activity with Nick, but it's minimal."

"How long before it improves?" I asked before the doctor continued. I wrapped my arms around myself and held on tight. It helped me feel safe. Dave put his arm around my shoulder and pulled me to him.

"We're not sure it will. There is a small chance it could improve; otherwise, Nick will stay in a vegetative state or his brain activity might stop altogether. The bleed in his brain is still bleeding a small amount and the trauma from the bleed has affected his brain tremendously. Even if he comes out of his coma he will have some damage. We just aren't sure how much."

The doctor's voice grew more distant. I barely heard him. I heard Dave calling my name in the background. He sounded so far away. And then everything went black.

I was still at the hospital when I opened my eyes. I glanced around the room and saw Dave and my mother and father looking down at me. I wondered why my parents were here.

What happened to Nick? Why was I in a hospital bed? I was very groggy. I felt as if I hadn't slept in days.

"How's Nick?" My voice was loud and full of panic and fear. My mom grasps my hand and pushed the hair from my forehead. I looked from her to Dave for answers.

"He's the same Rayna; no better or no worse," Dave spoke first, his voice sounded tired.

"Why am I in a bed? What happened?"

"You collapsed when the doctor spoke about Nick's condition," Dave stood up from his chair and walked over to the foot of my bed.

"Rayna, the device in your heart isn't doing its job properly. You need that new heart baby." My mom continued to hold my hand as she spoke quietly. "But if they had a new heart today, they can't do the surgery until the baby is ready. You're going to have to stay on the heart machine."

"So I'm going to be in the hospital for six months?" I sat silent for a few moments, contemplating not being able to see Nick. This wouldn't work for me.

"I need to see Nick." My voice sounded close to hysteria and I tried again to raise up, but it was no use right now. I lay back down in defeat.

"You can't go anywhere. The doctors said you are to stay put until the heart transplant. You can't leave the hospital. Your heart might fail at any time and the doctors want you monitored at all times." My dad placed his hand on my shoulder and gazed down at me with sad eyes.

"Then I need to speak with a doctor. I wanna be in the same room as Nick. I'll pay whatever it takes. I need to be with him." Tears streamed down my face and monitors started beeping above my head.

"Calm down Rayna, you need to stay calm baby." My mother pulled her eyebrows together causing her forehead to wrinkle.

The concern on her face let me know this was serious and I needed to listen to the doctors, but I needed to be with Nick.

Nurses showed up in my room to check on me and the monitors. They told encouraged me to calm down because my heart rate was irregular. I told them I needed to speak with someone about being moved. They looked at me like I was crazy, but I knew money could do wonders. And right now, I was ready to spend some.

After fighting with my doctors and the administration for a day, Nick and I were moved to a room in which we'd be together. I could relax. I slept more with the medication and the fact I didn't leave Nick's side, but I also worried more because I constantly watched him sleep, never moving. I dreamed more of Nick and started to enjoy sleep more than being awake. Nick and I were together when I slept; talking, laughing, and loving. I'd be moved up on the heart donor list, the closer the time came for the baby since I refused to abort. The baby and I would die if my heart failed. I I knew I'd have this baby and I'd pull through. I had a tremendous amount of faith that we would both be fine. In my dreams, Nick had assured me that both the baby and I would make it. I tried to find assurance that Nick would pull through, but none would come.

Twenty-Four

Weeks passed and we saw no change in Nick. My belly started to grow and I became weaker. I felt as if I wouldn't make it at times, but my faith kept me sane. I prayed a lot. Days and nights began to collide until I couldn't decipher between the two. I slept most of the time, only waking to go to the bathroom and to eat. My mom, Anna, Nick's mom, or Dave would feed me always trying to coax more food into me. My appetite waned. I didn't want food; I only ate what I forced down for the baby.

I slept so I could be with Nick. I didn't like my reality anymore. My dreams became better, so the more I slept, the better I felt. I wished I could sleep and never wake up some days. A few times when I would open my eyes, Nick stood beside me holding my hand. And then I would realize it was his brother, Dave. His hair grew longer and shaggier making him look more and more like Nick every day. It confused me sometimes. Some days I wished Nick would wake up and be fine and other days I'd wish we would both drift off together.

In my dreams, Nick loved me as much as he did before. I always tried to follow him and he always led me back to a field where we'd spend what seemed like hours lying in the grass holding each other and talking. It was so serene. My dreams started to overlap and became my reality. Nick was better. He didn't lay in a coma anymore. Nick always by my side, we wandered around the fields and down to a lake where we watched the sunset. I awoke to a beautiful sunrise and found I still lay in Nick's arms. His arms were warm and strong wrapped around me. I still melted when his lips touched mine. We had the perfect life.

I woke up to a dim hospital room with more monitors hooked up to me. I was weak and felt like a train ran over me. I realized I must've been dreaming. I scanned the room. Nick wasn't in the bed beside me. Nick was sitting in a chair slouched down sleeping. I couldn't see his face because his hair fell over it while he slept. He must be exhausted to be sleeping on the uncomfortable hospital couch. I gazed at him in awe, just being happy that he must've gotten better while I lay unconscious.

Nick jumped up and ran out of the room. A nurse came in and checked my vitals. She told me that everyone was worried about me. My eyes grew heavy and I drifted back off to sleep. I didn't dream of Nick. I dreamed of a beautiful baby boy with dark brown hair and mysterious brown eyes; Nick's eyes.

I woke up again and this time, my mother sat in the chair and we were in a different room. She jumped up and ran over to my bed when I opened my eyes.

"Mom?" My voice came out hoarse and my throat felt dry and scratchy.

"Yes, honey. I'm here." My mom kissed my forehead and grabbed my hand and held it. I still had monitors hooked to me, as well as oxygen.

"Where's Nick?" I scanned the room for him, but couldn't find him.

"Let me get the doctor. We've been waiting for you to wake up."

"Mom, where's Nick?" My words shorter and more to the point this time, but she still didn't answer me. She turned and hurried out the door ignoring me. I lay there wondering why she acted so odd.

My mom and a doctor walked back into the room. Nick walked in behind them. I let out a sigh and relaxed when I saw him, only to gasp as he got nearer. It wasn't Nick at all, it was Dave. My God, he looked like Nick right now with his hair long and shaggy. Where could Nick be? Of course he had to be here.

I glanced at Dave this time and asked where Nick was. He glanced at my mom but didn't respond. The doctor checked my vitals and my monitors.

"How are you feeling Rayna?"

"Like a semi drove over my chest. What happened? Why do I feel so bad?"

"A donor came through and you had your heart transplant. That was after you delivered a beautiful baby boy." The doctor smiled at me and waited for my response. I gazed from him to my mom and then to Dave. A tear trickled out of my eye, knowing I had a baby boy; of course that would be where Nick was; with our son.

"When can I see him?"

"He's in an incubator right now and you need to rest. He was born very early because of your heart. You both would've died if we didn't do an emergency cesarean. Your heart began to fail rapidly. You actually fell into a coma for a few weeks. But you've done wonderful for just giving birth and getting a heart transplant a week ago."

I gazed at the doctor in awe not knowing how my baby survived when I remembered only being a few months pregnant. I realized my days and nights were getting confused and couldn't be sure of how many nights I'd been in the hospital because most of the time I slept.

"How long have I been here?"

"You've been in the hospital for two months Rayna. You were in and out of it before you slipped into the coma; you slept most of the time. Your body became weak because of the baby and your heart. But a donor came through, so we had to take the baby. We hoped the baby would be strong enough, and so far the baby has gained some weight and his lungs are starting to develop beautifully."

"When can I see him?" This brought some excitement to me. I wanted to hold my beautiful baby boy.

"You're healing very well. I think in the next couple of days you'll be released so you can see him then. He's at Children's Hospital."

"A couple of days?"

"I took some pictures of him Rayna." My mom moved closer to my bed and pulled her phone out for me.

I examined the pictures. He was so small and weak. He had to make it. I already loved him. I loved him the moment the doctor informed me of my pregnancy.

"He's beautiful." I smiled and continued looking at the pictures. "Is that where Nick is? With the baby?

"We need to figure out a name for him Rayna. You might have a name picked out, but sometimes looking at your child helps you to decide." My mom avoided my question again.

"Where's Nick? Stop avoiding my questions." I demanded

"We need to tell her." Dave glanced over at my mother and finally at me. He walked over to my bed and picked up my hand to hold. "Rayna, Nick didn't make it. He passed away a week ago. I'm so sorry."

"No, no that can't be. I saw him when I was in the ICU. He slept in the chair."

"That was me Rayna. Nick is gone. We waited for you to wake up to plan his funeral."

"Before or after my heart transplant?"

Dave and my mom gazed at each other and back at me. They both stood silent for a moment.

"Before your transplant. My mom and I decided it would be better to let him go."

"Why didn't you wait until I woke up? I needed to be with him; to say goodbye!" I almost yelled now and tears streamed down my cheeks. I'd been robbed of telling Nick goodbye.

"Rayna, Nick was close to being gone for weeks; he had little brain activity. After you went into your coma, his brain activity stopped completely." Dave tried to make me understand, but I couldn't comprehend what difference a few days made.

"But I needed to say goodbye," I said between sobs.

"Rayna, there wasn't much we could do. Nick filled out papers before his surgery. He placed his name on the donor list if something happened to him. He was a perfect match." Dave ran his hands through his hair and moved his eyes away from me.

The room grew quiet. I gazed from Dave to my mom and then back to Dave. Reality set in. I understood now who my donor was. I thought I might be falling into a horrible nightmare I couldn't wake up from. The room spun. I heard a strange noise. I realized it was me gasping for breath.

Dave took my hand in both of his hands. I pulled my hand from Dave's and covered my face with them. Tears streamed down my face. I couldn't stop them. I sobbed. I couldn't stop the convulsion of my body. My chest hurt and the heart monitor beeped faster, but it must've not been anything of concern; nobody else rushed in. My mom pushed my hair back from my forehead.

"It's going to be okay honey."

"No it's not. Nick was my life. He was my everything. Now he is gone forever because of me; I can't live without him."

"That's not true Rayna. Nick was already gone. He gave you the gift of life. Now I truly understand how much he really loved you. He gave you his heart forever." My mom's voice came out soft, but shaky. It sounded like she was crying, but I didn't look.

"You can and you will. You have a little boy to raise; Nick's boy." Dave was stern. "You have two pieces of Nick with you forever; his child and his heart."

I continued to sob and sob. I rolled over and curled up into a ball and held my knees to my chest. Dave rubbed my back trying to console me; it didn't help. Even though I just received a new heart, it was breaking.

I lay in this position for a long time. I didn't really know for how long. Lunch and dinner had been served and the moon shone through the window, but I still lay curled up in a ball in bed without putting any food in my body. I drifted in and out of sleep. I tried to find Nick in my dreams. I called for him. I looked for him but I couldn't find him.

"Rayna." I listened to a soft voice that sounded like Nick. I thought I might be hallucinating, but then a warm hand touched my shoulder and I turned to see who touched me. It was Dave, standing there looking down at me with a forced smile on his face. He looked tired and weary.

"We need to make the arrangements for Nick." His voice was just above a whisper. I saw the sadness in his eyes.

"You do it. I can't. I trust you Dave." I forced the words out. I didn't want to speak to anyone or see anyone. I wanted to be left alone. I only answered him so he would leave. Nick didn't come to me in my dreams anymore. That was the only thing I had left since he had slipped into a coma. Now those were gone. I wouldn't see him anymore. Nick was gone from this world; my world.

Twenty-Five

♥

I was released from the hospital the evening before the funeral. Dave and his mom, Olivia, made all the arrangements. I couldn't try to make decisions on how to say goodbye to Nick. That would mean I had to face reality, and I wasn't able to.

My mom picked me up from the hospital and took me to a suite in a hotel she rented for a few weeks. I had to go to the hospital daily for my rehab treatment, she wanted to be close. I wanted to stay at Olivia's. My mom didn't fight me on this and Dave gave me and my mom his room. He said he could always stay at mine and Nick's place. I stayed away from our place; being there would bring back to many memories.

My mother bought me a new black pantsuit for the funeral. She also rented a limo that took us to the funeral. It arrived at Olivia's around one in the afternoon. My dad, Dave, Olivia, my mom, and I rode in the limousine on a cold and snowy day. The snowflakes danced all around my head as I stepped out into the dreary day. The day fit the way I felt; cold, dark, and gloomy.

I buried my husband in the middle of March with the weather still snowy. I had seven months with him, nine if you count the time in the hospital. I hoped to spend the rest of my life with Nick, not less than a year. I honestly didn't know how

I'd go on. I moved around in a trance and did what people told me to do; like a robot.

We arrived at the funeral home early for a private viewing with a small group of family and friends. I was still recuperating from the transplant and the grief of losing Nick, so I was fatigued. I leaned on Anna and my mom for support. Dave guided his mother who also had a rough time with the loss of Nick. Jeff, Travis, and Rick were waiting for us outside the funeral home. The funeral director met us at the door. My feet didn't want to move. They were concreted onto the tile floor. Anna and my mom pulled me along; my feet moved like bricks.

With heavy steps, we moved into the room. I saw the casket ahead. The room became a tunnel that seemed like it would never end. We started up the aisle between the chairs. Tears flowed down my face. Anna handed me a tissue. Everyone stepped over to make room for me as I staggered forward. There Nick was, lying lifeless in the shiny black casket Dave picked out. He wore a dress shirt and his hands were crossed at his midsection. He didn't look like the beautiful Nick that I remembered. They placed a wig on Nick that resembled his hair before they shaved it. His swollen face and discoloration made my new heart hurt; Nick's heart hurt. I held one hand to Nick's heart that now beat in my chest like a bass drum.

I touched Nick's face with my other hand. That's all it took. I crumbled. I lay across Nick and sobbed until I couldn't sob anymore. Dave pulled me away from the casket and held me. My knees buckled and he caught me, picked me up like a small child and carried me out to the car. He placed me in the backseat of the limo. I curled up into a ball on the seat. He covered me with a blanket and kissed my forehead and left. My mother slid into the seat beside me and held me. I'm not sure how long we sat in the car before Dave came back out to retrieve me for the funeral service. Time didn't mean anything anymore. I sat in the front for the service, feeling like I lived in an alternative universe. Voices sounded far away while I sat and stared at the casket, hoping I'd wake up from this nightmare. And then the service ended and the paul bearers lifted Nick from the stand and carried him out.

My dad took my arm and helped me from the chair and guided me toward the door. The funeral home was packed with people. I can't remember their faces; my brain drifted in a fog. People hugged me and gave their condolences. I tried to force a smile, but it wouldn't happen. My face stayed frozen in a state of sorrow. My dad put me into the car where I lay my head back once again. Dave put his mom in the car and then he slid in beside her. The car started moving forward driving Nick to his final destination.

We arrived at the burial spot on the hill. I didn't know how I'd face this. My father guided me out of the car and across the lawn to a chair. Black suits moved slowly as they carried the black shiny casket to its grave. They placed Nick in the spot where he'd be lowered into the cold hard ground.

My mother sat on one side of me and Olivia on the other. I kept my head down; it became too difficult to look at the black death box anymore. Olivia sobbed. I didn't think my body contained any more tears. I sat motionless like a zombie. Anna sat behind me with a hand on my shoulder.

The service started. The minister spoke about ashes to ashes and dust to dust. I never really heard what he said. I just stared motionless ahead, not really looking at anything. A twenty-one gun salute was fired for Nick since he served in the military. The sound of the guns going off caused me to jump. The tears and sobs began again when they started to lower Nick into the ground. Each member of the band placed some dirt on Nick's grave as they lowered him down. Anna put a flower on his casket. I didn't want to move, but I wanted to give him one last gift from me. So I forced myself to stand up and move to place a rose on his casket as they lowered him down into the dirt. I never wiped the tears away; I let them fall as the love of my life disappeared into the ground. I don't know how long I stood there, but Nick now lay at the bottom.

Somebody wrapped their arms around me and turned me to guide me back to the car. I peered up; Dave held me up. I threw my arms around him and never wanted to let go. He was the closest to Nick I'd ever have. I cried and cried. Snowflakes blew around us like a snow globe, but I didn't feel the cold; I was too numb. Dave didn't rush me. He stood holding me for however long I wanted. After a while, I let my arms down and Dave guided me to the limo.

At Olivia's house, friends and family gathered for condolences for the family. People brought in food that filled counters and the table. I had Dave take me directly to the bedroom. All I wanted to do was sleep. He got a fan out of the closet to help drown out some of the noise from the gathering. I lay down on the bed and curled into a ball. He took my shoes off and covered me with a blanket.

"Is there anything you need? You need to eat something."

"No, I'm fine. Just really tired."

Dave pushed the hair off of my forehead and leaned in and kissed the top of my head.

"I'll be right outside if you need anything. You can text me on your phone." Dave set my phone on the nightstand before he left.

It was dark when I woke up. I checked my phone for the time. It was eight in the evening. My throat dry from crying, I got up to find something to drink. The house sounded quiet so I suspected everyone left. Dave and my mom sat at the table drinking coffee or tea when I went out to the living room.

"Where's Olivia?" I whispered.

"She just went to lie down. All the company and the day's events wore her out." Dave said in a soft tone. "How are you feeling?"

"Tired." My mom and Dave glanced at each other.

"You need to eat something Rayna. I'll fix something for you." My mother said.

"I'm not hungry; just thirsty."

"Would you like to go visit the baby after your rehab tomorrow?"

"Yes, that's fine." I didn't want to talk, so I kept my conversation short. I drank a cup of water down and filled it up again to take back to bed with me. I walked back to the bedroom without saying another word to either of them; too numb and tired to care about anything right now. I wanted to close my eyes and not wake back up to this nightmare.

Nick didn't visit my dreams anymore. He was gone from this world and my dreams. I hoped every night I would see him again, but it was like he disappeared. I wandered around in my dreams like I wandered around when I was awake. When I was awake, he was gone and reality hurt along with my chest. But in my dreams, I searched everywhere, but to no avail, Nick had vanished. All I had left were my memories and the things that reminded me of him.

I went to rehab the next day and then to see the baby. I still needed to think of a name. Olivia and Dave met us in the lobby of the hospital. Olivia and then Dave gave me a hug. He held on tight and it felt good and bad at the same time. Being in the strong arms of a man brought back memories of Nick and it hurt.

"Are we ready?" My mom said.

"Yes, I want to visit my grandson again." Olivia forced a smile.

I gazed at both of them. I tried to make myself excited about this, but my only thoughts were of the baby being in an incubator with a breathing machine; I couldn't take another tragedy. I was afraid to have too much hope and be let down because the baby didn't make it.

We got off of the elevator on the floor for the premature babies. My mother and Olivia visited the baby before today, so they knew which way to go. Dave walked beside me while the two grandmothers walked in the front.

We reached the nursery and my mother spoke with a nurse. She told us only two at a time could go in. So since I was the mother and Dave hadn't seen his nephew yet, we went in first. They told us to put on blue gowns, face masks, booties, and a blue hat before we went into the nursery. I felt like I was getting dressed to do major surgery, but they explained to us the babies didn't have a good enough immune system to handle outside germs, so they took every precaution.

Five babies lay in incubators. Dave and I stood and gazed around at the small little bodies hooked up to multiple medical devices and inside a glass casket. A nurse guided us to my baby boy. He lay still; asleep I assumed. He was a little guy in an incubator with wires and tubes in his arms and up his nose. He also had a ventilator on. It frightened me looking at him so weak and fragile.

"You can touch him if you'd like. It's very helpful for him to have human contact. He's still too small for holding, but that'll come soon enough. The more touch he gets, the quicker his recovery will be." The nurse smiled at me.

"How do I do that?" I stared at the nurse hoping for guidance.

She showed me and Dave how to place our hands through the hole in the incubator to touch my little boy. He moved a little when I touched him, his skin warm. He wore a little blue hat on his head to help his warmth to stay with him. Just touching him made my heart feel a little warmer than it had been the last several days. Some of the numbness left when I touched my child's skin. He opened his eyes and looked at me. My heart automatically warmed. I felt a hint of joy trying to break free. But I was scared to let him into my heart because he was so fragile. I might lose him as well. A tear of happiness and one of sorrow escaped my eye. I thought I cried all of my tears away; I didn't think I had anything left. Seeing all I had left of Nick made the emotions seep up out of my soul I thought I buried with Nick. Dave stood beside me the entire time. He squeezed my arm when he saw me crying.

"Would you like to touch your nephew?" I took my hands away from the baby and wiped my tears away and looked at Dave.

"Very much." Dave moved over closer to the incubator and placed his hands into the small incubator.

He smiled as the baby grasped his finger with his little hand. Dave's finger appeared so huge compared to the baby's. I smiled when I saw Dave smile. It warmed my heart. I think I realized at that moment Dave suffered from as much loss as I did; he lost his only brother.

We spent some more time with the baby and then Dave let my mother and his mother come in to be with the baby. As I observed each person interact with him, I knew he had many people to love him. Just like Nick did. They would all be here for him and me. I could see that. I realized what I would name him as I watched my family interact with my son, He looked like a little Nick. I would name him Nicholas Scott Perry II. He was Nick's son, so he would be named after him; he would be his namesake. He would also be a constant reminder that Nick existed and our love was as real as he was. I can't be sure what it was, I think maybe God, let a feeling of joy and comfort consume me while I stood in the presence of my child. A strong sense of faith and hope overwhelmed me that gave me encouragement he would make it.

The days that followed were exhausting. I went to visit Nicky every day and then to rehab. I'd try to eat healthy for my heart and for Nicky. I'd go back to Olivia's in the evening and go to bed. I slept almost fifteen hours a day. When I was away from the hospital, I slept, life became easier that way. I didn't have to think about Nick. The next day I would do it all over again. Nicky gave me a reason to survive, but when Nicky and I were separated, it was difficult to exist.

My mother spent the days with me and Olivia at the hospital. She'd go back to the hospital in the evenings to be with Nicky when I went to bed. Dave and the band needed to finish the tour because the record company pushed them every day. They sunk a lot of money into the band and wanted to make their money back. Dave pulled Nick's lyrics off. Unless you met both of them, you wouldn't be able to hear a difference in their voices.

I stayed as long as I could at the hospital with my little boy Nicky every night. He grew a little each day and got a little stronger. He ate from a bottle now and I could hold him. The nurses encouraged me to hold him in a kangaroo hold. I'd lay Nicky on my chest, close to his father's heart, under my shirt. Skin to skin contact would nurture him and help him thrive. I understood skin to skin contact and bonding. It was extremely intimate, so I understood why my little boy would bond with me and heal.

I didn't know how I'd be able to deal with reality if I didn't have Nicky, He helped me want to get out of bed every morning and try to live life. But it was hard. The depression started to seep back in. I visited Nicky and slept. I did nothing else. My mother pushed me to find a house, but I ignored her and went to bed. I didn't have to think when I slept. Thinking caused me pain. I walked around like a zombie. I did what was necessary to act human and that was all.

Finally, weeks after the funeral, Anna and I stayed at mine and Nick's place for the first time. I didn't sleep well, but I needed to try and stay here because Nicky would be coming home in the next couple of months and I needed to have a nursery set up for him.

I unlocked the door I hadn't opened in months. It was strange being here without Nick. I opened the door and stepped inside. Everything looked the same. I don't know why I expected that anything had changed. Dave had been the only one here with my mother to get things for me. Without Nick, it stood empty and void.

"Do you want something to drink?" I glanced over at Anna as I carried bags of groceries to the counter.

"Yes, that'd be great." Anna put her bags of groceries on the counter and started putting things away.

I poured us each a soda and she got utensils out for us to eat our Chinese. I turned the TV on for some noise, it was too quiet here. We ate our food and talked about Nicky and how beautiful he was. Anna wanted to have me a baby shower, but I was really against it because having a party meant entertaining people. I convinced her to wait until I brought him home. I still tried being careful about getting hopeful. I went to the hospital every day and I began to bond with him deeply, but I refused to celebrate yet. I would never make it through another loss.

"Have you found a house yet?" Anna set her drink down on the counter.

"My mother has found a few she likes. She showed them to me, but I haven't made a decision yet. I understand I need to find a home for me and Nicky, but it's so hard to function."

"I can help you narrow it down." Anna offered.

"I need to pick one and let her get the process started. They're all nice, but I want to make sure I pick the perfect one. I told my mother I wanted a week to think about it and then maybe see the three I like again. I can show them to you on the internet." I set my drink down and walked over to pick up my tablet.

I opened the bookmarked pages and showed Anna the three houses I might consider. Anna liked all of them but liked the one with three bedrooms best so that she could stay over with me and Nicky. It did make sense to have three bedrooms so I had room for company.

Later that night, I laid down in mine and Nick's bed. I tried to hold back the tears, but it became more than I could stand and they began flowing. I had shut down my emotions so I could be there for Nicky, but now I let the tear waterworks flood. My whole body shook with sobs. I don't know how long I cried, it seemed like hours. I cried myself to sleep. I found myself in an empty room and no way to get out. It frightened me, I couldn't find a door. I woke up screaming.

"Rayna, are you okay? Anna looked down at me.

My clothes were soaked with sweat. "Just a bad dream." I wiped the sweat from my forehead with the back of my hand.

Anna stayed with me that night in mine and Nick's bed. She held me while I cried myself to sleep again; afraid of having the nightmare once more. But I did fall asleep; this time with no dreams or nightmares.

Anna stayed with me again for the next three nights. Nightmares invaded my sleep each night. I woke Anna up all three nights with my screaming. I started to grow fatigued from the restless nights and everything here brought memories back to my mind constantly. I found no relief.

I decided to go back to Olivia's until I purchased a house. I made the decision it was too hard to stay at Nick's place. Too many memories lived there. I'd always keep my memories of Nick, but they danced everywhere in the garage. I couldn't think because everything I looked at or touched made me break down and cry. It caused me too much stress and pain, so I searched for a new place.

Of course Olivia welcomed me back with open arms and I tried to take my mom's advice about keeping busy with the house purchasing. I decided on the three bedrooms. It had been foreclosed on by the bank, so I'd be able to buy it quickly. Anna and my mother took care of the moving company for me while I visited with Nicky.

I talked to Dave on the phone a couple of times a week. He wanted to know how Nicky was doing, but never asked me how I was doing. He knew not to ask. He understood how I was doing. I finished rehab and now had a new lease on life but I didn't understand how I was going to live with part of my life now gone.

The pain of losing Nick was still strong. The nights were the longest. But at least at Olivia's, I didn't have nightmares, although I cried myself to sleep every night. If not for Nicky, I couldn't see myself getting up each morning, but knowing he needed me, and I needed him, gave me the motivation to go on.

Twenty-Six

The purchase of the house went through without any difficulties in late June. With the keys to my new home, I moved in the same day. The movers brought everything and my dad, mom, Anna, her mom, and Olivia helped me to settle in. Nicky would be coming home in a week so I needed everything unpacked and put away. Anna just arrived back from the west where she flew out to visit the band for a few days. She was still in school, but she went to class and helped me in the evening with the unpacking. My mom and dad took a few days off from work to help and Olivia showed up after work. Everyone was determined to make sure Nicky and I were comfortable. Anna even planned the baby shower with everything else she did. We would host the shower a few days after he came home.

I got the house at a steal since the bank foreclosed. A beige colonial-style home with dark brown shutters and a large solid mahogany door accenting the house. It sat on an acre of land that was flat with rolling hills in the back. The forest sprung up about 200 yards behind the house. It was the last house on a dead end street. When you opened the huge mahogany door, you stepped into a beautiful entryway. A set of steps led up to the bedrooms. On each side of the entryway was a large opening; to the left was the living room and to the right a dining room. Walking through either one would lead you to the kitchen in the back of the house.

The kitchen was my favorite part with lots of cherry cabinets. The counters were dark brown granite and the floors were beige tile. I had a small breakfast nook table in the huge kitchen, but no dining table in the dining room. All of the extra amenities anybody desired were included in the design of the kitchen. The laundry room was just off the kitchen with a small bathroom and led out to the two stall garage.

I bought a new bed for my room and took mine and Nick's bed for the spare bedroom. I thought I'd sleep better in a new bed that Nick and I hadn't shared. Nicky's nursery was next to mine where we had everything set up.

My mother fixed dinner as Anna and I unpacked things in my room. Nick's boxes were all packed in the garage. I wanted Dave to be with me when I went through his things. I figured he'd want a lot of it. I kept a few of his shirts and hid them back in my closet. I wanted something to remind me of him. I also kept his wedding band and the gold chain necklace I bought him. I had our infinity necklaces put together as one and I wore them around my neck.

"Dinner!" My mom called from downstairs. It seemed like old times having her cooking us dinner and calling for us.

"We better go before she yells again." Anna smiled at me and picked up an empty box.

"Yep," I said and picked up another box to carry downstairs to add to the pile. I followed Anna down the stairs. I tried to keep my face looking like no pain lived in my heart, but it became difficult at times. I knew Anna saw through me, but she ignored it for my sake.

My mom made one of my favorites; Cajun chicken, and mashed potatoes with green beans. I was a little hungry and I had lost some weight; enough that people started to make comments. So I tried to eat for my sake and my mother's sanity. Olivia arrived right after we sat down.

"Come join us for dinner." My father said as he led Olivia into the kitchen.

"Dinner looks wonderful Carrie." Olivia grabbed a plate from the cabinet and walked over and kissed my cheek. "How are you today dear?"

"Okay." I placed a piece of my mom's chicken on my plate.

"You look really tired Rayna." My mom said after she took a bite of potatoes.

"I'm okay. I do have a new heart remember." I put on a fake smile and took a bite of food.

"I know that Rayna, but you do look tired."

"Well if Nick hadn't left me alone to live our life then I wouldn't be so tired."

"Rayna," my father reprimanded me.

I ignored him. "I guess I should feel blessed I have a healthy heart because I'm gonna need it to raise Nicky without a father."

"When are the boys coming home Anna?" Olivia tried to change the subject. But I did want to hear when they would be home.

"In about two weeks. They have a few shows this week out in California and then they'll start heading back. They'll stop and perform a couple of shows on their way back. So they should be back by the middle of July."

"That's wonderful. Dave's been missing his nephew. Nicky will be home by then, so it works out wonderfully. They've been gone for so long. I miss them all." Olivia said. She smiled at me as she stabbed her fork into a piece of chicken.

We finished dinner and Anna and I cleaned the kitchen. She helped me finish my bedroom while my parents completed the guest room. Olivia stayed and helped for a while and then headed home. Even though I let her collect the Nick's royalties on the band's album, she still got up early for work everyday. I kept the royalties from Nick's songwriting for Nicky.

Over the next several days, my parents and Anna worked in my house while I went to help take care of Nicky. My mom and dad or Olivia would go and visit with Nicky and help care for him when I came back to the house in the evening. They all enjoyed this time with him. Anna helped me in the evenings with the house. I slept a little better since I moved into the house. Anna stayed with me so I think that helped a lot. I didn't dream at all. I actually got a few restful nights of sleep.

The day I brought Nicky home, my parents went with me. It was wonderful to bring him home after all this time. I was so happy my little baby fought so hard and lived. I was able to bring him home and hold him without all of the IVs, monitors, and apparatuses. We brought dinner home that night and just enjoyed holding and bonding with the little guy. Still a little guy, he weighed 7 lbs. now and he had grown to 21 inches long. He was like a newborn baby, even though he was born months ago and fought hard to survive. He was a little fighter; my little fighter. A single mother of a little fighter, so I guess I needed to become a fighter as well.

I had a full house for the baby shower. My family, friends, and Nick's family and friends showed up to meet Nicky and bring him a gift. A few of the guests even brought a house-warming gift for my new home. Some of them were too much, but I appreciated all of them. Anna and her mom put the whole thing together; their gift to me and Nicky. They did a wonderful job. I was blessed to have such wonderful people in my life.

Olivia gave me Nick's baby rocking chair. She had the chair refinished for him. The gesture brought tears to my eyes for

Nicky to own something that belonged to his father as a child. It brought all of my feelings for Nick to the forefront. Every time I looked at Nicky, it brought tears to my eyes because he had his father's beautiful brown eyes. I would always be able to gaze into those beautiful eyes of Nick's through Nicky.

Dave was excited about the new house and Nicky coming home. He couldn't wait until the tour finished. He asked if he could stay with me. He wanted to spend as much time as possible with Nicky. I told him yes because it would be comforting having someone else in this big house. Plus, I missed Dave; he'd been gone so long.

Dave showed up the next week. He brought presents for me and Nicky. He bought me some beautiful picture frames for pictures of Nicky and he bought Nicky some outfits, toys, and his first pair of cowboy boots. They were so cute.

"How'd you find the place? I asked him as I opened the door. Dave looked more like Nick than he ever had. His hair had grown longer and shaggier like Nick's. He had the same dark brown eyes that Nick and Nicky had. He took my breath for a moment.

"Not too hard to find. You gave me good directions." He smiled as he stepped inside and set his packages down.

"But it's dark. I figured you'd get lost and need to call me." I forced a smile.

Dave pulled me into a huge hug. "I've missed you Rayna."

"I missed you too. Having you around for a while will be awesome. Are you hungry?" I let go of Dave and he picked his stuff up to follow me.

"Starving."

"Do you want to order pizza or eat leftover chicken Alfredo?."

"I'll take the alfredo. We eat pizza a lot on the road. Where's Nicky?" Dave searched the kitchen looking for the baby.

"He's napping. He should be up soon. He'll be ready for his dinner."

"I can't wait to see him." Dave smiled as he sat down on one of my wooden stools at the bar.

I fixed Dave's plate while he filled me in about the tour and the next album.

"We're hoping to start on the new album in a couple of months," Dave said. He took a bite of food.

"Already? Wow, that'd be great." I poured myself some iced tea.

"Yeah, it could take a while to put it together. The record company doesn't want to lose any momentum." He took another bite. "This Alfredo is fantastic."

"You can thank Gio's. Anna and I got take out yesterday." I heard Nicky. "There's your nephew," I smiled and put my cup down, and went to get him.

"I've missed you little guy," He smiled and took Nicky into his loving arms and rocked him while I fixed his bottle.

Dave enjoyed feeding Nicky. It warmed my heart watching him care for my son. At least I knew he would have a male role model other than his grandfather.

After Dave finished feeding Nicky, he leaned him up against his knees and talked to him like a little adult. I sat and enjoyed the show. It was encouraging watching the two of them bond. Dave helped me bathe him and dress him for bed. He showed a lot of interest in him.

I got Nicky to bed and then showed Dave where he'd be sleeping. I didn't sleep well the first night without Anna. I tossed and turned and woke up from a bad dream. I searched for Nick again without any avail. It disturbed me looking for him everywhere but never able to find him. I always looked for him in a beautiful empty house, empty mall, or out in the dark woods. The woods were the worse. It was creepy.

When I woke up I went to check on Nicky. He woke me up most mornings, but I didn't hear him this morning. I panicked. When I checked the bassinet, I panicked, even more, when he wasn't there.

"Dave!" I screamed as I ran down the stairs.

"In here," Dave called from the kitchen.

I ran into the kitchen and there Dave stood holding Nicky as he beat eggs in a bowl.

"Hungry?" He asked with a huge smile on his face.

"I couldn't find Nicky. I was scared to death." I took a deep breath and went over to take him from Dave's arms.

"I heard you last night in your sleep, so I didn't think you slept well. When I woke up, Nicky began fussing, so I brought him down and feed him so you could rest. Sorry if I scared you." Dave smiled at me. His smile brightened my day a bit.

"Thank you. I don't sleep well most nights. It helped when Anna stayed with me. I thought maybe the nightmares were over."

"You two get dressed and come back down for breakfast. I make a mean omelet." Dave smiled that smile again. He looked more like Nick than I had realized.

II took Nicky up and dressed him and then myself and then came down for a filling breakfast with Dave.

· ♥ · ♥ · ♥ · ♥ · ♥ ·

Dave and I spent the day playing with Nicky and talking about the house. Olivia was coming over tonight to fix dinner for us; her famous lasagna. It felt good having Dave around. I had missed him and he made me laugh a little. I hadn't laughed in quite a while. He told me the guys and Anna wanted to hang out this weekend. I dreaded it a little bit because I knew being with them would bring back strong memories. But I knew I couldn't keep putting the guys off. We had become a family. They all wanted to see Nicky.

As usual, Olivia's lasagna was delicious.

"You fixed dinner mom, I got the dishes," Dave said.

"I'll help," I said. "I don't think Olivia will object to watching Nicky while we clean the kitchen." I smiled at her.

"Not at all. I love spending time with my favorite grandchild." She grinned from ear to ear. "We'll be in the living room." Olivia talked to Nicky on her way out of the kitchen.

After Dave and I finished the dishes, he told me he had something for me.

"What is it?" I was curious what he'd brought for me.

Dave walked over and took an envelope out of his messenger bag.

"It's a letter from Nick," He handed me the sealed envelope.

I stood still for a moment in shock. What did he mean a letter from Nick? How could that be?

"How?" I gawked at him in disbelief.

"He wrote it before he went into surgery Rayna. He asked me to give this to you if anything happened to him. I kept it because so much was going on after the funeral and I didn't think you could take any more. I never read it, but I have an idea what it says."

I took the envelope from his hand and read my name on the front. Nick's handwriting stared back at me. A tear welled up in my left eye and slid down my cheek. I continued looking at the writing and turned out of the kitchen and headed for the stairs and slowly walked up to my room.

I sat down on my bed and stared at the envelope. Nick had written me a letter before his surgery; the surgery he never woke up from. My hands trembled as I held the letter. I turned it over and slid my finger under the flap. I eased the envelope open bit by bit. I let it fall to the floor as I unfolded the page with the last words Nick had written.

"Rayna, love of my life,

You just left for the evening and I have surgery in the morning. I understand you didn't want to leave, but you need your rest princess. I spoke with a doctor after you left and asked him to run some tests for me. The day I looked into your eyes my life changed. You changed my life. You made me see the world in a whole new way. I view the world through a lover's eyes. My gray skies turned to fabulous blue since the day you walked into my world. The happiest day of my life was the day you became my wife. I know we have only been married for a short while, but it has been amazing.

Knowing you need a new heart to keep you alive has motivated me to become a donor. To lose you would throw me into a hell I could never escape. So I would be forever grateful to whoever decided to give you their heart and keep you by my side. So I would like to be that lifesaver for someone else.

The doctor came back in today before you came in. He explained to me that my heart was 99 percent compatible with you. I guess you were right about us being twin flames. We match perfectly in every aspect; our bodies, minds, and souls. You are my true soul mate. So I made the decision that if I don't pull through this surgery, you will take my heart. And they will give me your heart. You will own my heart forever; literally. I need you to be alive, healthy, and strong if I don't make it. You have my child to raise. I gave you my heart the day I met you, now you will keep it forever. I love you.

I asked Dave to be there for you and to help raise our child. He has agreed to do what I ask. He hasn't read this letter, but he knows what my plans are if I pass.

Please Rayna, try to go on living your life happy. I know it'll be hard because I realize how connected we are. But you must for our child. Please tell our child how much I love him or her and I would have loved to meet our prince or princess. Also, please tell our child how much I loved their mother.

Rayna, I love you today, tomorrow, and forever. There is more after this life. The love I have for you today, I will take with me. Please know that in your heart. I will love you no matter where I am; forever.

In time, I hope you will find love again. I realize it won't be what we shared; you only have one twin flame. I hope you can at least find somebody to love in some way; somebody that will love you the way you deserve to be loved.

I will carry your love forever; until we meet on the other side.

All my love,

Nick.

The paper was wet from my tears. I read the letter again and again until I couldn't see through my eyes. I folded the letter and pulled it to my chest. I curled up on my bed in the fetal position. This letter brought back so many feelings I had tried to repress.

I didn't know how long I lay there. Dave showed up. He didn't say anything. He just lay down beside me and held me while I sobbed.

Twenty-Seven

I walked on the white sand beach with Nick. The roar of the ocean was thunderous. We walked hand in hand along the shore while the water tickled our feet. We stopped and Nick held my face in his hands. He spoke to me but I couldn't hear him over the sound of the surf. I read his lips when he said I love you forever. He leaned down and kissed me and I woke up. I hadn't dreamed about Nick in months; since he left this world. It was wonderful to be with him again. To feel his lips on mine and for him to say I love you.

I lay still wrapped in Dave's arms. It was weird being in his arms and dreaming about Nick. It felt similar being in Dave's and being in Nick's arms. I don't know how long we slept, but the moonlight beamed through the window now.

Although I couldn't hear Nick, I understood what he said. I jumped from the bed and startled Dave.

"What's the matter?" Dave gazed at me with concern.

"I need to write something down. Nick told me to." I hurried out of the room to find paper to write down what Nick told me.

Olivia stood at the sink in the kitchen bathing Nicky. "Are you okay Rayna darling?" Olivia glanced at me as she wrapped Nicky in a towel.

"Yes, grabbing paper to write on." I stopped and glanced at Olivia and Nicky. I smiled because I was genuinely happy for the first time in months. I had a beautiful son and a wonderful mother-in-law. I walked over and kissed her cheek. "Thank you for taking care of Nicky."

"My pleasure. I love this little guy."

I sat at the table and hurriedly wrote down what Nick said; the words were beautiful. Dave came into the kitchen and over to the table. He took the paper from my hand and read it. He stared at me in astonishment for a moment.

"Rayna, this is a song. When did you start writing music?"

"Just now. I dreamed of Nick and I woke up with these words. I think he gave them to me."

Dave gazed at me for a minute like I was crazy. Then he smiled. "Can you do this again?"

"I don't know. I somehow knew I needed to write the words down on paper. It's like they busted out of me." Joy spilled out of me. Nick spoke through me and it was the greatest pleasure I experienced in a long time. I ran upstairs to find Nick's song journal. He had some songs he didn't finish and I wanted to try and do it again.

I came back down to the kitchen with Nick's journal and opened it up. I searched through and found an unfinished song. Without hesitation, I understood what the words should be. I grabbed another piece of paper and copied Nick's words and finished the start of his song; just like that. I had never written a song in my life, but the words flowed from my brain to the page like I was a writer all my life.

Dave took the sheet from me and read the words. "Rayna, this is amazing. You are writing the band's songs for the new album. How are you doing this?" Dave's face was full of wonder and excitement.

"I think Nick is speaking through me."

"I read about people who receive a donor organ discovering new talents, but I never believed it. Wow! I am going to try and put some music to this tonight."

"Okay, I'll put Nicky down for the night and help you out." I took Nicky from Olivia and fixed his bottle. Olivia kissed my cheek and Nicky's and then Dave's.

"You two look like you have work to do and I work tomorrow. Good luck." She smiled at us, turned, and walked out of the kitchen to leave.

After I put Nicky down, Dave and I sat in the living room. He got his guitar out and worked trying to put a tune to the lyrics I wrote. He found a melody for three of the songs I wrote through Nick. We agreed we had an adequate start. He would work with the band in the next week to try and put the songs together. Dave, ecstatic about the new lyrics I wrote because he failed to write anything substantial when he tried, didn't think he would sleep tonight with the new discovery of my writing skills.

The record company wanted the band back in the studio within the next two months to start recording their second album and he'd been afraid they wouldn't have anything to work on. Now he worked his fingers across the guitar strings and allowed the music to flow with the lyrics. We worked for about three hours. Nicky would be up early in the morning so I excused myself to go to bed and Dave continued to work on the songs.

"Goodnight, songbird." Dave smiled up at me as I left the room.

"Goodnight." I smiled back at Dave with a light heart. Writing music refreshed me. I felt like I connected with Nick and Dave at the same time. It made me happy I made Dave happy. I hoped to have another dream with Nick; it had been so long since I felt close to him.

I wandered in the woods. It was dark with only a small amount of light from the moon. I listened to Nick calling my name, but I couldn't tell from which direction he called from. I kept searching in the woods. I began to run and panicked when I couldn't find my way out of the forest. I ran and ran until I stood sobbing and wailing. And then Nick appeared, touching my shoulder. I lay in my bed, safe and secure. I reached up and pulled Nick into me where I snuggled into him. He whispered a poem in my ear. I slept peacefully the rest of the night.

I kept my eyes closed when I woke up the next morning. I was wrapped in Nick's arms. I lay thinking all that happened over the last year must have been a dream. Lying in Nick's arms was serene. The dream was so vivid. I opened my eyes and turned so I would be able to see Nick's face. It seemed like I hadn't seen him in forever. As I rolled over, Nick opened his eyes. What!.......... It was Dave. I jumped up to a sitting position in the bed.

"What are you doing in my bed Dave?" I was shocked and angry he was here.

Dave held up his arms in defeat. "Rayna, you were having a bad dream last night. I didn't want you to wake Nicky, so I came in and sat down beside you and touched your shoulder hoping you would stop yelling and crying. You wrapped your arm around me and pulled me into your arms. Every time I tried to leave, you would grip tighter to me. I must have fallen asleep. I'm sorry if I upset you."

"I thought you were Nick."

"I understand, but it appeared to help you sleep better with me here."

An aura of transgression welled up inside of me; confusing Dave for Nick. I put my head down and covered my face with my hands, believing I betrayed Nick, I started to cry. Dave moved over closer to me and wrapped his arms around me. I sobbed into his shoulder.

"I miss him so much. I thought the last months were just a bad dream and I was in his arms."

"I know you miss him. I miss him too. It'll get easier. You need time. Rayna, you'll always love and miss him, but we have to move on." Dave pulled me tighter.

"It doesn't feel like it'll get any easier."

"It will; I promise. Writing the music yesterday put a smile on your face."

"Because I wrote Nick's words; I believe he's giving them to me."

"It's a possibility since you two were so connected and you have his heart. Maybe you're still connecting with him although he isn't physically with us. Maybe he's still here Rayna. In here." Dave pointed to my heart or should I say Nick's heart.

I pulled my head away from Dave's chest and gave him a weak smile. He might be on to something. I was happier when I wrote the lyrics that poured from me.

"Now that you mention it, I do have a tune in my head right now, but I can only hum it. I wished I played the guitar."

"Even if you don't know the cords, you can show me the rhythm of the song. Let's try after we feed Nicky." Dave gave me a huge smile.

We both peeked over at Nicky's bassinet because he started cooing. He was awake and not crying; such a happy baby. We smiled at each other. I stood and walked over to pick him up.

"I'll get his breakfast." Dave dashed out the door and down the stairs to fix Nicky his morning meal. I picked my beautiful son up and held him for a moment and kissed his cheek. I changed his diaper and took him to the kitchen where I feed him while Dave fixed our breakfast.

I put Nicky in his swing after I feed him and sat down on the couch. Dave brought his guitar over to me and I took the thing from his hands. I'd never tried to play guitar before. I knew how to hold it because I watched Nick many times. I put my left fingers on the strings and strummed down with my right hand. The guitar felt right in my hands. I tried to make the tune in my head on the strings, and suddenly something happened.

My fingers started to move like I played the guitar for years. I made music and I had no idea how. The music started to flow from me. My fingers moved to the correct cords to create a beautiful melody. At that moment, I realized the music coming through me came from Nick. I smiled from ear to ear.

Dave joined me with a smile. We both grinned from ear to ear as I played a tune that would go perfectly with one of the songs I finished of Nick's.

"This is amazing!" The enthusiasm radiated from Dave's face. He appeared more excited than me. "Wait until the band gets a load of this."

I laughed. Laughing only happened once in a while for me. A miracle began occurring right before our eyes. Nick's music would go on. I would write the lyrics and Dave would sing them. The band would take my rhythms and make them into wonderful songs; just like before. Now, Dave and I would speak for Nick. The band would be as wonderful as before.

Dave and I spent our days together working on music and taking care of Nicky. Weeks went by and we worked every day. The words flowed from my mind to the paper. It astonished me how I wrote these beautiful, meaningful words. By late August, we wrote a full album of songs. Working with Dave on music helped me make it through my and Nick's anniversary. It was a rough week, but Dave kept me busy writing lyrics while he played the guitar. Between music and Nicky, I was exhausted every night. Most of those nights, I cried myself to sleep without delay.

The band was ecstatic when I showed them the lyrics and played some music on the guitar. Everything started to move fast. The band practiced and put together the music to go with the songs. And before I realized it, they were ready for the studio a few short weeks later. They worked in the studio for over a week and put together what they thought was an amazing album.

My life started to have some purpose, but I realized by completing the album, the band would be leaving for the second tour. I liked having Dave around. He reminded me of Nick. He made me laugh and he kept my nightmares away too. Since the first time Dave held me while I slept, my nightmares disappeared. I only dreamed wonderful dreams of Nick now. I would wake up with new lyrics or a new tune for the band. Either Nick worked through me or having his heart changed something inside of me that now gave me the talent to write music.

The band was ready to promote the new album by late fall. Nicky grew rapidly and turned eight months old. Dave didn't want to leave him, but his career was in the music industry, and he needed to go. We had to keep Nick's dream alive. Anna graduated college so she would be going with the band this time. I would stay behind with Nicky. I wasn't sure if I'd be able to watch the band perform anyway, it would bring too much pain.

I talked to Dave and Anna on the phone a couple of times a week. Dave always gave me exciting news about the album. The first single climbed the charts to number one and sales climbed as well. He told me within a few months, the band would get an actual tour bus. The music business was working out for the band. Nick's dream was coming true and it made me jubilant.

Olivia and I spend Thanksgiving at my parents' house and we'd have Christmas at mine. I hadn't celebrated Christmas with Nick, so I didn't have any happy memories to flood my mind; only gloomy ones. Nick lay in the hospital this time last year in a coma. I experienced a few nightmares during this time, but they weren't as severe as before. It took the edge off of the nightmares watching Nicky on Christmas morning. He was trying to walk and running after him and worrying about him getting hurt kept my mind busy most days. The nights were the worst.

The band was gone until the end of January. I missed them so much. I missed having Dave around. He made me laugh and gave me company. I looked forward to the band coming home.

Dave called me a week before they planned to come home.

"Rayna, I have amazing news! The record company is having a big party for the band to celebrate this new album. The band did so well out on tour, they want to recognize us and help promote the new album. I need you to get my mom and your parents to New York next Thursday. We'll arrive in New York on Friday.

I sat for a minute without saying a word. "That's wonderful news Dave. It shouldn't be a problem. Should I make hotel reservations too?"

"Yes, that'd be great. I knew you would think of everything."

"Where should I make the reservations?"

"We are staying at the same place as before."

"Okay. Should we come early so we can find something to wear? How fancy is the party?"

"It will be ostentatious"

"Okay, we'll definitely all need to buy new duds if we want to impress." I joked.

I got off the phone with Dave and called Anna. I needed her support. She was beyond ecstatic. She wouldn't shut up for a few minutes.

"So how is Dave doing with the songs?" I asked.

"Rayna, he does an incredible job. Although he is a drummer, he is starting to take this singing thing as his own. And the girls go crazy!" she said. She stopped to take a breath.

"They love his voice huh?"

"They love everything about him. You should see his fans. The meet and greets take hours and the girls go crazy. It's amazing. The band's a huge success. I mean the girls go crazy for all the guys, but Dave is their favorite by far. The other guys are a little jealous I think."

"Hopefully, he doesn't let this go to his head and become reckless with the fans."

"I don't think that'll ever happen. He's always humble and a gentleman. I can't wait for you to see them play. I know you stayed away because you think it'll be difficult for you, but I think it'll help heal you some Rayna. You need to listen to your words being played live."

"Nick's word," I corrected her.

"I think they are both your and Nick's, together. I think Nick is smiling down at you and Dave; you for writing them and Dave for singing them. You have made him proud. Enjoy the success."

After I got off the phone with Anna, I thought about what she said. She told me to enjoy the success. I hadn't enjoyed or experienced any success. I made myself a hermit in this house with Nicky. We went places, the store, Olivia's, or my parents' house. I stopped living life. I wrote the songs with Nick working through me and I continued writing while the band toured, but I quit living. And then I thought about what Anna said about all the females going crazy over Dave; exactly like they behaved with Nick. A little bit of the jealous monster rose up in me but I had no right to be jealous. Dave owed me nothing, but I still wanted his time. He filled the hole Nick left behind.

・♥・♥・♥・♥・♥・

We all arrived in New York City on Wednesday morning. My dad moved a few things around with work, but we all came as a family, even Olivia. She'd never been to New York; so all the sights and sounds were new to her. The band wouldn't be here until Friday, so we had a few days to shop and sightsee. I took them to a wonderful restaurant we ate at while we visited here before on Wednesday evening. We shopped some throughout the day, but we didn't find the outfits we would wear for Saturday. Dinner tasted delicious, although I had some trepidation about going to this restaurant.

"Rayna, this is the restaurant Nick proposed to you isn't it?" Olivia asked after she took a sip of her wine.

I took a deep breath; Olivia got to know me and my moods in the last year well. "Yes, it is. I wanted to bring you all here because the food is spectacular and I wanted to see how being here affected me. I'll be in a similar situation Saturday and I wanted to experiment with my emotions before then."

"You're going to be fine honey." My dad touched my shoulder and gave me a gentle squeeze. I placed my hand over his and gave him a weak smile as a tear slid down my cheek.

SONGS FROM THE HEART

I wiped the salty thing away and smiled at Nicky who babbled while he ate from his tray. He smiled back at me and I saw the joy in his dark brown eyes; Nick's eyes.

On Thursday we shopped and the ladies decided to buy some leather pants for the concert. My mother and Olivia stunned in their new rock get -up. We toured the city some and after ate dinner. Afterward, we retired to our rooms so we could be refreshed for Dave, Anna and the band tomorrow. Later in the evening, Samantha, Rick's mom, called and said she would be in tomorrow afternoon. It had been a while since I saw her, so tomorrow would be a busy and exciting day.

After I got Nicky bathed and put to bed, I took a shower and climbed into bed. I pulled the covers up to my chin. I lay in bed thinking about seeing Dave and Anna after all these weeks. I grew excited for tomorrow. I hadn't been excited about anything in months, so the energy I had was new for me. I didn't think I'd be able to sleep, but I drifted off into a deep relaxing sleep and dreamed of the beach.

Twenty-Eight

♥

I found myself primping more than usual. I don't know why I tried to look best. My hair lay lifeless and flat. I tried everything, but nothing helped with this drab hair. My hair had grown down to the middle of my back and I could use a new style. I should've had my hair done yesterday. I wondered if I could make an appointment in the hotel salon before Anna got here. I checked the time and I had a few hours. They wouldn't be here until noon.

"Yes, I would like to make an appointment for a haircut before noon if possible. Okay, I'll be right down. Thank you." I hung up the phone and glanced over at Olivia.

Olivia grinned from ear to ear. "Would you like me to stay here with Nicky?"

"If you would please; I could use a little update in the hair department." I ran my fingers through my lifeless hair.

"You go ahead honey. You deserve a little pampering."

"Thank you Olivia. My parents should be over shortly. You guys can order some lunch if I'm not back." I kissed Nicky's cheek and then Olivia's.

She smiled up at me and then touched my cheek. "Take your time; have your nails done too."

I examined my nails and they were a little plain looking. Maybe I did need to allow myself some pampering. I needed to be stunning for the launch party. Since Nick passed away, I very seldom looked in the mirror. I now realized that I had let my appearance suffer as much as my heart had. Some days were better than others and Nicky took my mind off the sadness most days because he kept me so busy. My soul began to awaken again sometimes. Today it was awake.

I was truly impressed when she finished my hair. It was still straight but lay on my shoulders and had some texture and life. It didn't appear drab anymore. After my hair, I asked them to give me a French manicure and pedicure. They finished me up by 12:15. I stole a peek at myself in the mirror before I left the salon. I had to say, I did appear more vibrant than I did a few hours ago. Before I walked out the door, I turned around and made five appointments for me, Anna, my mom, Samantha, and Olivia to have our makeup done before the concert tomorrow. As I rode the elevator up to my room, I wore a smile from ear to ear. I felt more alive today than I had since Nick died. I began to believe I would survive.

When I put the key card into the door, butterflies danced in my stomach. The fluttering thrilled me. I opened the door and the entire band, Samantha, and my parents had joined Olivia and Nicky in my suite. They all sat around the table eating lunch and chatting. They looked up and stopped talking, every eye on me.

"Momma, Momma." Nicky said and held out his arms while sitting on Dave's lap.

Dave's mouth fell open. I walked over to pick up Nicky. I blushed with embarrassment as everyone stared at me.

"Rayna, you are beautiful," Dave said.

"Thank you," I said as I lifted Nicky from his lap.

Anna ran around the table and grabbed me and Nicky in a huge hug. "My God I missed you." She let go and held me at arm's length. "You do look wonderful."

I smiled, my mood glorious.

"You're breathtaking," my dad said as he laughed out loud.

"Well, if you think I'm wonderful now wait until tomorrow." I smiled. "I made appointments for the ladies tomorrow for makeup. I figured we all deserved a little pampering and to look fabulous for this tremendous party." I gave everyone at the table a genuine smile. They'd not seen my true smile in almost a year.

Dave stood up next and wrapped me in his arms. "You're beautiful as usual." He said in my ear. He let me go and smiled at me.

He smelled fabulous. And being wrapped in his strong, warm arms again brought security to my mind; security of home. I missed Dave more than I thought. Dave pulled a chair out for me to sit down.

We visited through the afternoon. Dave played with Nicky on the rug in front of the couch and the band got us caught up with everything that was going on. They'd be leasing a tour bus and it would be ready for them after they got back from Europe. They were leaving to tour the country next week. They'd be gone for three weeks.

We enjoyed a wonderful dinner and after we ate, my parents and Olivia took Nicky back to the hotel. Anna, me, Samantha, and the band went out on the town for a while. The night life was just as I remembered with Nick. Nothing about New York changed, except that Nick wasn't with us. This city brought back happy memories, but the happy memories always led to me missing him.

Dave walked beside me and kept me in his sight. He'd place his hand on my lower back when we walked into a place and guided me protectively in front of him.

Anna wanted to go dancing. I hadn't been dancing since Nick or out with Anna since before Nick's accident; almost a year now. I didn't want to let her down. Everybody had been patient with me while I mourned Nick. They understood that I still experienced days of loneliness, but they always tried to make the day better. So I didn't fuss when she pulled me into the dance floor. My mood wasn't conducive for dancing, but everyone's mood sort of rubbed off on me. I started to enjoy myself some, but it was difficult to totally allow myself to be free.

Dave and Travis joined us on the dance floor. I hoped to take a break, but they weren't allowing any. Dave spun me around the dance floor. He danced better than I thought. I saw him dance before, but it was different when you were his partner. We moved together easily. I didn't need to make an effort; I knew which way he would move. When he pulled me into him for a few moves, my stomach fluttered and I smiled. I enjoyed dancing with him, we'd grown close while writing songs and him spending time with Nicky. I became comfortable with Dave. Sometimes a little too comfortable, scaring me. But tonight, I threw my trepidation to the wind. I needed to let loose; at least for the night.

After a few dances, we all decided to take a break. Rick ordered us some drinks as we sat around the table. Our seats looked down at the dance floor that lit up with sparkling colors that moved to the beat of the music.

Travis slid out of the booth and onto his knee beside Anna. She was looking at me talking and didn't see his move. I smiled from ear to ear and poked her in the arm and pointed to Travis.

"Will you do me the honor and be my wife Anna?"

I leaned up so that I could see her face. Tears streamed down her cheeks. She put her hand to her heart and shook her head yes. Travis pulled her into a huge hug as she silently wept with joy. I know that they'd been talking about marriage, but she didn't know when Travis would actually ask her.

Travis let go of Anna so that he could place the huge rock on her finger. Anna admired the ring on her finger.

"Yes, yes, yes. I love you." Anna whispered.

"I love you." Travis pulled Anna in for another hug and gave her a long kiss. We all clapped and yelled congratulations.

I had a few tears myself. Remembering when Nick proposed to me with all of the same people sitting here. Dave pulled me into him with his arm that rested on the back of the booth. It comforted me to have his arm around me. I wiped the tear away and forced a smile for Anna. I was thrilled for her, so I needed to push my sadness aside. This was her moment and I didn't want my melancholy to cloud her day.

"Let me look at that ring girl." I said after I took a deep breath and straightened myself out.

"Rayna, it's beautiful." She said as she smiled at me.

I took her hand to admire her beautiful ring, a simple emerald cut diamond. It had to be close to a carat. It looked so huge on her small hand but showed the love Travis had for her. I pulled her in for a hug. I didn't want to let her go.

"I am so happy for you. You two are finally going to do it. I love you both." I stood up to give Travis a hug as well.

"We need some champagne," Dave said as he waved the waitress over.

Rick and Dave made a toast to Travis and Anna. We danced some more. I danced with Rick, Jeff, and Dave. The champagne helped to loosen me up some and we danced the night away. Later, a slow song came on and Dave pulled me to him. I felt at ease dancing in his arms, safe. I laid my head on his shoulder and followed his moves. I became a little intoxicated with his wonderful smell, his firm embrace, and the alcohol.

"Rayna," Dave whispered.

I glanced up and locked eyes with Dave. I couldn't pull my eyes from his intense gaze. Before I realized it, his lips were on mine for just a second. He gazed into my eyes again and the longing in his eyes made me crave another kiss. I pressed my lips to his this time. The passion increased with our kiss until it scared me. I pulled away and turned and quickly left the dance floor.

I found myself in the bathroom trying to catch my breath. What just happened? What was I feeling? This was wrong; it was Nick's brother. Did I naturally have feelings for Dave or the champagne and the fact that he resembled and acted so much like Nick? My mind shifted everywhere.

"Rayna. Are you okay?" I turned and glanced at Anna.

Anna's face was full of concern and confusion.

"Yes. I'm okay, just a little queasy; maybe the alcohol and all the dancing." I blotted my face with a paper towel. I peeked up at Anna and forced a smile, not sure if I should say anything about the kiss. It was perhaps just a moment between Dave and me. We had both been through so much and we spent a lot of time together on the new album. Dave was my rock when Nick left me. I was sure the kiss didn't mean anything.

But the moment still lingered in the back of my mind, the feelings that the kiss sparked. I took a deep breath and examined myself in the mirror. I shoved the feelings and the thoughts to the back of my mind and decided that I'd ignore them and act as if nothing happened.

"Ready to go back out?" I asked as I forced another smile on my face. I could tell by Anna's reaction that she didn't believe for one minute that I was fine. She knew me too well.

"I think everyone is ready to go anyway. They all know tomorrow is a big day and we should get some rest. It's past midnight anyhow." Anna put her arm around my shoulder and led me out of the door of the ladies' room and over to meet the guys.

I was worried about Dave's reaction. I turned and ran out after the kiss. But when we walked over to them, Dave just sat in the booth like he had been; relaxed and talking with the guys. He didn't appear any different than he usually did. Relief filled my mind.

"Are we ready?" Rick asked when Anna and I got to our table.

"Yeah, I think so. You all have a huge day tomorrow and I think I've drunk enough for the night." I smiled at Rick. I avoided Dave's eyes; afraid that he would see guilt in them. I planned to act like nothing happened; hopefully he would too.

Twenty-Nine

The next morning when I opened my eyes, I figured my head would be pounding. The only after-effect of the night before were thoughts of Dave and the yearning that he caused when he kissed me. His warm lips pressed on mine took my breath away and made butterflies swim in my stomach. I hadn't experienced those in such a long time. I forgot what it felt like, but soon after the guilt reared up. Guilty of having those feelings with Nick's brother. I still missed Nick and the betrayal engulfed me.

I pulled my robe on and opened the bedroom door. Dave sat at the dining room table with Nicky and Olivia having breakfast, I walked toward the table reluctantly.

"Good morning sleepy head," Dave said. "How did you sleep?" Dave smiled at me with his warm and gorgeous smile. Of course his smile was gorgeous, he looked almost like Nick. He could almost be his twin. This last year, he began to mimic Nick more every day. Maybe he always had and I never noticed or maybe I saw more of Nick in him because I wanted to.

"Good, and you?" I walked over and kissed Nicky on the cheek and smoothed his hair. He smiled up at me and said, momma. I sat down and poured myself a cup of coffee. I waited for the embarrassment to hit me. I peeked over at Dave and he smiled and went on eating like nothing happened last night. It made me think that possibly I read into this more than I should. He appeared to be at ease. I took the plate of food Olivia handed me and ate, letting the worries and guilt from last night fade away.

Our makeup appointments were for later in the afternoon. My dad volunteered to keep Nicky busy while we were being pampered. We enjoyed our girls' afternoon and came back and prepared for the concert. I wore a blush pink pair of leather jeans and a matching jacket with a silver camisole underneath and matching silver heels. I took a look in the mirror and wasn't sure that I recognized myself; I was captivated. My mom was stunning in her black leather pants and long silver sweater. Anna brought a pair of white leather pants she used for touring with the band; gorgeous as always. Olivia with her dark skin and hair looked enchanting in the long white leather skirt. We certainly fit the part of a rocker. And of course Samantha was rocking the red leather pants. My dad's mouth fell open when my mom came out of her room. We all laughed at my his face. He turned a little red. My mom simply grinned from ear to ear.

We were meeting the band at the venue. The record company had a car waiting to take us to the party. Champagne chilled in the back with enough glasses for everyone. We toasted to the band and how far they'd come in such a short amount of time.

Staff escorted us through the doors when we arrived at the 583 Park Avenue address. My stomach quivered full of butterflies; not only because of hearing mine and Nick's written words but also because I worried about how I'd react.

We had front row seats with the first table in the center. I guessed knowing the band and writing their songs did have its perks. We all took a seat at the table, with five chairs left for the guys. The venue was beautiful. Tables were placed all over with black table clothes. Glasses and small plates sat on each table with a pitcher of water. A balcony where fans would sit and watch the performance hung behind us. I grew a little tense listening to them do sound check. I took a few deep breaths and poured myself some water.

"How are you feeling?" Anna asked. She placed her hand on my arm.

"Okay, a little anxious. But I'll be fine." I gave her a weak smile and squeezed Nicky into me. Having him with me comforted me a little.

"I have to admit, Rayna; I'm a little bit excited. I haven't been to a rock concert for nearly 30 years." My mom said. She smiled and squeezed my arm.

I smiled at her. "I think you'll enjoy it mom. I'm glad you're here with me." She looked ten years younger in the rocker outfit we helped her pick out. My mom could always be a stunner.

"You are still so handsome dad. I'm so glad you came with us." I gave him a huge smile.

"I wouldn't miss this for the world. I'm proud of you honey," he said. He got up and walked over to my chair and pulled me into a huge hug.

"I love you dad," I said.

"I love you." He kissed my cheek and hugged me again. He walked back over to his chair and sat down and kissed my mom on the cheek.

"I'm so excited." Anna squeezed my hand and smiled from ear to ear. "This night is going to be wonderful. Having us all together to celebrate this success is amazing."

"I'm going to miss you when you leave tomorrow. You'll be gone a month." I frowned.

"I know, I'll miss you like crazy; and Nicky. He is growing so fast; he'll be walking before I come back."

"We'll skype every day." I hugged my best friend. I felt so fortunate to have a friend I could trust with my life.

We sat and enjoyed listening to the guys while they warmed up and got all the instruments tuned in. I peeked over at Olivia and she was all smiles. She'd never seen the band live. She was a proud mom.

"Dave has an amazing voice," my mom said. My dad shook his head in agreement. "Travis and Jeff play well also and the new guy on the drums is great."

I smiled at my mom and shook my head yes. The guy the band found to be the new drummer wasn't part of the band. They just hired him to play the drums. His picture didn't appear on the album, just Dave, Travis, and Jeff. He loved playing for them. His name was Mark. I didn't know much about him. I only met him a couple of times.

The guys finished the sound check and came down to the table to chit-chat.

"So what did you think?" Dave asked all of us.

"Wonderful, it sounded wonderful," Samantha said. Rick stood behind her grinning. He was ecstatic that his mother loved the band and supported them all the way. It was refreshing to have my parents join in with the band.

"You guys sounded amazing," my mother added.

"Thanks everyone. Rayna, what did you think?" Dave asked me personally.

"I think it sounded marvelous. I can't wait for the real thing."

"Well, you get your wish in about an hour. We need to change and grab a snack. They're going to be bringing out some things for us to eat before the party starts."

Like on cue, a waiter wheeled a cart out with appetizers and drinks for us. We all dove in and enjoyed some snacks before the party got started. The band ate a scant amount because of nerves and I was with them in that aspect. I ate a few bites, but my nerves put a stop to me eating.

We all talked and laughed while we waited for the party to start. The executives at the record company showed up and Anna and I made introductions. They were all optimistic and told us what to expect tonight. The band would mingle with radio hosts, journalists, and some fans. They'd play the new album and after the performance, socialize to celebrate the release.

At nine people started to flow into the party, all dressed for the red carpet. They wore leather, sequins, and suits. The party filled with fans, businessmen, and the media. The rush of anticipation flooded over me.

A few media people asked about the songwriter. The record executives pulled me from the security of my family and friends and wanted to speak with me about my songwriting and how it happened. I told them the truth; the words suddenly came to me; I couldn't explain how I came up with the lyrics. I didn't enlighten them with my theory; that Nick gave me the lyrics. They would've thought I was crazy. But they asked me the question. They asked me if I thought somehow Nick gave me the words. I told them it was a good theory. I believed their theory, but would never tell them.

The band did a short press conference and then took the stage. Everyone took their seat or their standing position at a table as the band opened up with their first single from the new album. I wrote the words but wasn't ready for the delivery. Dave commanded the stage. His voice sounded impeccable and the music astonishing. It was hard watching the band perform without Nick. A tear slid down my cheek. I wiped it away. My sudden sadness turned into joy as I thought about Nick looking down on us and smiling because he was happy for his brother and the band. He also smiled because his lyrics would live on through me.

The band played six songs off the new album. The enthusiastic crowd's applause told us they were excited about the new album and wanted to hear more. Luckily for them, the fans who attended the party would receive a signed copy of the new album.

I sighed with relief when the band finished their set. Not because I didn't want to listen to them anymore, but because I wasn't sure if I could keep it together any longer. I was still in awe.

Dave walked straight toward me. "What did you think?" He grabbed me in his arms.

"The band was wonderful Dave. It sounded beautiful." I smiled and gave Dave a tight hug.

Rick reminded the band this was a promotional celebration and they needed to mingle around.

"Sorry guys, but duty calls." Dave smiled at all of us and kissed my cheek. He turned and walked away disappearing into the sea of people.

I scanned the room and the band disappeared as fast as they appeared. Fans flocked to the guys for autographs and pictures. The press waited just past the fans.

"How do you do it Anna?"

"Do what?" Anna's eyebrows pulled down with confusion.

"Sit back while all those girls flock after Travis. I knew the girls loved Nick, but the band is so much bigger now."

"I let them have a few minutes and then I join the band or I offer to take the picture. Besides, most of them want Dave's attention." Anna laughed and put her arm around me.

The party was a huge success. It was getting late, but nobody seemed to notice except Nicky. He yawned and rubbed his eyes. He laid his head on my shoulder. All the attention from the press wanting pictures of Nick's son started to wear him out. My mom, dad, and Olivia offered to take Nicky up to the room. I think they were a little tired as well. Jeff's and Travis's parents were next to fly the coop.

When our table was almost empty, Samantha, Anna, and I headed to the bar. We had some drinks and laughs. We missed this girl time. Thanks to this celebration, we enjoyed some. It made my heart feel light, not having to think. I needed this.

"Well girls, while I have enjoyed our time together tonight, I have an early flight tomorrow and I don't want to turn into a pumpkin." Samantha hugged and kissed both of us before she left.

Anna and I were left by ourselves. I was saddened when I thought about Anna leaving soon as well. Anna felt my sadness and hugged me.

"You can come and see us while we are on tour. But if you don't, I understand. You and I will talk every day. You do need to help me plan my wedding." We both laughed.

We talked some more about her wedding and the upcoming tour. Travis found us and swept Anna away for a minute. I found the powder room to catch my breath. Thinking about everyone leaving tomorrow brought sadness to a wonderful night. I'd miss Anna and Dave; Anna because she had been my sister and Dave because he was part of my connection to Nick.

As I left the bathroom, I felt a little lightheaded; perhaps from too much champagne. I decided to go out on the balcony to breathe some fresh air. The air blew cool and brisk as I opened the door and stepped out into the night. I walked out to the balustrade and stared out over the beautiful lit-up city of New York. I inhaled deeply to refresh my mind while I enjoyed the amazing view.

So much had happened over the last couple of years. I met my soul mate and fell in love. I had his child and he gave his heart so I could live. And now his band was a success and I became the new songwriter celebrating in New York City. Now I had the task of raising our son alone. Part of my support system would be overseas on tour and promoting the new album and I'd be left behind again. It made me even lonelier in this big world watching everyone celebrate the success of the band and the new album.

"There you are."

I turned to the voice and saw Dave walking toward me. I forced a smile. He brought me out of my daydreaming.

"I've been looking all over for you. What are you doing out here in the cold?" Dave smiled and wrapped his arm around me to try and keep me warm.

"I needed some fresh air." The warmth of his body felt comforting against the cold.

"So, what do you think about the songs?" I could see Dave's breath in the air as he spoke. I guess it was colder than I thought.

"I thought you all did a wonderful job."

"No, I mean, how are you feeling about the songs you wrote?"

I paused for a moment, trying to understand his meaning.

"I felt sad, but I think the happiness seeing the band continue outweighs the sadness. This is what Nick would've wanted. And I'm sad because you and Anna will be leaving tomorrow."

"I'm glad to hear you say that the happiness outweighs the sadness." Dave kissed my head as I leaned on his shoulder.

It was nice being out here with Dave. It seemed like another world standing outside on the balcony in the quiet. We both just stood in silence for a few moments.

Eventually, Dave spoke. "Rayna, I'm glad I found you out here alone. I wanted to talk to you before I left."

Just the tone in Dave's voice made me realize I wouldn't like what he had to say. I turned my entire body so I faced him. I gazed up into his eyes. I expected to see sadness and sympathy. What I found was love.

"Rayna, I'm just going to come out and say it. I'm in love with you. I'm not sure when it happened, but I am."

I stood frozen, not sure what to say because I couldn't be sure if I heard Dave correctly. How could he be in love with me? It didn't make sense. I starred into the night.

"Rayna?"

He was my brother-in-law. I was married to his brother. I loved Nick.

"Rayna, say something."

I blinked and then glanced up at Dave who gazed at me with worry in his eyes.

"You can't love me. I'm married to your brother."

"But I am and I can't do anything about it. Believe me; I've battled with this for over a month. I'm in love with you." Dave touched my cheek with the back of his hand. It felt right, but wrong at the same time.

"You're going to ruin everything. You're Nicky's uncle. I love Nick, I can't love you and you can't love me."

"Who says I can't?"

I didn't answer him. How could this be happening?

"I'm leaving tomorrow for the tour and I wanted you to know how I feel; how I've been feeling for a while now." Dave grinned and leaned in to kiss me.

Angry with him for falling in love with me, I backed away from him. How could he do this to his brother? His brother had only been gone a year. He needed to love somebody else, not me.

"You can't love me. I can't love you; at least not like you deserve." I turned away from him and hurried back into the hotel. I didn't look for Anna. I rushed out of the party and down the hall to the elevators. I heard Dave calling my name, but I refused to stop and listen to any more of what he might say.

Thirty

♥

Olivia sat on the couch; still awake reading when I got back to the room. I told her I was tired and going to bed. I knew she sensed the tension in me, but she let me have my space and didn't ask any questions. I sat on the bed and tried to figure out if I ever led Dave on. I didn't think I had. At first I was mad at Dave, but then I became angry with myself. I should've seen this coming. We spent so much time together over the past year. He was the rock for Nicky and me; needing him led to him loving me. This was my fault. I should've never depended on him so much. He spent all his time with us.

A knock at the door caused me to jump.

"Rayna, will you come out and talk to Dave?" Olivia's voice sounded quiet.

"Tell him I can't right now. I need some time."

I couldn't be sure if Dave left or not because I didn't hear anything else from Olivia. I washed my face and got dressed for bed while trying to comprehend the events of tonight I heard another knock on the door and then the door opened. Anna stood gazing at me. Seeing her caused the buildup of my emotions to spill out. Anna pulled me into her arms. She held me while I cried.

After most of the tears were gone, Anna told me Dave explained to her what happened. He was worried about me.

He told her I refused to talk to him. I expressed my feelings to Anna; how I felt responsible and how I worried this would change my and Dave's relationship. I needed him in my life, but it wouldn't be fair to hold him back from having a relationship with someone else. I did love him and I needed him, but I didn't think I would ever be "in love" with anybody ever again.

"Rayna, I knew Dave was in love with you for a while now. I think everybody saw it." Anna said. She pushed my hair behind my ear.

"What? How did you know that?" I was so confused. How did everybody else know, but I didn't?

"Rayna, he adores you and the way he looks at you; the same look Nick..........." She stopped in the middle of her sentence when she realized what she said. "It's almost magical when you two are together. The other night when you two were dancing, you were smiling. It was wonderful to see you like that again; all because of Dave."

"Dave always made me laugh."

"This is different Rayna. Dave makes a difference in you."

"Yes he does. He makes the dark days brighter, but I still miss Nick. He's Nick's brother for heaven's sake."

"You can't look at it that way. Nick is gone and he'd want you to be happy. Dave makes you happy and he's in love with you."

"That all may be, but Dave deserves more than I can give him. I can't love him like he should be loved. Nick will always have my heart."

"You can love two people at once."

"How can I ever love anyone after Nick? He was my soul mate Anna."

"I can't answer that for you, but you need to start seeing your world without Nick, Rayna. He isn't coming back. You deserve to be happy."

I didn't know what to say to her. It seemed impossible to do what she said. I didn't think I'd ever be able to love anybody but Nick.

I didn't sleep well that night; too many things running through my head. The band had an eight a.m. flight, so they left the hotel around six. I never spoke to Dave or Anna before they left, but Dave left a rose with a note: "Sorry I upset you, Dave." It made my heart ache.

The day back home was quiet and sobering. Both Anna and Dave were gone. I was left with my own thoughts. Nicky kept me busy most of the day, but the house was very quiet when he napped. I couldn't put what happened out of my mind, and I couldn't wrap my head around it. I was miserable because I understood this now changed my and Dave's relationship. He would no longer be the happy-go-lucky shoulder I leaned on. When he found somebody to love, I wouldn't be able to have him by my side as my support system. It wouldn't be fair to him or her. But I didn't want to give him up. It tore me up knowing these facts. I drove myself crazy with what the future would bring. I thought more about Nick too; not having him here brought back memories I tried to bury for so long. While Nicky slept, I cried often.

I spoke to Anna and the tour was going phenomenal, but she noticed a difference in Dave. He'd perform and then find a party wherever he could. He'd party with the stagehands or at a bar or sometimes he would party with fans. She worried about him.

After days of sulking around the house and being depressed, I called Olivia and asked if she wanted to go to the ocean with me and Nicky for a week. She was happy to run away from the cold weather and into some sunshine. So I called and rented a house for a week. The beach was dead this time of year so it was rather easy to find a relaxing place. I would clear my thoughts at the ocean. Somehow the smell of salt and the sound of the ocean would always clear my head and put me into a better mood. I grew excited to be escaping for a little while.

The anticipation of relief swept over me as we made our way to the Florida shore. When we arrived at the cute little cottage, we unpacked our things and ran to the grocery store. This wasn't going to be a tourist vacation, it would be a relaxing, organize my thoughts trip. We needed to have our food ready even if we went out for a few dinners.

I spent the early mornings walking on the beach, trying to clear my head of all the negative thoughts. After Nicky woke up, I spent time with him playing on the beach. He loved the waves and the sand. He couldn't get enough of it. Dave would have loved to be with Nicky for his first visit to the beach. I tried not to think about Dave, but he kept filling my thoughts. At night, after I got Nicky to bed, I'd sit out on the deck or I would sit on the beach trying to calm my mind and trying to let Dave go. Letting Nick go was the hardest thing I ever did. But I needed to let him go completely. He was no longer part of my world. Letting Dave go would be hard also, maybe even harder, because I choose to let him go. I didn't have a choice with Nick, he was taken from me.

I prayed a lot. I ask God to help me cope with both of my losses. I cried a lot but slept less. After about the fifth night of minimal sleep, exhausted, I fell into a deep sleep.

Nick and I were walking hand and hand on the beach at sunset. His skin radiated warmth against mine; my heart full of love and joy. Beautiful as always; his hair blew in the wind and his deep chocolate eyes filled with love. We walked for a while without speaking. I embraced his arm while I held his hand and snuggled into his arm as we walked barefoot down the shore. The warm salt water kept brushing our feet as the waves rolled up on the shore. It was a beautiful evening in my favorite spot with my favorite person.

Nick told me he was alright. He also told me he watched over me and Nicky. And then he told me I needed to live my life. He made it sound like he was leaving again.

"Rayna, I will love you forever. And I will forever be here." He placed his hand on my heart and stared deep into my eyes. "But I need you to find love in your world; with Dave. He will love you to the end. He will love Nicky as his own. He will be there for you when I can't. He will make you happy; if you give him a chance."

"But I don't know if I can. He isn't you Nick. He deserves someone who'll love him like I love you. It wouldn't be fair to him."

"You'll love him deeply someday. You already love him." Nick smiled

"I do love him, but I'm not in love with him."

"I think you're falling in love with him. You just won't allow yourself to because of me. Don't feel guilty about it. I want you to love him with all your heart. Open it Rayna. Open your heart to Dave."

I didn't say anything to Nick. I was speechless. He wanted me to live my life with Dave. I was difficult to comprehend what he said to me. How could he want me to love Dave, his brother? I didn't want to love Dave; I wanted to stay right here with Nick. Being here with Nick made me realize how much I missed him. As I pondered what Nick said and wondered if he might be right, he slowly vanished away from me.

And then I woke up. Had I been waiting for Nick's approval or permission to love again? I felt he just gave it to me if that's what I had been waiting for. Seeing Nick again in my dreams was wonderful. I hadn't seen him in over six months. It felt amazing to see him again. I felt lighter, like a burden had been lifted.

Olivia must have sensed I was in better spirits during breakfast. I still needed some time to comprehend my dream with Nick.

"You looked refreshed today." Olivia smiled as she poured more coffee into her cup.

"I slept really good last night." I grinned over my cup. I didn't tell her about my visit with Nick last night. She wouldn't understand. Nobody really understood my and Nick's connection.

"Have you spoken to Anna or Dave?"

"I talked to Anna. She said Europe is wonderful. They haven't got to do much sightseeing, but the people are wonderful." I didn't tell her Anna told me Dave partied a lot and hung out with fans. I wasn't sure how much she knew about what Dave told me. I didn't want her to worry about Dave.

"You know it's okay to love him." Her eyes were full of concern. "Dave told me what happened." She sat beside me.

"It's more complicated than that."

"You two love each other. What more is there to it? Nick is gone Rayna, he'd want you to be happy and for someone to be there for you and Nicky."

I didn't respond to her, because I realized she was right. Anna told me, Dave told me, Olivia was telling me, and Nick told me last night. I spent the next couple of days on the beach thinking about the future and what mine might hold. I had two futures to examine; just me and Nicky living my life alone or me and Nicky with Dave. I had the same dream about Nick the next two nights

We flew back home and I still wasn't certain what I wanted for my future. I wanted Dave to be a part of my and Nicky's life. He wanted more than just a friendship. It wouldn't be fair to ask Dave to move on but to save space for us. He wouldn't be able to do that. But would it be fair if I never loved him like he deserved to be loved? I didn't think I could ever love anybody that way again; not the way I loved Nick.

Anna called that night and gave me an update on the tour. She also updated me on Dave. She said he was hanging out with random girls. Hearing this affected me more than I thought it should. I was jealous. Wow. I didn't want him to be with any other girls. It made my heart ache. I didn't like the feeling. I was restless in bed again; thoughts of Dave with other girls flooded the crevices of my mind. I didn't sleep well and Nick came to me again in my dreams. We were on the beach again. This time he stood far away, but I heard him like he stood beside me.

"Rayna, I am setting you free. I want you to be happy with Dave. Go to him. I will love you forever." Nick's voice sounded strong and at peace. He turned and walked away. I tried to follow him, but he kept gaining distance on me. Right before I lost sight of him, he turned and waved and then vanished.

Thirty-One

I woke up and felt a calm come over me that I hadn't experienced in over a year. There was only love, not sadness, loneliness or anxiety. I loved Nick, but I realized I loved Dave too. A rush of excitement and determination ran through me. I jumped from my bed and ran into Nicky's room, he still slept sound. Energized and ready to conquer the world, I ran to pick up the phone to call Anna. If it was four in the morning here, it would be nine in the morning in Europe. She'd be up by now from the late night before.

"Hello," Anna said, her voice flat. I must have woken her.

"Hey, did I wake you?" I said. I tried to keep my excitement in check, but it was hard.

"Yes, but I needed to wake up anyway. Got work to do you know." She groaned. "Is everything okay Rayna? You sound funny."

"Everything is wonderful." I couldn't keep the exuberance in anymore.

"What's up?"

"I'm coming to Europe."

"What?! We'll be home in a few days." Anna shouted in my ear.

"It can't wait that long. I have to catch a plane today."

"It's a nine-hour flight."

"I understand that, but if I catch a flight before noon, I can be across the ocean before the band finishes their set tonight. Can you pick me up at the airport? Can you make the arrangements for me?" I talked fast because I had plans to make and bags to pack. I needed to talk to Dave. I needed to tell him I loved him. My heart pounded trying to think and talk at the same time.

"I can do whatever you want me to do, but what is so important it can't wait a few days?"

"I need to tell Dave I'm ready. I'm ready to let him love me."

The phone was silent for a moment.

"Anna, are you there?"

"Yes, yes, I'm here. You just took me by surprise. You've got me energized now. What should I tell Dave?"

"Don't tell him or anybody else anything. I want it to be a surprise."

"Rayna, you sound wonderful; happy again. I love you."

"I love you. Now stay close to your phone and when I have everything ready, I'll call and let you know my flight number and time of arrival. You'll be in Manchester tonight right?"

"Yes, we're in Manchester tonight and London tomorrow. I'm so ecstatic right now. I don't know how, but I'll keep quiet."

"You better keep it quiet." I laughed. "Okay, I'm going to get off here and call the airport and then Olivia. I'll throw some clothes together and get out of here. See you soon. Love ya."

"Love you."

I hung up with Anna and got busy. I called the airport and they found me a seat in first class with British Airways Club World; departure time, eleven o 'clock. They had two seats left. I'd be flying in a top notch suite. It was four-thirty in the morning, so I tried to lie back down, but I couldn't sleep. I took a shower and packed my clothes. I packed light with a carry on bag and a clothes bag with a few outfits.

It was six thirty when I called to wake Olivia up. At first, she was startled because of the hour. I hated waking her up, but surprisingly she was excited as much as I was after I explained to her what I planned. She sprang into action and drove to my house within twenty minutes of me calling her. I threw Nicky's bag together and pulled him from bed and dressed him. After we loaded him in the car, I realized I forgot my passport. I ran back in and grabbed the gold decorative box I kept it in and ran back out to the car with it. The box also held all the pictures of Nick I'd hidden away from view.

I shuffled through the box and found my passport. I hurried through the box. I didn't want to spend too much time on the photos. I laid the box in the backseat beside Nicky and gave him a bottle.

"Dadda," Nicky said in his little voice.

I turned around to look at Nicky. He held a picture in his little fingers.

"Dadda," he said again.

I took the picture from his fingers to examine it. It was a picture of Nick I had taken on our trip when we got married. He stood on the beach. I hadn't looked at this picture in almost a year. How did Nicky understand this was his daddy? I had taken all of Nick's pictures and put them away, hoping it would ease the pain. I showed Olivia.

"How does he know?" I asked her.

She shrugged, "Maybe Nick visits him too." Olivia smiled over at me as she drove me into the airport parking lot.

I thought about it and last night before Nick said goodbye, he held Nicky and then sent him back to me. Nick had to be visiting Nicky in his dreams like he visited me. My mind wandered a bit for a moment wondering if Nicky saw his dad often. How would he recognize him? He'd never met him. I forced it out of my mind for now because we'd arrived at the drop off point. I kissed Nicky and told him I loved him and then gave Olivia a hug.

"Don't worry about anything honey, Nicky and I'll be fine. You go find your happiness. And tell my son I love him and miss him." She kissed my cheek and smiled. "You deserve this Rayna. Nicky deserves this. We love you."

"I love you. Take care of my little guy and I'll see you in a few days." I waved to them both, turned, and walked into the airport.

After the plane took off, the stewardess brought me lunch. I ate and took a Valium left over from last year. I needed to calm my mind from overthinking. The valium took effect quickly. I pushed the button and my seat moved into a bed. The stewardess brought me a blanket and pillow. I fell asleep while a movie played. I didn't dream at all.

I woke up in time for dinner. I ate and made myself presentable. I still had an hour before we landed and I was wide awake. My mind ran wild thinking about what to say to Dave and what he'd say to me? What if he didn't feel the same way he did a few weeks ago? What if he already found somebody? I couldn't control the gloomy thoughts. The plane started its decent and my stomach flipped upside down, not because of the plane, but because of Dave.

I hurried off the plane and into Anna's arms in no time. She had a car waiting for us. We left the airport at ten. She said the band had started at nine. She snuck away at the last minute to come get me. A ten minute drive and we were at the venue. I took a deep breath. I wasn't sure how this would turn out.

Anna gazed at me. "Rayna, what are you worried about?"

"What if he changed his mind? What if he doesn't want me anymore?"

"You worry too much. The man has been sulking this entire trip. He hangs out at the bars with strange girls to distract himself. He can't bear to think about you. You broke his heart Rayna." She wrapped her arm around me and we exited the car. She told the driver to take my luggage to the hotel.

"What?"

"He loves you. He fell in love with you a long time ago and tried to ignore it. He knew there was a chance you would reject him, but he wanted you to know he loved you nevertheless."

"How do you know?" I wondered if he told her this.

"Not in so many words, but he has spoken to me about some of his feelings. He still loves you."

Hearing Anna tell me this, made me more optimistic, but I was still nervous. Anna put an "ALL ACCESS" pass around my neck and we walked around to the side door. The guard smiled and let us in. Adrenaline pulsed through my veins and made heart beat faster. I hoped no one could hear it. We made our way down the halls and up the steps to the back of the stage. The closer we got, the louder the music. I recognized the song I wrote. Dave's voice sounded amazing and the crowd roared.

I saw the crowd first. All of their hands were in the air and they were singing the song with Dave. He looked wonderful out on the stage performing. Anna and I stood and watched it all as the band performed. Travis caught a glimpse of us and gave us a huge smile.

In the middle of the songs was a lyric break and Travis and Jeff played a guitar solo, Dave turned our way. When our eyes locked, a shot of adrenaline rushed through me and what felt like a little jolt of electricity. A huge smile formed on his face and his beautiful brown eyes lit up with love. His smile was contagious and I smiled from ear to ear. Heat rose up my neck and into my face. I had to be glowing. His smile was one of joy.

At that moment, he had to sing his next line. His persona on stage improved a little. His step was a little lighter.

It was hard waiting for the performance to end. I wanted to be wrapped in his arms. But I enjoyed the music while I waited. I sang along with the songs and danced a little. Nick releasing me allowed me to experience life again for the first time in over a year. I was having fun and Anna stood right beside me.

Dave walked directly to me when the band finished. He grabbed me in his arms and picked me up off of the ground and spun me around. The crowd yelled for an encore. Dave ignored them. He set me down and stared into my eyes.

"You look amazing. What are you doing here? We'll be home in a few days."

"I couldn't wait that long to see you. I'm ready Dave."

"Ready for what? Another song?" Dave's eyes were full of confusion.

"I'm ready to love again."

Dave stood in shock for a moment and gazed into my eyes; searching for what, I didn't know. He didn't say anything. He simply pressed his lips to mine and kissed me. His lips felt luxurious on mine and the warmth radiated from his lips to mine. I got lost in his kiss.

Travis cleared his throat and broke our kiss. We both gave him a grimace.

"If you two are finished, we need to give them an encore," Travis said.

Everybody laughed and at that moment Dave pulled my face up to his with both his hands.

"I'll be right back. Don't go anywhere." He kissed me again.

"I'll be right here waiting." I smiled at him as he slowly backed away not taking his eyes off of me until he began singing our songs.

SONGS FROM THE HEART

The love Nick and I shared is the kind of love that never leaves. It leaves such a deep impression in your heart, it marks you forever, like a brand. It's the kind of love that's with you for eternity. Although you can't see or touch the person you hold this love for, they are still with you. And you can love another and still keep their love in your heart.

♥

I would like to thank my husband, Todd, for allowing me the quiet time I needed to focus on writing my debut album. I also want to thank my boys, Drake and Lance, for putting up with me while I wrote and edited. And thank you Drake for brainstorming with me to help me come up with an awesome title. Thank you mom for being my first reader. I love you all.

Made in United States
Troutdale, OR
02/26/2024